SNAKE WIFE

SAMANTHA BURGESS-SMITH

www.samanthaburgess-smith.com

To Louisa, who made me a mother.

And to my father.
I am where I am because you are gone.
But I am who I am because you were here

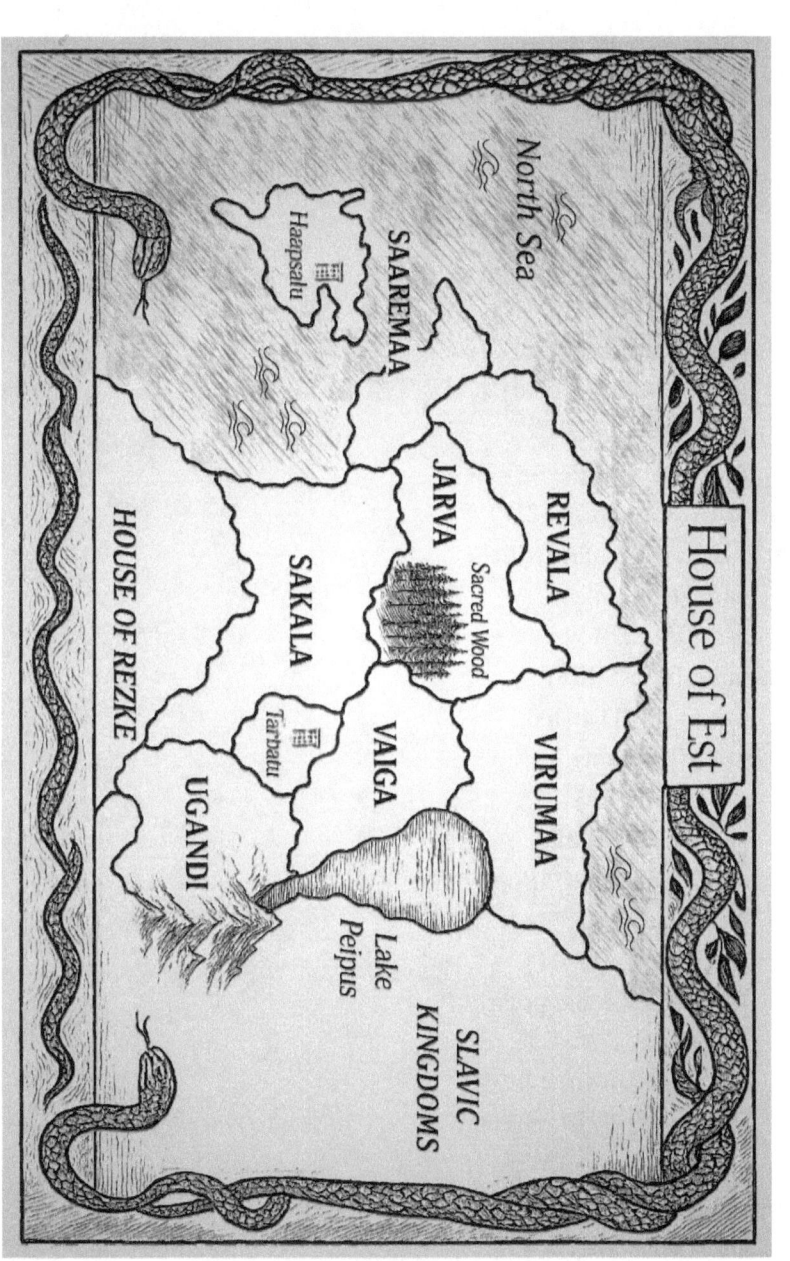

CHARACTER NAME PRONUNCIATION GUIDE

Aemilie (Ah-mehl-EE)
Barbüra (BAR-berr-ah)
Daemons (DEE-mohns)
Erga (Ehr-GAH)
Est (Ehst)
Hapsaluu (hap-sah-LEW)
Hariva (Huh-REE-vah)
Hiida (HEE-dah)
House Rezke (Rehz-KAH)
House Karsu (car-SEW)
Husandi (Hoo-SAHN-dee)
Jaarva (YAR-vah)
Jaasa (YA-sah)
Kallas (Kah-LUHS)
Kotkas (COHT-kahs)
Kurat (KER-aht)
Lekja (Lehk-YA)
Liama (Lee-AH-ma)
Looklema (Lew-OAK-lee-mah)
Maarja (MAR-jah)
Meevat (mee-VAHT)
Odypoeg (OH-dee-pohg)
Õnnev (oo-NEHV)
Rahuleid (rah-HOO-leed)
Revala (reh-VAHL-ah)
Saaremaa (sah-REY-mah)
Sakala (Sah-KAH-lah)
Suita (sew-TAH)

Tarbatu (Tar-BAH-tew)

Tuskjas (Tuhsk-YAS)

Ugandi (oo-GAHN-dee)

Vaiga (VAY-gah)

Vappers (Vah-PERS)

Varju Tütar (VAR-jah tew-TAR)

Vidar (vee-DAR)

Virumaa (VEER-oo-mah)

PROLOGUE

MY MOTHER CLAIMED that I could speak with the Moon Tongue. A subtle gift, a way of saying that which can only be seen in darkness.

Of making truth.

In almost all things, I am less sure than my mother.

There is some credibility to her claim, though. I have often felt a glimmer of that power, a hint. A soft settling of surety in my breast after a word has left my lips. But I have never been able to call it forth. I have only ever sensed it in the after.

I do not know if I can speak with the Moon Tongue, but I do not need it to be certain, absent from all doubt, that the time has come for me to breathe my spirit into the sky and seek out the place beyond this world.

And so I call my husband to me.

He argues. He cannot help it. He is desperate. He still has need of me. The work is not yet complete. I am young yet, he says.

But I am not. I know that I am not.

It is not the passage of years that grinds me to dust, but the passage of lies over my lips. The warping of my power has been my corruption.

Seeing reason holds no sway over death, he thunders. He paces and riots. He speaks of all there is left for us. All we have left undone.

I abide his anger. And in time it wears itself thin. He settles beside me reluctantly, his fine aged features bent in agony. I wrap his smooth hand in mine, breathing deep the air of this world, and I tell him one last tale.

CHAPTER ONE
THE BROKEN WRIST

Waster, woman, willing and free,
Go not from the Wood.
Go not from Me.

THERE IS A MAN in the Wood.

My power knows his presence before my body has sensed him. I go still, willing the babe at my breast to sleep. It is too fast, her immediate slumber too deep, but I cannot have her crying out when I slip my finger between her lips and break the seal of her suckle.

He is a young man, his body tells me. And he is not at ease, as an innocent traveler might be. As my daughter's father was when he wandered into my Wood.

This man has a heartbeat high and alert. He is aware. He knows whose Wood this is. He knows who dwells here. That is why he has come.

He moves slowly, acid leaking into the crouched muscles of his thighs. I lower my eyelids, pulling a silent breath in through my nose. Against the rough bark of the pine at my back, I will my own body down as I did my daughter's, stopping in the Shrouded place before slumber. I make myself little more than the grass below. I make myself as subtle as dew.

Closer. Closer he creeps. Into the space where my power can break his bones. If he finds me, I will do it. I will not go with him to do that Usurper's blood-letting.

I know when he stops. I know when he pulls in the smallest of breaths between his clenched teeth. I feel it color his lungs, blooming red. The delicate chords in his throat shudder as the whisper of his exhale passes over them, and he whispers.

"Liama."

The shock of my name pulls me up from the Shrouded place.

"Liama."

I crack the delicate bones of his wrist.

He cries out in pain. But he is not deterred. This time, when he calls out there is anger under his voice. He threatens me with my own name.

"Liama!"

I suck the fluid from his ears, drowning him in silence. Still he demands, his words warped without the sound of his voice echoing back to him.

"Leeeaaahma!"

Who is this man who dares come to my home and call me by my name as though he possesses the right to it? I will leech the blood from his heart, and I will look him in the eye as I do it. I will dump his body at the forest's edge, drained of its life.

I do not bother covering my exposed breast as I stand, settling the sleeping babe against my skin. This man will see me once and then see nothing more forever.

I turn, seeing him now crouched before me, his bent back, the frantic turn of his head as he swivels, unable to hear the world around him, yet sensing danger. I raise my fist to stop his heart.

He swings wildly towards me, one hand covering the mind-splitting pain in his ear. The other hand hangs limply from where his arm is tucked into his chest. His black-brown eyes meet my own, and my mouth begins to form the judgement that will end his life.

Before I can speak, there comes the oddest sensation of wriggling behind my eyes, like worms. The damnation stills on my tongue. My hand hangs benign in the air.

The man, young and handsome and delicate, grits his teeth. He pulls his hand away from his ear and looks at the blood on his palm. Then he turns from me, trudging heavily through the underbrush the way he has come, and I am no longer sure why I felt such malicious intent to raise my hand against him. Why, instead, I do not go with him to the place that he is going?

I pull my loose tunic up over my breast, tying the string at my chin with one hand and my teeth. And then I follow him.

It is middlenight when I flinch awake from the dream. That is how they come to me, the stolen memories. They come to me in dreams. Sometimes days after the events took place. Sometimes years. This one I have had more than any other.

It is no longer just a memory, but a haunting.

I pull in a long breath through my nose, dispelling the dream's weight on my chest. My mother told me once that regret eats away our power. There is already one parasite feasting on my own. I cannot afford two.

My husband has fallen asleep in my bed. He ages. And the more he ages the more his body demands of him for the things he demands of it. And so he comes to my bed and he pulses and throbs within me, and then he shudders his heaving sigh and rolls away. And he pays his body its price for the exertion.

I rise. I sleep poorly beside him. I sleep poorly beside anyone. There is too much noise, too much movement, inside the human frame. Slurps and slushes and squelches and squeals. The body never rests.

I pull the heavy dressing robe around my shoulders, padding on bare feet to the door. It is high summer, but the stone foundations of the fortress seem always to be freezing.

Hiida is there already, waiting on a low stool in the dark corridor. She rises when she hears the subtle squeak of the hinge. Wordlessly, she pulls a wrapped package from her apron.

I take it, the sour warm smell of its contents like my grandmother's embrace. Then we turn together and walk step for step down the wooden stairs, twisting and turning around the central tower of the fortress to its base.

Hiida dotes on me. The hearth in my husband's study is already lit and blazing. I sit before it on the woven rug, tucking my feet beneath me and wrapping my robe around my chilled toes. It is the only time I am allowed to sit thus. A Chieftainess is always under public scrutiny. Lounging on the floor hardly suits.

There was a time when my bed was often little more than pine needles, but that is all gone now.

I unwrap the rough hunk of rye bread and marzipan. Hiida says I am becoming too thin. She insists I fatten up if I am to carry another child. This is what she says in the daytime, when others can hear. In the night, my handmaiden knows that I will never carry that man's child. She knows that I have my daughter and there will never be another.

And so the marzipan, flavored this evening with cinnamon, is simply because Hiida loves me. As are the fire in mid-summer and the tea brewing now above it.

"Spent 'imself, did 'e?" she says, turning her wide hips and true face towards me. In the day, Hiida is silent and vacant and dutiful. But in these moments, she is blessedly crude and brutally direct. And so I love her just as she loves me.

"Thoroughly," I murmur.

"No such pleasure for m'lady, I don' doubt," she says, plopping herself down on one of my husband's plush chairs. I shake my head. I have known my pleasure. I shared it, however briefly, with my daughter's father. And then I bid him travel on from the Wood, and he did so.

But my husband has no interest in my pleasure. And I have no interest in using him for it.

"Call for him, Hiida," I command her quietly, my eyes enamored with the curling flames. She does not move to obey. Her body tightens, resisting.

"Call for him," I say again, firmer. And now she sighs, pulling herself up reluctantly to stand.

"I don' like it, m'lady," she says, hands on her hips. "Needa tell ya 'gain how I don' like it?"

"You needn't," I murmur.

She huffs indignantly, but still she goes.

Several moments later she returns, a dark traveling cloak over her arm to match the one she now wears.

"'e's ready," she reports, a little breathlessly. I rise, tying the dressing robe's loose strings and reaching for the cloak. When the stark white of my nightrail has disappeared beneath the layers above it, Hiida goes to the door, waiting on my nod. I send my awareness out, but there are no other bodies about in the middle of the night, save the guards on

10

the walls above. They are easy enough to blind in one way or another. A sudden dryness in the eyes that causes one to blink. A subtle wave of exhaustion that one only notices after he shakes himself awake from it. Or perhaps an ache in the back of the leg that another leans down to stretch out.

We both raise our hoods and proceed.

He has told me he does not often sleep in his quarters, those sparse rooms down in the town below my husband's fortress. For mutual protection, we exchange few personal details. I found it odd that a manservant would keep private quarters at all, but the quirk works to my advantage, and so I have never questioned him about it. Still, a device for drawing him from his master's presence undetected needed to be arranged. And so Hiida has her methods, and the man opens the door of his tiny chambers to her knock.

He steps back, nodding to Hiida, who goes in first. When I enter, he touches two fingers to his wrinkled forehead, bowing slightly. I return the gesture, but do not bow.

I would rather not have Hiida present for what follows, but as Vappers occupies only a single small room and a cloaked woman lingering about the alley would hardly escape the curiosity of a passerby, she stays, depositing herself in a rickety wooden chair by the door.

Vappers gestures to a much finer chair before his hearth, which is cold and dark. He did not have this chair when I first visited him. I suspect he has acquired it specifically for my use, as if finery were my due.

I sit. He takes a low stool across from me. A single candle has been lit behind him, casting his face in pooling shadow.

"Shall we begin, *Varju Tütar*?" he whispers, looking from me to Hiida. I was surprised when he first called me this. *Daughter of Shadow.* It is an old name for what I am and one not often spoken in these times.

He greeted me quietly in his master's home, his rugged fingertips brushing my palm as he placed a cup of tea directly in my hands. His master had chided him for the impertinence, reminding us both of my position, but I had heard little of the admonishment. I was too astounded by the sudden warm flood of peace that wrapped my bones and eased my chest at the touch of his skin.

When last I felt such quietness of spirit, when last someone called me by that ancient name...

"My Chieftainess?"

As always, Vappers' voice is respectful, yet open. Despite his role as manservant, I suspect from his dialect and cadence that he has been educated beyond the average servant. I nod to Hiida. She closes her eyes. After a few breaths, there is a subtle popping in my ears. She opens her eyes and nods. The room is sealed.

I hold out my smooth-skinned hand to my companion. His own weathered and freckled hand enfolds it. There is warmth in his touch. And goodwill. And harmony. I breathe deeply, sucking it into the center of my being.

He never asks me to share my burdens, but I find it is helpful to do so. It makes his power more potent to have direction.

"I dreamed again of when he took me," I murmur.

"The Heir?" Vappers asks. I nod.

"Perhaps you should speak it," he says softly, and with his words comes a compunction to do so, a kind of innocent eagerness, like a child longing to hear a story.

"My husband's son came to me in the Sacred Wood. He searched me out," I begin.

"How did he know of you?" Vappers beckons gently. We have done this before. He knows how to guide me through it.

"I had aided a woman with a corrupted womb. It would not cleanse itself as it should. She'd become sick with its rot, so I Wasted the corruption and made her fertile once more. I do not know how, but he found her. I suspect he changed her memory of me – made her see me as the one who had made her sick. She told him my name. She told him how to find me."

Her name was Erga. Erga the Weaver. How she had longed for another babe, a sister for her son. Yet, her womb would not yield it. She had wept when the blood had come, bright and thick and flowing as it should. She had thrown herself to her knees before me and kissed my ankles. She was so sure the babe, not yet conceived, would be a daughter that she asked permission to name the girl in my honor. But I could not grant her request. Liama is a Waster's name – the name of that Shadow Spirit of old, who had given life to Looklema, Snake Daughter, mother of us all.

It took me months to understand how Kurat had found me. And when I had, my broken mind had fixated on imagining the moment – the Heir standing before Erga's tidy little home, knocking brusquely to draw her out. The horror of how he had mutilated Erga's memories. What grisly image of me he had inserted in order to guide her towards betrayal. And always, in my own constructed visions, I am left with the inevitable void of what became of her? What became of the beloved son, not yet five? What became of the daughter not named Liama?

"Shall you tell us more, *Varju Tütar*?" Vappers interrupts the downward spiral of my thoughts.

"The rest you know," I sigh, suddenly weary. "I exposed myself to him for my own pride. I wanted to see his face when he died by my hand. And I damned myself in the doing. I damned myself and my daughter with me."

"And that is why you named her thus?" he asks, soft brown eyes round and sorrowful.

I nod, my own eyes burning with the misery of it all.

"That is why I named her thus," I whisper so I will not weep.

Maarja. Daughter of Bitterness. Stolen from the Sacred Wood. Stolen from herself.

I expect the void of all that has happened to open up below me, but instead my despair softens, turning buttery instead of barbed. It slides from my chest, which aches all the same, but does not bleed.

"There are some sorrows so deep even I cannot abate them," Vappers murmurs. "And for these we hope only to ease their passing."

I nod. Despite his tender words, Vappers brings to mind my mother. There was little in her of tenderness, but there was always honesty. A cutting, cleansing authenticity that I have grown to understand was worth the pain of the moment for the freedom that followed. I have grown to understand that her honesty was perhaps her earnest attempt at compassion. But I have grown to understand it too late.

Yet, it is not the only way this old man reminds me of her. There was a delicacy to her ability which I do not possess, though we both possessed the shared power of Wasting passed down from Looklema through countless generations. Each Daughter of that line has shaped the power to her will, to what is needed. My mother could Waste the very shame from a man's heart. She could seek out those shapeless forces of emotion – sadness, guilt, morose indifference – and starve them of life until they withered away, relief washing through in their wake.

Clarity washing through in their wake.

This was one element of our shared power that she did not offer to teach me. And I, who preferred the more tangible Workings of Wasting, did not ask to be taught.

It never occurred to me to ask her if she could use it on herself.

"This is not my only burden this night, Vappers," I sigh.

"I would not think so, my Chieftainess," he replies with a sad quirk of his lined mouth.

14

"I cannot hear Her," I mourn, the wetness pooling again at the corners of my eyes.

"Who, *Varju Tütar*?" he asks, his greying brows coming low over his eyes. For a moment I cannot speak in the face of his compassion. The words swell in my throat. And then a new wave of warmth spreads outwards from our joined hands, and the elusive peace this man offers eases my body enough to let me breathe.

"Looklema," I answer on the exhale. "The Snake Daughter, I cannot hear Her. I do not know what She would have me do."

Vappers' face softens even more. This is why I have chosen to trust this man, little that I know of him. For his worship of Her. And, if I practice my mother's honesty, his worship of me.

"You could hear Her before?" he asks, reverence in his voice. "She spoke to you?"

"She spoke to us. All the Wasters. But they are gone. And I am gone from them. And I cannot hear Her," I answer, the fleeting sense of peace disturbed like dust kicked from an earthen path. My mother had warned me – *go from the Sacred Wood and you will become deaf to Her voice.* And I had sworn I would never do so.

"Blessed child," Vappers breathes. "She is not gone from you. You know that She is not."

"But what if She is?" I cry. "What if all I have done – all he has forced from my hand –"

"You think She does not know?" he interrupts gently. "You are Her Daughter. You are Her legacy. If the others are gone as you say they are, then you are all that is left of Her line. You think She would abandon you for sins not your own? Would you so easily turn your back on your own daughter?"

"But they are my own," the condemnation spills from my soul. From all the shame at the center of me. "They are my sins to bear. Mine to wake from in middlenight. Mine to atone for, when I breathe my spirit into the sky."

"Surely they are not, *Varju Tütar*," he breathes, and I despise his reassurance. He can only see the goodness of folktales, but I am no longer a divine Daughter in a Sacred Wood. I am a crooked spine, a swollen wound, wretched with all the sickening puss in my heart.

"You do not know," I weep. "You do not know all I have done."

"Ack! Stop this, Liama," Hiida says behind me, and I hear the scrape of her chair as she stands, fists at her sides. I twist against the hardback of the fine chair to look at her.

"I'll no' stay silen' no longer, and do with me whate'er ya must for it, but I'll no' be quiet, not now," she insists. And I long for someone to say the words that I cannot say to myself. And so I let her speak, as if I could stop her.

"Three years," she goes on adamantly. "It took three years for ya to e'en remember how he took ya, it did. What with the rest of us not knowing ya weren't doin' all ya did for power itself. And I, one of 'em. I, the one that spoke agains' ya the most, when no one but my own could 'ear me. But since that first awful day when the dreams started comin' back, if ya havna done e'rything ya could to defy him, well I – I don' know, but ya have. Ya've done e'rything. And what's more, ya've shown yerself – yer true self – to all us that don' matter. All us that aren' livin' fat up on that hill, us down in the dirt and the mire of this House. Ya didna have to, he didna make ya do it and knowing that it was one of us betrayed ya in the first place woulda made me no' wanna do it outta sheer spite. But ya do it anyway. Ya heal 'em. Ya save the babes, Liama! I know ya say you canna heal but ya do, and well ya know it. And well e'ry one else knows it too, they do! So I won' hear ya speak againt' yerself, not on his account, or his son's. And each and e'ry one of the mothers whose babes are e'en now hale and whole against their breasts wouldna hear it either!"

Red-faced and breathless, Hiida stomps her foot as she ends her lecture.

"Just so," Vappers affirms her, a little half smile creasing the skin on his cheek. Then he turns back to me, squeezing my hand still held in his own.

"I shouldn't wonder if the Snake Daughter hasn't found a way to speak to you after all."

CHAPTER TWO
THE CHRONIC CHILD

Mother, at peace. Your child I take,
But health and resilience come soon in the wake.
Little Hurt, little prick, fever blooming on the cheek.
Yet when it cools, the child you keep.

"LIAMA," MY HUSBAND CALLS me forward. I drop my hand from the back of his chair and step up to equal him on the dais.

Tuskjas, Chieftain of House Est, is more his Slavic mother than his Estian father, this House's war hero. Tuskjas' size alone reveals that his heritage is not pure. He towers above the rest of us, shoulders broader and features blunter, his hair a mild brown in a sea of black.

Even with the truth of his powerlessness hidden behind the immensity of my own, he is marked as an outsider on sight alone. Thus my presence here. And Lekja's before me.

The son of my husband's first wife stands just below us on the dais steps to his father's right. Kurat is older now than when he pulled me from the Sacred Wood ten years ago. He is a man, just shy of his thirtieth year. In a way, we have grown old together from the youths we were then. I often wonder why he did not make me his bride, rather than his father's. He could have, if that had been his desire. I often wonder why he has not made his father's throne his own. He can, if that be his desire. And yet, he does not.

I have become convinced over the last ten years that loyalty is not the answer.

With my movement forward, the woman huddled before the dais whimpers. Perhaps she had hoped for mercy, or if not mercy, perhaps she had hoped that the cost of her transgressions would be the loss of a memory by the hand of the Heir. How foolish of her. They so often desire that. They deem it a lighter sentence, more bearable. What is one memory in the expanse of a lifetime?

Plead with your flesh, I want to beseech them. *Hold out your bones and your blood and your still beating heart and beg him to take them instead. At least then you will know what part of you has been severed.*

"It's really very charming, your tale," Tuskjas is saying, voice edged with sinister pleasure. "It does have all the themes of a good folktale, does it not?"

The woman, still dusty from the road, lifts her head, likely once more to plead. But Tuskjas gives her no such opportunity. This, at least, he has inherited from his father. The Usurper's son delights in theatrics.

"And yet, I confess, that its charm does not outweigh my disappointment," he goes on with a heavy sigh, leaning his thick trunk back into Est's throne. "I care little what manner of ancient creature you claim to have seen near the Sacred Wood that caused you to reconsider your assignment. Nor do I fear Looklema's judgement – see here. I have her very representative, her chosen daughter, to intercede on my behalf."

He lifts a meaty hand and wraps it about my wrist, tugging me closer, my hip digging into the carven side of the chair. And then he lets the air of playfulness drop from his countenance, leaning forward with glittering menace on his wide face.

"I wanted the niece dead, and yet, she is not, due to your 'sacred interaction with the divine'," Tuskjas spits. "You have doubts? You have guilt? Then you are not equal to the task. And if you are not equal to the task, then I have no use of you. And if I have no use of you, you have no use of that power of yours."

The woman's head whips up, frantic eyes pleading.

"Oh, no, my Chieftain, I beg –"

"Ah, ah," Tuskjas interrupts, wagging a finger, the jester once more. "I can't have you turning my Hall into a meadow of yarrow or my son into a pig."

And then he pulls me forward before him, leaning forward with his fingers wrapped around my forearms, his knees pushing into the back of my thighs.

"The tongue, don't you think, my love?" he coos into the crook of my neck, warm breath skittering over my skin.

The woman's horrified eyes flicker to me, glancing away from my gaze quickly, boring into my chest, as if looking for the heart there. She pants through her mouth, over that tongue which can make minor alterations to another's vision, replacing one object with another for a few moment's time. A skill she has used quite adroitly as Tuskjas' favored assassin, earning her latest assignment to murder the favored niece of the Kallas of Virumaa, an opinionated 14-year-old girl who Tuskjas believes will not uphold her uncle's advantageous policies when he names her his heir.

"Chieftainess, I beg –" but that is all she has time to utter before Tuskjas squeezes my arms so viciously that I nearly squeal, my fingertips flinching into fists. I do it quickly, if for no other reason than because she did not kill a child when she was ordered to do so. It hardly matters. Tuskjas will send another. And I will not intervene.

I have my own little girl to guard with my life.

The assassin's voice cuts off with a gurgle, her hands rising to claw at her throat, lips gaping like a fish. Tuskjas laughs at her frenzied pain, pushing me aside to watch it without obstacle. But as the guards at the doors of the Hall come forward to drag the writhing woman away, he pulls once more on my wrist, bringing my head close to his mouth.

"How placid you look, my dear," he purrs. "What a convincing mask you wear, stone-faced and indifferent. Nothing more than the weapon of the Chieftain. Yet, I know you, Liama – how you delight in savagery. I have not forgotten the true reason my father sought your grandmothers out. Are we not bonded thus, my love, wedded in violence? Who else would love your barbarity but one who is also bathed in blood?"

He presses his open mouth against my cheek, letting his teeth meet my skin, and then he releases me with a chuckle, turning now as another is led forward into the Hall, and a new audience begins.

Wedded in violence. Bathed in blood.

My husband's favorite of our marriage vows. And how eager he has been to enact them. Tongues. Toes. Teeth. Lesions, lacerations, limps.

The Kallas of....

The steward of ....

The wife of the ....

"What do you make of this report?" Tuskjas asks me, dragging my spiraling mind back into my body. The man on bended knee before us is my husband's spy from Jaarva, the region to the north, come to give his report on Jaarva's leader, Kallas Barbüra, and her family.

"Your desires regarding Barbüra's daughter are being fulfilled," I respond, releasing myself from the black wave of guilt that follows Wasting. "You wanted the line weakened. It has become so."

"I wanted the line destroyed," Tuskjas grumbles. "I only stayed my hand because my son advised me against indulging myself."

Kurat half turns from his place at the foot of the dais to respond to his father's complaint.

"The people believe she speaks for Looklema," the Heir says quietly.

"The people believe what I tell them to believe," Tuskjas sneers. "My father made Barbüra's grandmother from nothing. No one believed she had taken Looklema's blessing from the Wasters until my father used her to drive the Slavs out of the east. What's to stop me from claiming that Liama speaks for the goddess now, and ridding myself of Barbüra's line of bitches at last?"

"They may be bitches but they are king-makers," Kurat answers slowly, his eyes flickering to the spy, who surely hears every word. "Barbüra's grandmother put the crown on Kotkas' head. Barbüra put the crown on your own. Discredit her and you discredit your very right to the throne."

Tuskjas snorts.

"My ass has been in this chair for 30 years, boy. And it will be here 30 years hence. If Barbüra had enough influence to pry it out, she would have already attempted it. Especially after my beloved Chieftainess nearly killed her daughter," he says sardonically, turning a knowing look my way. One glance at my face has him chuckling darkly.

"See there, boy," he says. "See how she lusts after it? Like a bitch in heat. And they say she only heals the babes."

But Kurat does not look at me, nor I him.

"How old is she now?" Tuskjas asks the man.

"Five, Chieftain," he responds, head low.

"And you say she has been ill more and more as she ages?"

"Just so, Chieftain," the man answers. "My sources report that she is barely able to rise from her bed."

It's a simple thing, the Little Hurt. Prick the health of a babe just so. Expose the body to illness just enough to let it build defenses. Then let it guard itself on its own.

I'd pressed, and my husband had acquiesced, and now every babe born in Tarbatu is required to be presented before the Chieftainess within its first three months to undergo the Little Hurt. And then I had insisted on all the neighboring regions as well – Ugandi, and Revala, and Sakala, and Vaiga – until I'd orchestrated to spend nearly three months each year traveling between the Kallas' homes, pricking their babes.

Hale babes. Hale children. It is the little I have to offer. It is my recompense. And, should such a time arise, it is my way of purchasing the loyalty of the people.

A cruel grin deepens the corner of my husband's mouth as he half-turns his face to me. And I brace for what is surely coming.

"And how are the children of Jaarva?" he asks the messenger lightly.

Little tempted as I might be to forgive Barbüra her grandmother's sins, they pale in comparison to the Kallas' crimes against her own people. The self-righteous Barbüra earned my lasting enmity the day she refused to allow the babes of Jaarva the Little Hurt, insisted that the proximity of the Sacred Wood was enough to protect her people, as if my grandmother and my mother and all the women of Looklema's Wasting line had not spent their entire lives tending to the ailing and aching of the villages surrounding the Wood.

"There was an outbreak of leprosy north of the Sacred Wood," the messenger reports, having no doubt readied for this question. "As well as sweating sickness in the far west. I am led to believe that the children have been far more susceptible than adults."

"How wretched," Tuskjas says, mocking sympathy. "While in all the rest of Est the babes are hale and fat as piglets, are they not, Liama?"

He tries to goad me, and before I have been goaded. Though I hold her responsible for all the suffering, I know Barbüra's true motivations. For generations, the people of Jaarva have called out for a Kallas of Wasting power, a true daughter of Looklema. In murdering my grandmother and my mother and hauling me and Maarja to Tarbatu, Kurat had finally ridded Barbüra of the taint of the Wasters' presence in her region. She does not want me back, buying the loyalty of her subjects with my power.

"Truly, it was just, don't you believe?" Tuskjas prods me, looking up devilishly from his throne. "To deny her the Little Hurt for her own daughter was only fair, when she herself had denied it to so many others."

I would have done it for the babe's sake when Barbüra came to me in secret. And perhaps Tuskjas, who knew of the meeting in the uncanny way he possesses to know things he should not, also knew I would bend from my hatred for the sake of the babe. But it fit his purposes more to break the power of Jaarva – the power to crown Usurpers. He wanted Barbüra weakened. He wanted Barbüra's line tied to his rule.

Two years later, I woke up with the memory of flooding the girl's tiny body with disease.

"There are so few opportunities for retribution in this life," Tuskjas murmurs. "I am glad to see you avenged in this, my love."

And then, having toyed with me to his liking, he turns back to his spy.

"And Barbüra?" Tuskjas questions further, a pleased eagerness in his voice. "Does she seek healers?"

"I am told she has sought several," the man responds.

"See that she does not get them, for her daughter or her people," Tuskjas demands, sitting smugly back in his chair. "If it is a reprieve from the wailing of wretched parents she desires, I want her coming to me."

"Just so, Chieftain," the man's head bobs. Tuskjas waves him away, and he pivots after a low bow, striding on lean legs from the Hall.

"Proud of your work, wife?" Tuskjas turns to me, looking up from his throne. "Imagine, all of this would never have come to pass if your great grandmother had only given my father her blessing when he sought it against the Slavs." He sighs, slipping his thick fingers between my own and squeezing painfully.

"How grateful we are to her for her shortsightedness, are we not?"

I have stood over him for an age. His heart within my power's grasp. His thick neck a beacon before me, calling to be snapped.

Beyond Tuskjas' smug face, the slightest motion catches my eye. The fingers of Kurat's left hand flex, then fold, then flex rigidly again. And though he never turns, never pulls his gaze away from the open door of the Hall, I know, without knowing how I know, that he feels the echo of his father's crushing hold on my hand, even if only in memory.

Shuffling comes into the Hall with the next supplicant. I nod to Tuskjas, keeping the mask of the Chieftainess in place, then turn to observe the next audience.

"A report concerning the Kallas of Revala, my Chieftain," the steward bellows from the open door, and before the man has gained even a step into the room, Tuskjas is red-faced with old frustrations. The messenger does not even get to bow before he is interrogated.

"And have you found anything of use, this time?" Tuskjas demands.

The man pales even further than his northern complexion, genuflecting hastily.

"I believe so, my Chieftain, but I do not think it will be pleasing to your ear," he stammers. I raise my brows at his honesty, despite the hammering heartbeat that betrays his fear.

"Nothing pleases my ear," Tuskjas snaps irritably. "Have done with it."

"Yes, my Chieftain. The Kallas received your denial of funds to reinforce the northern fortifications, as well as your instructions to raise the required funds through internal taxes. I am afraid she has not yet levied such a tax."

"And so she will continue to publicly lament Norse raids and my lack of intervention instead?" Tuskjas asks bitterly, requiring no response. But the man has one. Unfortunately.

"There have been no recent raids, my Chieftain," the man begins. Tuskjas pauses in his grumbling, turning his cold eye fully on the messenger.

"In the warmth of summer?" he asks quietly.

"Eh, uh, no, my Chieftain," the man stammers, unsettled by my husband's sudden calm.

"Has she treated with them?" Tuskjas asks. "Has she composed some sort of agreement without my authority?"

"There is no evidence to support such a theory, but that does seem to be the general belief amongst members of her household," the man answers.

"There is no evidence or you have not found the evidence?" Tuskjas asks bitterly.

And in the pause before he answers, I see the man's indecision. I feel it, in the clench of his hands, the tightening of his leg muscles, which would have him run from the danger.

But there is honor still in Est, even if it does not sit the throne.

"If there is evidence, my Chieftain, I was unable to find it," the man answers, pushing what strength he has into his voice. "If the Kallas came to such an agreement, it was done secretly and under considerable stealth. Not even her maidservant knew of any correspondence or meetings, nor her master of horse."

Tuskjas' glittering eyes stare at the messenger for several heartbeats, assessing. Kurat, to his father's right, presses his lips between his teeth, squeezing the blood out of them. It is an old habit. The only sign of his unease. I do not dare cut my own gaze to him, though he too must be wondering the same as I. Which weapon will my husband employ? Which one of us will be called forth to mete out the punishment for this man's honesty?

"You understand the importance of confirming this rumor, do you not?" Tuskjas asks finally, his voice low and quiet.

"I do, my Chieftain," the man answers immediately.

"And yet, with your lack of success in doing so, you lack the motivation to succeed," Tuskjas murmurs, drawing his hands up underneath his chin, his thick fingers woven together into a single fist.

"I do not, my Chieftain," the man hurries to respond. "I will find it. I swear to you."

"Yes," Tuskjas grimaces. "I know this to be true. Because I will provide what you lack. Kurat."

And he lifts two fingers on his right hand, motioning towards his son. Kurat steps forward, and in the heartbeat before the man's eyes flicker towards the new threat, a warning barrels up my throat, slamming against the back of my gritted teeth.

Plead with your flesh!

And then it is too late.

The man meets Kurat's gaze and his face goes slack.

"What would you have me take, my Chieftain?" Kurat asks quietly. Tuskjas shrugs.

"Child, wife, favorite horse," he answers indifferently. "Whatever you feel he'd most long to get back."

"The man's wife is barren," I say, my voice cutting through the room too sharply. But by the time Tuskjas and Kurat turn to me, I have slipped my eyelids low and loosened my jaw, pulling all emotion from my face.

"She has come to me," I say flatly, with a shrug. "I cannot seem to convince her that I can do nothing for her."

Kurat turns his gaze immediately back to the man, though in that eerie awareness that I have of him I can sense that he knows I have lied. My husband's eyes search my face a breath longer, so I tilt my chin and raise my brows, as if to call him to challenge me outright.

My act of boldness succeeds. He turns back, resettling himself heavily on the throne.

"Wife it is then," he nods at Kurat. "Make him believe she has been unfaithful and Looklema punishes her for it with a rotted womb. Remove anything of fondness for her."

Kurat gives no indication that he has heard, but in barely more than a breath he steps away, breaking his shared gaze with the man, who shivers, then looks toward Tuskjas as if still waiting for him to deliver judgement.

Tuskjas smiles.

"Something has been taken from you," he says through yellowed teeth.

"My – my Chieftain?" the man stammers, unsure of his master's meaning.

"There is a lie buried in your memory," my husband goes on, narrowing his gaze over his grin. He gives a subtle nod towards Kurat, which the man's eyes follow instinctually. And then he understands.

"Oh, no, please," he stammers. "Please, no, my Chieftain. I will do –"

"Yes, you will do," Tuskjas interrupts his pleading. "You will do precisely as you have sworn to me, and bring me something I can use against Revala, no matter where you get it or what veracity it holds."

For a moment the man stands there gaping, laid bare at the crossroads between honor and desperation. Tuskjas twists the blade.

"Shall I tell you what will happen if you do not?" he says, leaning forward eagerly. "Shall I tell you how your own memory will haunt you, how the loss of the thing I have taken will eat at you, how you will wonder through the halls of your own mind searching for it, bringing forth and scrutinizing everything you've ever known, wondering which of your most precious recollections is corrupted?"

The wretched man just stands there, gaping up at the throne, all his honor pooling like acid in his gut.

"Shall I tell you how your own madness will drive you to destroy everything good in your life, everything you hold dear, trusting nothing and no one, until you are such a stranger to yourself that another breath is hardly worth drawing in? And then shall I tell you how it will feel, the blissful relief of sliding the blade into your own chest, cutting out the festering memory I have placed there?"

My eyes cut themselves away from the scene before me. It is not the first time I have heard these words on his lips, though he himself has never borne the burden of his son's power. And how did the words get there? How does he know how the mind shreds itself, clawing deep for the thing it cannot remember it has lost?

Because I have told him. In moments of abject misery, early in the years of our marriage, hoping for a morsel of compassion. My own blade at my throat.

No compassion came forth from him. Nothing but glee at my desolation.

And yet, the very night the fruitless words crossed my lips, my true memories began trickling back to me in dreams. *Looklema hears*, I felt my grandmother saying. *Looklema gives.*

"I will do it," the pitiful messenger promises at last, if only to make the horror of hearing his own fate cease.

"Yes, you will," Tuskjas nods. "And when you have done it, I will give back what I have taken. I will make you whole once more."

This is how he wields us, his son and me. One to destroy. One to devour. All so that others will destroy and devour in his name. And then the promise of wellness, of restoration.

Lies.

I can no more heal Barbüra's daughter than she herself can, now that the child has progressed five years in whatever ails her. And if Kurat can restore what he has taken, if he can unwrite what he has rewritten, I have never seen him do so.

I do not watch the man drag himself from the Hall. I watch my husband's thick neck instead, bent forward, his body tense and thrumming in its delight.

There, just before me, as hundreds of times before. Within reach, as if I needed hands to snap it.

How odd, I have always thought, the whistle in his blood, whining as it flushes through the passageways of his body. Whispering, as no other blood ever has.

As though it sings to me.

CHAPTER THREE
THE BELOVED BLOOD

Daughter of the Snake,
Daughter of the Wood,
Your mother's mothers' mothers
Have done all that they could.

Grace for those before,
Grace for those behind.
Forgiveness is the path,
Free from all that binds.

THE MESSENGER FROM REVALA has hardly stumbled from the Hall when a high, delighted peal echoes through from the yard outside.

"Mamaaaaaaa!" Maarja sing-songs as she frolics through the wide doors, pale brown skirts fluttering around her wisp of a frame. My Daughter of Bitterness has never known a bitter day in her life, save the one she cannot remember.

"Hold now!" my husband bellows playfully, all menace and violence forgotten. He rises from his chair, going down the steps of the dais like a bear in spring. "What is all this shouting for Mama? Am I first in your heart no longer?"

She giggles as she runs to him, tangled black hair flying. He kneels, scooping her into his big embrace and growling hungrily.

My eyes flicker to Kurat. His eyes flicker to me.

"I've come to get Mama for my lessons," Maarja squeaks out through giggles.

"Lessons on what? Sewing?" Tuskjas teases, now pretending to eat my daughter's neck. She wriggles and pushes against him, but he holds her fast against his barrel chest, his meaty arms banded tightly around her slim frame.

So tightly that I cannot act against him.

This vow I make to you, wife.

His words on our first meeting. His troth to me as we wed.

Should I receive a single scratch from your hand, your daughter will bear the same. Whatever you see fit to mete upon me will be meted upon her tenfold.

A promise he has kept to disastrous effect, evidenced by the slim scar that runs down the center of Maarja's chest, hidden beneath the fine embroidery of her gown.

And so I purchase the loyalty of the people with the Little Hurt. And my husband steals my own with my daughter's small bones in his hands.

"Not sewing!" Maarja squeals with obvious disdain. "Wasting!"

"Wasting?" Tuskjas asks. "You mean to tell me you need lessons on how to shit?"

It is an old line. And yet, his crudeness makes Maarja peal with laughter. Several moments pass before she has composed herself enough to correct him, and several moments more I have extricated her from her stepfather's company to begin our lessons.

32

I had intended to give Maarja her lessons in as similar an environment as I had when I received my own – the wild Wood, under ancient pines and among living, scurrying things with heartbeats. And when that was denied, Hiida and I had begun rearranging my own quarters to accommodate. That, too, my husband would not abide.

There will be no Wasting outside of my control.

His study, among his papers and his weapons and his scent and, occasionally, his very presence, was the only location that would meet his approval. And, when he is feeling disconcertingly generous, I am allowed to take her, under guard, to visit various locales within Tarbatu, seeing to the aching and injured and ill.

Hiida is in her customary place just inside the door to the Chieftain's inner study. When Maarja is settled, still a little breathless from her encounter with my husband, I nod to Hiida, and she seals the space. The bustle of the fortress outside the door fades, even from my awareness. It is another reason she has been such a blessed companion for both Maarja and I. Not only can her power lock in the sound of what takes place within, but it can also dampen, even entirely conceal, what is taking place without.

It is not my daughter's normal practice to seek me out for lessons, but today I have promised her something she finds difficult to resist. Today I have promised her a story.

"Are you composed, Maarja?" I ask her gently. She stills, a seriousness so mature it is nearly comical coming over her soft-cheeked face. For a breath, I only stare at her, the perfect slope of her nose, the featherlike hairs of her arched brows, the faceted richness of her brown eyes.

"I am composed, Mama," she says after some time, a small crease of confusion between her brows at my long gaze. I smile softly, nodding to her.

"You remember what our lesson is to be today?" I ask. She nods quickly, eager to show that she was listening yesterday.

"The Death of the Mother Snake," she offers. "You said you would tell me the story."

"And I will," I nod. "But first you must tell me something."

"What, Mama?" she squirms a bit, knowing I am readying to question her, and already impatient with it.

"You must tell me why Hiida seals the room during your lessons," I say, tilting my chin to invite her response. She sighs, pursing her lips.

"Because legacy is strongest in mystery," Maarja recites.

"And that means?" I ask. "And not just what I've told you. I want you to tell me in your own words."

Maarja wilts on her chair. She detests these interviews. I remember detesting them myself. But they are imperative to her training, more so than any other Waster that has ever lived.

I am my mother's daughter. And she, her mother's before her. Before her there was another. And before her another. And though I have never known how many *her*s stand between myself and Looklema, the Mother of House Est, for much of my life I never felt more than a few steps away from her. Before Kotkas came to power, to be an Estian Waster was to be worshipped as near divinity. And so the Usurper sought our affirmation. He wanted us to name him the rightful Heir to Looklema's throne. But he was a charlatan. He was a brute. There was nothing in him of Looklema's dignity and grace. We denied him.

And so he hunted us, though fruitlessly. My grandmother used to laugh as she retold stories of the men Kotkas sent into the Sacred Wood. Their vain bravado, calling forth Looklema's protection as they entered Her Wood to kill Her own Daughters. As if a Waster cannot sense a man's blood a league away, feel the acid burning in his muscles as he creeps through the underbrush.

We used to leave their heads on spikes, my grandmother, so peaceable and amicable and gentle, would giggle as she told us.

You must understand, my mother explained later, when I voiced my confusion. *She saw her father killed for love of her mother, for love of her. Where there is innocence, or even pure intention, a Waster will always give grace. But where there is greed or hatred, you must never relent. You must destroy it, and delight in the destruction, or be devoured.*

"We protect Looklema's legacy," my daughter begins confidently, but her resolution wanes quickly as she continues. "It doesn't matter if people know how we do what we do, they can't do it anyway. But the more we keep to ourselves, the more they don't understand it, the more _"

I wait for a moment for her to continue.

"If they can't explain it, they can't – they can't," she stumbles on, looking away from me miserably.

"Take a breath, Maarja," I say gently. "I know it's difficult to explain. That's why we are practicing."

Wasters have never kept their arts secret. There has never been a need to do so. One could know everything there is to the work, but if one has no Wasting power, the knowledge is fruitless. That I have Hiida seal the room is less about revealing the methods of the craft and more about veiling it in a mystery I fear it has lost.

"There is a reason our mothers and grandmothers have lived apart from others, away in the Wood," I prompt her, helping her find her footing in the tangled web that she and I are making together, apart and away from that sacred place all our mothers have called home.

"Because mystery gives us power," she says firmly.

"It does," I affirm. "It lets us reveal what we want to reveal and veil what we do not."

"So that we can be what we want to be," she says, meeting my gaze again. I nod gently.

"But there is a cost," I murmur. She breathes deeply.

"Loneliness," she answers, little more than a whisper. I smile sadly, reaching out to wrap the little bones of her fingers in my own.

"There is no one who can understand the nature of what you carry beneath your skin," I whisper back. "No one but those who have come before you, and those who will come after."

"But, Mama," she interrupts, tilting her chin. "We are not in the Wood. We don't have to stay apart anymore. I have Suita and you have Father."

I sigh through my nose, squeezing her hand gently. *Father*. Damn the man. Damn he take that name, when Maarja's true father was all gentleness and tranquility, his hands reverent, his eyes humble.

"Suita is a good friend, indeed," I redirect. "And while you are girls together, you should most certainly enjoy her company. You are lucky to have such a companion. But there will come a day when your power will be more important than hers, through no fault of her own. And you must be prepared for the loneliness that such power will bring."

Maarja twists her mouth, considering. I have mothered this creature now for ten years. I know that battle within. To argue on Suita's behalf would be noble, and perhaps satisfying. But there is still a story, promised yet untold, and she does not want to delay it any longer. I smother my smile, turning my head and pretending to straighten a fold of my skirts to keep from laughing.

"Shall we move on to our story then, my dear?" I ask her when I have composed myself. She nods, sighing with relief.

"This story occurs after Looklema left the realm of the living to live with her prince in the realm of the Daemons," I begin. "Shall you tell us a little of what happened before?"

"Ugh, Mama," she grumbles, her head falling back.

"You thought you'd escaped my questions, did you?" I tease her.

"But I already know all the stories from before," Maarja whines.

"Yes," I nod patiently, "but Hiida does not. Do you, Hiida?"

Hiida, ever loyal, shakes her head.

"Ne'er 'eard of this Looklema lady," she tells Maarja innocently. "Won' you 'elp yer poor Hiida and tell 'er a nice tale?"

Maarja nearly falls from her chair with the depth of her whining.

"Hiiiiiidaaa," she grumbles. "You know all the stories, too. You tell them all the time."

"What's a Day-mon?" Hiida goes on with her act, very convincing. Not a mite of amusement shows on her wide face. "Tha' somethin ya eat?"

I cannot help but laugh at her antics, even as Maarja looks between us, quite certain we are playing an elaborate joke but not certain enough that Hiida has not simply lost her wits to accuse us of it. We might as well both be Maarja's mother, for all that Hiida's hand has gone into her raising. For all that laughter has come into our lives because of the stout, red-cheeked woman that has made us her own.

"You'd better start at the beginning then," I instruct Maarja through my mirth. "And tell it simply. You know poor Hiida isn't terribly quick."

"Duller than mud," Hiida shakes her head apologetically, shrugging her round shoulders.

"Ughhhh!" Maarja complains, letting her head loll to her chest.

"Odd way to star' a story, I'd say," Hiida says to me, ignoring the shriveling look Maarja cuts her way. I chuckle.

When my own mother taught me this craft, it was through story. For each skill a rhyme. For each method a verse. She and my grandmother shared the work of teaching me, my mother learning from her own even as I learned from her. That was the way of Wasting women. If I stumbled in repeating or grew frustrated with half-remembering, they would still my hot heart and remind me.

Fear not, Liama. My mother had said, my grandmother bobbing in affirmation behind her. *For when you teach your daughter, you will not be alone. What your mind will not hold mine will. And what my mind cannot recall yours will. And with Looklema's blessing, it will be enough.*

But all that has occurred has occurred, and it is not enough. I lament all that my mind cannot recall. And I lament what will be lost in my mother's absence. What Maarja will never know because I could not remember. And what Maarja's daughter, and every Waster after her, will never know because Maarja never knew.

And so it is not enough that my daughter *remembers* the stories. She must know how to tell them. She must know how to wrap them around her wrist and wield them.

"There once was a Healer," Maarja begins reluctantly, and with little enthusiasm. "The Healer loved a spirit of shadow."

"She e'r told a story b'fore?" Hiida mock whispers to me.

"Hiida!" Maarja snaps. Hiida frowns, her brows high, and puts a hand over her mouth to signal her silence.

"The spirit's name was Liama," Maarja goes on, now with more feeling, "and she was the Lady of the Beings of Darkness, the mistress and queen to all the magical beings of the Wood – sprites and willen, spirits and fay. She married the Healer and gave him the power not only to heal the Beings of Light, the humans who lived in the Wood, but also her subjects of Darkness. And many powerful creatures came to him to be healed. And for recompense, he asked only that they grant a kernel of their power to a Child of Light, to make the babes of man stronger and better equipped to live among the Beings of Darkness."

Maarja stops to look at me, brows high, and I nod my approval for her to continue.

"In time, Liama bore the Healer three children. And on the days of their birth, each child was granted a kernel of power by a Being of Darkness. The oldest son was granted incredible strength and stamina by an Earth Spirit. The second son was granted immense wisdom and discernment by the Owl King. And the daughter, Looklema, was granted cunning and illusion and craft by the Mother Snake, the Austurica."

" 'ate snakes," Hiida shivers with a scowl. "Dev'lish scaly things."

"Hiida," Maarja complains.

"Can ya imagine?" Hiida goes on, serious and undeterred. "A snake tha's as big as a 'orse?"

"Was the Mother Snake as big as a horse?" Maarja asks, suddenly alarmed and very distracted.

"I've no idea," I answer. "Continue."

After a shared look of horror with Hiida, Maarja goes on.

"When Looklema grew up, she met a Daemon Prince from another realm."

"Tha's putin' it rather simply, I don' wonder," Hiida objects.

"A story for another time," I halt her with an upraised hand, waving Maarja on.

"They fell in love, and she gave birth to twin daughters. One daughter became the first Estian Waster. The other daughter was a mysterious being of Shadow who could slip between worlds as one might walk between rooms. Is it true that Kurat's mother was a Shade Walker?"

I sigh, feeling the focus of our session fracturing rapidly.

"Yes, go on."

"And can he Shade Walk?" Maarja ignores my tone.

"You know what his power is," I dismiss. "Please, Maarja, stay focused or we will be here til midnight."

"Looklema never revealed the identity of her lover to her brothers, which made them both mad. After a time, the oldest son and his children and the second son and his children lost their connection with the Wood and the Beings of Darkness, and Looklema made them all leave the Wood to go find places of their own to live."

Hiida cuts me a flat look that has me holding back a smile. I shake my head a little. We will work on Maarja's storytelling abilities later. For now I simply need her to remember the larger points, which she has done.

"The oldest son settled to the far south in what is now the House of Karsu. The second son settled to the west, on the sea, in what is now the House of Rezke. And Looklema and her daughters remained in the Wood, reigning over the Beings of Light and the Beings of Darkness in peace and harmony in the House of Est."

"Very good," I nod. "Until?"

"Until, eventually Looklema grew tired of ruling the Wood and longed to be with her lover, the Daemon Prince, in his realm, where he promised to make her Queen. And so she gave over her throne to her daughters, who became the Twin Queens, and then she slipped from this realm to the other, where she reigns as Queen of the Daemons."

"Lov'ly story, ma dear," Hiida nods her approval, "if no' a little 'asty in tha tellin'."

"Draw the Shroud, Maarja," I instruct, straightening myself for the task ahead. Maarja stills, her round brown eyes serious and focused. I observe her body, sensing as she dampens it, lowering herself into that half space. It is the first thing I taught her, to go to this place.

The Shroud. The place where all Wasting has its source.

When her heartbeat has stilled to a tranquil rhythm, I follow her into the Shrouded space. I have chosen this tale for this day. I have not yet decided on my course of action, but I must begin telling her. I must begin explaining, should I choose the path that beckons.

And so I begin.

"*In the days after Looklema departed the Sacred Wood to live with her Daemon Prince in his undying realm, her daughters ruled in unity and in justice, at one with each other and with all their grandmother's kin, the Beings of Darkness, and all their grandfather's people, the Beings of Light.*

40

Yet, in time dissent rose among the Beings of Light, for humans are changeable, capricious as the water's surface, and susceptible to greed. Fear set in among them in the darkness of winter when their bellies were not so full and their hearts pale, longing for the sun. And among themselves they grumbled, saying 'Are we not lords of this land? Have we not labored and hunted and worked the soil, and yet, the Beings of Darkness do nothing of the like? Why does the Wood simply give them all they need? Why does the Wood not provide for us as it does for them?'"

To the Twin Queens they brought their grievances, but the sisters heard their grumblings for what they were – empty bellies and weak hearts.

"What would you have us do?" the Shadow Queen asked the Beings of Light.

"How would you have us mete justice?" asked the Wasting Queen.

"Bind them!" the Beings of Light proposed. "Put to the Earth Giant a harness so that he may plow our fields. Put to the Water Spirit a net so that she might catch us fish. Could not they do in a day what we toil to do in a season?"

"We will not," the Queens answered together. "If you require more than the Wood can offer, then go forth from it as our uncles and their kin have done and our blessing on you. But if you stay, hear us now. We will not tolerate the binding of our brothers and sisters. And if you make attempt, you will find yourself bound in return."

But the Beings of Light were not satisfied with the Twin Queens' judgement. They departed from their court and met amongst themselves back in their hovels and holes.

"How shall they know?" grumbled one. "Let us subdue an Earth Giant ourselves with rope and leather. And, after we have made use of his strength, destroy him so he might not tell the tale."

"Nay, make it a kelpie for watering our fields," suggested another. And still another called for the capture of a leshy, and another one still for the

binding of a fay. And so the Beings of Light argued among themselves as to which of the Beings of Darkness might make for them the better slave.

At last, a man stood from among the throng.

"Brothers," he bellowed. "Sisters. Kinsmen and beloved. None of these will save more than a single drop of sweat from our brows. Will we wrangle an Earth Giant each spring, only to destroy it in the autumn? How long, then, will the Twin Queens remain blinded to our sport? No, the being which we possess must provide for us endless reprieve if we are not to toil once more as we have done. We must choose it not for its strength or its cunning or its wealth, but for its precious value. It must be that for whose life the Twin Queens will stand aside and allow us our due – to bind whatever Being of Darkness we desire for whatever task is at hand and for however long we require its service."

"What is this creature of which you speak?" the Beings of Light questioned the man. "For whom will the Twin Queens give up the freedom of all others?"

"For the Mother Snake herself," the man responded, and the Beings of Light agreed and made him their leader. And he was called Odypoeg. So they set about to trap the Mother Snake, the very serpent who had gifted Looklema a kernel of her power, and who by our tongue we call She Who Reaches High.

But the Twin Queens were not deceived. For as the Beings of Light had departed their court, the Shadow Daughter had slipped among them, unseen and unknown. And there she had heard all.

"Sister," said she when she returned to the Wasting Queen's side. "The Beings of Light have devised all manner of wickedness against the Mother Snake, to seize her and so force their will upon us for her freedom."

"She must be given warning," the Waster Queen agreed. And so the Queens traveled to the court of She Who Reaches High.

Now, it had been many years since the Mother Snake had blessed Looklema. Though she had made for herself great fame among her den

42

sisters for the peace she had ensured between they and the races above, and though she had birthed and raised many princesses of her realm, She Who Reaches High had long grown weary of this world and longed to breathe her spirit into the sky.

And so, though the Twin Queens pled with her to guard herself against the threat, She Who Reaches High proposed to offer herself as a sacrifice instead. Awed at her proposition (for the Mother Snake was not known for her selfless nature), the Twin Queens and all the Snake Princesses of the realm refused to hear of such an act. Impatient with their clamor, She Who Reaches High silenced them with a deafening hiss and a sharp crack of her long tail.

"You misunderstand me, Daughters," she addressed her court. "For I do not intend to give myself over to these guileless fools without cause and without recompense. If I am to breathe my spirit into the sky and shed the weight of this aged spine, then so too will I snatch the spirits of these villains from their meaty shells."

"But how?" asked the Waster Queen.

"By what power?" asked the Shadow Queen.

"Was it not I who gave you your own power, daughters of the Snake Daughter?" She Who Reaches High answered. "Do you think, then, I know nothing of what I have bestowed? If so, you are fools, for Looklema and I ruled as Queens together, she of her realm and I of mine. And in the course of our sistereign she gave me knowledge, should I choose to use it, of how to join her in her new kingdom when my time here was complete."

"Tell us of this," the Twin Queens insisted, "For we, too, long to join our mother and father in their realm."

"The time has not yet come for you to do so," She Who Reaches High answered. "But I will tell you so that you might go to Her when it comes. There is a place outside the Wood. A glen beside a lake. And within the glen, a stone. And within the stone, a door. It is from this door that your father first entered the Lighted Realm, in search of your grandfather's healing power, and so met your mother and loved her. Beyond the door lies the realm of the Daemons, where your mother reigns on high. No human may venture there, or lest be bound to that cold place forever. But the door can only be opened by a great sacrifice of blood. A self-sacrifice. For no being, be they of Light or Darkness, may carry through the door its body. It must be cast off of one's own free will, or otherwise ripped away by the doorway itself."

"This is what I propose," the Snake Mother continued. "To this glen will I lure the Beings of Light, telling them that within it you have no power. And when you have come to ensure my release, I will strike at myself with fang and cover all with my blood. Then, when the door is opened by my sacrifice, I will tangle myself among their limbs and pull them through with me to the realm beyond. And so will I be rid of the weight of this life and so will you be rid of the weight of their greed among your people."

"We will agree to this plan," spoke the Shadow Daughter, "and She Who Reaches High will be worshipped in our realm for her sacrifice by our children and our children's children, for as long as Looklema herself is remembered among them."

And so the Twin Queens departed the court of the Mother Snake. Though She Who Reaches High had not slithered forth from her den in many years, she bore her long and aching body from its coil and out into the world above and there was captured by the Beings of Light who lay in wait for her. And so their Chieftain, Odypoeg, went forward to the court of the Twin Queens once more to treat for her freedom.

But She Who Reaches High had given instruction to the Queens as to how to answer the Beings of Light and lure them into her trap. And so, when Odypoeg came into the Twin Queens' court, this is what he said.

"My Queens," and he bowed with great pomp, touching his nose to his knees. "You will remember, in your wisdom, that my kin came to you with a plea to take for themselves a single Being of Darkness as laborer and so save themselves from the toiling curse of this land, which requires of us, and only us, that we break our backs and bleed our blood into its soil year after year. And yet, you, in your wisdom, denied my brethren this small request, though surely a Being of Darkness can do in a single day what it takes us an entire season to achieve."

"We remember," spoke the Queens together.

"So have we been forced, in the absence of your intervention, and to save our children from lives of ceaseless toil and sorrow, to take for ourselves that which you would not give freely. With great cleverness, we have seized a Being of Darkness, and for its freedom have I come to treat with you, for, as you told my brethren, you would not, in your wisdom, allow a Being of Darkness to remain bound in your realm."

"Lay your terms," the Twin Queens commanded as one.

"That being which we have in possession is She of utmost value to you and to your realm, the Mother Snake, She Who Reaches High, with whom your mother made peace and to whom you owe your power. You know the terms of the law made between your realm and hers – that should harm come to any serpent by the hand of man, so will the land be flooded with the wrath of her den sisters, and no being, be they of Light or Darkness, safe from their vengeance."

"And yet, it is you, not us, who have made threat against her," answered the Wasting Queen. "Why then would we not tell her many daughters to seek their revenge against the Beings of Light and leave unharmed the Beings of Darkness?"

"Would you offer up the innocent to the mouths of snakes?" answered Odypoeg, thinking himself cunning. "Would you give to them our babes, who have done naught but suckle at their mothers' breasts?"

And the Twin Queens remained silent, pretending to consider Odypoeg's words.

"So do we propose these terms for her release," the leader continued. "First, that a treaty be drawn between the Beings of Light and the Beings *of Darkness which requires each season for a Being of Darkness to be given over to us to do our labor. And more, that no recompense be sought against us for our actions, but that pardon be granted by yourselves, for what else could we have done in the face of our trials?"*

"Bring to us the Mother Snake and we will agree to your terms," answered the Shadow Queen.

"Do you think us fools?" laughed the leader. "We will not release her until your mark is upon the page."

"And you will not do so here, I suppose," said the Wasting Queen, as She Who Reaches High had instructed. "Or do you have no fear of us, here in the seat of our power, such is your pride now that you have captured what we hold dear?"

And as she spoke, she reached out with her power and leached the color from the leader's eyes, so that the world around him became muted and grey, as if he stood at the very door of the Daemon realm.

"Cease your Wasting or your sacred serpent will die!" Odypoeg yelled, fear now in his chest. The Wasting Queen released her hold upon him and the color of the earth flooded back into his sight. When he saw himself restored, the fear left him.

"The Mother Snake is eager to be back in her den," he said. "She has told me of a place where you have no power and there, and only there, will she be given back to you once you have made your mark upon our treaty."

And so the time and place for the Mother Snake's freedom was set for the glen outside the Sacred Wood, three days hence, and Odypoeg strode from the court of the Twin Queens as though a victor.

Then the fateful day came. The Queens, with all their court and all the Snake Princesses of the Serpent realm, came forth to the edge of the clearing. So, too, did the Beings of Light, with the Mother Snake bound among them. Then the Queens strode together into the glen, carrying with them the treaty required by the Beings of Light. And Odypoeg met them at the great stone in the center of the glen, with all the other men dragging the great body of the Mother Snake behind. And so, when the Mother Snake came close enough to the stone, she broke from the hands of the men, striking herself with her fang, and lashing and writhing until all the Beings of Light were covered with her blood. The door within the stone opened, and from it the chill wind of that place beyond began to howl, pulling in all of the beings covered with the Mother Snake's blood. The Shadow Queen grasped her sister's arm and slipped the Wasting Queen away to the safety of the forest, where the Snake Princesses wrapped themselves around the Twin Queens, holding them against the solid trunks of pines so as to escape that yawning void.

When they saw that they had been deceived, the Beings of Light screamed their terror, grasping at each other as they were dragged beyond the world, their souls shucked from their bodies as nuts from their shells. And among them, She Who Reaches High reared her great head, her laughter a hiss upon that awful wind, and from her heavy and aching body her own soul sprang free, disappearing into the doorway, which sealed once more to stone.

And so did the Twin Queens rid themselves of the greed of the Beings of Light. They gave the children of their enemies over to the Beings of Darkness to be raised with an abiding respect for the creatures of the forest. And for many generations after, there was once again peace between the Beings of Light and the Beings of Darkness.

And within the glen where She Who Reaches High gained her freedom, the body of that great snake was left as a monument to her sacrifice. And though it withered and decayed over time, it is said that if ever the greed of the Beings of Light once more should compel them to violence, the body of the Mother Snake will wrap itself around the great stone in the glen's center, ready to sacrifice itself once more.

Maarja takes the end of my tale as permission to rise from her Shrouded state. Her round brown eyes open, showing me their delight.

"Oh, Mama!" she squeals, squirming in her chair. "I do like that tale. Why have you never told it before?"

I try to smile at her. I do not want her to remember me always scowling. I am determined to be something more, something different in her memory than my own mother is in mine.

"I have told it to you now," I answer her lightly.

"And is it true? Did She Who Reaches High go on to be with Looklema? Is there really a glen like that, and can we go to it? Do you think her body is still there?"

Hiida and I share a look.

I know what lies in that glen now. If there was ever a boulder with a doorway into the realm of Daemons, it has been crushed beneath the weight of time. And there is no giant snake spine coiled within its clearing, only the rise and fall of moss and lichen and heather over the dead trunks of fallen trees.

Still, I know it to be the place of my grandmother's story. I have felt the power there, dormant yet present, like the buzzing of a thousand bees. Perhaps the time is not yet right, perhaps the greed of man is not yet swollen enough for She Who Reaches High to save Looklema's realm once more. Though if it is not, I shudder to think of what level of avarice will be required to fulfill the door's conditions.

"When my grandmother told me this tale, the first thing she told me about it was that it was not true," I explain. Maarja's eyes fall at their outer corners, her mouth opening in shocked disappointment.

"Hold now," I go on softly. "I was just as disappointed when I heard the same. But my grandmother wanted me to know, just as I want you to know, that there are tales beneath tales, and within them and without."

"Whatever does that mean?" Maarja grumbles, impatient for me to get on with whatever I am trying to teach her.

"It means that there are tales told by the common folk of Est, and within them countless magical and miraculous things occur. But behind most of them, whether mentioned or not, is a Waster. We do not choose to share all that we do. We do not choose to be remembered by it."

"Whyever not?" my daughter asks.

"Many reasons," I answer, which clearly disappoints her, thinking it an evasion. "But I think in the case of this story, it was perhaps for the purpose of peace."

She presses her lips together, lowering her brows. For though she hurried me on to this lesson, she hates being taught things. It is part of being separated from herself, from the Wood of her ancestors. I devoured all that my mother and my grandmother had to teach me. It had purpose. Here, she has no purpose. Here, her own power has little meaning to her, other than as a novelty. A thing for which other people can point at her and say, *Ah, she is a Waster. How fine!*

"In truth," I explain, "my grandmother told me that She Who Reaches High did not offer herself up to be sacrificed but that the Queens persuaded her. And it was the Queens, not the Mother Snake, who knew of the glen and its power and contrived to lure the Beings of Light there. In the story, the Mother Snake speaks of her close bond with Looklema, which was true. The Twin Queens suspected that their mother would open the door to Her realm only for someone whom She deeply loved, and as they were not yet ready to join Her in that place, they needed someone who had grown weary of this world and longed to move beyond it."

"But to the realm of the Daemons?" Maarja asks doubtfully. "Wouldn't she rather breathe her spirit into the sky?"

"I don't know, my love," I answer her. "Perhaps even so cold a place as the undying realm is made warm by the presence of those you have loved in life."

"Is that where you want to go when you die?" she asks innocently, as only a child can consider death.

"I would go wherever my grandmother has gone," I smile sadly. Maarja nods, coming to her own easy conclusion.

"Then I will go there too," she answers simply. "Is there more in the story that isn't real?"

Her redirection draws a huff of laughter from my throat. To dismiss death so lightly is a gift of the young.

"There is," I continue. "The Twin Queens knew that the door would claim any who bore the blood of the one who sacrificed herself to go through it, for it devours the body, the whole body. To avoid getting the blood on themselves or any of the Beings of Darkness, She Who Reaches High did not strike herself with her fangs, rather, when the Beings of Light had dragged her into the clearing, it was the Wasting Queen who pulled the serpent's blood from between her scales and pushed it into the bodies of the Beings of Light. And, rather than being dragged into the other place by a howling wind, the Shadow Queen, being half-Daemon herself, was the only person who could approach the doorway without being required to give up her body. She pushed the Beings of Light and the Mother Snake through to the other side."

"But that's wretched of them!" Maarja objects.

"Why?" I prod her.

"Well –" and then she hesitates, searching within herself for the source of her unease. "I suppose they should have – why didn't the Wasting Queen just Waste them all –"

"All at once? Suppose there were tens of them? Hundreds?" I ask.

"Could they not have given over the Earth Giant for a day?" She tries an alternate argument. "Surely it would not have been so horrid to – well, surely an Earth Giant might have even agreed to help for –"

"And do you suppose a day of the Earth Giant's labor would have satisfied the Beings of Light?"

"If they needn't work so hard, perhaps they would be happier," she reasons.

"If they had not been slave to their own greed, they would not have needed to work so hard in the first place," I propose. "Our people lived in the same Wood for generations, and it provided for all of our needs."

Maarja screws her mouth up, thinking.

"But still, couldn't some sort of agreement have been worked out between them? Couldn't they have paid the Earth Giant or –"

"Maarja, hear me well," I warn her. "There are no terms under which greed can be satisfied." My grandmother's exact words, waiting patiently on the back of my tongue since before the story began.

Her little thin brows lower, but she does not speak.

"Treat with it," I go on, pressing my words into the air between us. "And you will find yourself giving over all you hold dear for a peace that never comes."

"Is this my lesson, then, for the day?" she says grumpily.

I smile.

"No," I answer, shaking my head. "Your lesson for the day is how to draw blood from one body and give it to another, as the Wasting Queen did with the blood of She Who Reaches High."

And so I cover my intent with practical application, and Hiida loses a little blood.

CHAPTER FOUR
THE LITTLE HURT

Build up the mother, measure her health.
Restore to her peace in abundance and wealth.
When challenges rise and illness draws near,
Build up the mother and lessen the fear.

I DO NOT CLAIM to know my husband's reasoning. I had expected him to deny my request to administer the Little Hurt to the babes of Tarbatu when I'd first made it eight years ago. And yet, he had granted it, giving no reason, and I have been left to speculate.

Perhaps he truly saw the advantage in strong babes and peaceful mothers.

Perhaps he understood that allowing me a purpose might keep my attention from designing his demise.

But I most suspect that he had only just stepped out from the darkness, seven years after her death, of Lekja's reign of terror. She had made his throne secure, striking at his enemies from the shadows in the upheaval after Kotkas' death. But Tuskjas was more than 20 years into his reign by the time I became his Chieftainess. His rule was unchallenged, but also unloved. And so, it has become politically advantageous to allow me to win the hearts of his people, rather than use me to carve them from their chests.

When I step through the wide doors to the Hall, a hush shudders in the room. I nod to the mothers waiting in line along the room's back wall. They dip as well as they can, giving me whatever version of the sacred greeting the babes in their arms will allow. Several of them are not alone – their husbands holding the hands of older children, hoping to earn renewed blessings on their heads. I halt beside a woman whose body is limp and languid. Her worn face is pale, the skin hanging from its bones and muscles in a way that exceeds the typical fatigue of a mother.

Her pale brown eyes widen when I turn to her, and she bows deeply, the babe against her chest stirring in its sling at the sudden motion.

"You are unwell," I say to her softly. Her exhausted face warps, her thin brows reaching down at the corners around morose eyes. I know that she has not dared to admit the same to herself. I know that she has looked around, comparing herself to the other mothers, wondering if they, too, feel as wan as she.

"What is your age?" I ask her, drawing her forward with a gentle hand on her elbow. She follows reluctantly, looking back at the others, noting their narrowed gazes. She opens her mouth to answer, but only a thin cough comes out.

I am relieved, at least, to see color bloom on her cheeks in her embarrassment.

"I'm in my forty-first year, m'lady" she finally croaks.

"And this is your first child?" I murmur, parting the cloth of her sling and looking down at the babe, little more than a few months old.

"Aye, my Chieftainess," she whispers in response. "My first husband died too young. I took o'er the brewing – the ale, I mean – when he breathed his spirit into the sky. I didna take another husband until two years ago."

I dip my chin, giving her a small smile.

"Because you have been too successful to need one," I guess. She nods, the ghost of a grin on her grey lips.

"I didna expect a babe, not at my age," she says, her voice gaining a little strength.

"And yet, Looklema has given one," I say.

"Aye, my Chieftainess, but I fear it'll be the death of me," she murmurs, her voice breaking over her words. Her face crumples, eyes glistening. "I canna – I do not – that is, I see the other mothers –"

"Do not compare yourself," I chide her. "These women have half your years and half your wisdom. Their bodies are still in bloom."

"And mine decays," she mourns, clutching her babe to her chest.

"Yes," I confirm. "But only because it requires more to recover from bearing and birthing your child. You have asked of it more than these other women, and it has given it, as the body longs to do. But you must give it something in return."

"What?" the woman breathes, shaking her head. "I am empty. I've nothing more."

"Your husband is a good man?" I ask her. She closes her eyes, nodding.

"I didna rush to choose," she murmurs. "I chose well."

I nod.

"Then when you return to him, this is what you will do," I say, placing my hand on the small of her back and guiding her forward towards the dais. She comes willingly, her eyes widening the closer we get to the great stone chair.

I step away from her at the bottom of the stairs, sharing a wordless nod with the Lady Hariva, who takes my place beside her, a comforting hand on her shoulder. Kallas Rahuleid's wife has become something of an assistant to me during the long days of the Little Hurt. I have found that, despite bearing witness to countless variations on birth and child rearing, the touch of a woman who has borne and lost – a woman of this specific sorrow – is often more welcomed than the touch of a woman with a hale daughter in her tenth year.

I suspect Lady Hariva finds some healing for herself as well.

I ascend to Looklema's throne, but I do not sit. Instead, I turn before it to face the wide, crowded Hall. Babes yelp and fuss. Mothers shush, and fathers lay heavy hands on squirming bodies. I look out, pushing my voice to the room's corners and beyond, and deliver the customary welcome.

"I am Liama, Chieftainess of House Est, Looklema's daughter and Heir to the Wasting Queen's power. You have come on the promise of health for your children. I will do what is within Looklema's will to grant."

I am even still a bit surprised when I see them lining the walls of the Hall, spilling out into the yard, all the way to the fortress gates and down the steep hill beyond. Bundles at their feet, dust on their clothes. It isn't just the babes of Tarbatu that I see every three months but the babes of any and all who find their way to me.

It is a risk, bringing their children here to be made ill. And yet, they come.

And they believe.

I intone my grandmother's favorite rhyme.

"*Mother, at peace. Your child I take, but health and resilience come soon in the wake. Little Hurt, little prick, fever blooming on the cheek, yet when it cools, the child you keep.*"

I look down at the haggard woman below, gesturing her to bring her babe up the stone steps. Hariva gives her an encouraging push, and she ascends on shaking knees.

I part the cloth covering her child, looking down at its sleeping face, petal lips pursed in the shape of its mother's nipple. And then I touch the fingertip of my third finger to its brow.

I do not need the touch to perform the working, but the mothers are comforted by it all the same.

"It is done," I murmur to the mother. She looks up at me with awe-filled eyes, edged in harsh red lines. "Expect a mild fever within a day, followed by a few days of fussiness or irritability. If a rash develops, bring her to me at once."

The woman nods, her age showing around her worried mouth.

"Now," I go on, looking her intently in the eye. "When you return to your husband, you will put the babe in his arms. And you will rest. Your husband will return here on the morrow and present himself to the kitchens. There will be a supply of cow's liver. You are to eat of it twice a day so long as you nurse this child. Do you live in Tarbatu?"

She nods, eyes wide.

"Then you will have no trouble finding liver after what I provide is gone. Do not allow miserliness to keep you from it, yours nor your husband's. I command this of you. I expect it to be done."

The woman's face bends once more, this time around her gratitude. The wetness finally escapes her eyes, trailing down her hollowed cheeks in fat rivers.

"M'lady," she breathes, shaking her head subtly in disbelief.

"I expect it to be done," I repeat, gently but firmly. She bows, bringing her fingers to her brow. Then Lady Hariva helps her back down the stairs and waves forward the next woman in line.

And one by one, I prick the babes.

My mother did not let me perform the Little Hurt until I bled.

She had insisted that the young had no delicacy, no understanding of what the life of a babe meant to its mother. If she could have, I suspect she would have kept me from performing it until I became a mother myself. But my grandmother had swatted her thick-knuckled hand at my mother's caution, telling her to forgive herself at last.

I did not understand my grandmother's admonition until many years later when I asked why we did not go to Husandi, a small village on the northern border of the Wood. We emerged once a month at one of the 12 other settlements that surrounded Looklema's home, pricking the babes and seeing to the health of the mothers. But we did not go to Husandi.

For in Husandi, I learned, lay the source of my mother's caution. They had buried both babe and mother together right in the middle of the path from the Wood, laying a flat carven stone overtop.

The message etched upon it was simple.

Waste here. Die here.

She was blameless, my grandmother explained. *But she was too young to know that one can be right, or powerful, or blameless, and still carry the guilt of all that lies outside of one's control.*

And so we did not go to Husandi.

I bled, the pains of my moon cycle giving me some framework for the pains of birth, and my mother finally allowed me to administer the Little Hurt, now that I knew, however inadequately, what a child would one day cost my body.

She could not have explained, and I could never have understood, how the cost would mean nothing when I held my child to my breast.

I cannot fathom her, my mother. She has always been an enigma. I thought perhaps motherhood would bring some new understanding, some insight into her character.

In small ways I admit that it has. I understand now her fatigue. The pervasive sense that I was a bother to her, something to be tolerated. I understand now the balance all Wasters must strike between being a Daughter and being a mother. I understand that protecting Looklema's legacy is not always the same as pursuing one's own flourishing, nor the flourishing of one's child.

I understand now that my mother was more than my mother. That she was a woman, whole and apart from me, with the power of a goddess in her blood.

I am that woman now.

I snap. I spit. Occasionally I turn my back on my daughter, seething in frustration. But always I find the strength to turn back. Always I find the strength to encourage, to understand, to open myself when I long to shutter all that I am behind an impenetrable wall, if only to breathe my own air.

My mother was bold. She was courageous. Unyielding. But, now that I see the strength in myself, I do not believe that she was strong.

She had the delicacy to Waste shame from the soul, but she did not have the delicacy to show her daughter tenderness. Pride, certainly. Direction, guidance, yes. It is from her that I learned justice. It is from her that I learned control.

Her faith in my power, in my place in Looklema's line, was unwavering. Absolute. To her, I was a Daughter, more than I was *her* daughter.

My faith in Maarja is not so absolute. Nor is my conviction to make of her a Daughter of Looklema. I am yanked, tugged, displaced unceasingly in the thin space between raising my child in the fullness of her heritage and making of her another weapon to be wielded by powerless men. And the guilt, the shame of the choice, of both options – I am born down into the dust each time I think I have arrived at what is best, not only for Maarja, but for the land. I am no goddess, but I hold the legacy of one in my hands, dripping through my fingers into the pitiless void of time with each sun that sets over Tarbatu.

No, my faith in Maarja as the last of the Estian Wasters is not so absolute. And so I am determined to give her all that I have of that other well. I am determined to give her what my mother did not give me.

I will give her all that I have of myself.

CHAPTER FIVE
THE SHORN LOCK

What cannot be done with power can be
done with fear.
When force has been tried, give thought to veneer.
What terrifies most? What bends men to the knee?
A woman whose beauty she gives to be free.

I REMEMBER very little from those early years. I wonder sometimes if Kurat can feel the memories as he rewrites them. I wonder if he remembers more of my coronation, more of Maarja's infancy, more of the workings of my hands than I do.

Despite his actions, a time did come when I relinquished my anger against my husband's son. I came to realize that Kurat was only a tool, like myself. He gave no outward sign of this – he is as he has always been, unquestionably dutiful to his father. The powerful, reserved, calculating future Chieftain of the House.

Yet, when the memories began returning, I could sense in them his reluctance. I could sense in them the same grim determination to survive that I myself possess. And then I began to do what my anger had not allowed me to do before. I began to observe him, not as an adversary seeking out weaknesses, but as a fellow weapon, honed and held by the man who owns us both.

That is how I learned what my grandmother had tried to teach me. Anger is a livid fuel for a moment, channeling new depths of power. But long anger is a parasite, eating away the eye, the ear. Long anger warps the senses, corrupting all that flows through them. It blinds. It deafens.

Long had I been deaf and blind to Kurat.

Perhaps there is not a power forcing him to do his father's bidding as he uses his own to force me, but Tuskjas still possesses a kind of control over his son that goes beyond both fealty and power. I do not know the nature of that control, but for a man as capable as Kurat to remain loyal to a man with no power at all, it must be considerable indeed.

Still, I cannot trust Kurat enough to make of him an ally. Surely together we could rid ourselves and this House of the corruption squatting on its throne, but beyond that what is there? I do not desire to be Kurat's Chieftainess any more than I desire my role as his father's. Yet, I am Looklema's daughter. I am Her throneless Heir. Now that I am out of the Wood, everywhere I go I am a threat to power. No one will abide my presence.

The irony is bleak. My daughter, and I as well, are safest in my enemy's hand. And Tuskjas knows this. He has made it so.

And so he directs his son to steal my memories and rewrite them, shoving them back into my head to bend me to his will. To use my power as his own. And my husband believes that doing so will make me hate his son. And I let him believe that I do. And I let Kurat believe that I do.

Because the deception may one day be of use.

So when I close the door between myself and the wretched world, breathing in the familiar scent of my private quarters, and feel Kurat's body pulsing and thrumming from within my bedroom, I wrap his heartbeat around my wrist and yank.

I hear his grunt as he stumbles forward from the shadowy gloom of my bedchamber. "Peace," he wheezes, his hands raised in surrender.

"Get out," I whisper.

He shakes his head. His dark eyes are just visible in the darkness. He has the same grimly determined expression he wore when he charged forward to capture me in the Wood, seeping blood from his ears and cradling his shattered bones.

"Then speak your business and be gone, you fool," I hiss, stepping around him to the candle on the little table beneath the darkened window. I release his heart as I light it, then turn the harsh light upon his face. He winces, straightening.

He is handsome, the Heir of this House. If he had wandered into my Wood for any other purpose, I might have taken him as a lover. Kurat is slim and fine and self-possessed. He looks nothing like his father. There is nothing of his grandmother's Slavic heritage in him. He is all Est, from the black hair swept neatly away from his face to the black-brown of his dark, enigmatic eyes.

"I cannot speak it here," he murmurs, lowering his hands.

"Then why have you come?" I ask. I do not bother to chide him with all the reasons he should not have done so, which will only prolong his stay.

"I would speak with you elsewhere," he answers, stepping towards me, deeper into the light. His face is earnest and pinched, unlike the cold mask of indifference he wears in his father's company. Perhaps that is why I do not force him from my quarters immediately.

"There is no elsewhere," I answer instead, impatiently. "If the risk is too great to speak your mind here, then the risk is too great for whatever your words might contain."

He is undeterred.

"Yet, you have found an elsewhere," he says meaningfully, eyes narrowing. Alert prickles across my skin.

"What would you know of this?" I ask, not bothering to deny it.

"That which Tuskjas knows as well. And that which he permits, to keep his Waster as sharpened as his axe. Where do you suppose the old man got such a fine chair for your company?"

So my husband knows of my meetings with Vappers. I am unsurprised. He has a way of knowing things he should not.

"And when I next see the old man, will he remember my prior visits?" I ask, brows high.

"So long as you agree to meet me and hear my words," Kurat counters.

"Perhaps you should simply shove them inside my head now and save us the risk," I answer.

"It doesn't work like that," he shakes his head subtly.

"And you would tell me how it works," I ask, my terms beginning to take form. "If I were to agree to meet with you, you would tell me how it works?"

His eyes narrow further, attempting to pierce my words for what lies beneath them. He is too calculating to be ignorant of what he is asking of me. I will agree only when he extends his neck as well.

He studies me with dark eyes a moment longer, and I wonder if he, too, has learned to observe me not as the adversary that snapped the bones of his wrist in the Wood, but as something apart from what we once believed the other to be.

At last he nods sharply, then steps cleanly around me towards the door, listening for other souls moving in the stairwell beyond.

63

After less than a breath, he is gone. It occurs to me then that he has not told me where or when to meet him.

"Mama," my daughter calls in her singsong voice.

"Here, my love," I answer. I feel her body follow the sound of my voice into the back room of my chambers.

"Are you ill, Mama?" she asks, her little face bending in precious concern as she comes on dirty and bare feet, pattering on her toes to my bedside.

"No," I answer, giving her a small smile. I reach out, tracing the curved slope of her nose to its point. She scrunches her eyes, abiding the tickle of my touch.

"Only resting," I say. "And what have you been doing?"

She clambers up, all elbows and knees and sharp hips. I move over, making room for her to sit in the curve of my body.

"What have you been doing?" I ask again after she settles herself. She smells of sweat and tangy dirt and animal musk, and underneath, herself.

"Seeing to the horses," she answers, fidgeting absently.

"And how are the horses?" I ask, lifting her sweaty braid from her nape and pulling it over her shoulder. A thousand tiny hairs have escaped from it along her neck and her ears, rising like low-lying clouds to hover around her beautiful face.

She flicks the braid back over her shoulder, swatting my hand away. To be near, so near, and yet desire my touch only on her own terms. That is my daughter.

"Hale," she answers shortly. I study her profile, the high bloom of the heat of the day on her pale cheeks.

"Mama, can animals be Wasted?" she asks, her thin brows coming low over her dark brown eyes, looking out the window.

"Yes, they can," I answer, letting her lead us onwards. My mother and grandmother had often taught me to Waste on animals, what with the stark lack of other human bodies in the Wood. Maarja has thus far had the benefit of a town full of aching and ailing people for her own studies. But her awareness of animals should flow to her as readily as her awareness of humans.

"I thought so, but I didn't know how," she says lightly, sitting up a little straighter at something she has just seen out the window. She jumps up, padding over to it and rising on her tiptoes to look out over the trees.

"What do you mean?" I ask, rising up onto my elbow.

But my daughter is not concerned with such things.

"Mama! Look, a hawk!" she says, pointing to something below. "It's on the wall!"

And then she races from the room, leaving the door ajar as she goes.

I wake three nights later from a dream I have never had before. In it I leave from the fortress under cover of night, but instead of seeking the solace of Vappers' power, I slip beyond the gates of Tarbatu into the fertile wood that surrounds the city, a foreign sense of longing driving my legs.

I rise from my bed, which is blessedly empty, besides myself. Maarja was given rooms of her own only last year on her Name Day. I had thought her departure would mean deeper sleep for us both – she suffers the same insomniac affliction as do I in the presence of others.

Then my husband had begun visiting.

Hiida is not outside my door, and so I dress myself quickly in light wool to keep from getting too hot beneath my traveling cloak. And then I follow my dream-self out from the city and into the woods, Wasting the guards and townsfolk with subtle distractions as I go.

I do not question my instinct to follow this path or that, nor do I stop myself when I come to the small herding hut at the edge of the woods. The moon is sharp and bright above, soaking the open grazing fields beyond in its blue light.

He is there when I open the door, lit by candle, his own traveling cloak thrown over the top of a well-worn stool. He greets me with two fingers to his forehead and I return the gesture, then he motions to the stool.

"I have been here before." I say, though I have no explicit memory of the place.

The corner of Kurat's mouth tucks in grimly.

"The Chieftain met us here when you came from Jaarva," he answers, looking around the place. His eyes linger on the cot pushed against the far wall.

I stare at him.

"You mean to say I was married in this hut?"

He nods. I sit.

"Say your peace then," I prod him. "I've no wish to linger here."

"Do you not remember it?" he asks, his question genuine. "You have no memory of this place?"

"I remember threats exchanged," I answer sharply. He presses his lips together, but does not speak. "But I have no memory of the place," I go on, looking around at the shabby surroundings.

There is a purity to nature. The open Wood, with its soil and rot and dew, is a cleaner place than the finest chamber in the finest fortress. Perhaps once this place had been comforting to those who rested their heads here, but negligence has left it to decay.

"How did you know I would dream of it this night?" I ask him in return. "How did you know to meet me here?"

He does not answer.

"I trust you remember our bargain," I remind him, fingering his heart beat.

"I remember," he answers darkly, rubbing his chest. The candle light flickers, the flame consuming itself for a moment, then wiggling back to life.

Long silence stretches between us, tense and heavy and tight, like a swollen wound.

Finally, he speaks.

"I have long considered how I might go about this," he begins, looking down to his folded hands. "I had thought perhaps you would need to be forced," he continues. "There have been times when your performance has been most convincing."

I resist the urge to scoff. If I have given a performance, it is only with him directing every twitch of my hand. But I contain my instinct for a sharp-tongued response, giving him nothing.

"You have no love for the Chieftain. I did not expect you to," he goes on. "Still, I thought perhaps you had grown to love the power, grown to love being Chieftainess. That, even if not precisely happy, you had become contented by it."

He looks up to me for my response.

"I assure you I have not," I murmur quietly. He nods, then drops his eyes from mine.

"You told Tuskjas the wife was barren, but the Revalan spy has four children," he says, just as quietly. I hold my tongue.

"I do not regret bringing you here," he continues. "I can say with honesty that I regret how it was done, but I cannot regret your presence."

67

"Because you mean to use me in some way," I clarify, ushering us past his fruitless self-reflection and towards the point of this visit.

He huffs a dark laugh at my bluntness, then answers simply.

"I do."

A moment of silence passes between us.

"Do you suppose you can push him through yourself?" he asks, finally raising his eyes to mine.

I should not be surprised, but I am. Still, his question needs no clarification. I know he speaks of the doorway in the Glen. I know he has managed to hear the tale I told my daughter.

"And who have you corrupted?" I ask, matching his calm tone. "My daughter or my maid?"

"Rest assured I have touched neither of their minds," he answers. "Maarja gave up the tale willingly."

"And are you in the practice of speaking with her on the subject of her lessons?" I ask testily. He shakes his head.

"Little as you might believe it, it was she who instigated this particular conversation."

"And you encouraged it," I press.

"And I encouraged it," he shrugs, unapologetic. "But I wish your daughter no ill will."

Now it is my time to laugh. I shake my head at him, unsure, for a moment, how to express the depth of my disbelief.

"You brought a lifetime of ill will down on her the day you stole us from our home."

I am beginning to lose my patience with this tedious exercise.

"Even so," he answers, unaffected by my ire, "The life she has now is a good one, if you can bring yourself to see it. And I would not mar it, so long as she does not intervene in my plans."

"And now we come to it, then," I say, straightening in my seat.

"Your intent is to move against him, is it not?" he asks, narrowing his gaze. I say nothing, my spine as straight as a pine.

"It must be, for you to consent to meet with me," he reasons. "You must know that I intend the same. What other reason would I have to request of you a meeting, and you to accept?"

I look at him, mouth tight, brows high.

Now he begins to grow frustrated. His body begins to tighten.

"Is that not why you told her the story?" he presses, leaning forward. "Because you intend to contrive his death via the only means that would ensure your daughter is not punished for it? Because if he dies at the hand of Looklema's Doorway you can claim Her intervention and who would stand against you? Who would dare punish you or oppose you if Looklema Herself removed your obstacle to the throne?"

Still I do not speak. He presses his lips together, brows lowering as he becomes more agitated with my silence.

"Is this not your intended method? You truly believe some fabled doorway to another realm will simply suck him up and you'll be done with him?" Kurat pushes, leaning forward in his chair, fighting the burning urge to stand, to tower above me. He holds himself back in a way that his father has never done. He holds himself back from the unspoken threat of violence. He is determined, for whatever reason, not to force my hand. And so he is left with persuasion.

How terrible it must be for him to feel powerless. How I relish witnessing it. Why would I speak now, when his undoing is so satisfying?

"You have come all this way but you will not consent to speak," he scoffs, leaning back in his chair as if dismissing me. "Perhaps you do love being Chieftainess!" He tries to goad me, but I am not prey to such petty insecurities.

And so his self-restraint ends, as I knew it would. I have watched him for a decade. I know that honor binds him only to the end of his patience, and from there the pursuit of his will justifies his darkness.

Now he rises in the way a man rises. He steps towards me in the way a man steps towards a woman he wishes to bend to his will. He clenches his fist, his jaw.

Then he is brought to his knees.

There is a subtle thread woven through the back of the knee. Pluck it just so and the mind loses its connection with everything below. And so Kurat kneels, catching himself with his hands before he tastes the soiled thresh of the floor.

In his father's court, I have been nearly powerless against this man for ten years. And though I am not so blinded by anger that I cannot understand his motives, I am not so benevolent as to wholly forgive him for what he has brought against me and mine.

Fool.

He has brought me here. He has forgotten the blood pooling in his ears so long ago. He has forgotten the audible *snap* of his shattering wrist as it echoed between the sacred pines.

Fool.

When he looks up at me, he knows it. There is the anger, of course. But his fear is a pleasant tang on the tip of my tongue.

"And have you now remembered to whom you speak?" I say mildly. He sneers, pressing his lips together, but does not speak.

"Have you now realized your folly in bringing me here, where threats against my child are meaningless and you leave yourself open to my power? I hesitated before, to indulge my own greed. I will not make the same mistake twice. Speak what you have come to speak, offer what terms you have come to offer, and if anything besides leaves your lips, I will complete the work I began ten years ago."

I expect him to argue that to move against him would be to move against his father, and to do so would ensure Maarja's own demise. And so I have already devised a series of torments that I can do and undo in the span of a few hours' time.

But then the oddest thing happens.

He narrows his eyes and fills his chest with a deep breath.

"I intend to kill the Chieftain," he murmurs, almost as if to himself. And then he is gone.

In one moment, he is prostrate before me and in the next, as I stare at the empty space where he knelt, I remember with a sinking horror that he is Lekja's son – the child of a Shade Walker.

Before I can even rise, he is there once more, standing, though with a pained twist to his mouth. And from his fingertips dangles a lock of my daughter's thick black hair.

I come to my feet slowly, staring at it.

For several breaths, neither of us speak, our gazes locked together on the delicate artifact between us, still smelling of sweat and horse and girl.

"You're a Shade Walker," I breathe.

He nods grimly.

There is only one question that is important now.

"Why have you not done it already?" I whisper. "Why have you not killed him?"

He reaches out with his other hand and I allow him, perhaps in a stupor of shock, to take my own. Despite his show of power, his palm is clammy, his fingertips unsteady.

He brings my hand between us and slowly lowers Maarja's hair into a coil in my palm, then folds my fingers over it.

"For the same reason you have not done so yourself," he murmurs, releasing me and stepping away.

"Maarja?" I ask, doubtful. He shakes his head.

"I wish her no ill will," says the man who only just cut a lock of hair from her sleeping head to prove a point. "But I will not alter my designs for her sake."

"Then who?" I ask.

And then he looks at me, weary and open and angry. The hairs on my nape electrify, the shiver running down the backs of my legs.

"Me?" I breathe, astounded.

"Perhaps we should continue as we were," he says, moving away and motioning to the stool I have abandoned. He lowers himself to his own.

"I rather think that impossible," I answer breathlessly, but I sit nonetheless.

"It is not for the reasons you might think," he explains, crossing his lean legs and straightening the tunic that covers them. "I have found it a convenient and effective method to allow Tuskjas to believe that I am in love with you, but I would make it clear to you that I am not."

"Whyever would you –" I start, struggling to consume his logic. "He fears an alliance between us more than anything else –"

"Certainly, but a clearly unrequited affection works to his advantage in numerous ways," Kurat explains, raising his fine hands to tick off his reasons. "First, there is no chance of you ever returning the feeling, which is evident to anyone at court or beyond. Second, to believe me weakened by such an affection allows Tuskjas to feel himself at a great advantage in his dealings with me, primarily in keeping himself safe. Third, he relishes in my misery, and that indulgence blinds him to my intent."

"So if you have no true affection for me why 'alter your designs' for my sake?" I ask him in his own words.

"That requires considerably more explanation than simple unrequited passion, including several items which I am not prepared to reveal to you until I better understand your own intentions," he answers tightly.

"Then why reveal it to me at all?" I ask.

"What, precisely?" he asks, cocking his head.

"Any of it – all of it," I say, sweeping my hands wide. "Why show me the Shade Walking? Why tell me you intend to kill him?"

"What do you know of Shade Walking?" He answers my question with his own.

"I know that it originated with the Shadow Queen. That it allows the Walker to step between places from one breath to the next."

He nods subtly, crossing his hands carefully over one another in his lap, tight and tidy.

"There is something you do, I have noticed," he says slowly. "When you are preparing to use your power – you go within yourself. You –," he waves a hand around, trying to bring forth the right word, "– quiet yourself. Are you summoning it, the Wasting?"

A note of warning tickles my neck, but if I were to have heeded every one of my body's warnings, I would never have reached this place. I am here. I suspect there is no returning to whence I came. So I dare.

"We call it the Shroud," I begin slowly, not familiar with the sharing of such secrets.

"It is a part of your power? A thing you cover yourself in then?" he asks, his chin tilting slightly with the curiosity in his level gaze.

"It is a place, in some respects. A state of the body. A state of equanimity and objectivity," I explain. He nods.

"And from that place you draw your power?" Kurat guesses.

"No," I shake my head. "The power comes regardless of the state of the Waster. But Wasting from within the Shroud gives one better control over the working."

He nods, murmuring, "I have often wondered." Then he straightens his shoulders and breathes deeply.

"Shade Walking requires something similar," he offers. "An ideal state of being. One of purity."

I cannot help my disbelief. The man before me must surely be anything other than pure. He deals in untruths.

My condemnation is visible to him. He grins slightly, grimly.

"Yes, I would imagine you find it difficult to believe me a man of purity," he admits, looking up to the moldering thatched roof of this place. He sighs deeply.

"Balancing my two powers has been the greatest challenge of my life," he goes on with his strange and unfamiliar honesty.

"With one I create falsehoods, and yet, to use the other I must be free of them. And that is why I do not often access my mother's power."

"It forces you to confess," I say, remembering his murmured words before he disappeared. *I intend to kill the Chieftain.*

His gaze falls heavily on me.

"It is as you say," he answers carefully. "The power comes, in some form, regardless. But complex practice requires sincerity. An unapologetic scoundrel may manage to pass from one side of the room to the other, but to cross distances, and do so with accuracy, requires the Walker to travel lightly."

"And so you have told me that you intend to kill your father," I say.

"I have not dared to Walk more than a few feet since the moment I first contrived it," he confesses.

"But now that you have confessed it, you can threaten my daughter freely," I accuse.

"Is that what I have done?" he asks, head tilting away from me in the candlelight. I bring my hand out between us, opening my fingers slowly. My palm has grown damp, and Maarja's lock limp within it.

He does not look at it. He does not need to.

"And if I told you I took that from your daughter's head several weeks ago? If I told you that I only Walked outside and returned?" he asks.

"I would require proof. I would require you to Walk *now*, saying nothing before you go," I answer.

"Good," he nods. "Then this will be your practice each time we meet from this day hence. If I make a claim or reveal a truth, demand that I Walk to prove it. Though, do keep in mind that I can only Walk to a place I have been, or to the presence of someone with whom I am familiar."

"Then Walk," I demand. "Prove you took the lock from her weeks ago."

He does not patronize me by showing any surprise. He simply opens his hands, palms up.

"You cannot," I accuse. "Because this still bears my daughter's essence as surely as it did when you cut it from her head a moment ago."

He shrugs, unapologetic.

My fingers close back over my daughter's hair, nails biting into the thick base of my palm.

"Walking proves nothing," I say, looking back at him. "Whatever test I might devise you can simply pluck from my mind or change my intention at will."

"What I have given you thus far is not enough?" He scoffs indignantly. "Now you ask after that other power? You require that I reveal all my secrets on our first meeting?"

"If you desire for there to be another, yes."

Kurat studies me with all his desire for my cooperation written into the lines of his face. I say nothing. I prod no more. He will either risk or he will not, depending on how greatly he desires the outcome.

"I have no power to see that which is in your mind," he confesses finally into the silence.

"I can only presume what might be within a person's mind based on what I know of them, and then lay another story over it. The closer my revision is to what one has actually experienced the more effective, or perhaps the more subtle, I am able to be. If I have no inclination as to what a true memory might contain, the illusion unravels quickly or the person I am attempting to influence becomes aware of my intervention too quickly."

"In the first years that you were here, I was present for nearly every moment of your waking day. I knew what your memory would contain from each interaction, and so I was able to alter it for Tuskjas' purposes and then lay it gently over your true memory. That is why it took you so long to discover my influence."

"And the dreams?" I breathe.

"Dreams?" he asks, brows lowering.

"They come to me in dreams," I murmur, throat tightening on the words trying to push through. "My true memories come to me in dreams."

He purses his lips assessingly. "You are the only person I have influenced as often and for as long as I have. I do not know if all the memories I alter eventually reveal their true selves in dreams or if that is a particular quirk of your own power."

"Yet, in the moment, I know nothing of your influence. I have no way to guard against it, even now," I argue.

"I don't think that entirely true," he says, shaking his head. "There are times when I have thought you had learned to resist me, but then I would try again after a time and find no opposition. Over time I began to notice a pattern – the Shroud, you called it? I cannot affect you there."

Draw the Shroud, Liama.

My mother's voice. My grandmother's. The first of all the things they taught me. To find the stillness. The well. The vast heart of power.

76

All this time. All this time, resisting him has been as simple as drawing the Shroud. The realization is battering, a solid punch to my belly. My fingertips feel numb.

"Are you now satisfied?" Kurat asks, tilting his head with brows high. But I cannot speak.

"Liama?" he asks, narrowing his gaze, and I am back in the Wood, hearing my name from his lips like a threat.

"Why have you revealed this now?" I whisper, even as I draw the Shroud around me. He studies me, but I do not let the truth of what I am doing into my eyes.

"I should think that clear to you at this point in the conversation," he answers softly.

"How can you be so arrogant?" I say, sitting forward. Gaining strength. But I can tell he does not understand me.

"You have no weapon now," I clarify. "You have no means –"

"I do not think that you can live inside your Shroud anymore than I can keep impurity from crossing my lips," he argues, sitting forward as well. "Power always has limits. What I offer is an alliance – the one Tuskjas so fears – and whatever power over you I have given up to acquire it should indicate how strong my motivation is to see my desired ends achieved. Whatever I have given up I consider nothing in comparison to what I may gain. But hear me well, Liama."

His black-brown gaze bores into mine. His jaw sets, pointed and firm under his pale skin.

"Everything depends on the most delicate subterfuge. Everything depends on his ignorance. I will not risk it. If I have to rewrite every memory in your head, I will not risk it."

"And you hope to win my loyalty with such a speech?" I bite, but my voice lacks heat. It is the Shroud coming down, its detached indifference leaking into my voice. And he is right. I cannot live inside of it forever.

"I want nothing of your loyalty," he presses. "I only want your power. If I can obtain it willingly, and something of your trust along with it, then that is what I desire. But if I cannot, I will not hesitate to take it by force."

It falls between us, the threat I have known would come from the moment I sensed him shadowed in the darkness of my chamber. I know his character well enough to take him at his word. And then I ensure that he will take me at mine.

It is a complex working, one that can only be achieved from within the Shroud. Bringing a man to his knees or breaking the fine bones of his body is a kind of Wasting that more likely results in anger. Anger is useful. Anger corrupts the thoughts. It brings out weaknesses and exposes insecurities. It dulls reason.

Yet, anger is simply the compass, exposing the path. There is something that lies deeper.

The delicacy of this practice lies in understanding that, though I change before his very sight, it is his body, not my own, that I am Wasting. I cannot hope to achieve the effect that my mother could with her decades of experience. But I have always had a deft touch and an affinity for the eyes.

He feels no pain at all, the Wasting is so minute. And though the space between us does not change, I know what he sees within it. The candlelight darkens, shrinking until it is nothing more than a sliver of dancing light, as red as blood. What was once golden around us mutes to a dull maroon. My face is cast in red, my eyes the color of dried blood. His heartbeat kicks and wobbles. He does not understand what is occurring. He can feel his pulse in his palms. All the light fades from the surroundings. There is only my pale face, disembodied, floating in the pitch.

"What are you doing?" he asks, trying to keep the shudder from his voice.

I smile, baring my teeth.

"What are you doing?" he calls again, alarm growing. He makes to rise but he finds his legs will not hold him. His hands will not obey.

Now I turn my touch on myself. I stare back at him with hollowed cheeks and wide, blood-shot eyes. With shriveled lips pulled back over the darkness of my open mouth. I thicken the delicate chords within my throat, preparing to push my voice deeper.

"Liama!" he demands, one last attempt to saddle me with my own name. He knows it is an illusion, but he cannot escape the body that does not.

It is the curse of these vessels we carry. They cannot be reasoned with.

I lean over him, bringing my ghastly face within his exhale. And when I speak, it is with the voice of the grave.

"I am not your weapon, to be wielded for your whims," I growl. He tries to recoil, horror fighting rage in his eyes.

"Say it," I command. But he bites his lips together, refusing. I pull the light further from his eyes, casting him in total darkness.

"Say it," I command again. He shakes his head bitterly, pale gaze searching blindly for the source of my voice.

Darkness has been his home. His inheritance. Let him know that I will turn that safety into terror.

And so I wrap his heartbeat around my wrist and pull.

He stutters, gasping for air, and the fear in his blinded eyes wins out.

"You are," he croaks through empty lungs, "not my weapon."

I smile, releasing his heart. He shivers and shakes, heaving in air, but the rage burns back into his eyes as his sight returns, and the gaze he turns upon me is more livid than any I have yet seen from him.

"Now walk, boy," I demand, making him acknowledge the truth of what I have forced him to say.

He sucks in a final, gasping breath.
And then he is gone.

The figure stands over me in the darkness. The fear rolls from her in spikes, glinting as brightly as her upraised blade in the moonlight. She had not expected me here. She has realized she was misinformed.

But she swallows the hesitation. Her mistress has ordained her. She will not turn away now.

I open my eyes.

Our gazes embrace.

And then I turn from her, giving her my back.

She breathes in. Three quick breaths booming red across her lungs. And then she tenses, the acid flooding into the muscles of her shoulders, her upper back.

With a final, bracing, inhale, she slams the blade downwards, her own anguished cry echoing in her ears.

I allow the tip of the blade to knick my husband's thick chest, and then I drop her, breaking her arms as she falls under paralyzed legs.

Tuskjas rises like a startled wolf, bellowing even before his eyes are fully opened. He leaps from the bed, grabbing the lame woman by the head and snapping her neck in one powerful twist of his arms.

He does not need to know who sent her.

Guards barrel into the space, candles lighting and voices filling my husband's chamber. But the big, heaving man turns his enraged eyes to me, livid with betrayal. A single trickle of thick foreign blood winds its way down his hairy, muscled belly. From somewhere I hear the sound of faint whistling, like a window cracked open in the wind.

"Bring the girl," he whispers, low and rough.

"No," I whisper, rising to my knees, despite my nakedness. The guards look away, but I do not heed their embarrassment.

"I stopped her," I argue, crawling towards him on all fours. "I stopped her, Tuskjas. It is only a little scratch."

But his narrowed gaze is unconvinced.

"Bring the girl," he orders again, but my daughter is already being carried through the door.

She has only just learned to walk, but when they put her on her fat, rounded feet she falls, still half asleep and already whimpering.

I scramble towards her, but Tuskjas slams out an arm, knocking the breath from my chest. Still, I fight and scratch and scream empty screams and Maarja echoes them, wailing fat wet tears from red eyes, snot flowing freely from her nose, arching her little back and trying to drop out of the guard's hold. The men holding her hesitate, looking between the Chieftain and the child.

Tuskjas throws me back on the bed a final time, ordering guards to hold me down. I drop the first one and Tuskjas spins, the assassin's dagger now in his hand, striding forward to hold it to my throat.

"Tenfold," he seethes into my face.

Whatever you see fit to mete upon me will be meted upon her tenfold.

His promise to me on our wedding day.

I am beyond reason, but still I do not Waste him.

Why do I not Waste him?

Maarja screams as he towers over her, kicking her feet and smacking at him with her tiny hands. He snatches them both in one hand, holding her chubby arms above her head and laying her back on the cold, hard stone.

She screams harder, choking on thick, globby sobs. I kill the first man in my desperation to get free of his hold, blinding the next and breaking

81

all the fingers on the third. Then Kurat is there, leaning over me, his gaze depthless and black and hollow.

"Stop, Liama," *he breathes into my face, and as I breathe in the breath he exhales, I do.*

I can smell her blood, I can hear her shrieking, terrified cries, every other word my name.

And yet, I lie there, limp and staring into his endless eyes.

Suddenly, there is a silence there has never been in all the times I have relived the horror of the night my husband carved his mark into my daughter's tiny chest.

I breathe. Kurat breathes with me.

In this body, this sleeping body, I remember the delicate touch of his shaking hand as he lowered Maarja's lock of hair into my palm, curling my fingers gently over it.

And then the dream unfurls.

"Tenfold," *Tuskjas seethes into my face.*

Whatever you see fit to mete upon me will be meted upon her tenfold.

His promise to me on our wedding day.

I am beyond reason, but still I do not Waste him.

Why do I not Waste him?

Maarja screams as he towers over her, kicking her feet and smacking at him with her tiny hands. He snatches them both in one hand, holding her chubby arms above her head and laying her back on the cold, hard stone.

I cannot see his hands, but I feel the tense of his muscles as he flips the dagger deftly in his grip and brings its tip to the collar of my daughter's nightrail to slice it open. She screams harder, choking on thick, globby sobs. I kill the first man in my desperation to get free of his hold, blinding the next and breaking all the fingers on the third.

"Stop!"

Kurat comes running in the door, pushing a guard to the side in his haste. He skids to a halt over his father, who is even now ripping the delicate fabric of Maarja's nightrail in two.

"Stop!" Kurat yells again, dropping down beside Tuskjas, but he does not dare touch man or child for fear of misdirecting the knife's point.

"Think of what word will reach Barbüra," Kurat reasons into the side of his father's livid face. "All the fortress has heard the screaming. Do you think the assassin has come alone? Barbüra will know – the whole House will know she has moved against you."

"Let them know," Tuskjas seethes, undeterred. He turns the dagger again in his grip, this time to carve. Maarja shakes and whimpers, her baby cries all given out, her lashes thick and black with vain tears.

"And will you show them the flesh of a babe?" Kurat argues, spreading his own hand under the dagger's point, his pale fingers over Maarja's pale chest. "Drag the assassin's body out for all to see and put her head on a spike, but do it with your wife and child hale and victorious beside you."

Tuskjas growls, hating to let go of his vengeance.

"But let them know your Waster has failed you and you dull your own blade," Kurat murmurs, this time for only Tuskjas to hear. "Let them know she is not here willingly, loyally, and they will never fear her again. You will find yourself embroiled in plot after plot with her at their centers."

I leap from the dream prematurely, gasping into the night. But even though I do not witness it, I wake with the memory of Tuskjas' reluctant hiss, the way he pulled back suddenly, jumping to his feet and spinning on me, still held prostrate and naked by his men on his bed. The way he held my eyes with his hot, violent gaze as he ordered everyone out of the room and turned the blade on his bedding, carving the outline of my body into the mattress below, his careless knicks sending my blood flowing into the down.

And I had whimpered, too relieved to be humiliated or afraid. I had only cried my sweet mother's guilt into my hair, letting him have his way with me.

And now, when I draw the Shroud and tiptoe into my daughter's chambers, dampening my body so as not to wake her, and part the ties of her soft nightrail over her thin chest, I let the same tangy relief flow down my cheeks and into my mouth at the sight of her smooth, unmarred skin.

CHAPTER SIX
THE PINE SAP BOIL

The womb, the darling, the giver of life.
Holy of power, riddled with strife.
The body bears the womb as the womb bears the babe.
Heavy the burden of birth and decay.

I ASKED my grandmother once why we did not call Looklema's twin daughters by their names. Why only Wasting Queen and Shadow Queen?

I was concerned about my own naming. My mother and grandmother had chosen to name me after Looklema's mother, the Shadow Spirit Liama, wife to the Healer and mother to the three founders. When I questioned her, I could tell my grandmother had misinterpreted my intention. She had thought that I felt unworthy to carry the same name, the name of the Most Sacred Mother. In truth, I knew that Liama was known, not for her power, but for her quiet loyalty, her grace, and her womb. I did not want to be quiet or graceful.

Of the Twin Queens, my grandmother had only said "If they had wanted their names on the lips of their descendents, they would have put them there."

"But why?" I had questioned. "Why would they not want us to know their names?"

She had grinned, eyes gleaming.

"Perhaps because their reign is not yet complete," came her cryptic reply.

"But are they not dead, then?" I asked.

"Daughter," my grandmother had chided warmly. "One need not be living to be reigning."

I think about her words more often than I ought.

I do not tell Hiida.

She will only fret and fuss and advise against the very thought of any agreement between Kurat and myself. So I hold my tongue, not because she is wrong to do so, but because she is right. And I cannot hear her and proceed.

And yet, I must proceed.

I do not chide Maarja either for revealing the contents of our lessons to her stepbrother. I have been possessed of a nagging worry now for many years. I suspect that my daughter is missing something vital, something essential. Some nutrient or element which can only be obtained from Looklema's forest. Her age is so tender, and her spirit even more malleable. I am not surprised to hear that she was eager to share her knowledge with someone. She is eager for Kurat's approval, no matter his detached exterior. She has the same desire to please my husband, to earn his praise.

I've spoken my worries to Hiida many times. I've spoken my worries to Vappers. They assure me, in their own ways, that Maarja's softness is a sign of growing grace in the world. Hiida says I have had to be rugged to endure what I have experienced. She says Maarja does not need that strength. Maarja will be adored, and that will be protection enough for her.

Hiida's friendship and her service have been invaluable to me. And her bluntly delivered truths, refreshing in their ineloquence, have set my heart to rights more often than I can count. But I do not consider her to be a terribly wise woman. Hiida sees what she longs to see.

And so I fret over my daughter, and I do not chide her.

Kurat makes himself scarce for several days following our encounter. On the third day, my husband and I occupy our places upon the dais. He, seated on Looklema's throne, and I, a menacing pillar behind him, hearing the dispute of an official of the woodcutters' guild against rising fees extracted by local mills. My husband finds these administrative duties to be tedious. He far prefers the reports of his spies on the Kallas and their families. Tuskjas slumps on my ancestor's chair, his large head held aloft by the rough and hairy knuckles of his left hand.

My power reveals what my husband's senses cannot. The official's body pleads for justice just as his words do. The heart beats high and tight. The ache of his anxiety presses against his sternum, squeezing his voice and bringing high color to his cheeks. His forehead beads sweat, and I can hear the buzzing intensity of his mind, releasing and absorbing the emotions that drive his plea – stress, fear, anger. He has been sent here to plead on behalf of his fellows. There is no counting how many souls he speaks for. How many wives and children his words are meant to represent.

He has long considered what he will say to the Chieftain. He has ruminated over the words, their intensity. His fellows have given him advice. His wife has placed her hands on his shoulders at the door of their home. She has looked into his eyes and blessed him with the tongue of the Mother Snake, to speak wisely and persuasively. His children have all kissed him, blessing him with their innocent trust. He has walked all the way to Tarbatu, steadying his breaths. He has waited in the Hall for his turn before the Chieftain, praying to the Snake Daughter for her guidance. And now he has delivered his well-constructed plea as well as he can, and the man before him has done little more than stir briefly from his repose.

I do not know that any of these events have taken place specifically, but I know that all of them have in some way. My husband sighs, as if raising himself from deep thought. His reluctance, his indifference, is written in every coarse line of his rugged face.

Tuskjas is at his ugliest when he is bored. They say his father was a handsome man, and his mother was considered beautiful by her people's standards. Tuskjas has nothing of their famed appearances. It is as if all the features that drew the approving eye to his parents' faces have rearranged themselves ungracefully and untidily. A nose too thin and long on a face too wide. A thick-lipped mouth on a delicate chin. And eyes too small, too muddy, too close together.

"Have you not taken the matter to the steward at Gratu? Why have you come here with your troubles?" Tuskjas says wearily. The woodcutters' official works the slouchy cap in his hands between anxious fingers. I watch as he rubs his thumb over and over the tidy seams of a new patch. He is pulling his wife's presence with him into this space. He is thinking it should have been her here before the Chieftain. He is thinking she would not have felt tempted to cower. He is thinking she has never been afraid in her life.

"We did, indeed, my Chieftain," the man begins his explanation, stopping to calm himself with a steadying breath. He has already explained this to my husband, but he readies himself to explain it again.

"The steward felt the matter should come before you, my Chieftain, as it pertains to the setting of fees across multiple regions and therefore cannot be resolved by –"

"You seek to instruct me on interregional policy in my own Hall, do you?" Tuskjas grumbles, though he is not really offended, merely annoyed. This is a tactic often employed. He seeks to weaken the resolve of the man before him. He doesn't want to have to consider a judgement on something so trivial as mill fees. He wants the man to take his troubles away and reconcile them on his own.

But the man presses his lips together, thumbing his wife's handiwork once more on his worn cap, sets his shoulders, and pushes forward.

"The steward has provided me with this letter describing his hesitations in detail," the man goes on, pulling the leather satchel on his shoulder forward and producing a rolled parchment. The seal of the steward of Gratu, with its twin bridge towers, is evident on its front. I step forward, descending the dais to take it from the man's hand. His eyes drop, head bowing, and he brings two fingers to his forehead, whispering '*Varju Tütar*' as the letter passes from his hand to mine. But he does not release it. He holds me there with him, his lowered eyes flickering towards my husband behind me. Then his other hand slips just inside of the sleeve of his tunic, emerging as a fist, which he lays over my curled fingers, wrapped around the parchment. I open my palm just enough to feel the scratchy pine needles tucked into the gap, and then the man releases me, stepping away and bowing his head.

All of this has passed in little more than a breath. I slip the token into my sleeve as I turn, ascending the dais once more and passing the letter to my husband, who maintains his air of reluctant tolerance.

I do not need an explanation to know what I hold against my skin within my sleeve. I know the oils, the smell of these needles, as I know my mother's open palms.

The audience goes on. My husband offers the man nothing more than a commitment to consider the matter and deliver his judgement directly to the steward of Gratu within the moon. The woodcutters' official makes no attempt to meet my eye as he goes, hat in hand, from the Hall. More supplicants enter and depart. We hear reports of Norsemen sightings off the coast of northernmost Revala, heading south through the North Sea. My grandmother once told me her mother's mother had battled Norsemen in her time, sending the vicious barbarians scurrying back to their longboats with their braids between their legs.

An hour finally comes when the business of the House is done. The sun slants low through the Hall's high windows. The smells of the kitchen across the yard begin to seep through the large open doors.

My husband waves me out from behind his throne, leaning over its carved side to murmur with his steward, who stands in Kurat's customary place in the Heir's absence.

I step from my place, back aching from standing so long behind him. Hiida will be expecting me upstairs to dress for end-day meal. She will need to find me something to wear with long, gathered sleeves. The pine sap against my wrist has begun to burn and itch.

I turn, giving my husband the customary respects before leaving his presence. His business concluded with the steward, Tuskjas returns the gestures, drowsy and bored.

But when my foot falls on the final step from the dais, he speaks.

"Liama," he calls. I turn, looking up at him. His half-grin sours my stomach.

"Are you not going to show me your little gift?" he asks innocently, tilting his heavy head just so. I know the expression too well. A kind of restrained delight in impending misery.

"I have no gift," I answer flatly. My wrist itches.

"No gift?" he asks, smiling now in full. It is a wretched thing to behold, unproportioned to his thick lips. "You needn't be coy about it. I am not so vain as to be jealous of how my people adore you. Come here. Show me what token of their worship they've bestowed upon you this time. I love to see their little offerings."

What my husband lacks in power, he makes up for in this way. This uncanny ability to know what is being kept from him.

I pull the token from my sleeve, looking at it now for the first time. It is a simple thing – a single frond from the end of a pine bow, only six or seven needles. Wrapped around it is a frayed ribbon of old cloth, what was once the deep rust color of a favorite work apron. I can see it on Erga's delicate frame. She was too thin by far when I came to her. The long straps of the apron were tied twice around her waist.

Smell is such a powerful sense. I had never met Erga's husband as I treated her, only a sister and her son. Her husband had been away. But I had spent several hours in her home. I had smelled him in all the ways one leaves one's body behind. His scent on her bed, in her clothes. In her son's fine brown hair.

And the moment the woodcutters' official pulled the token from his tunic, the sparkling scent of pine tied him to that place in my mind, and there was no mistaking him.

I hold the little offering out in my palm, but make no move to take it up the dais to my husband. His close-set eyes fall on it, derision in the set of his brows.

"You will not take the finest clothes and trinkets from me, not even a circlet upon your head, but this little thing you let rest against your skin, bringing it to boil? How terribly precious it must be to you,"

Tuskjas sneers, eyes narrowing further on the token. He presses his fat lips together, and when they release they form once more into a derisive grin.

"Tear it up," he commands.

I do not hesitate. I rip the pine needles apart, throwing them away from me to mingle with the thresh. Their destruction releases their scent sharply, and I breathe it in, victorious. The smell of home.

"That as well, whatever it is," he nods, indicating the string of Erga's worn apron. I let it fall to the stones. I raise my eyes to his. Obedient. He studies me for signs of resistance, but I give him nothing. I think of Kurat's terrified face instead. I think of how he stepped frantically into Shadow, fleeing. I hold the fear of my husband's son in my gaze. I lay it over Tuskjas' features. I relish, knowing that there will come a day when he looks at me with all the knowledge of his own death in his eyes. That is all I need to do what must be done now.

After a moment he waves me away. I turn, striding from the Hall, making my heeled boots strike harder and ring louder in the cavernous space. The token is not a keepsake. It has already done its work. My wrist itches, and I scratch it for the first time, my nails ripping the skin, peeling back the barrier. The wound burns, and I rejoice, sacred pine sap seeping into my bloodstream.

I charge Hiida with finding the woodcutters' official before he leaves Tarbatu. She will not complete the task herself, but she will find a way. She is used to these little jobs I give her. So long as she knows that whatever I am about will ultimately deepen the people's love for me, she makes no argument. She thinks that adoration, worship even, is a weapon.

It is likely that she is right. But it is a weapon I have not yet learned to use. Still, I store it up, like the Little Hurt. If I cannot wield it, then at least I may bestow it on my daughter when the time comes.

Hiida tells me that the man is found and pressed to extend his stay. She reports that he was unsurprised by the request. I suspect that catching my attention may have been a secondary motive for presenting himself to the Chieftain. Still, there's nothing more I can do until Kurat shows his face again, which causes several days to pass.

The Heir presents himself in the Hall at midday meal, dusty and disheveled from travel, greeting his father with the Estian greeting and a deep bow. I am wholly ignored – the only indication he gives that our last encounter remains in his mind. If his father notices the slight, he does not make note of it.

"Clean yourself up and join us," Tuskjas commands, indicating Kurat's typical place to his right. Kurat nods, accepting his father's direction, but approaches the table in his travel clothes nonetheless. He leans forward on Tuskjas' left side, murmuring loud enough for me to hear.

"I have matters of extreme urgency to report from Ugandi."

Tuskjas studies him with narrowed black eyes, then nods. Kurat backs away, bowing once more and then striding from the Hall. My husband rises from his chair well enough, but I catch the subtle groan and strain of the bones in his knees. The weight of his big body is beginning to thin the delicate membranes there.

At his rise, all the Hall's many occupants come to their feet. There are more people at court this time of year, when Tarbatu, high on the central plains of Est, is cooler than the low, forested regions that surround it, save perhaps Vaiga on the shores of Lake Peipus. And the warm afternoons tempt the members of court to linger over their meads and sweet pies, enjoying the cool interior of the stone Hall.

The tables are arranged in long lines running along the walls, with proximity to the Chieftain's raised table on the dais, indicative of one's general standing at court. Kallas Barbüra once occupied the foremost seat, but she has since been replaced by the young and ruddy Kallas of Vaiga, whose freshwater fish and minerals have brought considerable wealth to his region in recent years. Kallas Rahuleid's charisma has certainly assisted his rise, as well as his wife, the Lady Hariva, who has a propensity to give expensive, carefully-curated gifts.

Farther down Rahuleid's table is the venerated Kallas of Ugandi, an ancient man who fought alongside Kotkas himself to regain Eastern Est from the Slavs nearly 70 years ago. It is whispered that he was among the most outspoken protractors of Tuskjas' ascension to the throne, having been unable, even during the 40 years of Kotkas' long reign, to come to terms with a Slavic Chieftainess. Still, his heroics during the war ensured his longstanding place at court, although I suspect the shine has worn from his reputation, as well as his sword, in recent years, so few left are there who remember the war.

The man's age, especially considering his profession as a warrior, is astounding, and yet, his straight-backed posture and the sinewy strength of his uncovered forearms might tempt one to believe he has at least one more war in him before he expires. His son and heir sits by his side, nearly an aged man himself, so long has he waited for his father to breathe his spirit into the sky and pass the title.

The Kallas of Sakala sits beyond with his daughter and heir, Maarja's little companion Suita. Bordering House Rezke to the south, it is said that before the Rezkans denied Kotkas aid in his battle against the Slavs, Sakala was a place of open interbreeding between Looklema's people and those of her middle brother, Erasts, blessed by the Owl King with great wisdom and discernment. Nothing of that heritage shows in Meevat or the young Suita, as petite and sharp-featured as the rest of us. However, Maarja has told me that Suita's intended back in Sakala is a tall, self-contained youth with a gift for languages, and as such, has become quite the object of the two girls' youthful romantic fantasies.

In and among the Kallas are their entourages and advisors and stewards, as well as their children and nieces and nephews and grandchildren, all traveling to and from court for their education. An education that has, since Kallas Barbüra's departure, been in name only. What Barbüra lacks in honor she makes up for in profundity – there is perhaps no one with a more meticulously curated knowledge of Est's history. Tuskjas has been unmotivated to find capable tutors in her absence, claiming that the few Estian scholars who have presented themselves as candidates were too biased against the Slavs, his mother's people. Another indication that the war is long over. Still, for the young, the prestige of being seen and known among the court of Tarbatu holds substantial weight in the consideration of marriage contracts and favorable political terms.

More notably, absence from court indicates the Chieftain's displeasure. In Lekja's day, her father, the Kallas of Saaremaa, was said to have occupied the highest seat of influence, but he has not been seen in Tarbatu since her death. Nor has the Kallas of Revala, who long insists that Norse raids on her shores are the primary reason for her absence. Virumaa, the poorest of the regions, whose heir apparent Tuskjas is seeking to have murdered, is rarely represented at court either.

Tuskjas could easily fill their empty seats at the back of the Hall with willing occupants, but he leaves the three places open, insisting his invitation to the missing Kallas is always extended. The dust gathering on their chairs is statement enough to the double-edged nature of the claim.

When the Chieftain has exited the Hall behind his Heir, the members of court all regain their seats, falling back into abandoned conversations, which drift like smoke into the rafters, filling the Hall with sound. I am not expected to follow my husband to the private conference in his study, and so I make my way, trencher in hand, down the dais and to the open chair beside Kallas Rahuleid's wife, the Lady Hariva, who sees me coming and slaps her husband's hand away from the last remaining hunk of dark rye bread at the table's center. Rahuleid looks up, breaking from his conversation with the visiting steward of Bainu on his other side, a playful tease on his lips for his wife's sudden violence.

Rahuleid's eyes are always kind, but when he sees my approach, they soften further. I do not know if the Kallas of Vaiga is aware that I order his manservant from his quarters late in the night to take my hand and ease my many burdens, but I suspect that if Rahuleid were aware, he would not object.

Man and wife both greet me with two fingers to their foreheads, but that is the extent of the formality between us. Hariva pushes the small trencher of bread towards me, smiling her knowing smile.

"If only the Chieftain himself could be won over by bread," Rahuleid laments theatrically. "I'd have a fat purse and an even fatter ass by now."

Hariva shakes her head, long accustomed to her husband's antics.

"As if anything you ate ever put an ounce on your figure," she says, pressing her lips together. I grin at them both but do not speak. It is a particular luxury of my friendship with these two. They do not require anything of me other than my presence and the occasional affirmation that they are, indeed, delightful companions and the most humorous of my many acquaintances.

"Maarja and Suita came to see me, did you know?" Hariva reports, a smile tucked into the corner of her prim mouth. I raise my brows in question, beginning to pick the hardened crust off the loaf to get to the soft middle.

"Quite a few interesting questions, those two had," Hariva goes on. "I advised them both to take their questions to their mothers, but Suita would not be denied, and Maarja I'm sure was just as eager, even if she let Suita do all the talking."

"Do I want to know the nature of these questions?" Rahuleid asks.

"I suspect you already know the nature of these questions," Hariva answers sardonically.

"Ah, well. And with that, I return to the far more intelligent talk of men, who never dwell on such things," Rahuleid answers, dramatically turning himself away to continue his conversation with the steward on his other side.

Hariva rolls her eyes. Despite his playacting, her gossip-hungry husband is surely still bending an ear to our conversation.

"Did you answer them?" I ask.

"Of course I did," Hariva waves my question away. "I certainly gained nothing of value from my own mother when I asked the same, and, meaning no offense, I suspect your answers would bend towards technicalities, being what you are."

She raises her thin brows and tilts her small head, waiting for me to deny it, which I do not.

"Anything I need to revisit with my newly-educated daughter?" I ask saucily, though in truth I'm glad Maarja has gotten her knowledge from a woman who is so clearly adored by her husband. Perhaps she will know better than I how to determine compatibility, having learned from Hariva.

"She seemed to have some trouble with the impetus behind a few of the more, shall we say, exploratory expressions of desire," Hariva says, waving one of her delicate hands in the air between us.

"Snake's teeth, Hariva," I exclaim. "How detailed did you get with them?"

"I only answered their questions!" She defends herself quickly.

"And where on earth did they get these questions?" I ask.

"They didn't say exactly, but Suita seemed to be operating from a rather detailed perspective, one I suspect she gained from hiding unseen somewhere while certain acts were taking place," Hariva explains, brows waggling, now beginning to smile again.

I glare at her knowingly.

"Not me!" she suddenly exclaims, understanding my unspoken meaning. "I grew up with seven sisters, I'll remind you. I'm quite adept at locking my door!"

"Hariva," I sigh, shaking my head. "Suita is a Clasper."

The other woman stares at me for a moment, then her brows rise and her mouth forms into a long 'o'.

"Then you think –" she starts, realization dawning.

"That she's perfectly capable of unlocking your door and hiding herself away in your chambers," I explain.

"But whatever for? Surely she wasn't there for the sole purpose of witnessing –"

"She's 13 now and considers herself quite a bit older. I am certain she was there for the sole purpose of witnessing exploratory acts of passion between a woman she idolizes and a husband who so obviously adores her." I say.

"Snake's pit," Hariva curses. "I'll skin her alive."

"Who are we skinning, my love?" Rahuleid turns, inserting himself once more into the conversation, as if he has not been listening all the while.

"No one," Hariva and I answer together.

"A shame," Rahuleid sighs. "I've been considering a new saddle."

Hariva had made me laugh.

It had shocked me, barreling out of my sternum, wild and unkempt. I had been four years at court then, alone, save for a child and a lady's maid who had only just begun to see me as something other than a sacred disappointment.

Certainly I had not welcomed Hariva's friendship when she arrived with her husband, the new Kallas of Vaiga, to present themselves before the Chieftain. And yet, she had seemed determined. At first I believed it to be strategic, a way of ingratiating herself and gaining influence for her husband. Her extravagant gifts quickly became well-known among the ladies of court, and yet, she never sought to win my favor with one. It had not taken long to discover that, at least in matters of personal affection, Hariva lacked subtlety as much if not more than I lacked experience.

And so, after weeks of attempting to engage me in conversation and facing my cold rebuffs, she simply approached me one evening as I left end-day meal and asked, in the guise of complete innocence, if I wasn't rather disappointed in the perk of my breasts now that I had weaned my daughter.

And I had been so shocked that I laughed.

She'd explained quickly that she had no children of her own yet, but she did have seven older sisters, all of them openly lamenting the sag of their once ample bosoms after the laborious job of lactation.

Then she looked down at her own breasts assessingly.

"Rahuleid swears he won't mind," she'd sighed. "But I rather think I will, having to roll them up every morning and pin them at the top."

I'd laughed again, picturing it.

"Is that what you've done with yours?" she asked, eying my chest brazenly. "They look quite nice that way. Perhaps you could teach me, when my time comes."

The surprise of it all had answered for me. I'd acquiesced, not even sure what I'd agreed to since my breasts were not, in fact, pinned to my chest, but unable to deny this delightful woman anything.

And then she'd become pregnant and miscarried early. And then she'd become pregnant and miscarried late, the wretched lump of her baby's half-formed body like a river boulder in my hands. And then Rahuleid had bitterly declared that he'd never touch her again, to put her through the same, and she'd spat at him from her bed, red blood still staining the sheets, and told him he'd better present himself as full and able the next time she called for him or she'd find someone who would.

If I hadn't loved her before, I'd loved her then.

Apparently Rahuleid had overcome his reservations in the face of his wife's threatened infidelity, because little more than a year later Hariva was pregnant once more. This time, however, I knew from early on that the babe would not make it to its first breath, and I told her so, my tears thickening my throat. The heart, with its many chambers, was growing too small on the left side.

She'd looked at me straight on and asked if she carried this one, would she ever be able to carry another.

I did not think so.

And so she lay back and gritted her teeth as I slipped the little life from her womb. And then I held her as she held the babe, its tiny face warped and stunningly beautiful all the same, until he breathed his spirit into the sky.

We did not tell Rahuleid that time. Neither of us spoke the agreement aloud. Together we simply knew what needed to be done.

And so to see her now, waddling and fat, the babe within her whole and hale and vital, and to hear her confess that her husband still indulges in the "more exploratory expressions of desire," is perhaps my most preciously-held happiness.

I do not hide my relationship with her from my husband – she would not let me. But I do not express my affection either, not in ways that he can see. Let him think I am doing no more than what my position requires. Let him see me silent and reserved in her company, abiding her tedious tongue.

But, it is because of Hariva that I am convinced of my own selfishness. I have allowed her to love me, and to go on loving me, knowing all the while that I will soon be gone.

CHAPTER SEVEN
THE LONG DEAD MOTHER

A child, the boy longs to be touched.
In youth he wants freedom to stand.
The young man desires closeness again,
the feel of soft skin on the hand.
Aging now, he searches for youth,
older, for something long fled.
And when death comes calling for him,
he wants only to lay down his head.

And what of the girl? Is all the same true?
Does she walk the same path to her death?
No, my daughter. In youth or in age,
a girl wants a crown on her head.

AFTER REFLECTING on the events of that first night, I have come to understand how it was that Kurat gained entry to my rooms without my awareness. I had admonished myself for not observing his body behind my closed door. Now I see that his Shade Walking surely allowed him to slip within my chambers from his own rooms below, likely at the very moment I entered.

And so I am not surprised to see him step from Shadow a breath after I close my door behind me.

There is a lingering wariness to his gaze, as if he cannot help but search my face for the ghast that once possessed it. I turn my most pleasant of smiles on him instead, but say nothing, waiting for him to explain his presence.

"I have need to speak with you," he murmurs. He is no longer road worn, but precisely rearranged into the brooding Heir of House Est.

"Then speak," I say, moving to sit in one of the receiving chairs of my outer room. He looks at me darkly.

"Elsewhere," he says tightly.

"It is not yet end-day meal," I shrug. "And I no Shade Walker. How do you propose I extricate myself from your father's company for this conference?"

"Call for your handmaiden," he instructs.

"I will not," I refuse. He presses his lips together, not needing my reasons. I suppose he was merely testing to see if I had already involved her in whatever this is.

"Very well," he says, turning towards the window beside him. It looks out over the back wall of the fortress, into the dense dark pines beyond. It faces south. Hiida has told me these were not Lekja's rooms. Those were on the floor above, facing east.

He puts us where we cannot even gaze towards home.

"Tonight. We will Walk," he commands. But I expected this.

"Under a certain condition," I amend. His chin tilts back to me, brows low. He is unused to disobedience.

"Name it," he snaps impatiently, surely nervous to linger so long in my chambers. That is why I have kept him here.

"There is a man I wish to see," I answer simply, smoothing the wool over my knees. His eyes narrow, but he knows I am not fool enough to engage him in a lover's rendezvous.

"Where is he?" Kurat asks.

I shake my head.

"I will arrange the location. It will be somewhere you are familiar with."

"So long as it does not take a quarter of the night," he grumbles.

"Not so long, I don't think," I answer lightly. He presses his lips together once more, assessing me. I hold his gaze with wide, innocent eyes. Then he nods, and steps into darkness.

I ring the bell, calling for Hiida to dress for end-day meal with a smile tucked into the corner of my lips.

Tonight, Kurat will face his deeds.

"Mama," my daughter mumbles. I shush her, brushing the downy hair from her fat cheek. She moans sharply, then turns, never once opening her eyes. Her little hand reaches out, searching. I slip the poppet Hiida has made for her back within reach. She grasps it, tucking it under her chest, between her knees. I pull the quilt up around her ears, rubbing her little back and dampening her heartbeat slowly.

She falls back to sleep instantly, with that special grace of the very young. And I lay next to her through the night, beating back the terrors of motherhood with every one of her indrawn breaths.

With plotting occupying most of my thoughts the remainder of the evening, I do not take time to consider what it might be like to Shade Walk.

Kurat is agitated when he appears in my rooms. I wonder what he has had to divulge in order to purify himself of untruth. Taking me along with him through the darkness has surely cost him a great falsehood.

After so long staring at the wall of his impenetrability, I confess I find his new unease delightful.

He says nothing, simply motions me forward to him. He wears a traveling cloak not unlike my own, its hood already drawn up over his features.

I do not step to him.

"Prove yourself," I demand instead. He stills, then slings back his hood.

"I've just Walked here, have I not?" he snaps irritably. I shrug.

"Tell me you have no intent to harm me or mine in any way," I say. "If you are so eager to be off."

"Intent?" he asks, scowling. "You are more clever than that, Liama. What good is a promise of my intent? I can surely change it, should I desire."

"I'm well aware," I respond. "Even you are a slave to fate. But intent is all that can be accounted for. And I call you to account for it."

He rolls his eyes. "Yet, of all the truths you could wring from me, you ask for the truth of my intent?"

"And grow ever more suspicious that you defer from giving it," I answer, increasing the weight of my gaze.

For a breath we stand there against each other, my hands on my hips, his arms crossed before him.

And I know, without knowing how I know, that we have done thus before.

He turns his chin quickly away, breaking the intensity gathering in the space between us.

"Very well then, foolish as it is," he says dismissively. "You have my promise that I do not intend you, nor your daughter, harm in this present endeavor. My devious maneuverings this night do not extend to locks of her hair."

"*Your* devious maneuverings do not interest me this night," I answer, coming to my feet and pulling my hood up and over my hair.

"That is hardly comforting. And what, if I may be so bold, does interest you this night?" he asks sourly. "Where are we going?"

"Acker's Inn, the room on the eastern side of the third floor, if you please," I say, putting my hand out between us.

The action stills something in the air. His agitation halts, enigmatic eyes locked on my open palm. I want to draw my hand back, but I will not wither under his gaze.

After a moment, he shakes himself free of hesitation but does not take my hand.

"Snuff the candles, as if you've gone to sleep," he instructs.

"If your father thinks me asleep, there is a chance he will seek me out," I say.

"He will not seek you out this night," he answers. I narrow my eyes.

"And what have you done to ensure this?"

"If you're inferring that I touched his mind, I have not," he answers testily with no intent to go on.

"If there is a way to keep him from my bed, rest assured it will be negotiated as part of whatever bargain you're envisioning between us," I answer, brows high. Then I step away to snuff the candles as instructed.

"I have only plied the beast with enough mead to down a heifer," he grumbles.

"Surely he is too clever for that," I say, disbelieving.

"We will have to hope that he is not," Kurat answers.

This time it is he who puts out a hand when I return to him. I fight the urge to stare at it, his finely kept hand, just as he stared at mine. But I slide my palm over his own, smooth-skinned and dry. He cocks his head, indicating that I should stand beside him. I move to do so.

"Breathe, Liama," he murmurs, drawing in a breath of his own.

I do the same, bracing for the darkness.

But instead he speaks once more, keeping his eyes forward all the while.

"If there is a surer way to keep Tuskjas from your bed, I will give it over to you gladly."

I am still inhaling his words when he guides us into Shadow.

"What have you brought me, son?"

Kurat's eyes are hooded, black pools in the candle light.

"The last Estian Waster," he answers softly.

The big Slav – the Chieftain – assesses me, his eyes too close together on his wide, meaty face.

"To kill her?" he asks. Kurat looks at his father balefully.

"If you desire to be wasteful, I suppose."

"And what need have I of a Waster?" the Chieftain asks after a moment, cutting his eyes to the sleeping babe in my arms. "Or her whelp?"

"I care not what you do with her," Kurat says, shrugging. "But what my grandfather began is done."

"You are certain she is the last?"

"She is the last in the Wood," Kurat answers. "If there are others, they've been so long from the Wood they can hardly be a threat."

"You think it true then?" the Chieftain asks, still dragging his eyes over me and my child.

"Her power has already diminished in the short time since I took her," the Heir replies, adding his assessing gaze to his father's. I brace, watching him in return, waiting for something within his dark eyes. "Yet, it is still considerable. Whatever you mean to do with her," he says, as if I am not present before them, "do it with caution."

The big man ends his assessment, his too-thick lips smearing into a cruel smile.

"There will be no need for caution, will there, my dear?" he asks me. Still, I wait.

"Give me the babe," he commands in my silence. My eyes flicker to Kurat's. He presses his lips together, nodding. I narrow my gaze in a challenge, wrapping my power around his still-shattered wrist, which he has tightly bound to his chest.

Tuskjas watches the exchange, his beady eyes going to his son's injury for the first time.

"I see she has gotten the better of you, boy," he sneers. Kurat's brow slams down.

"A certain vulnerability was required to draw her in," he says, simmering.

"A certain vulnerability," Tuskjas repeats in a murmur, his eyes flickering between us.

"Yes," he says after a moment, his smile deepening. "Perhaps I can make use of her."

And then he stands, erasing the space between us with a single stride. He pulls my child from my arms, waking her. She cries out, but he lays her gently against his massive chest and she settles, having never really woken.

"This House has long been in need of a Chieftainess," the Chieftain says, looking greedily down at my daughter.

"And one can never have too many Heirs."

Perhaps I had expected it to be cold. One of Looklema's twin daughters, the first Shade Walker, was half-Daemon, creatures who are said to live in a realm of cold darkness, emerging into our world in search of sunlight and warm skin.

Perhaps I had expected a whipping wind, the air of all the spaces we are moving through grabbing at my skirts, objecting to my passing. Like the feeling of being on a skillful horse, galloping against the will of the earth.

It is neither of these. And yet, I cannot say exactly what it is before Kurat gently tugs my hand in a new direction, and we step out of wherever we have been.

We are greeted by the damp summer night air.

"Where have you taken me?" I ask immediately, making to pull my hand away. Before me is the back of a structure, the thatch of the roof slumping down its pitch. Yet, the inn I had directed Kurat to take us to is a fine, well-kept place.

"Never seen the back of Acker's, have you?" Kurat answers, tightening his grip on my hand. "The man tends to spend his purse on what can be seen and ignore the needs of what cannot. Hold now."

He pulls me back a step, Tarbatu's stone wall at our backs. A figure emerges from the crooked doorway of the inn, slings a bucket of something putrid into the yard, then clambers back in.

"Wits about you, Liama," Kurat murmurs, squeezing my hand.

"Why didn't you take us directly into the room?" I murmur back. His hooded head is moving back and forth, searching.

"That would be the height of folly. I've given you ample tools to use against me should I prove deceitful, and yet, you've provided me with nothing to prove your own sincerity," he explains objectively.

"Nevermind that you can alter my very memories any time you like," I argue, ire rising. Nothing in return, indeed.

"Nevermind that you can shrivel my eyeballs to husks any time you like," he murmurs back. "Can you discern if the room below the man's is occupied?" he asks, his hooded head turning towards my own. I cut my eyes away, looking up to the lighted windows of what must be the inn's back staircase, sending out my awareness.

An onslaught of sensation greets me. Bodies pulsing and thrumming in all corners of the structure, healthy and ill and ailing and hale. I narrow, drawing the Shroud up only enough to focus my power's sight.

I find his heartbeat.

"He's there. There's a woman in the room below but not in the room across the Hall," I murmur.

"That will have to do," he grumbles.

"Why risk being seen in the Hall? Why not Walk straight in, since we know he is alone?"

The incredulity on his face makes me feel roughly Maarja's age.

"And reveal my power to this man?" he scoffs.

"He is certainly no one of consequence," I argue.

"Whoever he is, he's drawn the honor of receiving the Chieftainess of the House, who happens to be dragging its Heir along with her. I would hardly call him no one of consequence," he argues back.

"Can you not simply rewrite his memory?" I ask.

"Would you have me do so?" he returns, knowing my answer. I scowl.

"I didn't think so," he concludes, agitated. "Can we be off now, or have you more objections to raise as to my methods?"

He does not expect me to answer, tightening his hand around my own once more and turning to face forward.

"Does your father know you are a Shade Walker?" I ask, before he can fling us forward.

The question startles him. The large breath he'd been inhaling wooshes out in a rush.

His hooded head turns to me once more, but his fine features are barely discernible in the gloom. For a moment, he does not answer.

"You do not know what you ask," he says at last, barely more than a whisper. "But since truth is required for us to finish this ridiculous journey, then no, Tuskjas does not know I inherited my mother's power."

His confession complete, we step into Shadow.

I have to send a man to sleep on the stair below, but we cross the hallway with few other obstacles. I do not bother to knock or present myself in some formal way. We simply open the door and step inside, closing it quickly behind us.

To his credit, the woodcutters' official manages to maintain his composure in my presence, having received a message from Hiida to expect me. He stands from his chair by the empty hearth, raising his hand to give the Estian greeting. But it stops midair, his eyes widening when he sees who accompanies me.

I expect him to be afraid. He is not.

My power tells me that his body is preparing itself for something, his brown eyes slitting like a snake's, the blood speeding through the tiny passages of his body. I have made no promises to Kurat about my own intentions for his wellbeing, but this is not the reckoning I have designed.

"You are Erga's husband, are you not?" I say, stepping into his gaze and slicing it with my own.

The man remains rigid, fists clenching, but nods after a moment, pulling his eyes to mine with effort.

"I was, *Varju Tütar*," he answers, his voice strained. My chest tightens at his wording.

"What happened to her?" I ask softly, stepping towards him to gain his full attention. My approach breaks his anger. Before my eyes, it warps into grief, bending his shoulders and bowing his head.

"Dead these eight years, m'lady" he answers, his mouth wrapping around his still-fresh sorrow.

"How?" I ask. Erga's husband slumps to the chair behind him, bending forward with a great moan.

"By 'er own hand," he laments, his words garbled between his knees.

"How?" I ask again. I am being unmerciful, I know. Hiida would urge compassion. But any harm I inflict on this man in the remembering, I intend tenfold on the man behind me.

Erga's husband raises a face aged ten years beyond the one that greeted me moments ago.

"She didna know, *Varju Tütar*, I swear it," he pleads. "She was faithful, so faithful. She woulda rather died. He did somethin' to 'er," he points a vicious finger to Kurat, the anger leaking back into his face.

"Who is this man, Liama?" Kurat murmurs behind me. I tuck my chin over my shoulder to answer.

"Have you not guessed, Kurat?" I say, using his name as a whip. He does not answer, but I feel his heartbeat tighten and rise.

"Tell the Heir who you are," I command, turning back to Erga's husband. "Tell him what business he had with your wife before she thrust her own spirit into the sky."

The man clenches the carved arm of his chair, rising on its weight. He stands once more, the terrible rage building around him as he

112

prepares his testimony. I wonder if he has imagined this moment before. I suspect that he has, never once expecting it to come to pass.

"I am husband of Erga the Weaver, and father to the children of 'er womb," he begins, jaw clenched. "We lived in peace in Urtic, on the border of Looklema's Sacred Wood, as our people 'ave for generations. And we are loyal to the Wasters of the Wood, as our people 'ave been for generations."

His boldness surprises me. He has openly admitted treason to the Heir of the House. Still, I am no stranger to mourning. To grieve is boldness in and of itself.

"Ten years ago," the man goes on, "my Erga sent word into tha Wood that she was in need o' a Waster. 'Er womb hadna healed from the birth o' our son as it ought. It bled wi'out ceasing and she couldna conceive, but she wanted another child. The *Varju Tütar* came. I wasna there. I was clearin' the lands east of Urats with my guild. But the *Varju Tütar* cleansed 'er. She caused 'er womb to 'eal itself. When I returned, Erga was haler than I'd seen 'er in years. She blessed the name of Liama and burned off'rins to Looklema e'ry night. And soon, so soon," tears stream from the man's eyes, his throat closing over his words.

"She was with child again," he barely manages to push the words into the room, and when he has done so, he hangs his head once more and weeps.

"Liama," Kurat breathes harshly behind me. He has stepped closer. "This man is not what you think."

"You would be so bold as to deny him an audience? To deny him his own misery, caused by your hand?" I say, half-turning to address him as I step outside his grasp. Then I turn my face back to the wretched man before me.

"Looklema's blessing is on you, husband of Erga the Weaver," I say formally. He nods, accepting my words, and gathers himself to go on.

"Liama," Kurat warns once more, but I hold my hand up, silencing him.

"I canna describe 'er 'appiness," Erga's husband whispers. "She might as well 'ave carried a Waster 'erself in 'er womb, such was 'er joy. She was convinced the babe would be a girl of great power, like the woman who cut the path for 'er inta tha world."

He clears his throat, bracing himself for what comes next.

"I wen' once more with my guild out past Urats. My men worked themselves to the bone tryin' to meet the quota in time ta get me home for my daughter's birth. But news reached us that the babe 'ad come early, and when I saw her," his face crumples again, tears trekking worn paths down his weathered cheeks.

"When I saw my Erga," he pushes on, "I knew why."

The man turns, yanking a soiled cloth from the pocket of his tunic and wiping his face in a brusk, hard motion, as if punishing his eyes for their tears.

"She was a husk," he says, sucking in a big breath. "It was terrible. I 'ad left 'er hale and warm and 'appy. And when I returned she was naught but a withered, cold shade. The babe was barely alive, but Erga wouldna take it to 'er breast. No one who 'ad known 'er could accoun' fer it. It was as if 'er spirit 'ad wandered away. I sent word inta tha Wood but no Waster ever came. I went inta tha Wood m'self, beggin' Looklema's forgiveness."

Erga's husband raises his head, hard eyes pushing past me to the man at my back.

"But I needna tell you what I found, do I?" he bites. Kurat remains as still as an oak in winter, silent and cold. I do not dare to speak. After a moment, Erga's husband goes on.

"By tha 'and of Looklema, my daughter lived, if you can call it that. But Erga ne'er returned ta me. She was empty. She didna speak. She barely ate. The townspeople began ta speak of Daemons. But I cared for

114

'er. I ne'er left 'er to go with my guild again. I was too afraid to leave 'er with the children. I didna think she would 'arm 'em, but I didna think she would keep 'arm from 'em either. In time, word came that tha Chieftain had found 'imself a Waster a' last and married 'er. I began to wonder, then, but I couldna put the pieces tagether. And I couldna imagine Erga betraying the Wasters in any way. She'd never 'ave. Never."

He shakes his head, all the rage and the grief wrung out from him at last.

"Two years later, she startled in the night. When I went to 'er, she pushed me away. She screamed, and it was my Erga's voice. The babes woke cryin'. She leapt from the bed and ran from tha house. I stopped only long enough ta comfort tha children, then went after 'er. I found 'er on tha banks of tha river, knee deep in the spring flood. I made to run in after 'er but she screamed for me to stop. I didna make sense of anything she said until after. I was just tryin' to get 'er out. She was tryin' to explain, but she was frantic. She'd gone mad. And then between one word and the next, she slipped 'neath the water and was gone."

"My son 'ad followed me," he murmurs, his eyes on a distant shore. "Otherwise I mighta plunged myself 'neath the rapids with 'er."

His tale is done, his heart wrung dry of its turmoil. He slumps once more to the chair, hanging his head in his hands.

"How did you discover the truth?" I ask softly. He stirs, but does not raise his head. Kurat speaks instead, stepping up to my back once more.

"This is not the truth. The man lies, Liama. I swear to you, he is not _"

I squeeze the air from his lungs, ignoring the wheezing gasps that follow as he sucks it back in. I nod for Erga's husband to go on.

"It took weeks," he murmurs, his frightened eyes jumping to Kurat's heaving form behind me. "I scraped my memory fer what she'd been sayin'. I remembered rumors of the Heir travelin' through Jaarva on business with tha Kallas. And then I pieced it together with what I knew of yer own departure from the Wood, and finally I made some sense of it. She said a man had made 'er hate ya. 'E'd made 'er believe you would return and Waste the babe. She 'adna remembered it, only that when 'e left, she'd laid down to rest. Then she'd woken in tha night – tha memory of your goodness and 'er betrayal 'ad come to 'er in a dream. I didna think she knew that two years 'ad passed between when she lay down and when she woke up. But my Erga –" he shakes his head.

"I canna blame 'er," he whispers. "My Erga would rather be dead than live with tha knowledge tha' she'd betrayed you."

The silence that follows is as hollow as a rotted stump.

Moments pass.

Finally, I break it.

"What ails your daughter?"

Erga's husband lifts his head now, surprised at my question.

"She's as cold and distant as 'er mother was," he rasps. "Yet, she's still a child. She longs for things, I can see it in 'er eyes. She knows more than 'er mother did. It's as though she simply canna muster 'erself to grasp at life."

Now I turn myself to Kurat, gathering his lean limbs back underneath himself. His gaze meets mine immediately, hard with silent rage. I ignore it.

"Can it be undone?" I ask.

I believe, if given the chance, he would like to slap me.

"I cannot undo what I have never done," he grits out between clenched teeth. "You don't know what you ask." I narrow my gaze at him.

"I know very well what I ask," I go on, indifferent to his tone. "You have robbed this man of his wife, not to mention what you have taken from me as well. But I commit to you this day that I will seek no recompense for what you owe me so long as you make right what you owe him and his children."

"You can't remember, Liama. You don't know – this is all an imperfect art, but this man –" he starts, but I hold a hand between us.

"I have no use for your excuses. My power is no more perfect than your own and still I have managed to contain myself from destroying lives for my own purposes, excepting your interference, of course, and your father's."

"You had someone to teach you to control it. I had no one. Can you not imagine the destruction you might have caused if you'd been left to discover your power on your own?" he argues.

"You stand here before me, before this man, and seek to convince us that you meant no harm? You did not seek out his wife for the purpose of forcing her to give up the whereabouts of the Wasters that your line has hunted for three generations?" I demand, my own anger pushing past my teeth.

"I *did* seek her out, but not –" and then he stops himself, red-faced with frustration. "It matters little. You wouldn't know the truth if it spit in your face. I am the Heir of this House. I will not be put on trial in a damned inn like some common criminal!"

"You *are* the Heir of this House!" I bite back. "And now you are asked to make recompense for your actions. Or are you outside the law, Heir of House Est?"

"You *do not know* what you ask!" he seethes, voice rising. "You have no idea –" But with every repetition of the phrase, I have become more and more convinced that he is the one who does not know what I ask. So I make myself clear, matching his volume, uncaring what ears might hear.

"CAN. IT. BE. UNDONE?"

"Have you not heard me?" he nearly yells, raising his hands between us. "All that I know of this power I have had to discover on my own! I have no idea of its limitations. I have no idea if it can be undone! But even if it could, whatever ails this man's child, if she even exists –"

"You are no fool, Kurat," I snap. "Perhaps once you carelessly wielded a weapon you did not understand when you still possessed the illusion that it could earn you your father's favor. But you have long since ceased to be that youth. We both have. You are too clever to plot against him without accounting for every variable, your own power included –"

"*Liama*!" Kurat exclaims, his eyes flickering wildly to the man behind me, alarmed at what I have just revealed. But I am not yet done exposing him.

" – and you are too powerful to give yourself over to his will any longer. You must see –"

"Shut your mouth!" he snaps, stepping forward to silence me himself before I can divulge any more of his carefully guarded secrets.

I drop him to the floor under failing knees, spinning now to Erga's husband, who has risen to his feet with a look of utter shock and awe, mouth agape and eyes wide. I give him no time to compose himself.

"In two months' time the babes of Tarbatu will be gathered at the fortress to receive the Little Hurt. Your Kallas has forbade me enter Jaarva and provide the same to your people's children, but you cannot be stopped from bringing your daughter here to receive it. When you come, I will ensure this room is made available to you once more. Provided you do not speak of this encounter, or anything spoken between us, the Heir and I will inspect your daughter further to determine if there is anything to be done about her condition."

"Liama!" Kurat roars behind me, fisting his hand into my skirts and jerking me back. I can feel his lungs widening, his power circling around us.

"Tell no one of what you have seen here," I barely manage to command before the darkness descends.

He Walks us, and so I know he is speaking truth about his inability, or perhaps his ignorance, to undo the effects of his power.

In the inbetween space, I lift the Shroud, preparing for his attack the moment we emerge.

It does not come.

We tumble from Shadow into open night air. I spin, ready to defend myself, but his violence comes only in a vicious shove, knocking me back several feet. He turns from me, cloak whipping wildly behind him, and stalks several paces away.

Suddenly, he spins back, something barreling up his throat which he barely contains, releasing instead an enraged howl, then spinning away once more.

He has brought us to the road beside the decrepit little shack we met in before. The moon is high and bright above, leaving its smeared shadows across the open fields of mossy grass. We stand in the path outside the hut, the structure behind me empty and dark.

Within the Shroud, there is little feeling. It dampens all emotion, subduing the wily heart and enhancing instead the senses of the body. Within it my awareness of myself fades as my awareness of the bodies around me heightens.

A detached sensitivity. A sense of objectivity. A watcher, gazing indifferently out from a safe and peaceful harbor.

The further I drop into it, the greater my control. The further I drop into it, the less my attachment to this world.

My own anger washes away. In its wake, I observe Kurat's.

He is right to be jealous of my upbringing. I was covered over and under with the women who made me, who shared my power and had walked its varied paths long before I walked this earth. Still, it is by his hand that those women are gone. It is because of him that I possess only a fraction of the knowledge that my ancestors cultivated carefully over untold generations, and of which my own child, and every Waster who comes after me, will possess even less.

My grandmother was capable of very nearly reading my mind. She explained that it was as much a careful observation of my character as it was an expression of her own power. She herself rarely drew the Shroud, such was her learned control and ability. Perhaps her subtlety would have been my own if Kurat had only left me in the Wood long enough to grow blissfully aged.

If I were my grandmother, perhaps I could read Kurat's mind.

But I am not.

He heaves air into his red-blue lungs, clenching and unclenching his fists.

"Erga's husband will not betray us," I say dispassionately, prodding for the source of his anger. My voice is hollow and flat in my ears.

He turns, the moonlight illuminating his forehead and leaving his eyes in shadow. But I can feel their movements, the tightening of the delicate cones within, trying to make me out in the gloom.

"Come out of there, Liama," he growls, stalking a few steps towards me before stopping again several feet away.

"Come out of there and face me," he challenges.

My mother often warned me that unspoken thoughts had a tendency of finding themselves exposed if one was not careful within the Shroud.

I am past being careful.

"You have always said my name as though you possess a right to it," I say slowly. "It is why I meant to kill you in that Wood."

"Yet, here I am," he says darkly, spreading his arms out as if to prove he takes up space in the world.

"And you still dare taunt me?" I say flatly.

"The Walking is done," he answers. "You have nothing with which to bargain, and I have no obligation to truth."

"I seek no bargain," I answer, tilting my head.

"No?" he asks, unbelieving. "Have you not promised the man that I will try and heal his daughter? You expect me to do so willingly?"

"It is you who seeks a bargain," I begin, moving towards him in a measured, menacing step. "Say it now. What terms, Heir? What would you trade for the throne?"

The distance between us is cut to barely a handsbreadth. This close, I can sense every unit of his existence. I can feel them, stacked in infinite amounts against each other, squirming, squeezing. The tiny round discs of his blood, bouncing through his veins, drowning in the expanse of his body, only to resurface with every inhaled breath.

But he does not speak his terms. Perhaps I've finally made him see me for the creature I am, the brittle fiend beneath the dutiful Chieftainess. Perhaps now he is afraid.

He sets his jaw, refusing to meet my challenge, yet refusing to back away.

If he thought he would have me on his terms, he is little more than the youth that clutched his broken wrist to his chest so long ago. But I am not she who needed to meet his eyes for the sake of her own pride. I need very little now for the sake of my own pride.

Kurat is clever, to be sure. He is calculating and manipulating. His equals in power are few and far between. He has considered himself in control of all that has transpired between us. Perhaps he has even found a way to fool himself into believing my ghastly display from the other night did not affect him as I know it did.

Yes, Kurat is clever, to be sure. But in this, he has been a fool.

I am the last of the Great Estian Wasters. And he has given over himself to gain my allegiance.

I am Queen of his body, and any other I might desire to possess.

"Speak your terms, Heir," I say again.

Slowly, achingly, the strength leaks from his jaw as I Waste the strength from the muscles around it. He clenches once more, resisting. Still I press, unfolding his tightened fists into limp hands by drawing out the tendons there. My power here in the Shroud is so immense. I am barely skimming its surface.

I press my open palm to his chest. He recoils, tilting his chin backward to look down his sharp nose at me.

But the body tells no lies, and his black gaze is heavy with resentment.

With hunger.

"Speak your terms, man of Shadow," I whisper, letting my breath shiver against his lips.

His lidded gaze sparks, catching fire. It flames and then subsides, burning his strength away with it. He exhales a heavy, shuddering breath, surrendering.

And then he drops his forehead gently against my own, sighing deeply and closing his eyes.

"Looklema's power is leaving the House," he whispers. "My terms are simple. Kill Tuskjas. Marry me. Heal the land."

CHAPTER EIGHT
THE WANING LAND

When blood is lost, take care to replace.
Only a Waster knows tenor and taste.
Let sentiment not sway you to take from a friend.
The wrong blood given will be friendship's end.

I JERK AWAY from Kurat, horrified. The Shroud slips in my surprise.

He watches me, his jaw set once more.

"Why – why have you done this?" is all I can manage to say to him.

"Ask a better question," he demands arrogantly, like a man who was not reduced to meat in my hands only seconds ago.

"What are these terms? These are – these are – you cannot possibly believe –" but he shrugs.

"These terms are what I offer, and you will not get better."

I gape at him.

I expected his plot would involve the death of his father, how could it not?

The rest, however? I've always known there is no way to return to all that was lost, even if Tuskjas no longer held me captive. Certainly I would outlive him anyway. The man was nearly 60 years old, and I half his age. But I had imagined myself in some honorary title, Kurat married to his own pitiful wife to take my place as Chieftainess. Perhaps I would travel the land freely as my mothers and grandmothers did once before, giving out the Little Hurt. Perhaps I would go south to House Rezke to have their scholars document all that I knew of Wasting, so that future women of my line would not be so dependent on absent mothers.

And perhaps I would seek out that doorway in the Glen, and give my body over as a willing sacrifice to join Looklema in her undying realm.

But to take the throne alongside him? Never. Never had I considered such absurdity.

"The power is going out from this place, Liama," he presses, stepping towards me. "I've seen it myself. You and I are among the very last of Looklema's line. If we sit the throne together, as her twin daughters once did, there's a chance we can save it."

"Walk!" I demand, charging him. He shakes his head at me, making me feel ridiculous. But still, his chest expands, and then his pulse and flow disappear from my awareness, reappearing less than a breath later behind me.

I spin on him, ready to do battle.

He holds out a ragged shape between us – Maarja's worn poppet, long since abandoned by her but kept by me, honored on the table beside my bed. And I have a sense, from the weight of his eyes, that he is aware of how I press the little thing to my nose deep in the night, devouring the lingering scent of her soft baby smell, and that only makes his choice of token more alarming.

He raises his brows, waiting.

"You only think you've seen it," I argue past the heat in my face. "How can the power go out from the land? This is *her* land. Maybe in Rezke or Karsu, but not here."

"Think, Liama!" he argues back, shoving the little doll into my chest. "Are you as powerful as your mother? Your grandmother? I am not. In a single step, my mother could Walk from her chambers in Tarbatu to her father's Hall in Saaremaa. Yet, I can manage no more than a half day's ride. My child might be able to pass a league, and their child from one room to the next. I've been everywhere. I've seen it in every region. Barbüra can no more see the future than I can, and yet, her grandmother predicted every move of Kotkas' enemies unfailingly. There are five-year-olds in Ugandi who have not yet developed any power at all. I could recount an hour's worth of similar stories. It's going out, Liama."

"Maarja," the whisper slips out from my mouth around the dawning horror in my throat. He sighs, dropping his hands, knowing what he's cost me.

"I had thought it was because she wasn't raised in the Wood," I reason to myself.

"Likely as not, that's precisely the cause. No one is raised in the Wood. No one is raised in the seat of Looklema's power, and now a man of foreign blood sits Her throne," he responds softly.

"You think he is the source?" I ask.

"I think when Kotkas defied the Wasters and took power for himself, it began, though no one knew it. All his actions, and Tuskjas' after him, have corrupted Est further," Kurat explains.

"You think She's leaving us?"

"I am not one of those who believe Her to linger in this world. She left us long ago, Liama, when She traded this kingdom for another."

But I am Her daughter. I know Her touch.

125

"I used to hear Her, in the Wood," I shake my head. "Something of Her lingers here."

He shrugs, unwilling to argue.

"Regardless, I doubt you would hear Her now, even in that place."

The humid summer air has grown suddenly chilled, even under the traveling cloak. I wrap my arms around my chest to ward it off, holding my daughter's poppet to me, but the bitterness does not fade.

I begin to turn away from him. I cannot think with his body pulsing so close. But then a thought strikes me, turning me back.

"You said a man of foreign blood sits the throne," I say, narrowing my eyes.

Kurat says nothing, but his face is hard-set, waiting.

"You are not his blood," I whisper. His jaw clenches and relaxes. His shoulders tense, and then drop subtly, as if I have lifted a heavy load from them.

"I am not his blood," he whispers back, his eyes softened. Pleading.

He does not speak further, but his plea is in his gaze. He is asking forgiveness, in his way. Or, if not yet forgiveness, understanding. He is asking me to understand, finally.

A firm foundation of belief cracks. I do not yet know if beneath it there is forgiveness. But perhaps there can be understanding.

"Your mother," I murmur, prompting him.

"It was not as it is now," he begins, sorrow in the corners of his mouth. "When Tuskjas brought my mother from Saaremaa to be his Chieftainess, the House was in turmoil. Kotkas had no other Heir, but had never acknowledged Tuskjas formally as his chosen accessor. Whatever respect and loyalty Kotkas had demanded, it did not pass to Tuskjas."

"Nor did his power," I add.

"Just so," he nods. "Little though it was known. You and I have both experienced his uncanny ability to know what should not be known. I suspect he honed other skills as you or I might hone our power. I suspect his Slavic mother had far more experience in the subtle art of manipulation than Kotkas, who simply bent the world to his will by force."

"Still," he goes on, "a talent for manipulation does not make up for a lack of visible power in the fortress, and so Tuskjas sought out a power of legend. Something that would demand respect. He could hardly break from his father's position and get a Waster who could have rivaled his own right to the throne. And so he sought a daughter of Looklema's other line."

He stops a moment, rocking back on his heels and looking up to the bright moon. It spills its touch over the fine features of his face and I am reminded of another man, a lifetime ago, who spilled his own touch over me in the silver dawn of the full moon.

Kurat goes on speaking, sending his breath upwards into the sky.

"You keep babies from being sick and give his enemies bad knees," he says. "She was slipping daggers into backs. She was pulling children from their beds."

I dismiss his gross understatement of the ways in which my husband abuses my power. I am not so proud as to press a petty defense in light of what he claims was required of his mother and what, if his Shade Walking power were to be known, would be required of him.

Lekja. So little is her name spoken among the court, despite reigning alongside Tuskjas for nearly 15 years. And when it is spoken, it comes on the breath of horror.

"What did he have to command such from her?" I ask quietly, though I don't need his answer to know how this works. Still, his whispered reply washes over me with a force so strong I have to plant my feet against it.

"Me."

Something settles between us. I do not know its name. But I imagine Maarja in his place, burdened with the terrible knowledge of all that I have done to keep her safe. And I see for the first time the shame of it – the guilt. How heavy the weight of my love on her shoulders, even if she does not yet know it.

Sometime in the silence that follows, he pulls his gaze down from the moon. And I pull my gaze away from his face. We both look out over the grey-dipped fields, dewy in the warm night. I do not ask more from him. And I do not ask him to Walk. I trust him no more than I did when we set out from my chambers an hour ago, but I do not require proof of his mourning. I have seen him under the moon.

"Believe what you want," he says finally, resigned, "but that man at the inn is not what he claims."

"I know him to be her husband," I argue, though not harshly. "I can smell it on him."

"That may be so, but I am not the cause of his daughter's ailment. I will see the girl if that is what you require. I do not know what can be done, but if it ensures your allegiance, I will see her."

I do not thank him. Nor do I fully believe him. I would have found a way to ensure his participation in keeping my word to Erga's husband, but his willingness is one of very few good things between us, even if it is my due.

"He will not betray me," I say, pressing my conviction into my voice. He shakes his head, unwilling to continue discussing it.

A long silence stretches out in the moonlight, companionable perhaps. Still, he does not turn to me, and I do not turn to him.

"You have a design?" I ask after a time. "This is not just youthful folly? There is no glory in what you're conspiring. He may be of foreign blood, but he has been the Chieftain of Est for more than three decades. They will not accept us easily, no matter our mothers' names."

He laughs darkly.

"I have not been a youth since the day I took you from that Wood, nor have you. If there is folly, I cannot blame it on inexperience. I think you underestimate your influence, but I do not. I am forming a design. But I can move no further until I know where you stand."

"I will not stand against you," I offer.

"But you will not stand with me," he finishes.

"I do not yet know," I answer in a murmur.

"I need a Waster, Liama," he turns to me now, pressing. "The land needs a Waster."

"You've told Tuskjas of what you've seen?"

"Of course," he answers tersely, not appreciating the change of direction.

"And your suspicions as to the source as well?" I press. He cuts his eyes sideways at me.

"My title as Heir, no matter its veracity, is somewhat critical to achieving my designs. I do not seek to jeopardize it. And what would be the purpose of speaking my thoughts openly? Do you think he will simply step aside for the good of the land?"

"That is not my meaning. No one possesses more hatred of the man than I," I argue, recoiling at his suddenly biting tone, "but he is no fool. He wouldn't let the House go to seed –"

"You think my own hatred of him does not amount to yours? You think you can tally more sins against him than I can?" Kurat barks.

"Yes!" I spit at him, quite ready to forgo power and put my fist inside his chest cavity instead. "Yes, I can tally more of his sins, starting with every time he has been inside of me!"

Kurat's brows shoot up, eyes wide. Then he looks away quickly, working his jaw, but I stay after him, the heat in my chest escaping on my tongue.

"You are justified in your resentment for what he did to your mother, and certainly I am sure you have had your own suffering at his hands, but you have never been his wife. And if all that you have revealed this night is true, then you have only chosen to be his Heir for your own ends."

"They are hardly my own!" he exclaims.

"You will not delight in being Chieftain?" I ask sarcastically. "You will consider sitting the throne a chore to be undertaken for the good of the land?"

"Of course not," he scoffs.

"Then do not pretend that you are any more selfless than Kotkas himself! At least he had a foreign army at his gates to justify his means. You have nothing more than a handful of powerless children and rumors of doom!"

"I do not pretend! I have not pretended!" he yells, throwing his hands in the air. "I delight in the thought of being Chieftain! I delight in the thought of sharing that throne with you, wretched intolerable as you may be!"

"Sharing as your father has done?" I spit.

"He is not my father!" he roars. The sound sprints across the open fields, bouncing for a moment against the trees beyond and rushing back to us where we stand panting in the dust of the road.

We heave our tandem breaths, flinty eyes caught on one another's, hating the sounds of our pain leaking out through our teeth.

And yet, how sickeningly satisfying to fight something that can be fought.

Someone who *wants* to be fought.

"He is not my father," he repeats, quiet now. "And he rejoices in the loss of Looklema's power. He rejoices in anything that gives him power over another."

"Does he know you are not his son?" I ask. Kurat nods. I am beginning now to understand.

"He has made you his Heir because of your power. But if Est has no power, he does not need a powerful Heir."

"He hand-picked my father," Kurat explains. "His reign was young and unstable. He did not want to risk passing on his powerlessness while still living in the shadow of Kotkas' great rule. But it's been 30 years, and that has all changed now,"

"And your father?" I ask, trying for tenderness. He cuts his chin away from me, breathing deeply.

"Served his purpose," he answers tightly. And then he rubs a long-fingered hand down his face, wiping away the loss. His reluctance to speak more is a spike driving out from his body, and so I pull us back to the horrors of the present.

"You think the power is going out that fast?" I breathe. "You think he can yet risk someone weaker on the throne?"

"I am only one of his sources," he shrugs. "This is not the type of information one discusses in the open Hall. What I have seen would take two or three more generations to completely die out, but I do not know what other information he has gathered. But yes, I think he believes if he can manipulate it, it will be gone before our grandchildren are born, especially if he can warp the land's greatest power into something ceremonial, something benevolent and superficial."

And he looks at me heavily.

Tuskjas had allowed me the Little Hurt. Of course.

"But who would he name as Heir in your place?" I ask. Kurat pulls his eyes from mine, pressing his lips together.

"There are two options at his disposal," he answers, looking down into the dust at his feet. "Either he gets a babe on you at last, a babe likely as not to be powerless. Or he names the only other Waster left in the land, then marries her to an outsider, cutting off the very heart of Looklema's power at its center."

"Maarja," I breathe.

131

"His affection for her is widely known," Kurat says, unable to keep the sneer from his voice. "A Slavic husband would do nicely for easing tensions with our old enemies in the east, and between one generation and the next, the Estian Wasters are gone."

"The court, though," I wonder to myself. "The court would never stand for an alliance with the Slavs."

"And who do you think would stand against him?" he asks, raising his hands. "With your support behind it, which he will surely demand, who would stand against him?"

"Hariva, for one," I answer, "Her father was killed by Slavic raiders."

"Ah, yes. The clever Lady Hariva," Kurat responds, shaking his head a little. "I rather expected the two of you to overthrow Tuskjas yourselves when you became friends."

"What do you mean?" I can't help asking. Hariva is terribly clever, of course. But I had not considered her intelligence to be even faintly political in nature, other than furthering her husband's success.

"Tuskjas' missives pass through Rahuleid's fortress at Mustvee en route to the Slavic king. I've become convinced that Hariva has managed to get her hands on several of them, including one or two negotiating a potential marriage contract for Maarja," he explains.

"Why on earth would you surmise that?" I question, appalled.

"Because she's here, in Tarbatu, where no other Kallas' spouses reside, befriending you and trying desperately to get a son in her womb," Kurat shrugs, as if all Hariva's efforts to do so consisted of little more than courtly ambition.

"You do not know her," I argue defensively. He narrows his eyes at me for a breath, then concedes.

"No, I do not," he admits. "But neither, I suspect, do you."

The ire rises to defend Hariva's intentions, but I am not so blinded by my love for her that I cannot admit there may be reasons beyond my warm and inviting presence which have caused her to pursue this relationship we share. Had I not thought the same as Kurat when she first came to court? That her attentions towards me were more than advances of simple friendship.

"If I am a poor judge of character, it is your power that I blame," I say sourly. "How am I to determine what I cannot remember or cannot trust in the remembering?"

"I never said you were a poor judge of character, only that Hariva may be above and beyond what you already know her to be," he responds, looking out once more to the grey-lit field. We have stood in this dust nigh on an hour or more now. The moon shadows in the grass are stretching themselves towards dawn. Perhaps there is more to be said, but I know it will not be said this night. There is no space between us for any more revelations.

"Kurat," I say, stretching my open hand out towards him. He turns to me, seeing my invitation and sliding his palm against my own.

"I never want to return to this place," I finish, casting my eyes to the darkened hut just behind. He senses what lies beyond my words, studying my face for some other meaning. But even I cannot fully explain the sadness I feel here.

He nods.

"I will do my best to avoid it," he murmurs, though his eyes linger on the little hovel when he turns back.

Then we pull in our collective breath and Walk.

CHAPTER NINE
THE FLAYED SKIN

Within two moons, the beat of a heart.
Within four, movement will start.
Six will bring the shape of the babe
(Take care! Ensure the heart is well made).

At eight advise red meat and rest –
Do not let the father protest!
At nine observe the opening womb.
Turn the babe to welcome the bloom.

When pains repeat and quicken to come
Mother and child will cease to be one.

"*YOU WILL FORGIVE* me my unbelief," I say, dismissively.

"Then if not for this reason – if not to save Looklema's House, why do you stand against him?"

Kurat and I are, once again, in the shepherd's hut. And yet a fire blazes in the hearth.

"It is enough for me that he is the son of the Usurper," I answer, indignant and impatient with an argument that is wearing thin between us. "I will peel him from Looklema's throne on that sin alone."

"And I, his son? Will you peel me from the throne as well?" he asks, eyes narrowed.

"You are no more his son than I am," I answer, rolling my eyes. It is long since

time to dispense with this particular untruth between us. Yet, there is no surprise on his fine features that I have unmasked him. He has known that I have known.

"My grandmother was there," I say, shaking my head at him. "She was there when Kotkas came, when he asked for her mother's blessing and she refused him."

His brows lower, not understanding. There is much between us that has yet to be understood.

"She knew his blood – she knew its taste, its tenor," I say, struggling to explain the complex sensitivity of a Waster to tell one man's blood from another. "Even twice diluted as yours would be, she knew the moment you stepped into the Wood that you did not share his blood."

He stares at me for a moment, pressing his lips together. He is terribly young.

"That is why she did not leech it from your body on sight," I say haughtily, bluffing. My mother, perhaps, would have done such a thing. But my grandmother is far too curious.

He stares a moment longer, studying me. Then he turns his chin away.

"I suspect," he mutters, "you will soon make me wish that she had."

I give him no answer, and he does not press me further.

I had thought to ask him where he had been before. What urgent news he brought back to Tuskjas. But what was said between us is all that was meant to be said. Still, when he, once again, disappears from court a few days later, I begin to regret not asking after his errand.

I turn my attention instead to his suspicions about Hariva.

She has a subtle power, Rahuleid's wife. Generally among the court, the nature of one's power is not considered entirely appropriate for polite conversation. Power is hinted at, carefully from the corner of the mouth, rather than openly discussed on the tip of the tongue. I do not know the precise reason this is so, but I know enough of my husband's father to assume that Kotkas likely believed as I do in this one thing.

If power must be discussed to be known, it is hardly worth the knowing.

It goes in my husband's favor. He having no power whatsoever to discuss.

Using one's power on the other members of court is similarly frowned upon, but in both cases, subtle rebellions are common enough. And so Hariva weaves her little manipulations, mostly for her own amusement. Occasionally for more nefarious purposes, but as those have been most often in defense of me, I do not find them objectionable.

But I am careful enough with her, knowing what she can do. Hariva is next in my heart to Maarja, but she does not have my full confidence. I would not dare mark her with all that I know.

And so she thinks my marriage politically convenient but terribly dull. She thinks my husband a negligent and unskilled lover, hence my long-empty womb. And I suppose she thinks that I am, at heart, a person of serious and somewhat depressed nature, likely as not due to my power. How could one who makes things rot and wither be lively and gay? And she thinks my insistence on subduing my affection for her in front of others a kind of overprotective diligence born from my tendency towards paranoia.

But for this investigation, I am especially careful to keep my intention from falling victim to her uncanny ability to recognize subterfuge when she sees it. I even draw the Shroud just so, dampening my unsteady heartbeat, as I knock on her door.

By design, the Kallas and their companies do not reside in the fortress itself. Rahuleid and Kallas Meevat of Sakala share a wide, grand house in town, high on the hill below the fortress. This is what allowed Meevat's daughter, Suita, ready access to Hariva's quarters. I suspect that Suita had long endured the noises of Hariva's "exploratory expressions of desire," the walls being thin as they are. I cannot blame her for eventually falling victim to her own curiosity.

I have come under the guise of a professional visit to see to babe and mother. I make no expression of familiarity when Vappers answers the door to his master's home, and the old man remains the picture of indifferent servitude, bowing low with his fingers to his brow and guiding me to Hariva's outer sitting room. From the care he gives to his master's home, one might never know that he himself occupies a one-room, sparsely furnished chamber half a mile down the hill, accessed from a putrid alleyway of scraps from the tavern beside.

Hariva waves a lazy variation of the formal greeting at me from her repose, stretched out along a plush couch with her feet inclined in her husband's lap. Rahuleid makes to rise but halts, balancing for a moment between formality and his wife's comfort. I hold my hand up, excusing him, and he nods pleasantly instead, bringing two fingers to his brow and bowing as well as he can.

"Well I kept from skinning her but I certainly scared the little chit away from any future explorations," Hariva says by way of greeting, and I feel a pang of pity for poor Suita, who is likely still smarting from Hariva's tongue.

"Most gracious of you, wife," Rahuleid affirms, his words an obvious jest despite his serious tone. Hariva kicks up a foot at him playfully.

"Rahuleid is unaffected by shame, as you know," Hariva goes on. "When I told him about Suita's spying, he said he might see if she'd be willing to give a third party assessment of his performance."

Rahuleid shrugs his wide shoulders.

"Well, it's hardly as if the opportunity had presented itself before," he says. "And I doubt it shall do so again until our own mite is old enough to go sneaking about in search of things he ought not to know."

To this Hariva can only laugh, and then, as women with child are want to do, she begins to cry.

"Hold now!" Rahuleid exclaims, alarmed, wrapping her feet in his hands. "What's this? No tears, my love. I swear I won't ask our child to assess my sexual performance until he can at least get it up himself."

The sniveling Hariva transforms once more, giggling between sniffles.

"Good tears, my love," she laughs, wiping them unceremoniously on her very fine wool sleeve. "Now away with you, before you make me piss myself again."

With her words Hariva raises herself laboriously from her recline, bringing her bare feet to the rug in a wide, unladylike pose. Rahuleid's concern does not immediately abate, but he follows instructions, rising from the couch and straightening his fine blue tunic, the symbol of Lake Peipus, the pride of his region, emblazoned on his breast.

I am reminded of my task.

I step towards Hariva, allowing Rahuleid to pass from the room with his bow and a passing word to his wife. Ever since Hariva's second miscarriage, when she'd carried the child halfway to term, he does not linger for my appraisals of his wife's progress.

I help Hariva to stand, guiding her back to her sleeping chambers and closing the door softly behind us. She is in her eighth month now, yet certainly agile enough to walk on her own once she gets a little momentum. She is one of those women who carries her child on the outside of her body, as though someone has simply stuck a boulder to her belly. All her petite limbs, her slender shoulders and small breasts are unaffected by her state. I am struck, for the umpteenth time in attending pregnant women, how incredibly different they all are.

She takes a wide chair beside the bed, spreading her knees and leaning back into its frame.

"Any pains?" I ask, kneeling before her, my awareness going out from me into her body.

"None," she answers simply, shaking her head. "Other than aching of course."

"Your hip again?" I turn my senses to the bone there. She nods. There is a build up of acid in the muscles entwined in the joint, but nothing more. I suck at the acid, pulling the swelling down. She relaxes deeper into the chair.

"Nothing quite like that, is there?" she breathes. "It's funny, I never truly know how much it's bothered me until it's gone, and I realize what it ought to feel like."

"Many things are that way," I murmur, moving my awareness back to her belly. "It's the body's way of enduring itself."

"Endurance, indeed," Hariva murmurs back. "That is all childbearing is, isn't it?"

"And child rearing as well," I answer. She gives a little huff of laughter.

"And will I be doing any child rearing this time, do you think?" she says, her light tone betrayed by her words. I pull my senses back, focusing on her face.

It is not in a Waster's nature to give false hope or fan fickle flames. We do not deal in idealism anymore than we deal in false fear. I have told Hariva this. I have shown her in my manner as we have walked this road together. I know she puts great trust in my words.

"There's no reason to believe you will not be," I answer. "The babe is hale. He grows as he should. All is wholly well."

"Yet, we have been here before," she murmurs, looking away from me.

"We have," I nod. "But we are more prepared."

"Rahuleid says he's serious this time," she goes on quietly, eyes locked in the middle distance.

"I suspect that he is," I return. "He will not risk losing you again, not even for an heir."

She nods, swallowing, but does not break away from wherever her mind has gone. I do not prompt her towards what Kurat claimed about her intentions to carry a child, though I consider ways I might. And so I am half-amazed that she goes on in the very direction I came here to guide her.

"It isn't just an heir, Liama," she murmurs. "Not for Vaiga, at least."

And now her warm brown eyes come to my own. We are not young women, Hariva and I. Her age lines may surround her smiling mouth, and mine my furrowed brow, but we have earned them together. I know, without knowing how I know, that she is thinking something similar. I know, without knowing how I know, that she is preparing to risk on behalf of what we have shared.

"I know why you seek a son," I stop her before she can speak. Her brows bend, eyes watery once more.

"You do?" she breathes. I nod.

"And I would welcome it," I say, taking her hand in my own. "I could imagine no greater happiness than to unite our children. But it is too late now, Hariva. You must know that."

Her mouth bends, warping under her sorrow. She knows as I do, but she has not wanted to abandon the hope.

"I had thought – if it had been the first time, or even the third," she struggles, tears now streaming from the corners of her crinkled eyes.

"What is done is done," I murmur softly, squeezing her hand. "You must not put this pressure on yourself now. Or on your babe. Maarja will wed whomever Looklema has chosen for her."

Hariva nods dutifully, but does not break from her sorrow. My words will perhaps mean something to her later, but not now.

"You can't let him do it," she mourns, glistening eyes pressing into my own. "It will be the end. You know it will."

"What will be?" I ask lowly, pretending confusion for fear she will see through the farce.

"I've read the missives, Liama," she goes on, near to whispering. "I know he intends to marry her to the Slavic prince."

"I know you feel strongly about the Slavs because of your father –"

"It isn't that," she interrupts, pursing her lips impatiently. "I *know*, Liama. I know he has no true – I know there is nothing within. And I know *why*."

"Don't say such a thing, Hariva," I warn her, squeezing her hand harder this time. "Never again. Swear to me."

She doesn't speak but she nods, setting her jaw. She does not wipe the tracks of her tears. I have felt it too, before. The power in those wet markings over hot cheeks.

"It might not be so with her," she says, leaning forward over the swell of her belly. "Rahuleid says her power might be great enough –"

But I shake my head. She stops, mouth ajar.

"Maarja has been raised outside the Wood," I answer simply. Hariva's thin brows rise in her forehead.

"You mean to say it's true then? The power in the Sacred Wood is greater?" she breathes.

"I do not know," I answer, shrugging gently. "I am the first Waster to leave it in generations. Maarja is the first one to be raised completely isolated from it, perhaps ever. But I know her power is not like my own.

And I know her child's power will be even more displaced, even more diluted, unless Maarja returns to the Wood."

"Then you cannot let him do it," her voice rises as she turns her palm in my hand to wrap her fingers tightly in my own. But now we enter territory for which I am unprepared. I have come for confirmation of what Kurat claimed - that my dearest friend sought an heir to secure Maarja's future, and perhaps her own. To bind us together in ways that simple friendship cannot. Machinations can be forgiven, but this new direction to her words borders on treason, and I will lead Hariva no further down this path.

"My husband is no fool," I say, pouring my conviction into my words so she will not sense the doubt in me. "He will have considered what such a union means. I would not be surprised if he does not have designs within designs."

Hariva narrows her eyes.

"Then you will support this, even if it means ending Looklema's line?" she asks warily, assessing me anew. The surprised accusation in her eyes is cutting, but I endure it.

"My grandmother once told me that Looklema's twin daughters did not give us their names because their reign was not yet complete," I say, untangling my fingers from hers. "I think she meant to assure me that what may seem to be an end is often a beginning."

Hariva's keen eyes flicker back and forth between my own, her look of critical disappointment unabated.

"And you are willing to leave this to Looklema's will?" she asks. "You are willing to leave your own daughter's fate in the hands of a being no one has heard from in a thousand years?"

"There is nothing else I can do," I say, rising to my feet. Hariva's eyes go with me, trying one final time to peel back what she senses, but cannot see.

"I don't believe that," she argues, rising herself. "You don't either."

"Anything else is treason, Hariva," I scold.

"*You* are treason," she bites back. "You and Maarja are treason simply for drawing breath. I cannot believe you would do nothing to protect your daughter or your line. Lie to me if you must, but I cannot believe it of you. I won't."

"Hariva, cease this at once –"

"Why have you not taken the throne, Liama?" she asks baldly, crossing her arms over the swell of her belly.

"Hariva!" I gasp, surprised anew at her boldness. And terrified by it.

"He has nothing and you have everything," she goes on, undeterred. "You *are* everything."

"He has *her*," I argue. She nods, pursing her lips.

"Then it's as I've always thought. He has some hold on Maarja that you cannot break. But *how*? Tell me how, Liama, and perhaps together we –"

I turn from her, gathering my skirts in my hand to flee, rather than hear her spew her own death wish. Because Kurat was right. Tuskjas knows things he should not know. Always he does. And I do not know how. And I would not know, with Kurat's power, if it were through me.

"Liama!" she calls after me, wobbling forward. "*Liama!*"

But I do not stop. Not when I push open the closed door to her chambers. Not when I brush past Vappers tidying the couch where his master and mistress have just reclined. Not when I hear her call after me a final time.

"I have carried dead babes I was willing to give more to save than you will for your hale, living daughter!"

It lodges in my throat, her accusation. I choke on it, sputtering as I stride from the room with her knife in my heart. She may have managed not to skin Suita alive, but she has not spared me.

CHAPTER TEN
THE SHATTERED FEMUR

When bone is shattered, eat of its shards.
When glistening smooth, straighten its parts.
Bind thus together, sealing the skin.
In time the bone will grow whole again.

I REMEMBER their hands the most. The living rarely consider how well we know the hands of those we love. My grandmother had short, thick fingers, wrinkled at their joints with her age. Sun spots stuck to the backs of her hands, layering over each other like the smooth rocks along the river bank.

Her palms were dry and cool. Her nails shaped like fat half moons. She said her hands came from her father. He had been a farmer, his land butting up against the edge of the Wood. That was before Kotkas, when she and her mother and her grandmother could come and go from Looklema's forest without fear. When the shrines at the edges of the

Wood were heavy-laden with offerings, and the people came from all corners of the House to be blessed or healed or simply known by its Wasters.

In those days my grandmother had known her father, and he had known her. Delighted in her. And she had seen his body strung up from the trees when Kotkas had come hunting them.

But I am more of my mother than I am my father, whoever he might have been. Perhaps there were subtle differences in the angle of our eyes, the shapes of our nostrils. But I have her hands. I have her long, thin fingers. I have her nails that grow too fast, needing always to be trimmed so they won't break in jagged edges. I have the same slight curve in my middle fingers, bending outward. I have the same rugged calluses – or at least I had.

My mother never knew her father. He came and went through the Wood just as my own lover did. By then, all but the loyal folk at its edge had begun to believe it cursed. They had begun to believe Kotkas had achieved his aims, and that our spirits were lingering, longing to go on to be with Looklema, but unable to leave the land without its Wasters. Women were more likely to pass through it than men, and only the most faithful. The ones who knew Looklema's grace and trusted it. We might show ourselves to them. Might share a meal, asking after people we'd healed in the villages nearby. My grandmother might bless them in the Snake Daughter's name before we sent them on their way.

But the men we did not show ourselves to. Not unless we sought pleasure. And only then after several days observation of their character. Did he stop to lay a pine bough on the shrine beside the path? Did he stand in awe of the stag barely visible between the trees, or reach for his bow?

The ones who reached for their weapons did not emerge from the Wood with the hand that held them.

My grandmother had been long past pleasure. At least not the kind my mother and I sought. She'd laugh at us, returning unsatisfied after many days' absence.

"One day you'll realize a man is not worth the distance you must walk to find a good one," she'd cackle.

Their faces I have to drag up from the grave, much as my eyes lingered on them in the first 19 years of my life. But their hands are always waiting for me when I close my eyes. I would have long ago been lost, if not for their hands.

"What's 'er name, m'lady?" Hiida asks, angling her head to look into the little basket where my daughter sleeps.

"She has none," I answer simply, not pulling my gaze from the window. It faces south.

It faces away.

"No name?" my handmaiden asks, straightening in her surprise. "She's surely old 'nough now to name."

"Wasters are not named until their power appears," I answer her lamely.

"Whate'er do ya call 'em, then?" the round woman asks, looking back down at the babe. "Howe'er do they know it's them yer speakin' to?"

I sigh, pulled reluctantly into the conversation.

"There's only one child at a time in the Wood," I say, turning to her.

"So it's true, then?" she asks, brows raising. "Ya only have one babe."

I nod.

"Well," she says after a moment. "There's more'n one child in Tarbatu, m'lady. We'll need to call 'er somethin'."

"Maarja," I breathe, speaking aloud what I had decided the day he brought me here. "Call her Maarja."

146

Hiida looks up at me, her nose crinkled in disgust.

"Surely no', m'lady," she says boldly. "She'll ne'er 'ave a 'appy day in 'er life with a name like that."

I turn away from her once more.

"Then the name will be true enough."

"Please, my Chieftainess," the woman presses the little parcel, still emitting warmth, into my hands. A small smile plays in the corner of her young mouth, despite the circumstances. "I've a cousin in the kitchens a' the fortress," she says quietly. "I've 'eard you never turn away fresh rye."

And I smile. My daughter. Hariva. Hiida – this unspoken thing threaded through us, unknown until the moment we are tugged towards each other, even only for the exchange of a small favor, the passing along of a kindness. I had thought once I would not know mirth again, or the kind of tenderness that makes one *want* to share it with another. And then all these women grew into the soil around me, each a different bloom, and in them there was something of what had been lost, until I found myself amidst a wild chaos of fragrant flowers.

And yet, the thought gives me pause, the wilting stem of Hariva's bloom like a softening bone, no longer holding up what it ought.

"Do not let that stubborn man rise for at least three days," I instruct the young woman again, looking back over her shoulder to her father, who is even now trying to do so, his young son pushing him back down by the shoulders.

"We'll do our best, m'lady," the woman says in a sigh, turning as well. "You've 'eard 'er, 'aven't you, ya ol' dolt? Three days, an' no' a moment less!"

"I expect it to be done," I add firmly to her admonishment. "Or there'll be no more help from my hand when it worsens."

That stills the man, however temporarily. He grumbles something only his son can hear, which causes the boy's ears to redden, but lies back down, letting the boy prop another folded blanket under his gout swollen foot.

"Keep him off beef and ale," I say, reaching my hand out to take Maarja's.

"It'd be easier to make 'im Chieftain," the daughter grumbles, then slams a hand over her mouth. "I mean no disrespect, m'lady."

Beside me, Maarja giggles and I smile again, taking my daughter's hand and pulling her through the low door of the bedroom, out into the main room of the man's tannery, stinking vats spilling hot, putrid steam up into the air. Maarja covers her nose, but the young woman following us out stops by one, taking a deep sniff and giving it a displeased stir.

We pass through the main door and out into the street, turning to give the tanner's daughter the Estian greeting. She returns it, adding a deep bow, then disappears back inside of her father's workshop, no doubt to give a stern lecture to the vat that displeased her.

"That was disgusting," Maarja says, her little nose a snarl, as we step into stride behind the guards that awaited us at the end of the alley.

"Which aspect?" I ask her.

"All of it," she answers, her mouth turning down. "How do you get a thing like that?"

"Gout?" I ask. She nods. But before I can answer, her attention is already drawn into the business of the street. We emerge into the backside of the marketplace, hawkers and craftsmen calling out, one on top of the other, like birds looking for a mate.

My eye stays on my daughter, watching the wonder flicker across her face as we weave through the crowds, which part like a stream around rocks, the people stepping aside, two fingers to their foreheads, as we pass.

They have so few chances to see us, Maarja especially. My position allows me some freedom to pass through the fortress gate, but Maarja is kept mostly within it, save for these little excursions to observe my Wasting. There would be more opportunities – if my will was the authority, I would spend all my days thus – but Tuskjas hands out my power like tokens, exclusive and precious, to those who make themselves valuable to him. The Little Hurt is the only working I am able to give to one and all. The tanner makes my husband's prized saddles, the finest in Tarbatu, and he cannot do so when he is swollen with gout.

Dappled sunlight, dyed a soft orange, flashes across Maarja's pale face, catching her eye. I watch her turn, the fraying braid slipping over her shoulder and down her back, and then I am jerked by our intertwined hands to a halt.

She says nothing, her mouth slightly agape. I press my lips together to keep from smiling.

The little amber hunk is rough-hewn, the tiny white flower at its center hardly visible except for a single polished side, which refracts the light across my daughter's cheeks like freckles of daylight.

Finely dyed wools and embroidered dresses, polished copper brooches and delicately knit gloves. All the precious things thrown hastily and carelessly to my daughter's floor when she's done with them. But here she stops, transfixed before a hunk of hardened tree sap. Perhaps she is not so removed from the Wood as I thought.

I am opening my mouth to offer the little trinket to her, when a ghastly scream rends the air.

Heads swivel and bodies turn towards the sound. My husband's men tighten around us, pressing Maarja and I together, our backs against the little table.

The splintering crack of bone hits me in the stomach, my vision sparking at the pain flowing into the body I can sense but cannot see. I drag the Shroud up, putting the protective lair between myself and the broken thing, then turn to instruct Maarja to do the same, but she is still staring, unaffected, at the object of her fascination.

"Maarja, draw the Shroud," I instruct anyway, shaking her shoulder. She looks up, surprised, then around her, as if noticing the tumult for the first time. But she blinks, pulling in a long breath, and I feel a distance grow between us, her own Shroud swathed around her form.

"Stand aside," I order the guards, and when they do not do so, I shove the one whose back is nearly pressed against my chest. It hardly moves him, but he does turn his head over his shoulder.

"Apologies, my Chieftainess," he says, not unkindly. "I cannot let you through until we've assessed –"

"It's a boy, out in the street. His leg is shattered. You will let me by," I command. The guard turns high brows to another man, then jerks his chin towards the main road. The man stalks away at once, shoving people from his path until only the shining top of his helmet in the sun is visible. It turns back and forth, then makes its way back to where we are cornered.

"It's as the Chieftainess says," he tells his leader.

"You will let me through," I bite. "There's little time."

The first guard nods and the men form an arrow shape around us, spearing through the crowd, which no longer stands aside to genuflect.

"Make way for the Chieftainess!" the spearhead yells, frustrated when heads only turn, eyes peaking through the men's shoulders, to get a glimpse of this new development. But the bodies do not part for us.

I can feel it, just below where I linger in the Shroud. That well of beckoning power. The same as when I stood before Kurat in the moonlight, melting his body to my will. My fingers tighten around Maarja's hand, unsure if they will keep their hold the deeper I descend.

And then I allow myself to slip further within the Shroud, like sluicing through deep water, sleek and slim and inevitable.

And then I slide one wet tendril of power through the crowd like a needle, staking itself in that broken body, and with a little shudder of will, bodies begin to bend themselves away from the thread, muscles bunching and joints bending and weight tilting just so. A thin path opens between all those pulsing, thrumming things and I walk through it, unsure and uncaring if the other little Waster follows.

Though my awareness of its corruption increases the closer I get to the broken thing, the Shroud keeps the splintering pain from my senses. Still, I am not yet so deep as I have gone before. And it is the Shroud itself, the detached objectivity it provides, that prods me to rise, pushing higher towards the surface, or risk the working that is to come.

You must be a body to heal a body.

My grandmother, who grew so familiar with her own power that she hardly needed the Shroud at all.

Go deep in that well, she advised. *But not so deep that you forget you have toes.*

One of her common sayings, and always a little different, for her own humor.

But not so deep that you forget hair grows from your chin, same as mine.

But not so deep that you forget you have to piss.

And so I pull myself up, driving towards the light, until I hover only just beneath the surface.

It is the mother who is screaming.

She holds her boy's head in her lap even as he sweats and heaves and thrashes, her sinewy strength keeping him from turning his head towards the putrid wound, the white bone glistening in the sunlight as its shattered head protrudes from what was, only moments ago, his leg.

Beside them, a heavy-ladden cart is still lurching back and forth, the boy's father trying in vain to calm the frightened horse that pulls it.

"The Chieftainess!" someone screams as I emerge into the street. The mother's head whips up, her skin pulled tight across her cheeks, eyes red-rimmed and desperate. Seeing me, she lets out a horrible, aching wail, fear and despair and blistering hope in its tenor. The boy's thrashing renews, responding to his mother's call, and the useless leg wiggles and jars and spits blood out into the dust.

The mother first then. I slide her heartrate down, forcing a deep breath into her lungs, wishing for my mother's subtle ability to beat back panic and fear, knowing I will have to settle for tricking her body into calming itself. She chokes on the first inhale, coughing and gasping, one hand clutching her chest, and in that horrid second, her son's head, free at last, jerks towards his body, mouth opening in the breath before a horrified scream.

But his mother's hand comes down over it, wrenching the boy's face away and smothering his shriek in the softness of her own belly. Behind her, the aged manservant huddles over them both, one hand on the mother's back, the other extending towards the boy's nape. I've no idea how the man hobbled through the crowd underneath my awareness, but I have no time to acknowledge anything other than an extreme relief that he is here. When Vappers' palm meets the bare skin there, the boy slackens, his body loosening and shuddering and shivering, but calmed.

The weathered face comes up, brows long and grey under a forehead wrinkled in concentration, and the old man nods.

"*Varju Tütar*," he breathes. "Please begin."

"Someone get a healer!" I call, sweeping aside my fine skirts and kneeling in the dust. Behind me, I feel Maarja approach, obedient but reluctant, hovering over my shoulder.

"Pay attention," I instruct her, feeling her body's disgust, her stomach trying to force itself through her throat. "Hold his hand and observe."

She slips down, reaching out hesitantly for the boy's sweaty palm, his fingers still twitching until she wraps her own around them. And then she closes her eyes.

When bone is shattered, eat of its shards.

My awareness fits itself over the shape of the boy's broken femur like a glove, torn asunder in the middle. The angle of the break and the width of the damage tell me the wound's story. Likely as not, something on the wagon began to tumble and the boy jumped down trying to steady the load, only to fall beneath the wooden wheel himself.

"I'm putting him to sleep," I explain, meeting the mother's eyes, which are still red-rimmed but now steely under Vappers' hand. She gives a firm nod, tightening her grip on the boy who has long since outgrown her in both size and strength.

I pull down his heartbeat, slowly but firmly. As it lowers, so do his eyelids, the hand in Maarja's going slack.

"Maarja, keep him asleep," I command her, and her head pops up in surprise. Outside of my husband's study, she has only ever observed my Wasting. But the task is simple enough and the time has long since come for her to participate.

"You will do it," I murmur to her, brows high to broker no argument. Her soft brown eyes are wide and wet, but she presses her pale lips together and nods.

The wound is a pulpy mess of bone shard and glistening yellow fat and seeping blood, slowing now that the heart is subdued. My mother used to say that a Waster should be awed at the speed of rot, the way the body begins to decay immediately, wasting no time in destroying itself in its attempt to heal. Good Wasting works with the body, not against it.

So I do not stop it. I spur it.

I sicken the muscle, turning it upon itself, the body's own poisons eating away in mere breaths what would take weeks without my prompting. In the crowd, there is retching and gagging, the smell of the decay crawling across the ground. Blood sours, feeding the rot. Fat blackens and wilts, until the shape of a clean hole begins to form at the wound's edges. And then, when my eyes can see the pale glisten of bone deep in the meat, I hold my hand out to Maarja, palm upwards, raising it up and up, and she allows the heart to quicken once more. Blood, clean and red, gushes into the wound, washing away the gore as I Waste the rot itself, withering the tiny moldering mouths too small for the eye to see until they are shriveled husks, easy enough for the blood to wash away.

Then I turn my palm over, bringing it down, and Maarja pulls the heart down once more. The blood slows to a gurgle.

"Where is the healer?" I ask to no one.

"C – coming, my Chieftainess," a man answers. "I've sent my girl. She's fleeter than a fox."

"I'll need the smithy as well."

"Yes, my Chieftainess," the man says, then pushes back into the crowd, bellowing the smithy's name.

My power slips over the fragmented ends of the leg bone like prodding fingertips, and then I flush a wave of something akin to hunger into that touch. After a breath, the bone begins to bubble like water in a pot, the shards glistening and melting, softening and smoothing.

The bone continues to weep, eating itself clean, marrow dripping in sizzling rivulets over the clean edge of the wound. There is little to save. The bone cannot be fitted back together.

I feel her coming before she arrives, screeching like a goose for the crowd to part. Then the healer slams down to her knees on the other side of the boy. A heavy satchel spills half its contents as her chest heaves from exertion and her keen eyes flow over the wound.

"Wha' would you 'ave me do?" she asks breathlessly, wasting no time on formalities. A good healer, then.

"It cannot be repaired. It will need to be held in place. We are holding him stable long enough for the smithy to assess the shape and form, but the loss of blood will kill him if we keep him open any longer. You will need to bind and sew it as well as you can while the plate is made."

"Aye," she says, twisting to the spilled contents of her bag. With impressive speed, she prepares her long, hooked needle threaded with sheepgut, and procures a bottle of spirits as well.

"You won't need to cleanse the wound," I tell her. And for the first time, she looks up at me, cheeks red but eyes steady.

"No, m'lady," she says, and her eyes crinkle at the corners. "I keep this one fer celebratin' afterwards."

I would laugh if not for the Shroud.

"Feeling confident?" I ask her instead, feeling as though I could be talking to Hariva. She waggles her brows, cutting her eyes to the mother, then slamming a mask of sobriety down over her wide face.

"Is no' e'ry day someone comes callin' with news of a Waster a' work," she murmurs to me. "I had to trample three other healers ta get 'ere first."

The big smithy breaks through the crowd with a bellow, shoving the man who fetched him nearly to the ground. I motion him forward and he strides over, barely containing his wild look of horror at the scene.

"*Looklema*," he swears, heavy brows bending over eyes beginning to glisten. "Igna," he says to the mother. "I didna want to believe it. What in –"

"The boy fell beneath the wagon," I interrupt him. "The bone is shattered and cannot be put back together. You'll need to devise a plate to hold it. Assess the form and size as quickly as possible."

"Aye, Chieftainess," he nods, leaning over the healer. Only a handful of breaths later, he nods grimly. "I've got it. Roughshod, it'll take a few hours still."

"I don't want it roughshod," I argue. "This will be inside of him for the rest of his life. Your finest work, and nothing less."

His brows lower, eyes sincere.

"You'll have it," he says, then turns to the mother. "You'll have it, Igna. Immeld. Give me til sunset."

And then he strides off, thick torso and muscled arms brushing the shoulders of only the first few people he passes, before the crowd parts for him like a man ordained by a goddess.

I turn back to the healer.

"Bind it," I instruct. Without warning or preamble, the healer puts one thick palm against the protruding bone, the other over the muscle below the wound, and with a heavy grunt, she shoves the protruding bone back into the hole I have made.

It would have taken a Waster three times more powerful than Maarja, and perhaps twice as old, to hold the boy under. He comes up squealing like a boar, but his mother is ready. Her elbow around his neck, her spindly leg around his waist, she throws her own weight back on the ground, holding him to her as Vappers fumbles to regain his touch. Another man – the one who went after the smithy – launches forward from the periphery, throwing his weight across the boy's hips while still another woman grabs his ankles. And between them all, they hold the squirming child to a bare wriggle while the healer aligns the bones and sews the wound.

When it is done, several people assist in the unloading of the wagon to make room for the prostrate boy, who still sweats and shivers and moans even under Vappers' hand. And when he is pulled, slowly and carefully from his mother's lap, all that resolve and sinewy strength goes out of her, like water from a broken dam, and she crawls on her knees, collapsing into my lap where I still kneel in the dust, and weeps with her arms around my waist.

Something breaks in the father as well, who steps for the first time away from his horse where he has stood murmuring to it all the while strangers tended to his son. He lurches forward, arm outstretched, as if to stop his wife from embarrassing herself in the crowded marketplace.

It is time to go.

I stand, pulling the weeping woman up with me and, as if summoned, the healer comes, taking the woman into her own arms. I murmur instructions to the healer for how to implant the plate, but I suspect she is keen enough in her art to not need them.

"That man there, in the brown tunic, as well as the woman with her three children, you know them?" I ask quietly. The healer follows my direction, nodding.

"I know the man. I can know the woman, if need be," she answers, all the while stroking the head of the crying mother.

"Should you feel his blood loss is too great, they can supply him with some of their own. Send word for Hiida at the fortress and I will come. Do not let anyone else attempt it, and accept blood from no one besides those two, not even her," I say, nodding to the mother.

"Why them, m'lady?" the healer asks, brows low as her eyes search over the man I've singled out.

"Not all blood is the same, even between kin. When blood is lost, take care to replace. Only a Waster knows tenor and taste. Let sentiment not sway you to take from a friend. The wrong blood given will be friendship's end," I quote the Waster's rhyme for her.

"Is tha' so?" She asks surprised. "No' much sense in tha', innit?"

I like this woman terribly. It is time to go.

"I expect it to be done," I command her, putting formality between us.

The healer nods. "Aye, m'lady Chieftainess. I will."

"If there are any signs of infection, send for me. Do not hesitate. I haven't done all this for the boy to die of fever."

The healer nods once more. Maarja slips in beside me, fisting a hand in my skirts as she once did when she was half her age. I put a hand on her shoulder, squeezing slightly, and turn to slip into the crowd, guards be damned.

"Oh! No! Please, m'lady!" a sudden shriek splits the air, and when I turn, the mother has roused herself from the healer's shoulder and is hastily backing away towards where her wagon is being unloaded, one arm extended as if to keep me in place, the other hand wiping the tear stains with the underside of her wrist.

"Please, take – take –," and she begins throwing aside parcels and baskets and sacks, looking for something of value. "Take it all!" she finally screeches, grabbing a fat sack of grain and beginning to waddle it over towards me. The men unloading the cart stop to watch, unsure of what to do. She dumps the grain a few paces from my feet, then scurries back to the pile to grab something more.

"Igna! No!" the father finally speaks. Scuffling over to intercept his wife, he spreads his body out in front of the goods. The wife pays him no heed, reaching around him for a basket, wilting carrot stems cascading over the side. She hurries it over, dropping it next to the sack of grain, then turns back for more.

"Igna, stop! Stop it!" the husband stammers, abandoning the pile to come and retrieve what his wife has already offered. They go on like this for several more trips, the woman dragging goods to the pile, the man hastily following behind, dragging them back. Snickers begin to wind their way through the onlookers, starting, I believe, with the healer.

"The good Chieftainess 'as no use o' our stores, I'm sure," the man says hastily, pointedly not looking my direction. "Certainly no' that ol' wool, see 'ow fine 'er clothes are?"

But the wife stalks towards me, a rolled up length of the rough brown stuff on her hip.

This is enough.

I untangle Maarja's hands from my skirts, setting her gently behind me, and step forward.

The woman stumbles to a halt at my movement, as if I have been nothing more than a figure above a shrine. Her husband nearly rams into her from behind. All around, the snickering stops, heads turning, bodies stilling, waiting.

I cast my gaze towards the woman, wondering if I have seen her before. If she brought her baby boy, or perhaps another child, and stood in the cold or the heat or the rain amongst the other mothers lining the fortress gates so that a Waster might prick her babe and keep him well all the years of his life. Only now to watch with sickening horror as his foot slipped, his weight tilted, his head slammed against the ground, and her own body jolted as the wagon below her thumped over his thin, beautiful, perfect leg and crushed it. The audible snap that must have careened through all the chambers of her heart, and echoed in the horrified silence before her scream pierced the air.

Her coarse brown eyes are still red-rimmed, and as we gaze at each other, they begin to glisten, and I know, without knowing how I know, that all of this is true. It has happened just as I imagine it. The Waster was there that day when it snowed up to her shins, and her husband scolded her for taking the boy out, but she bundled the babe in every garment she had, including her own shawl – the fine, thick one that her mother had given her, that her brother had wanted to bury the woman in, but she couldn't bear to be separated from forever. The Waster had been there that day, and pricked her babe to save him.

And the Waster was here now, had been here this day, and rotted that beautiful boyish leg to save him again.

I hold out my hand, palm upwards. Her gaze drops to it, staring for a moment in confusion before she understands. Then she takes the final step, placing the heavy wool in my arms.

"A fine weave," I say without looking down at it, letting my voice ring out. "How warm it will keep my daughter and me when winter comes. I thank you."

The woman bows low, two fingers to her forehead, her other hand over her heart. I do not even acknowledge the father as I turn, looking out over the gathered crowd with two fingers to my forehead.

I pretend I do not see it. I keep my step steady, my hand soft against Maarja's small back, our eyes trained to the top of the hill and the wooden gates, the stone fortress beyond.

But what Vappers begins spreads through the crowd, and I sense it all the same.

He puts two fingers to his forehead, returning the greeting. And when he drops them to his downturned lips, changing the sign, all the people gathered do so as well, their fingers resting on their lips long after I have left the crowd behind.

The sign of Looklema. The sign of the goddess.

CHAPTER ELEVEN
THE CALL OF ROT

Beware the powerless man, my daughter.
Do not treat with him.
For if you lay him open,
you will disappear within.

"*WHAT OF* my grandmother?" Maarja asks, winding a loose thread from the hem of her nightrail around the tip of one of her fingers. It turns white, then a deep pink.

"What would you like to know about her?" I ask, breathing into the space in my chest where my mother's memory resides.

"Is she dead?" my daughter asks, with the frankness of the very young.

"She is," I answer, trying for the same.

"How did she die?"

"I –" I hedge, quickening towards an answer. "I don't know, exactly."

"How do you not know?" Maarja goes on, ignorant, in her child's way, to any discomfort but her own.

"I was not there when it happened," I answer, striving for safe, generic responses. Such, I am learning, is motherhood.

"Then how do you know she is dead?" Maarja asks, unwinding the thread.

"I know," I answer. "Shall we get you covered up then?"

But my daughter is at no other time more focused on having her way than at bedtime.

"I want a story about her," she declares, as if she has not heard me.

"I've told you several stories about her," I chide. "Now it is time to sleep, and stories of your grandmother before bedtime hardly make for restful slumber."

"Because she was bad," Maarja says, looking up from strangling her own finger.

"Certainly not," I argue, surprised. "Have you heard such a thing from someone else?"

"Father said she was cruel – that all the Wasters before me have been cruel."

And now we come to it.

"Tuskjas is not your father. Nor is he to be trusted on matters of Wasters. Your grandmother was not cruel. She was just and faithful and powerful. And her mother before her was compassionate and graceful and even more powerful."

"So I am not the only good Waster?" she asks, in such a way that I do not know how best to answer. And so I do as these women we discuss have taught me. I do so with honesty.

"You are a very good Waster, but you are not the only one," I answer, hoping that she is still too young to see the gaping hole below my words.

But she is not.

"Are you?"

This was her trap. Her test. And I do not know how to prevail in it.

"You might as well tell me what you've heard," I murmur, cutting to the quick.

She casts her soft brown gaze outward, catching on the candle that still burns across the room.

"I've not heard anything, Mama," she mutters, fidgeting with the thread in her clammy fingertips.

"I know you lie, Maarja," I admonish her gently. "Nothing can come from your lips that I've not heard before. Let's have out with it."

But she will not be persuaded.

"Nothing, Mama," she says, pulling her legs up and turning away from me, finally lying down, as I've been begging for the last half hour.

"Maarja, my love?" I ask.

But she never answers. And I am too tired to press.

My husband has little to say about the boy in the marketplace, though I know word has reached him, likely from the mouths of my own guards. He gives me nothing more than a knowing glare when I join him at the high table for end-day meal, and I am reminded of what Kurat claimed – that Tuskjas longs to warp the land's greatest power into something ceremonial. Something benevolent and superficial.

Perhaps that is what my husband thinks is occurring. Perhaps he does not know, or does not understand, the sign of the goddess. How could he? Surely his Slavic mother never taught him.

Hariva shows herself less at court, Rahuleid delivering her excuses that the pregnancy tires her more as she climbs closer and closer to its end. But he insists she does not need my services, and so I know the lie for what it is. And what would I say to her, should she come? I can do nothing to refute her perceptions of my loyalties. And so I leave her as she wishes to be left and save us both the effort of a farce. She is safer, no doubt, away from court, away from Tuskjas, who might sniff out her disloyalty like he sniffed out the pine bow hidden in my sleeve.

As for Kurat, he has once again disappeared from court after our last meeting. Despite the weeks that pass, I do not dare ask Tuskjas where his son has gone. I do not even reveal to my husband that I have noticed his absence.

When Kurat does return, there is no presenting himself in the Hall. The remnants of end-day meal are being swept from the tables when I feel his body barrel through the gates outside. I am lingering with Maarja, who takes an age to finish the tiny amount of food required for a child's sustenance, when he passes quickly before the open doors of the Hall and disappears, my power tracking him to Tuskjas' study, where the Chieftain is lingering over his first cup of krupnikas.

I slip the Shroud up over my head, lightly enough that Maarja does not suspect, and cast my awareness out deeper. And so it is that I know that Kurat argues heatedly for several moments, and Tuskjas sips his liquor, indifferent.

"How much more, Mama?" Maarja grumbles. Hiida is making her way across the Hall to fetch me up to my rooms for the evening.

"That will do," I say in a long sigh, surprising Maarja who surely expected me to demand several more bites. But she does not linger for me to change my mind. She jumps to her feet, nearly upending her trencher in her lap, and shoves it away so hard it topples my untouched cup of mead.

"Maarja!" I chide. "Slow down, child."

But she is off, looking, no doubt, for stolen moments with Suita, who lingers restlessly beside her father, before they are both relegated to bed.

Hiida mops up the spilled mead with her apron where it is racing towards my lap, *tsk*ing at me when I reach to help.

"Are ya ready to retire, m'lady?"

Kurat spins in Tuskjas' study, shoving himself towards the door, then stops abruptly at a word from my husband. Whatever is said, it burns in Kurat's heaving chest, but he calms himself, striding from the room with purpose but not panic.

I see him pass again by the open doors, out into the yard, and through the gates, where my awareness of him fades. I let the Shroud fall.

"I am," I answer Hiida, gathering myself up.

When we pass beside the closed door of Tuskjas' study, I feel him lumber to his feet, the krupnikas beginning to swirl in his blood. The door opens, my husband sneering in the dimness beyond, backlit by firelight. Hiida immediately steps back behind me, bowing her head low and folding her hands.

"Wife," Tuskjas purrs. "Will you not come in and share a cup with me?"

My incredulity at such a request must be evident on my face, for he laughs darkly.

"Ah, yes, I remember. Wasters do not imbibe," he says. "A pity. A little fire in the gut would make your bed far warmer, since I won't be coming to it tonight."

I move to step past him, but he grabs the crook of my elbow, pinching the skin beneath the light wool of my sleeve. I yank away from him, wincing. He snatches at me again, wrapping his big hand around my upper arm and dragging me towards him, liquor rolling off his breath as he murmurs against the side of my face.

"You will not join me, so I will have to issue my warning here for your little maidservant to hear." I turn my chin away from the tickle of his mouth over my ear, slamming my eyes shut to keep violent thoughts from my fingertips.

"You Waste when I tell you to Waste. You heal when I tell you to heal. What use is your power to me when any common boy in the marketplace can gain it for himself?"

I don't bother to argue, little purpose it would serve.

"Here me now, Liama," he murmurs, rubbing his blunt nose against my hairline. "Should I hear of you casting your power about without my direction, I'll find a better purpose for it. And it won't be some stranger in the marketplace, to be sure."

He shoves me away so hard that I stumble into Hiida, who wraps her thick arms around my waist and keeps me from the ground. Before I have even righted myself, Tuskjas has slammed the door of his study, and I can feel him pouring himself another glass of krupnikas behind it.

"Ne'er ya worry, Liama," Hiida whispers as she sets me to rights, straightening the dress she'll pull over my head in less than a few moments. "I 'eard what they did in tha' marketplace. I 'eard they gave ya tha sign o' the goddess."

"Hush," I warn her, hurrying towards the stairs before I lose yet another friend to treason.

"Jus' a little further now," she murmurs, following behind, and I know that she isn't speaking of the distance to my chambers. "Jus' a little longer, ya'll see, ya will."

We reach the first landing, turning past the door to Kurat's chambers, when I feel him flicker behind it. And perhaps, though I have not given him my answer, we have reached some sort of truce between us, because I can feel his heartbeat reappear in my own quarters just above. It is a new and small courtesy, but I recognize it for what it is. He is giving me the opportunity to turn away, to find some other occupation for myself, should I desire to deny him.

I ascend the stairs at a measured pace, not wanting to alarm Hiida even as I conspire ways of getting rid of her.

"Hiida," I say quite loudly as I turn back to her, especially considering that we've just been whispering. "I need you to stay in the kitchens tonight. Or the yard."

"Whate'er for?" she balks, halting on the stair below me.

"I'd forgotten," I go on, putting a hand to my head, "I told the healer that she should find you if she required any help inserting the plate into the boy's leg."

"They'll fin' me ready 'nough if she comes callin'," Hiida says, confused.

"It may be quite urgent, and I don't want word spreading with the other servants," I say, nodding meaningly below us, towards Tuskjas' study.

Still, Hiida looks at me suspiciously, and I am beginning to think of ways to make her leave without her knowing.

"Please, Hiida," I beg simply. "I'm worried over him."

That is enough. She softens, thinking I have confided in her.

"Liama, love. O' course ya are," she comforts, putting her hand over mine in the railing. "Would ya feel bett'r if I sent fer word on 'ow 'e's doin'?"

"Can you go yourself?" I ask, a little too quickly.

She grimaces, no doubt thinking of the long walk down and back up the hill, but finally sighs.

"Course I can, m'lady. So long as ya can see to yerself –"

I wave her off. "I did so for 20 years. I can manage a single evening on my own."

She *tsks* at me, but doesn't argue further, patting my hand once more and then turning to descend. "I'll bring ya word soon as I return," she says quietly, and there's little I can do now to keep her from doing so without giving myself away.

When I reach my door, I pause, waiting for Hiida to step off the final step at the base of the stairway and back into the corridor to the Hall. Then I ready the Shroud, but I do not lift it.

Before I have even turned from closing my door, I can feel the charge of anxiety around him. It refracts against the skin at the nape of my neck, sending chills to my fingertips. I had not considered until this moment that things would be different between us after our last encounter. Suddenly, I am leaden. I cannot turn around.

I am resolved not to ask where he has been. I am resolved to show no interest in his long absence.

He spares no time.

"I am reluctant to ask you –" he murmurs, his voice dry and tight. "I had designs on letting you come to it yourself. I will not say I have been a fool, but I have been proud. And now I am reluctant to ask you for your decision at the very moment of my return, but I am hoping my time here will be short indeed."

I turn now, my hesitation overcome by the desperation in his voice.

Kurat is still in his traveling cloak and boots, covered over with the dust of summer's paths and wrinkled from long overwear. His hood is back, his fine features open and drawn in the late twilight gloom, a hard twist to his mouth.

"Something has happened," I breathe. His brows lower, sharpening his gaze.

"You must answer now," he whispers, soft but firm. "I am sorry for it but you must answer now."

"What has happened?" I ask again, but he only shakes his head, his jaw tight. He will not tell me until I have given him my answer.

"I will not give myself wholly over to your designs, but I will assist you where I can," I say, pressing my own gaze back into his.

"Where you can?" he repeats skeptically.

"Insomuch as Maarja's safety can be assured," I clarify.

"I cannot assure you that," he says.

"I have not asked you to," I answer. "I will ensure it myself. But these are my terms. If she comes under attack, do not depend on my assistance. It will be elsewhere."

It is not the allegiance he wanted from me. But I suspect he was not fool enough to believe he would get my help without conditions. *This* condition. After a moment more of careful study, he nods.

"What has happened?" I ask once more.

"Get your cloak and call your maid," he instructs by way of answer. "She was bound to be brought into this at some point."

"I will not," I say, using the voice I raise from the dais in the Hall below, when I am permitted to use it. "I go no further until you have told me what has occurred to put you in such a state."

I can tell he would rather spit at me than answer, but it is he who seeks my help. I have been bent around Tuskjas, shaped to make space for his will inside of me. But I will not bend around Kurat. If he wants my assistance, it is he who will need to bend around me.

"Where have you been, Kurat?" I ask him directly.

"Everywhere," he breathes, deflecting. "Is it true what they said of the Wasters of old?"

"Is *what* true?" I ask, narrowing my gaze. His own flickers up and down my body, looking for something.

"Is it true that they were warriors?"

His question startles me into a breath of silence.

"In a manner of speaking," I answer after a moment.

"Damn it, Liama!" he hisses, stepping forward. "I have no time for vagueness. *Is it true*? Is it not the real reason Kotkas sought them out? To destroy his enemies?"

His words are like the click of a lock. The swing of a rusty grate. Something begins to unfold inside of me. Something starved.

"It was true," I breathe.

"And you?" he asks, his eyes raking my face. "Are you one of them?"

For a breath I do not answer. I have hidden it, this part of myself. I have not even dared to think on it.

"Are you?" he presses, grabbing my shoulders and shaking. I let him.

"If I show this to you," I whisper on ragged breath, "if I reveal this, what will it become in your hands?"

His face softens, warping, all the anger from a moment before pushing away to its corners. His hands come up to my cheeks, cradling my jaw.

"I do not know," he whispers, those enigmatic eyes bent at their corners. "I do not know, Liama. But I must ask it of you all the same."

He does not try and deceive me, and that is why I give him what he asks for.

"Who has come against us?" I whisper, burning.

"Norsemen, in Saaremaa," he answers, his face transforming again, split with fear and rage, fingers clenching gently around my jaw.

"Raiding?" I ask, surprised at him. Norsemen have been raiding our shores for decades. They come, they plunder, they go. It is the very source of the rift between the Kallas of Revala and my husband.

"Not raiding," Kurat answers, shaking his head. His tongue passes over dry lips. "Liama, they are killing them. Hundreds. They are tearing the countryside apart." He swallows hard.

"They are *killing* my mother's people."

"You have always been told that Looklema's daughters were queens. Just. Fair. Powerful. Compassionate," my mother says, her face stern.

"But remember," my grandmother joins in, placing her thick-palmed hand over my own. "There are tales within tales, and without. The truth seeps its way into legend. When Looklema's eldest brother, blessed by the

Earth Giant with enormous strength, came against her in violence, seeking to force the identity of her lover, her Daemon Prince, from her lips, her daughters defended her, overcoming their mighty uncle with ease. The Wasting Daughter withered the man's heart, driving him to the doorstep of death, where the Shadow Daughter stood at the ready to pass him through."

"Do not be fooled as the common folk are," my mother takes up the lesson in her terse voice. "They remember only Looklema's grace in the tale, when she allowed her brother to leave with his life, though exiled forever from the Sacred Wood. They do not remember what her daughters did. How they did it so easily."

"We have crafted good from this power," my grandmother says, turning her hands over and cupping them, as if she holds all that good in her palms. "We have crafted life from death. We say we cannot heal, and yet, we heal. We say we cannot create, only destroy, and yet, we create."

"But I have always thought there was a reason Looklema was drawn to a Daemon, charming as her Grey-Eyed Prince surely was. I have always felt the same tug towards darkness. We all, every Waster since that first one, have felt the call of rot. The temptation to destroy."

"And that is why, although we bend ourselves to heal, we are at our most honest when we shatter."

Despite Kurat's urgency to be away, he cannot deny that steady thought and planning are required to sweep the Chieftainess of the House away from Tarbatu under cover of night without putting her daughter in considerable danger.

Taking her with me into battle is unthinkable, though I confess I am tempted, if only to have her close. And perhaps as well, for her to see this facet of her heritage, which I have not revealed.

It is a mother's constant work, assessing which danger is greatest. Which risks can be borne, and which cannot. But I am not given the choice, in the end. Kurat claims he cannot Walk her as well as me.

"Hariva," I breathe, casting aside the doubt that lingers from our last encounter.

"You are sure enough of her to leave your daughter in her care?" Kurat questions.

I have carried dead babes I was willing to give more to save than you will for your hale, living daughter!

"Yes," I nod, Hariva's shrill accusation aching behind my eyes. "Can you Walk her here?"

"I don't dare, not with the babe," Kurat shakes his head. "I've no idea what that could do. Nor do we have the time."

"We will have to leave instructions with Hiida, then," I say, trying to conjure ways to draw back the woman I have just sent from the fortress grounds.

"Call for her," Kurat says again.

"She isn't here," I shake my head.

"Where is she?" he asks impatiently.

"I just sent her on some errand to protect *your* secret power," I bite back, not liking his tone.

"Well, where has she gone then?" he returns testily.

"To see after a boy I Wasted in the marketplace today," I answer waspishly. He gapes.

"Why on earth did you Waste a boy in the marketplace?"

"Little it matters now!" I snap. He sighs heavily through his nose, shaking his head at me as though I have disappointed him greatly.

"There's no other choice," I tell him, hands on my hips and brows high. He purses his lips, rolling them between his teeth as he stares flatly back.

I raise my brows higher.

"You have to reveal your power to someone in order to gain mine in defense of your mother's people. You either put your faith in a loose-lipped ten-year-old girl or you put your faith in a shrewd woman who has served me loyally for a decade."

"You don't recommend your own daughter?" he sneers.

"I wouldn't recommend trusting a ten-year-old with a secret so consequential even if it were Looklema herself."

"This is going to be far more dramatic than I have the patience for," he sighs.

"She won't be far, still on the hill, I suspect," I instruct. He glares at me a moment longer, but then he closes his eyes, pulling in a long breath through his nose.

"My father's name was Tasuja," he murmurs, and then he is gone.

It takes only a moment, Hiida likely having stopped off at the kitchen for some offering of goodwill to take to the boy's family. I am standing at the ready, alert for their return, which is the only reason I am able to silence her shriek before it leaves her throat.

They tumble into the room, Kurat releasing her quickly, his hand going instead to a bloody scratch on his chin. Hiida, Looklema help her, is near to choking on her own tongue, the effects of Kurat's Walking and my Wasting compounding for what I am sure is an unpleasant experience.

I snatch at her shoulders, trying to get my face in front of her own wild eyes before she takes another blind swipe at anything that moves. Her frantic gaze catches on me, bloodshot eyes going impossibly wider as she hauls in a gasping breath.

"Hush, Hiida," I soothe her. "All is well. Hush. All is well."

"Snake's tits, Liama!" she wheezes. "I – oh, Looklema –" and she drops to her knees, a hand on her heaving bosom. "What in all the –"

"He's a Shade Walker, Hiida," I explain gently. "I asked him to bring you here."

She sways, putting an arm out, which I catch. She gapes, murmuring something between stiff lips, and I lean down to hear her better.

"Ne'er again," she murmurs. "Goddess 'elp me, ne'er do tha ta me again."

"Liama," Kurat warns, as if I need a reminder that time is of the essence. I glare at him, but then turn back to Hiida.

"Hiida," I say firmly, trying to cut through the fog. "I've need of you." She blinks a few times, then nods, pulling herself up to standing with my help.

"O' course," she murmurs, coming back to herself. "O' course, Liama. What need?"

"I am going with the Heir," I begin. "We may be gone for some time. I need you to ensure that Maarja gets to Hariva, and deliver a message with my instructions."

"Yer goin' with the 'eir?" she repeats breathlessly, turning now to Kurat behind her.

"To –" but Kurat grunts loudly, cutting me off.

"And what if they have need of me?" I bark at him incredulously.

"They'll know soon enough where we've gone," he answers darkly. "The whole House will know. I would give us cover for a night at least."

"Does Tuskjas know?" I ask. Kurat only looks at me with hooded eyes.

"You went to him first," I conclude, remembering their argument. And then I remember his warning. *Should I hear of you casting your power about without my direction, I'll find a better purpose for it.*

"He refused to send aid?"

Kurat sneers. "Saaremaa is too independent. He's wanted them cowed for years. Now the Norse will do it for him."

"Did you ask him for my assistance?" I ask, stepping towards him.

"No," he says firmly, shaking his head. "He doesn't know that I am here. There's no reason for him to believe I would seek you out."

174

"He knows," I breathe. "Or he suspects. I thought he was talking about the boy in the marketplace..."

"Then ya canna go, Liama," Hiida joins the argument.

"You would have her damn Saaremaa?" Kurat bites.

"Hiida," I cut through them both, "go make sure Maarja is still in her quarters."

"I'll go," Kurat declares before Hiida can take a step, and then he is gone, reappearing in little more than a breath. "She's safe. Asleep."

"You have to Walk her to Hariva, immediately," I command him.

"No," Hiida argues. "Liama, no. Ya canna trust 'im. Not with yer babe. I'll get Maarja to safety. I'll 'ide her down in the town if I need ta."

"He'll tear it apart before sunrise tomorrow," Kurat snaps.

"It has to be Hariva," I say. "She has the best reason – if they're caught –"

"They *will* be caught," Kurat claims.

" – then she can claim she's only taking Maarja for a small journey, or has urgent news from Vaiga and needs Maarja to go with her in my absence."

"He'll never believe that," Kurat shakes his head.

"He doesn't have to," I insist. "It only needs to give her enough cover that he cannot act against her in front of the court, not without isolating Rahuleid and Vaiga."

"Then let me take Maarja to 'er, I beg ya, Liama," Hiida pleads. "I'll see 'er safe with Lady 'ariva, I swear by it."

I look once more to Kurat, close to pleading with him to conjure some better solution. Or recant his request to me entirely. But he only looks helplessly back, shaking his head. Empty.

"Do it," I turn to Hiida. "Get her to Hariva. They must leave immediately. Tonight. And Rahuleid must stay. If he goes as well it will appear to be fleeing."

Hiida nods firmly.

"So help me, Hiida," I stop her with both hands on her round shoulders before she can move to the door. "If she –" but I cannot go on, choking on the possibilities, endless, that I have set in motion. Hiida's face softens, her chin wobbling as wet pools in her eyes.

"I made a vow to ya, Liama," she murmurs, her calloused hands coming up to cup my cheeks. "Ten years ago, I made ya a vow. I'll no' let any man, no' even a Chieftain, make me break it."

And then she leans forward, stretching up on her toes to press a kiss to my forehead.

"Looklema keep you, m'lady," she whispers. "And whoe'er yer enemies be this nigh', let there be nothin' left of 'em but blood."

And then the warmth of her eyes and her hands and her bosom slips away, my ears popping as she opens the door, having sealed the room to protect us sometime while we spoke. And even though I see her close the door behind her, I cannot hear it, nor her tread on the landing outside my door.

I turn to Kurat.

"I hope you understand what you have asked of me this night," I say, leveling my gaze at him. "I hope you understand what I am risking on your behalf."

He nods seriously, almost humbly.

"And you understand that if my daughter comes under threat, I will rip the air from your lungs until you return me to her side."

This time he pulls in a long breath, and then he nods.

"I understand, Liama," he murmurs, stepping towards me. "And if Maarja comes under threat, you will not have to force me to bring you back. I will do so willingly."

And then we share a long gaze, passing these understandings between us until they form the pillars of a bridge.

"You said you can only Walk a half day's ride? How on earth are we to get there?"

"I can only Walk a half day's ride in a single jump. We'll be stringing several together. But you must heed me, Liama," he says, eyes sharp and anxious. "Raise your hood. It will not be like the other times. I will lose speed as we go on, and perhaps clarity. Piecing together several Walks can be dangerous, and that's on one's own. If I had another option, I would certainly utilize it –"

"I will draw the Shroud," I interrupt. "I might be able to Waste your fatigue as we go."

"If there is some method for that, I invite it," he says, holding his hand out, anxious to be away. I move across the space between us, already reaching for him. "As it is, I'll need to keep you much closer. And I suspect you'll need to remind me, at times, where it is we are going, and why."

As he speaks, he draws me in slowly by the hand, making his intention evident and giving me the opportunity to refuse it. His caution is ridiculous. As if I would leave the people of Saaremaa to the Norsemen's sword on grounds of refusing my old enemy's embrace. I am tempted to remind him again that he is not Tuskjas' wife and so does not know the half of what I have allowed, but the comparison sours on my tongue, no longer as true as I once thought it was.

I pull the Shroud lightly around myself as he pulls me into his arms, prepared to dive deeper if needed.

And so it is that he guides my hand behind his back, tucking my head gently into the crook of his neck. I can smell the smoke on him and the tang of dried blood under layers of salt and dust and briny sand. His arms clasp firmly around my back, and he slides his foot forward in between my own.

"Clasp your hands," he murmurs. "And do not let go."

I nod into his shoulder, interlocking my hands around my wrists.

"Breathe," he whispers, and our chests expand together, pushing against each other. I close my eyes, expecting the darkness, but it is held off a moment longer.

Then he speaks, so softly I can barely hear him.

"This is not the first time I have held you thus."

His confession hurtles us into time and space.

CHAPTER TWELVE
THE BLEEDING ISLAND

Ooze, squelch, glisten, bore.
Rotten, weeping, seeping, sore.
Bodies molding all around.
A Waster learns to love the sound.

MY ARMS tighten reflexively against the sense of depthless falling. This is what I had expected upon that first Walk. Yet, in the chaos, I am still able to make sense of a new sensation. We are crossing miles upon miles, where before we had only crossed from one part of the city to the another. Still, there is no sound but the whipping wind across my skin, curling its warm summer fingertips into my hood and trying to yank it free. It lasts less than four breaths before we slam to a halt, a darkened sky and sentinel pines barely materializing around us before Kurat throws us to the wind again.

We carry on thus for several more jumps, as he called them, making our way across the thick forests that border Tarbatu to the west. Then at our next halt, the moon is suddenly brighter. I can just make out its fat, waxing shape, a sense of openness all around us, before we hurtle back into darkness. We have reached the long expanse of Sakala's open moors.

Somewhere in their vast, pitiless eternity, Kurat begins to flag. Within the Shroud, my power observes his fatigue before my senses do. I begin to hunt his body for weaknesses, sucking out acids in his muscles and stabilizing his wild heart. His only acknowledgement is a tight squeeze around my chest, but I suspect that my intervention has been helpful in some way. It holds the strain at bay for a few more jumps, but then a rapid decline begins, his body beginning to fail in more ways than I can shore up at once, my attention rapidly shifting from one system to the next, like a fisherman trying desperately to plug a sinking boat. His grip on me loosens, and I begin to recognize his trickling murmur below the sound of the wind, though I cannot make out the words.

"Kurat!" I scream into his neck, squeezing as hard as I can. "We go to Saaremaa. We go to save your mother's kin!"

We slam to a stop. This time his arms do not brace me, and I am held onto him only by my own grip. My body is thrown sideways, bringing him down with me, my fists clenched into his cloak.

There is grass and stabbing stalks, a sense of wetness on my back and shoulder, seeping. His body lies limp across my own, and I am struck by how light it is. The moon is no longer high above, but drifting to the west, washing the moor in pale light.

"Kurat!" I yelp, pushing at him, trying to find his head, his face, in the yards of tangled cloak. He moans painfully, murmuring what sounds like my name. I heave him off of me, rolling him to his back.

His face is ghastly, made even paler by the moon. He looks as though he has aged to his final day, his eyes open and staring into the sky above.

At some point in the wreckage of our landing, the Shroud has been torn away. I can still sense the life left in his bones. Otherwise I would think him dead.

He had already made this journey once this night, coming in urgency for help. The thought had come to me as we stood in my chambers, as he explained what would be required to make it this great distance, and as I pressed my face into his neck, smelling salt and smoke. Now I suspect it was folly to have attempted it twice. That is perhaps why he'd felt the need for such a great confession, to heave off the weight of impurity.

Perhaps I should have made mine as well.

Yet, how could I have told him that I remember his embrace? That I have begun to relive it in dreams, not knowing when or how it occurred, but growing ever more sure that my body has not forgotten it, even if he has taken it from my mind with his own hand.

How could I have told him the sense of familiarity, of rightness, that had washed me from scalp to heel, even from within the Shroud, when he'd drawn me to the cradle of his chest?

"You mustn't stop," I command him, rapidly pulling the fatigue from his limbs. "Your purpose is Saaremaa. You must get us there."

A little color is returning to his cheeks, but his eyes stare vacantly upwards still. I ramp up his heart, sending the blood pulsing rapidly through his body, and he begins to suck in thick, heavy breaths to support it.

"I will not tolerate this weakness from you," I say, forcing steel into my voice. He blinks, his fingers stirring in the grass. "How ridiculous you look, lying here when your mother's people are calling out. How ridiculous she would think you, she who could Walk from her chambers in Tarbatu to her father's Hall in a single step. And here her son lies, unable to manage it in ten."

He blinks again, this time flickering his gaze to my face, eyes growing keener with every word from my mouth. He coughs dryly, then begins to hack in earnest, his chest shaking itself out. He rolls, slamming a hand into the grass to stabilize himself, sending his heaves into the earth.

The fit subsides, but he stays prostrate, sucking in the moist air, forehead pressed against the squelchy moor.

"You think to use shame against me," he finally says, voice broken and weak.

"Has it not succeeded?" I answer, brows high. With a groan he pulls himself up to sitting, his back against my side.

"I suspect your Wasting has made a greater impact," he says hoarsely, raking a hand over his face and squinting out into the vastness.

"Have you any idea where we are?" I ask, trying to make my own assessment of our surroundings.

"Not in Saaremaa," he murmurs bitterly.

"Then we had better carry on," I say, rising. He turns just enough to look up at me over his shoulder.

"And if I cannot?" he asks, looking for a moment as he did before, haggard and old and despondent. I cannot bear the expression on his face. I will not tolerate it.

"Then I would consider it treason, and think you pathetic," I judge him, meaning every word. "And I would require you to Walk to prove it, so you might as well get off your ass and take me with you in the direction of my people, if you please."

I cannot say precisely how his expression changes, only that it hardens, not against me, but around me.

He raises a hand and I heave him upwards, flushing his legs with blood to strengthen his stance. We fold each other once more in our embrace, and this time as I tuck my face against his neck, I sense something more familiar than smoke and salt and blood.

"Raise the Shroud," he murmurs against my hood. "Whatever you were doing before, keep doing it."

I obey, but find that I am reluctant to lose that nagging sense of a memory to the Shroud's indifference.

"Ready?" he asks, inhaling deeply. I expand my chest within his arms in response.

And we Walk once more.

"Mama!" my daughter squeals. "Mama! Mama! Mama!"

"Yes!" I nearly scream, exasperated. "Yes, my love. What? What is it?" I have just spent the day standing on the dais through the tedium of Tuskjas' administrative duties, longing for nothing more than to be here, in my daughter's company instead, and yet, now I could beat my own child with bare fists if pushed only a little further by her unceasing need for my constant attention. There are days when I can hardly stand the sound of her voice, much less the constant touch of her grubby hands, tugging at my arms and pulling at my clothes.

She has no awareness of herself. She smacks and yanks and thuds and stabs with abandon, her sharp little limbs like the cruelest weapons honed for the softest places of my body.

"Tell me a story," Maarja demands, unfazed by my frustration. "Tell me the best story you know. Tell me one about the Daemon Prince where he goes to meet Looklema's mother and she gives her blessing for them to marry."

"You hardly need me to tell it if you know it so well," I grumble, feeling around in my depths for any measure of grace and finding the well empty.

"Please," she begs, yanking on my arm and throwing me off balance. "Please, Mama, please, please."

"Maarja, let go," I pull my arm from her grip. "You know I hate it when you pull on me."

"Please, please, Mama," she continues on, this time reaching for the front of my tunic. I swat her hands away, but she is too persistent. I try and turn from her, but she simply wraps her arms around my leg, tangling us both in skirts. I stumble, barely catching myself against the wall.

"Let go of me!" I scream at her, tightening my hands into fists against the cold stone so as not to beat her with them. I just barely wrangle the loose tendrils of my power, already whipping out to force her into obedience.

Maarja stumbles back, her face crumpling at my tone. But I cannot reach for her. If I do, it will be with claws.

She stares at me with her eyes bent downward at the corners, her lips forming around the blistering sob.

But she is too old now to be soothed by the very hand that strikes her.

Before the sob can release, she turns and runs away.

I should follow her.

I do not.

I lean against the wall, pressing my fingertips into my eyes to the point of pain, and breathe through the shame.

I shore up his body, and he keeps us going in a steady rhythm for several jumps. I am not sure how many have passed when I begin to sense the sea. When we stop in the sand near the surf, he breaks the pattern with a short halt, leaning back from me to meet my eye before I have even gathered our surroundings into a cohesive whole. Across the black, roiling water, the lights of the island Saaremaa are flickering.

"This will be the final one," he says, panting. "I should be able to drop us in the Hall from here. Prepare yourself. I did not tell them who I would be bringing, only that I had gone to seek help."

I nod, and he tucks me back into his chest, flinging us the final distance.

Our arrival is greeted with shrieks and yells, the feeling of bodies scurrying away. Kurat pulls away from me immediately but keeps a hand under my elbow to keep me steady. Or perhaps to keep himself steady. He stumbles, and I reach out with my power, holding him up.

We are in a Hall, though it looks nothing like my husband's in Tarbatu. There are windows only on the eastern side, which I suspect is the side away from the sea. The room is warm with candlelight. That is where my body's senses cease and my power breaks in.

If I did not already have the Shroud drawn up, I would be overwhelmed by the flood of observations my power begins to pull inside itself. I spin, sensing the hundreds of broken, bleeding bodies before I see them. The front of the Hall is filled with them, dropped haphazardly in loose groups, a dozen women or more scurrying hastily between them, tending what can be tended.

I let my weight carry me down deeper into the Shroud, reaching for the calm that I know awaits. I have a sense of Kurat speaking to someone behind me, but I care little what he says. My feet begin to move before I have made a conscious choice to order them. I come upon the first body, observing its need – an arrow tip in the meat of the left shoulder. Standing over it, I Waste the rotted flesh around the foreign object and open a clean hole behind it, much like I opened a hole in the boy's leg in the marketplace. The arrow tip drops through and I flush the wound with blood, only long enough to push out any remaining rot, then cut it off, sensing that this body has already lost a considerable amount. Distantly, I register screaming, drawing heads and eyes towards where I work, but there is no time to move slowly. All of this I complete in little more than a breath. I grab at a woman rushing past me, instructing her to wrap the wound immediately and sit the body up. Then I move on to the next.

A jagged slice in the thigh of the next body. It is simple enough to eat away the rot already festering there, flush it, and move on.

A fractured head wound in the next, likely from a war axe. The meat of the brain is too vulnerable. I drop the heartbeat instead, letting the body slip into blissful unconsciousness. It will expire within minutes. I move on.

By the seventh body, my awareness of the surroundings alerts me that I have the attention of an audience. I ignore it, walking past each body in need and addressing it without slowing. I have never worked with this speed before, or addressed so many bodies at once, but I find that I am not limited. I could carry on at this measured pace for hours.

He approaches me from behind slowly, following me at a short distance past several bodies before coming close enough to catch my hand in his. He pulls me to a gentle stop, leaning over my shoulder to murmur in my ear.

"The dawn has come. The Norsemen have pulled back to their boats. The Kallas suspects they will not strike again until nightfall. Do your working, but do not overtire yourself. You will be needed, Chieftainess."

Perhaps I nod my acceptance. His body slips away, one more in the mass, but I sense it nonetheless, close by, as I Waste the people of Saaremaa back to health.

There are more. I can sense them, when I have seen to every body in the Hall, just beyond its doors and spread throughout the remainder of the fortress. But I keep his words close. I will be needed. This is not my greatest responsibility. I must rest.

I pull back the Shroud and fall with it. Small, agile hands catch me against what feels like a girl's body. Then there are several more, lifting my limbs from the ground. An instruction goes out from one of them. I am half-aware of being carried into dimness, a place cooler and quieter than where I was. Then I am laid in repose on softness. A command is made to call for the Heir.

I do not know if he comes. I pull down my heartbeat and sleep.

CHAPTER THIRTEEN
THE FESTERING WOUND

Hot the cheek, yet cold the shiver.
If swollen the wound, look to the liver.
Corruption can foil the most precise of Workings.
Seek out the poison within that is lurking.

"WHO IS HE, that you would stand with him against me?"

"We would have you hear what he has to offer," my mother says.

"Hear his offer," my grandmother presses. "And then make what judgements you will."

I have not woken like this in a lifetime, not since I was a child, stretching the limits of my power under my grandmother's guidance. She would brew her tea of peppermint, dolloping in a huge glob of honey for healing, and flush my tender limbs and aching head for me while I drank it.

I am left to my own devices now. I do as she would have done, finding my body sore but my power undiminished from the working of the night before. Or the morning. In the dimness of the room where they laid me, I can sense nothing of the day's progression. When once more I can point my toes and reach my arms over my head without aching, I rise to meet whatever the day holds.

In Tarbatu I pass through the fortress as a known presence, gathering greetings and gestures of respect, but hardly worth more than a pause in the course of business. I am not surprised to find it different here, but neither am I completely prepared for it.

I go only a few steps from the door of the small room, likely a servant's quarters, before encountering a flock of women flying through the hallway on hurried feet, baskets of still wet, hastily scrubbed cloth on their hips. They skitter to a stop like chickens, squawking and dipping and bumping into one another, their shock and awe staining the air around them.

"Oh!" squeaks a little woman at the front, her face lined around the mouth with years of sternness. "Oh, my Chieftainess! Apologies, so many apologies!" And then she throws down her basket as if it contained a wasp's nest and falls to her knees.

I suspect that under other circumstances I would be horrified to see a woman – now women, as the others have followed suit – who is so obviously about the work of caring for the sick and dying fall to her knees on my account. As it is, though, groggy and smarting and still with considerable feats of power to undertake, I am more annoyed at the obstruction than ashamed for it. And so I give them what they want, or rather expect, simply to have done with it.

"Rise," I say, using the voice of the dais. They clamber up in all manner of fussiness, unsure what next to do.

"Where is the Heir?" I ask.

"Just on," the older woman says, dipping another bow. "To your left at the end of the hall and then a right after – ack," she sputters, waving a hand in the air. "Agda! Take the Chieftainess to the Kallas study at once!"

A younger girl peels off the back of the group, cheeks burning, and dips what must be seven or eight times before I am able to convince her that I would rather have her guidance than her genuflections.

And so it is that I come to the Kallas of Saaremaa's study in the wake of a laundry girl. I ignore however many more times she dips before scurrying away, pressing my palm firmly against the aged woodgrain and entering the space without announcement.

Heads rise all around a wide table, several chairs in various states of occupation, and a whole host of men filling the space. At the head of the table I see Kurat.

But it is not him. The Heir of the House stands to my right. I had already searched out his heartbeat before I entered. But the Kallas of Saaremaa possesses in his face what I had always looked for in Tuskjas' before I knew he had not fathered his own Heir. Kurat's straight and slender cheekbones, high below keen black-brown eyes. The pointed jaw, hard set against his foes. Only his mouth is different, and something about the brow.

In this breath, I am gifted something I did not know I was looking for – the vision of Kurat as an aged man, honed and weathered with time, but straight-backed and steady and wise. A man of some suffering but, perhaps also, a man of some joy.

Then chairs are scraping and knees are unbending as the men rise in respect, heads bowing, two fingers coming up to foreheads in their formal greetings. I read the wariness in each body, the way eyes catch from across the room, bracing themselves.

I return their gestures with a curt greeting, but no bow. I have not come here for these men, but for the men and women even now shifting in their posts on the beach, and their wives and husbands and children holed up in every defensible nook and cranny in Saaremaa. But to save them, I will have to go through this chamber.

"Kallas Õnnev," I say, acknowledging Kurat's grandfather. "I require a briefing on the current state of your defenses and your expectations of where the Norsemen might next strike, as well as any explanation you have to offer as to why they have chosen to do more than raid your land and leave it."

Even Kurat's brows rise, but what did he expect? He and I have shared countless hours listening to the reports of Tuskjas' informants. Did he think I would be less informed than he? Norsemen do not invade, nor do they attack a place more than once in a single campaign. They seek no land or influence, only plunder. The fact that they have chosen to engage in repeated attacks on Saaremaa is an indication that they desire something more than what little resources the coastal villages have to offer.

For a moment no one speaks, though a few eyes flicker to Kurat, as if to see if he will intervene. He does not, turning instead to his grandfather, awaiting the man's answer to my questions. Then Kallas Õnnev gathers himself to his height, inclining his grey head in a sign of respect.

"You show your intelligence, my Chieftainess," he says in a raspy voice. It sounds overtaxed, as if he has been bellowing instructions for hours. "Yet, I pray you will allow us our caution in addressing your requests, considering the circumstances."

"And what circumstances are those?" I inquire coldly. Õnnev raises his pointed chin.

"Those of your husband's refusal to assist us," he says, not withholding the anger from his eyes. "And though I know the Heir has undertaken considerable risk to bring you here, and your assistance with the wounded last night has not gone unconsidered by this council, I am still wary of your help, my Chieftainess. As are my advisors."

I do not look at Kurat nor does he look at me, and yet, I know what he is thinking. I picture him, turning from Tuskjas' denial of aid, enraged only to have the beast warn him that any appearance of disloyalty would be punished. And so Kurat checks himself at the study door, sucking in a reluctant breath, his mind already whirling with possibilities.

I see his sharp eyes as he does the mental calculations, closing the study door behind him. He is determining if he has revealed enough of his true self to earn my trust. He is assessing what he knows of me and if I will hate violence against people I do not know more than I will hate putting Maarja in danger. He knows any agreement I might give him will have to include provisions for her. He knows, as I did the moment he made his plea, that at the end of this we will be exposed. He is assessing whether putting me into play in Saaremaa is worth risking his long-term objectives for the throne.

And he is deciding, with the closed door at his back, that his mother's people cannot be abandoned in his pursuit of the throne.

And that is why I had walked into his embrace.

Here, in the council room of Saaremaa, Kurat does not speak in my defense. He watches. And waits.

I see the opportunity for what it is.

These men do not know I am more slave than Chieftainess. And so I can be something more.

"In this matter the Chieftain assesses poorly," I say, chin high, eyelids low, letting my gaze fall heavy on the Kallas before me. "I am Chieftainess. Moreover, I am an Estian Waster. And as such I am free to act as I see fit in defense of the Snake Daughter's House. You may question my reason for doing so, but I will not allow you to question my loyalty. Take your risks, if you dare. I will either fight alongside you in accordance with your wisdom or I will fight on my own in accordance with my legacy. It is your choice."

There is a moment of silence as the men look around. Then a woman's voice from my left.

"I believe I am owed a considerable sum," she says haughtily. I turn to her, having already deduced the truth from her heartbeat and the tenor of her blood. Kurat's sister is dressed for war, her thick leather chest plate already swiped with dried brown gore. Her pitch black hair is braided through, the pleats tossed haphazardly over her rigidly held shoulders. She is terribly striking, staring down her thin nose at me with her family's black gaze.

"Can we cease this foolishness now?" she asks, turning her disdainful look on the men around her. "Or will the Chieftainess and I be required to destroy the Norsemen on our own?"

Still, Õnnev holds his defensive stance for a moment more, looking about to the others in the room. I grow impatient with their silent communing.

"You sent a request for aid to the throne of this House, and the throne has answered you. Perhaps you expected legions. Fighting men marching across the moors in three days' time, your people dying and your villages burning while they squelch in the mud, arriving exhausted and reluctant to give their lives for a remote land that has long fallen out of favor with their Chieftain. This is what you hoped for, is it not?"

And I stare at them, letting my eyes go from one diverted gaze to another, forcing them to respond. And yet, not one of them opens his mouth to admit that they'd still rather have men under my husband's banner than me. Cowards. Even Õnnev does not speak, though he at least has the courage to meet my eye as he purses his lips in frustration.

"Fools," I murmur, and then I drop two of them to the floor.

The other men jump back as if snakebit, hollering, chairs scraping and tumbling. A few go down on their knees around their fallen comrades, sleeping like babes, trying to shake them back to life. In the tumult, I let my eyes flicker to Kurat's. The bastard has the audacity to raise his brows at my theatrics. I shrug, turning back to Õnnev, who is leaning over the table, looking down into the mass of bodies with a grim expression.

Kurat's sister, among the first to drop down to the slumbering man beside her, suddenly gives a stark chuckle.

"Sleeping!" she snickers, her face breaking from the backs and shoulders of the men crouched around her. "They're only asleep." And then she rears back a greaved hand and slaps the man next to her across his slack face.

Which does absolutely nothing to rouse him, his heartbeat held tightly within my power.

She laughs again.

Õnnev blows out a long breath between his lips, shaking his head. He presses his lips together in an expression I have seen countless times on his grandson, and nods to me, however reluctant.

"Very well then," he acquiesces. "We are not in any position to deny assistance readily given. Rouse them."

I release my hold on their hearts, letting them awaken naturally in the loud chamber. One man sits up rubbing his shoulder where he fell, his fellows moving back to give him space. Then the two victims are brought slowly back to their feet, looking groggy and confused.

"There is still the matter of recompense," Õnnev begins, looking at me warily.

"There will be none," I assure him.

"I highly doubt that," the older man growls back.

"If there is, it will be against us all," I say without having to explain my meaning. His eyes narrow, seeking it out. After a moment, he finds his answer.

"Yes," he murmurs softly, and his eyes flicker to his grandson's hardened face. "I suspect it will."

His words break the tension in the room. The War Council of Saaremaa acknowledges, as a whole, what risk I take in this endeavor, and something about the shared nature of our stakes erases some of the remaining suspicion they have held against me.

"The Norsemen have made their wealth in harassing Revala to the north for years," I say, gesturing for us to move on. "Why have they chosen to move south now?"

"Revala's building defenses, my Chieftainess," another man says from across the table.

"With what resources?" I ask skeptically. Only a month ago, my husband denied the Kallas' request for support in the building of defenses.

"That isn't clear," Õnnev answers. "Yet, they're building them all the same."

"So the Norse seek out new prey," I say, letting my eyes trace the coastline on the roughshod map stretched out on the table before us. "But that does not explain why they have suddenly begun behaving like invaders."

I raise my eyes, looking around, watching them all look away. Another layer of suspicion. Something they did not want exposed.

"What have you that the Norsemen so desire?" I press.

It is Kurat's sister who steps forward and speaks, her black-brown eyes like shards of granite.

"My daughter," she says, voice edged in rage.

"They want my Aemilie."

CHAPTER FOURTEEN
THE NAGGING HEART

What is beauty but skin?
A vessel to hold blood within?
If the face that you bear is a cage,
Spring yourself free with the gift of old age.

"WHY ON earth would they want a single girl?" I ask.

"For her power," Kurat's sister responds bitterly. "We do not know how they heard tell of it, but they sent a missive, demanding her by name."

"Her power is new among us, and considerable," Õnnev supplies.

"I should think so," I say. "What is it?"

"She's an Illusionary," Kurat's sister answers.

"That is no new power," I argue. "We have those traveling through Tarbatu often enough with their troupes."

Kurat's sister shakes her head.

"It's more than that," she says. "She can do more than spin tales. She can make you believe them."

"That is still nothing new," I press, growing frustrated. "Any well-trained –"

"Not because her illusions are thorough," Kurat's sister interrupts, growing frustrated herself. "She can *make* you believe – she can get inside your mind and *make* you wholly convinced that what she is showing you is true."

I cannot help it. My eyes search out Kurat's. Surely they know the man standing here can do the same? His gaze is already on mine, expecting my question before I ask it.

"Not like mine," he says, shaking his head. "Aemilie can spin a tale and influence the beliefs of anyone who hears it. It is not altering memory. It is changing the very pattern of a thought outright, even before it occurs."

"And," his sister adds, cutting her eyes at Kurat, "she also speaks with the Moon Tongue."

"We do not know that, Jaasa," Kurat argues, shaking his head.

"She is of the Shadow Queen's blood," I say, looking between them. I am familiar with the old tales of the Shadow Queen's second gift – that of speaking the future. But the Wasters have long since believed the Moon Tongue to be lost to the dilution of the Shadow Queen's line.

"A direct descendent," Jaasa answers firmly.

"As are you and I, yet we have no –" Kurat cuts in.

"Aemilie's tales have a tendency to come true," Jaasa argues, pressing her palms to the table between them. The rest of the council watches on, heads volleying back and forth as the siblings exchange arguments.

"It is just as likely that they are nothing more than self-fulfilling prophecies," Kurat returns.

"And yet, they come true all the same," Jaasa snaps.

The horror of what Jaasa claims about her daughter strikes me first. The power of this girl in the hands of someone like my husband. Someone like Kurat himself.

"Where is she now?" I ask, interrupting their momentum.

"I would not tell you that if you held a knife to my throat," Kurat's sister answers, her hands forming into fists, knuckles digging into the wood. I assess her cooly, but all I see is another mother.

"I do not need to know her whereabouts," I respond calmly. "But I must insist she be taken from Saaremaa at once under the protection of your most able warriors."

"She is already gone," Õnnev cuts in. I nod.

"When did they first make the demand?" I ask, moving on.

"Six days ago," Õnnev answers. "They came ashore in the night at Rooslep, just south of the Revalan border. We keep a small company of warriors there, as well as a Shade Walker to take messages up and down the coast. I've no idea how they knew that, but it appears to have been their aim. They killed the lot of them, save the Walker, and sent the woman with a message demanding we give up Aemilie to them in a day's time or they'd set fire to the town."

Unlike the Waster Queen, who ordained that her power be passed from mother to a single daughter in each generation, the Shadow Queen had passed her own gifts to several children, and they to theirs. Still, I had not considered that there might be so many Shade Walkers still traipsing about in Saaremaa. Kurat had made it seem like he was the last of the Walkers when he proposed that we marry to restore the throne, but perhaps his assertion had been based on being a direct descendent.

I resolve to berate him for his slippery tongue later.

"And I assume they did set fire to the town?" I prompt. Heads nod.

"Did you offer them tribute in her place?" I ask. The men in the room shuffle. One spits. Another swipes his hand across his brow. Õnnev looks around, his frustration evident.

"We were yet undecided on the wisdom of doing so when they attacked," he grumbles, looking pointedly to a few of the other men, who look away.

"And so you've let them carry on burning the coast for five days while you debate amongst yourselves?" I ask incredulously.

"They pulled back after the first attack," Õnnev answers testily. "We thought they'd burned Rooslep in revenge and given up."

I stare at the man, unable to keep my disbelief from seeping into my expression.

"You denied the Norsemen something they wanted and you thought they'd simply go home?"

Õnnev stiffens at my tone, eyes cut all over the room as men suddenly form up sides, and I know from the tension that tightens across chests that this council is far from unified.

"Pardon my frankness, Chieftainess, but Wasters and Chieftains haven't been in Saaremaa for generations," Õnnev grits out. "We've had relative peace with the Norse for years. Many of our grandparents were half-Norse, which is why they've let us be for as long as they have."

But I am not to be goaded. Arguing the point would only delay a decision, and I did not come for diplomacy's sake.

"Shared blood matters little now," I say firmly. "Your defenses then?"

Õnnev looks unready to yield, but he presses his lips together in an expression he passed down to his grandson, and relents, motioning for a man to his left to step forward.

Over the next hour, as the midday sun sinks in the windows behind us, the men, who I learn are mostly stewards of the various towns up and down the coast, take turns reporting on where, when, and with what number the Norsemen attacked their villages, raiding as they went and repeating the same demand for the girl Aemilie. *Köngulóar Silki,* they called her in their tongue. Spider Silk, for the woven webs of her tales.

The Norse method proves itself to be simple, yet effective in nature. They have moved along the coast, starting in the north and working their way down towards the fortress in Hapsaluu. Two nights ago, a smaller band of four longboats raided Einbi, the village just north of the delta of the Great Bay of Hapsaluu. The council had not thought they would venture into the bay itself, sticking to the coast, which put Saaremaa's capital under threat. They had shored up defenses, abandoning the lower town outside the fortress walls and sending the citizens deep inland into the moors for safety. The old and wounded who could not travel had been packed inside the fortress itself.

The Norsemen had been expecting it. They had gone further south, all the way to Pasku, instead. They'd set the town ablaze as a sign of their impatience.

"And so they have made themselves unpredictable," I conclude. "You do not yet know where they will strike tonight."

The men tighten their jaws against my words, disliking my acknowledgement of their ignorance.

"Survivors from Pasku saw them heading north again," one of the stewards supplies unhelpfully.

"We've Walkers posted up and down the coast," Õnnev says. "The trouble is, once we get word that they've come ashore, we have nothing more than knowledge. We cannot get any sizable defense there in time, even with the Walkers."

"Then you must draw them to us," I answer simply. "Why have you not done so already?"

"We have no hope of facing them in force," another man says. His chin is weak. I look around at the other faces at the table.

"Surely this is not the opinion of the council as a whole?" I ask. They look about one another for a man bold enough to answer, which is, of course, not a man.

"It is not," Kurat's sister bites, eyeing the men. "Yet, the Norsemen have at least 10 longboats. That's nearly 400 warriors, seeing as we've not been able to kill many of them. Their strength is considerable, and we've yet to devise a way to overcome it."

"Powerless men?" I ask incredulously.

"As I said before, we've lived here in peace for generations. The people of Saaremaa, even with Looklema's gift, have not been warriors for over a hundred years. They use what power they have to make lives for themselves and their families. Even the Walkers are little more than messengers," Õnnev says, defending his people.

"You mean to tell me the coast of House Est has been largely undefended all this time?"

Õnnev pulls a long breath in through his sharp nose, growing frustrated.

"We've a small company of trained warriors and guards at Hapsaluu, led by Jaasa, but we've not needed organized warriors since the time of Kotkas. And even then, we sent only what could be spared from the daily toils of surviving. What challenges come from the sea are mostly raids from wandering bands, and while the loss of goods is unfortunate, they have been so few and far between that mounting a defense against them is not worth the blood such a defense would surely require."

"And yet, have they not shown you the same?" I ask, looking around at these men who call themselves a Council of War.

"What is your meaning?" Jaasa asks icily.

"They bypassed Hapsaluu, did they not?" I go on. "They've not the strength or the resources to take it, nor the desire, I suspect, to hold it even if they could. Perhaps by now they know Saaremaa does not have the Chieftain's support, but taking the fortress would surely cause him to act. They are trying to wait out your patience, thrusting spirits into the sky as they go. And you are letting them."

"We had hoped to gain the assistance of the Chieftain," one man grumbles.

"And Revala and Sakala?" I ask. "Have you sent requests for aid there as well?"

"We have. Of course we have," Õnnev spits. "Denied, both of them."

"Under what cause?" I ask, surprised at Suita's father, Kallas Meevat of Sakala.

"Forbidden by the Chieftain," Õnnev answers bitterly.

"He wants Saaremaa broken," Kurat interjects, repeating his assertion from last night.

"And have you not considered using the very weapon they seek against them?" I ask, watching the surprise that ripples about the room.

"What?" Jaasa says. "Aemilie?"

"Can she not compel them against this campaign?" I ask, brows high.

"She's only a child," the girl's mother says breathlessly.

"She isn't a child, Jaasa," Kurat interjects.

"She's 16," Jaasa argues, her face taking on a rigidness that I can tell must be familiar to it.

"And how old were you when you killed your first man?" Kurat fires back. Jaasa rears back, as if slapped, her cheeks brightening.

"I wasn't being asked for by name by rabid Norsemen," she spits. "They wanted to kill me, not rape me or who knows what else."

"We are out of options," I interrupt. "You say you cannot face their numbers in direct battle. I propose we feign to give them what they seek. We offer Aemilie, demanding tribute for her and demanding they leave the Saaremaan coast for as long a time as we can negotiate. I will pose as her maid. Give us over to the Norsemen, let them depart with us. If she is what you say she is, she and I will have no trouble overcoming them once at sea."

My words land on the table between us.

An indrawn breath, and then the room explodes.

In the dramatic scene that next unfolds, Kurat and his sister find themselves united against a common enemy.

"Have you lost your mind?" he barks, striding across the room, pushing away the other men in his wake. I glare at him, brows high, inviting him to do his best.

"Absolutely not!" shrieks Jaasa, coming at me from the other side. They meet me at the same time, so close in appearance they could be twins, opening their mouths in identical expressions of poorly contained rage.

The sun slants low, its narrow beams seeping across the floor. We have no time for their shortsightedness. The Norse will be on us in a matter of hours.

I drop both Kurat and Jaasa to their knees. If Kurat slams down a little harder than his sister, it is only because he should know better by now.

And he does know it. He grunts, then growls my name, setting his jaw and shaking his head, and I know he is thinking he's growing weary of being brought down by my hand.

"You bitch!" Jaasa screeches, trying and failing to bring her feet underneath her. Somewhere beyond the three of us, Õnnev bellows Jaasa's name, no doubt to silence her. I lift the Shroud, hoping it protects me from whatever her power may be. She is Kurat's sister, after all.

"Are you prepared to see reason?" I ask smoothly. Kurat only presses his lips together, breathing sharply through his nose. But Jaasa is not yet done fighting what she cannot hope to overcome. I let her do it, though it wastes some time. I am a mother too. I cannot make her feel as powerless to protect her child as I have been made to feel in protecting mine.

"I will not for a single breath hand her over to you. I don't care who bore you or who beds you!" Jaasa yells, eyes wild

"Jaasa!" Kurat snaps, watching his sister toe the line of my patience. She does not heed him.

"You'd not hand your own daughter over. You'd not risk a hair on her head. They could tear Tarbatu down brick by brick and you'd rip them to pieces before they touched her," Jaasa goes on, face mottled in rage. She is not wrong, of course. I would. But then Jaasa goes too far.

"Go get your own brat! Go offer her up for tribute. Though I doubt they'd want her. I hear she's a simpering chit. I hear she's a pathetic –"

"Jaasa! Cease this now!" Õnnev bellows, moving forward. I can smell the heady spike of fear, the beginning of a nervous sweat on his palms. Surely he must see his own daughter. Surely he must be thinking of how he gave up his own Lekja for the good of the House. How he lost her to it. And now his granddaughter asks for her death before Lekja's successor.

He need not worry. I will not kill her for raging against the threat to her daughter with whatever she can grab in her hands to hurtle. And I am within the Shroud, which has blunted her insults. Still, I cannot let her carry on. Not if I am to do what needs doing.

I wrap her heart around my wrist and tug. It stumbles over its next beat, missing it entirely, then picking up unsteadily once more. She clutches at her chest, wilting to the side, her face paling.

"Liama, no," Kurat says softly, reaching out to catch his sister.

"Forgive her, I beg you," Õnnev pleads, trying to step between us. I hold up a hand, spearing Jaasa with my eyes until she meets them.

"I will remind you," I say quietly, "my daughter has lived nearly every day of her life in the hands of the man whose father hunted my people for sport." As I speak, I pull back the Shroud just enough to let the anger deepen the lines on my face. "And yet, I am here, saving yours. Every moment I delay returning to Maarja's side is a moment she is left open to threat, and you waste my time telling me that I know nothing of what you are experiencing? And you think that I will abide your judgement without shriveling your tongue in your very mouth? You forget to whom you speak."

And then I lock her jaw, silencing her, to further my point.

She writhes against my power, rearing back and turning her jaw side to side as if she could break free from it. I look up to the others.

"This is no longer under debate. I assume you have sent the girl with a Shade Walker?" I ask, brows high. No one answers, and it is answer enough.

"Very well, bring her to me." I command cooly. "Bring me this child you are all willing to let others die for, and I will assess if she is worth my own life, and my daughter's. And if I judge that she is as you say, you will send an envoy to the Norsemen within the hour."

For a breath, no one moves.

"I expect it to be done," I command, letting my gaze fall heavily on Õnnev.

He nods, fear shaping his lined eyes.

We are agreed.

I lay my eyes on her. Always, my eye is upon her, now flitting through the Hall on tiptoes, now giggling into the cold air, her breath going before her. Now standing still, her back turned to me, watching the horses come into

the stables. Now simmering in a near rage, refusing to eat the food growing cold before her.

My eye is always upon her in this world. And yet, it is not my only way of seeing. I see her in a second place, a place only a mother's eyes can go. I see her stumbling as she flies across the worn stones of the Hall. I see her slipping into the cold air and never returning, lost and screaming for me in the winter night. I see her trampled beneath those horses' hooves, hear the crumpling of her delicate bones as the blood seeps into the dark places inside of her. I see her tangled in the bed clothes, her face captured in the pillow. I see myself rolling over her lifeless form, the soundless horror blooming in my chest.

The scream that never comes.

A mother sees her child's death in a thousand ways and at a thousand times. It is the nagging echo after the cry of delight, happiness' shadow trailing just behind. For every wonderful moment, every breath of gladness, there is the threat of sorrow. The two cannot be separated. If there is joy, so too will there be despair.

They say it will take an hour's time to collect the girl.

In the interim, I see to the wounded.

I do not lift the Shroud. I need an acute awareness of my body's fatigue in order to ensure I am prepared for what next comes. And so I move slower, and I leave more to breathe their spirits into the sky.

I make my way through the crowded corridors surrounding the Hall. After a time, I notice I have gained a little following. Several women are moving behind me, binding and sewing and closing vacant eyes. I give a command and it is followed.

And yet, they are not like the laundry women from this morning, hooting and genuflecting in my presence. These are nursing women, steel-spined and level-gazed. They do not thank me, and I do not thank them. We simply move as one through the bodies, doing the work that needs doing.

Twilight has come when Kurat finds me. We did not speak after the council departed. We do not speak now. He simply makes his way towards me, his heartbeat going before. I finish my work on a woman who has lost most of the fingers on her right hand. Even washed in pain as I know she must be, she lifts the bleeding stump to her forehead in respect, leaving a trickle of blood down her face. I reach down to wipe it away, nodding my respects in turn.

I straighten and meet his eyes. I suppose I am forgiven my invasion of his body in the council room, because he lets me see his fatigue, and I let him see mine.

Then he nods his head back towards the Kallas' study and I follow him.

Aemilie is here.

She is tiny. It is only that Jaasa claimed she is 16 that I do not assume she is still a much younger child. And then I begin to sense the womanliness of her body, fertile and ripe. Jaasa's fierce protectiveness comes into clearer focus now that I have seen how little the girl takes after her warrior mother.

Aemilie stands, her mother and her great grandfather to her back, at the far end of the study. If they have told her of what transpired before, or of what I have proposed, she does not show it on her small, pale face. I have lifted the Shroud, wary of her power; otherwise I might wonder if she was not painting the bravery there in my mind.

She is a woman. She desires to be seen as a woman, so I treat her as such.

"Have they told you what I will require of you?" I ask cooly. I cannot be kind. The Norsemen will not be. And I must know what they will see on her face when unkindness comes her way.

She sets her jaw, pointed like her mother's, and nods.

"Yes, my Chieftainess," she murmurs in a girl's singsong voice. I suspect it captures many an ear when she uses it with her power.

"And you will submit to this?" I ask. The family chin comes up.

"Yes, my Chieftainess," she says, firmer this time.

"Then I have need to see your power at work," I command. "I would know its ability, before putting it to use."

"What would you have me do, my Chieftainess?" Aemilie asks, unable to hide the wary edge to her voice. I suspect she is sensitive to her power in the hands of others. That is wise of her. She will need to be sensitive to it, and more.

"Leave us," I demand to Jaasa and Õnnev. Jaasa hardens, daring me with her gaze, but her grandfather grabs her arm, nearly dragging her out. Then the door is shut behind them both, leaving Aemilie alone facing Kurat and me.

I move, pulling a chair away from the table and lowering myself to it.

"You know of your uncle's other power? Not Shade Walking," I ask. Aemilie's warm brown eyes flicker to Kurat. I feel the muscles of his neck clench as he nods to her. She looks back to me.

"Yes, my Chieftainess," she says, uncertain with my line of questioning.

"Ten years ago, he used his power to compel me to leave the Sacred Forest of Looklema," I say, watching the girl's eyes widen.

"What's your game, Liama?" Kurat growls behind me. I ignore him.

"He then took me to Tarbatu, where I was further forced to marry the Chieftain and submit myself to use as his weapon," I go on. "In the course of this, your uncle has rewritten a considerable number of my memories. I want you to undo what he has done."

"Liama, no," Kurat argues, now coming around to face me.

"You would deny me this, now?" I ask him, brows high. He hardens his jaw.

Perhaps I have become familiar enough with him now to do as my grandmother once did and read his thoughts. Or perhaps I myself have a little of the Moon Tongue, because when he parts his lips to speak, I intone right along with him.

"You do not know what you ask," we say together. After shock, his face mottles in anger.

"I overheard a woman in the Hall," I say, speaking only to him. "She said the Shade Walker who took the request for aid to Revala had returned with some kind of sweet from its capital, still steaming, for his wife who was born there. She was damning the man for stopping for a pastry, considering the circumstances."

His fine features break their mold, shaping themselves into an expression I cannot name on him. Perhaps it is guilt. It should be. His lips part on justifications that do not come. His keen eyes plead for a mercy I am not yet ready to give.

"How far away is the capital of Revala, Aemilie?" I ask her without looking away from Kurat.

"Tallinn?" she answers, surprised. "I don't know, my lady."

"More than half a day's ride?" I prompt, watching Kurat's guarded face.

"At least, my lady," Aemilie answers uncertainly. "Two days, I think. I don't know. I've never been there."

"Will you confess it to me now, Heir?" I murmur to him. His lips press together, sealing the truth inside them. I shake my head.

"You know that I know the truth now, and yet, you still will not give it willingly. Your mother was no more powerful than you are – than any other Walker in this land. It isn't a declining power that restrains you. There's nothing wrong with Looklema's House. You cannot Walk more than a day's ride because you drag too much untruth in your wake."

He cannot stand the saying of it. He closes his eyes over the truth, reaching out to brace himself on the table beside him, head hanging low.

"How much of it is mine, Kurat?" I whisper.

He releases a pained breath but does not answer.

"My arms remember the shape of your body. How much of it is mine?"

Now his hip thumps against the table. His hand comes up to cover his face.

"Too much," I hear him whisper.

I raise my eyes to Aemilie, staring open-mouthed at the scene before her.

"Undo it," I command her. Her eyes flicker to mine, scared, then return to her uncle's back.

"I –" she stammers. "I do not know if I can. I haven't – that is –"

"It should be simple enough," I say. "You needn't address each memory individually. Simply convince my mind to release its secrets. Make it believe that it is not susceptible to his power."

"But I've no idea how to do such a thing!" she blurts, her alarm growing.

"Do compose yourself," I command. "I won't have you slicing my mind in two from sheer panic."

"Can I not instead tell you some tale? Perhaps the ballad of Looklema and her Grey-Eyed Prince?"

I shake my head slowly.

"I have no need of tales," I deny her. "And you could not compel me to believe them any more than I already do. Tales will not be enough to save us from your pursuers. This is my requirement. It will not alter."

"I can't – I couldn't possibly –"

"You have no choice, in truth," I say coldly. "You can either make your most valiant attempt, prove yourself, and come with me to save your land and everyone in it, or you can refuse, be whisked away to wherever your mother deems is safe, and know that your people died in your defense, myself and your uncle included. Or do you expect all the rest of us to show the same level of cowardice as yourself?"

"You ask too much of her, Liama," Kurat intervenes from behind his hand. "She tells stories," he adds, looking up at me desolately.

"And yet, I demand more, just as what she will be required to do will demand more," I argue unflinchingly. "More than she considers herself capable. More than anyone has ever believed she can accomplish. Once we have been taken aboard, you will be required to convince more than 40 warriors that you do not have this power they seek, all while using it against them so subtly that not a single man suspects your intervention. Do you think you can tell them some tale to accomplish it? No, you must rewrite what they already know. You must erase yourself from their memory even as you stand before them filling their ears with your voice."

Now the girl shows what has always been there, her true fear. She may have chiseled a brave face before, with her mother and her great grandfather looking on, but here now she shows herself as she truly is.

"The night approaches," I say sharply. "Will you or will you not make an attempt to do as I say?"

Kurat sighs, turning away, knowing better than to argue but showing his opinion of my methods. Aemilie is frantic, looking between us, twisting her slim fingers painfully as she considers her options. I bore my gaze into her, giving her no reprieve. Her pulse spikes suddenly, her body flooding with sharpened fear, the kind that releases in sudden bursts of bravery.

"I will do it," she says in a rush, hurrying to get the words into the air before her courage falters. I let her words land between us for a breath, echoing in the silence.

"You will do no such thing," I answer, rising. They stare at me, the two of them, with wide eyes, for a breath or more. Kurat recovers himself first.

"Damn you," he breathes, shoving off the table and stalking away. The door to the study opens behind me, then slams shut.

"What?" Aemilie stammers. "What – what has happened?"

"Your uncle is shrewd. If he assesses your power to be capable of what I ask, then I believe him," I answer. "Your mother as well, though we certainly have our differences. She would already have whisked you away, regardless of the consequences, if she'd not believed you capable."

"And so, what then was this?" she asks, her cheeks beginning to pinken.

"I needed to ascertain if you would bend to my will under duress," I answer simply, turning to leave the room.

"You mean you had no intention of letting me – of making me –"

"Flay open my mind?" I finish for her, turning to spear her with my gaze. "Certainly not."

"And Kurat?" she asks boldly. "Has he really done as you said?"

I turn away from her, striding to the door. I intend to give no answer, but she asks once more, and I feel a nagging in my bones, a warning on my tongue.

"The most dangerous of men is he who will do for love what should only be done for the vilest hatred," I answer over my shoulder. "Kurat is one such man. And I am one such woman. You would do well to remember that."

The word is given. The missive is carefully worded by Õnnev's War Council after an aggravatingly tedious argument over every phrase.

Several copies are made, then sent by Shade Walker up and down the coast. Outside the fortress, down on the shoreline, a white flag is raised, lit from underneath by a broad, flat fire, illuminating the night.

Less than an hour later, a single longboat splits the sand before the fire, 40 Norsemen within it. A smaller group clambers from their ship, sloshing up to the shore with their hands steady on weapons, ready at the slightest threat to fight their way back to the safety of the boat. They do much to show that they are not afraid, and yet, from where I watch high above on the fortress' outermost wall, I can taste the metallic tang of their wariness. I sense the soft shushing of their eyelids, shifting back and forth, searching for treachery.

Õnnev strides out of the gates and onto the beach, his best warriors assuming formation behind and alongside. Their shadows warp across the sand as they approach the fire, keeping it between themselves and the Norse.

I lose the words exchanged to the lapping of the waves, but within minutes Õnnev turns, pointing up to where Aemilie and I stand on the wall, heavily cloaked despite the summer's heat. Aemilie takes her great grandfather's signal, throwing back her hood and revealing her face in the flickering firelight.

The Norse leader, an immensely tall man, thick of chest and meaty, hoots his approval, calling out to her by the name they have given her. Spider Silk.

She does not alter her countenance, staring down at them with cold, hard features. And she does not shrink away from the leader's assessing gaze, his low whistle at her beauty. He turns to his fellows and mutters something for which no one needs translation, sending a ripple of laughter through the group. I am reminded of Jaasa's words – rape, or worse. And I am reminded of what we risk if either of us falters.

I'll shrivel the ballsacks of any man who lays hand on us before I let such a thing occur.

Suddenly there is umbrage. We had expected this. Õnnev has denied the Norsemen their prize this night. The other councilors had offered up flimsy excuses – Aemilie desires to make offerings to Looklema before giving herself over to them. Aemilie is ill with her menses and cannot go. Jaasa and I had both rolled our eyes at this paltry comprehension of menstruation, exacerbated and yet unsurprised.

In the end I had demanded simplicity. Aemilie will not go this night. If you want her, come back tomorrow and get her. As I suspected, the Norsemen can do little about it. They haven't the fighting force to demand her, tucked up behind the fortress walls. The leader curses and bellows, but finally agrees.

A final bargain remains to be struck. My own. Once more, Õnnev points back at us, explaining that Aemilie desires to take along her old nursemaid for companionship. I pull my own hood back with shriveled hands, showing my ancient, aged face, withered and harmless. The Norseman grunts his approval. I will be no threat.

Aemilie and I do not remain on the wall to witness the end of the discussion. Jaasa meets us at the bottom of the stairs, tucking her daughter under her arm and disappearing into the shadows of the wide yard.

I release the hold I have over my face and hands, feeling the youth return, joints bending freely and skin pulling back into place. I seek out my own chambers, pausing long enough in the Hall to see to a fever that has suddenly spiked. A nursing woman asks me to remain to treat a few more, but I deny her as gently as my mood allows. I tell her if I do not see to my own needs, she and her sisters will have even more bodies to care for, including my own.

I make my way unaided and uninterrupted to my rooms. I hold back my awareness until the last breath before my hand pushes against the wooden door, forcing self-control, but his heartbeat is not behind it, and I will not search him out.

As a younger woman, perhaps I would have tossed and turned, restless and unsatisfied. But I feel as aged as the face I showed to the Norsemen. And so when I set my body to rest, it does so without delay.

It occurs as it always occurs.

There is my sense of a man in the Wood. There is the soft yet insistent tug of Maarja's petal lips on my breast. There is the sound of my name, the cracking of bones. I turn, breast bared, to shove the man's spirit into the sky.

But when I cast my eyes upon him, he is not bent over, his wrist cradled to his chest, but standing tall, his fists clenched. I stop, stricken with shock at the sight of my mother and my grandmother at his back. I had not felt their bodies approach. They had hidden themselves from my power.

"Stop, Liama," my mother says, her voice flat and empty. She has drawn the Shroud.

"We would have you hear what he has to offer," my grandmother adds with more feeling. Years of experience have lent her the ability to go into the place without losing the warmth that makes her who she is.

"Who is he, that you would stand with him against me?" I ask, and in this sleeping body of 30 years, the voice of the girl in the memory sounds terribly, terribly young. Yet, I remember the sense of instant betrayal, a severing of something sacred between myself and the women who raised me.

"Hear his offer," my grandmother presses. "And then make what judgements you will."

When the man between them raises his eyes to mine, he is no youth. Kurat looks out at me from my memory of his face as it was in the Kallas study hours ago, his eyes dark and keen and angry.

"Damn you," he says, just as he cursed me before.

I rally my power, forcing my mother and my grandmother out of the memory, and sucking the liquid from the delicate drums of his ears. They rupture; yet, as the blood trickles down his jaw, making for his neck, he goes on repeating himself, his voice warped where he can no longer hear it echoing back on itself.

"Damn you, dahm you, dayou, you, you, you, you, you."

I push out from sleep in horror, the scream captured in my throat by instinct alone. I leap from the little servant's cot, wrapping my skirts hastily around my waist, and stalk into the stillness of the night, hands still shaking.

I can no longer leave this undone.

CHAPTER FIFTEEN
THE CALLOUSED HAND

Will you? Won't you? Can't you, please?
Desperate the plea. Weak the knees.
Do not be swayed by pity or hurting.
Honesty, daughter, is sacred to Working.

THE BONE-WEARY Saaremaans are making good use of the night's reprieve from terror. I step around countless sleeping bodies in the passageways, shutting out the demands of those inside the Hall. I could draw the Shroud, letting my awareness seep further out and, likely as not, find him all the quicker. But I am not willing to release my ire long enough to do so. When I face him, I want him to see all that I hold inside my body written across my face. There will be no cold mask of the Chieftainess. He will receive the same as he got in the Wood, when I was only an indrawn breath away from ending him.

And so it is that I do not sense him coming until he steps from the shadow before me.

I reel, forcing myself not to leap back and shriek.

He doesn't speak, his face cast in darkness. But I feel his expectation for me to be the first to act. He has come. He will do nothing more.

"Would you like me to redress you here in the corridor?" I hiss.

"That would require you to undress me first, would it not?" he responds icily. His uncharacteristic lewdness catches me askance.

"Are you drunk?" I ask, though certainly I would have sensed it by more than his choice of words.

"Certainly not," he bites back.

"Ah, I see," I press. "Only miserable then, and determined to stain the very air with it."

"Is this what you have come prowling through the night to say?" he mutters.

"Is this how you'd hoped to begin your defense?" I bite right back.

I hear his indrawn breath. His long, slow exhale.

"What defense is there to make?" he says at last.

"The one I am due," I answer. "The one where you spare me your self-pity and tell me, finally and in full, what you have taken from me."

He is a silent shape in the darkness for a moment, and then he speaks.

"No good will come of it," he murmurs. "It changes nothing."

"And yet, I demand it all the same," I answer, unyielding.

He sighs.

"I'll not bare my soul in the corridor," he grumbles. I do not answer his complaint, only turn and guide us back to my chambers, stopping to instruct him to step this way and that over the sleepers.

And then the door is shut behind us, leaving the dim, flickering light behind. For a moment I do not step to where I know the candle stands in its thick wooden holder beside the cot. For a moment we simply stand, inches apart, breathing the same darkness.

And then I do step, striking the flint, and the warm yellow light flickers madly in the space, warping our sense of each other before it steadies into something present. Something faint, but true.

He stands rigid just inside the door.

I go looking once more for my anger, but it has gone. In its place is a kind of silent keening, a low, thrumming desperation to end all this misery between us. And that is more unbearable than rage.

And so I step to him slowly, reaching out and wrapping my hand around his clenched fist. I draw it between us, and he lets me open each long, slender finger, exposing his palm.

"You took these from my memory," I murmur, tracing my fingertip softly over the hardened calluses there. On the night when we first Walked, when I took him to Erga's husband, I remember his hands being smooth and soft.

He tries to twist his hand from mine, but I clench my fingers in his to the point of pain, trapping him in my touch.

"Why?" I demand.

He does not meet my eye but ceases his attempts to pull away.

"Why did it matter so much that you would want me to forget?" I ask again, firmer this time.

He closes his eyes, pressing his lips together.

"What I have here is more precious to me than the throne itself," he murmurs tightly. "Saaremaa has always been my refuge. It is one and the same with what I remember of my mother. It is the wholeness of me, in a place. I cannot have that wholeness in Tarbatu. There must always be subterfuge, and refraction, and multiplicity. I must be a man whose power does not require the lifting of a finger. I must be a man singular, without allies, a man who does not need others to gain his desires. If I am not that man, if instead I am a man who must knot a rope, or swing an axe, or string a bow, then I am no different than any man. And any man cannot sit the throne."

"And can you?" I ask softly. "Can you knot a rope, swing an axe, and string a bow?"

He nods grimly.

"All my youth, I was the Kallas' grandson here, nothing more," he murmurs, looking at the rough bumps on his palms. "Jaasa is Heir. I am only an accessory. I have no need of that other power, my father's power, to bend the world to my will. But I have need of my hands. I have mucked stables and built boats and dug graves."

His final comment settles between us. I do not need to know whose graves he has dug.

"There was a time when my hands looked like yours," I whisper.

"I know," he whispers back.

"Tell me, then," I nudge. "Tell me how you know."

He shakes his head, pulling his hand from mine and turning away.

"Why?" he asks. "Why do you insist on these memories? They have nothing in them but sorrow."

"Why do you insist upon hiding yourself within them?" I return. "What do you not wish for me to see?"

"The folly!" he insists, turning his hard eyes on me. "The ridiculousness. The ignorance and stupidity and pride."

"And yet, you are still too proud!" I argue, jamming my finger into the center of his chest.

"I am not proud, Liama! I am terrified. Can't you see?" he pleads. "All that power, and yet, you still cannot see that what lies underneath this skin is not blood and bone, but fear! I am all fear, within and without. I am nothing but waking nightmares, with you at the center of each and every one."

"You think I will haunt you? You think I will stalk you through this life for revenge? I have told you I will seek no recompense for what has been done, so long as you –"

"You still do not see!" he heaves, fisted hands in the air between us as if he might crack my skull between them and drive his meaning in.

"I cannot see what you will not allow me to see!" I fight back, finding my anger ready once more.

"I cannot undo it, Liama!" he shrieks.

"Then give me what I need to undo it myself!" I shriek back. "*Tell me* what you have taken from me. *Tell me* what I cannot remember, or continue on as a coward."

"You cannot fling me around as you did, Aemilie," he seethes.

"I can fling you around however I like if that is what is required to drag the truth from you!"

"Then drag it from me, if you must!" he yells, all pretense of composure lost.

We stand there heaving, glaring into each other's eyes with his challenge exploding in the space between us. For a long, long time there are no more words. Then he shifts away, turning his shoulder to me, his hand coming to his brow to hide himself beneath it.

"I desire it freely given," I say at last, my voice so soft I know it stings.

"You ask too much of everyone," he murmurs from behind his hand.

"If I ask too much of everyone, it is because too much has been asked of me," I counter.

He swipes the hand over his face, shaking his head. I use his silence to press my point.

"You are in my debt."

"Have you not just said you will not seek recompense?"

"You are in my debt, not for what you have done to me, but for what I once was to you," I clarify, opening the door to the truth for him. But he cannot bear it. He turns fully away, giving me his back.

"I recant my pledge to you," I go on firmly. He stiffens, but does not turn. "I will not act to put you on Looklema's throne, even at my side, if your cowardice runs so deep as this. If you lack the justice required to pay your debts. You are not worthy of it."

I speak without heat, impartial and distant. I do not say these things in anger. I do not say them to wound, though they do. This is my judgement given. My right, as Chieftainess.

I wait and wait and wait.

He does not turn. He does not speak. He chooses fear. I have had enough.

"Leave me," I command. "For today I go into battle on your behalf."

And the coward does.

The dam has broken. The memories come on thick now, one after the other, their edges frayed and tangled. The dreams that carry them trip over one another until I cannot be sure where one ends and another begins.

"I am wholly given over to recklessness in your name," he confesses in *a growl, and as his mouth crashes into mine, we Walk.*

"Will you take this from me?" I ask, panting.

"There will come a night," he promises, *"years from now, when you wake from the dream of this memory, and when you turn, it will be me beside you, and we will make it all over again."*

"Will you take this from me? Do not take this from me."

"Look at me, Liama. I already have."

It is not sleep. It is remembering, and longing, and mourning, and, above all, resenting.

And when I give it up, rising in the dark stillness of my little room, I am weary and wrung out and bitter.

A good day to meet an enemy.

My attitude is surely written on my face, for the bodies part before me in the corridors like starlings taking flight. I refuse the heavy-laden trencher offered to me and insist on the same rations as all others, taking the hunk of rye and hard cheese with me to the Kallas' study. A few members of the council are already there, looking measurably more resilient than they did the day before. Several even offer my voluntary nods of solidarity.

Õnnev gestures for me to take his chair at the head of the table. I refuse it, staying on my feet. Unlike the others, he looks as weary as I.

"You have your wits about you?" I murmur as I draw close.

"Yes, my Chieftainess," he rasps. "I have never slept well before battle, but I have never failed for the lack of it."

"I thought there were no warriors left in Saaremaa."

He huffs a dark laugh.

"Battle does not always include swords, my Chieftainess."

"What *have you* failed for lack of?" I ask. He looks at me, narrowing his eyes.

"Help," he answers quietly. I nod.

"Then you will not fail this day," I answer, mustering conviction into my voice.

"And if help is not enough?" he asks. It is a moment of softness, of something like trust. He is seeking reassurance.

"It will be," I answer. *I* will be. "But if it is not, you may take some joy in knowing that Tuskjas' punishment for what we have done cannot reach us in the sky."

Õnnev smiles grimly, huffing another dark laugh.

"I do take some joy in that. And in meeting my Lekja there, Looklema keep her."

"You would leave your grandchildren for her company?" I ask, curious to know his response, having passed his best years in this world long ago.

"It is not just her," he sighs, shifting to lower himself slowly into the chair I have denied. "My other daughter waits for me there, and my wife. My father. My mother. My children's children bring me some joy, but they have not made me what I am. I carry a longing always to be with the ones that have."

His words smooth something out in me. Something had hitherto been jagged and sharp. I sigh, letting the healing balm sit for a moment on the wound.

"Why is Jaasa not at court?" I ask several moments later. Õnnev's fine brow lowers.

"Why would she be?"

"She too is Lekja's daughter. I suppose she is second-born, but she could have a place there, if she desired it," I explain.

"Jaasa is not Lekja's daughter," he rumbles.

"She is not?" I ask in surprise. "She is so like Kurat, their bodies are built from the same material. I had assumed they were brother and sister."

Õnnev shakes his greying head.

"If they are built from the same stuff, it is because their mothers were as well. They were twins," he explains. "As alike as two can be, even in temperament. My wife used to say it was as if one soul was split into two bodies."

"And yet, Lekja went to Tarbatu," I say. Õnnev nods sadly.

"And Kelja stayed."

"I would ask you what I have never been able to discern myself," I say softly. Õnnev looks away across the room. More stewards are shuffling in. The War Council will soon begin.

"You want to know how she died," he murmurs. I nod. He closes his eyes, breathing in deeply through his nose.

"If one day you are able to discover the truth, I would ask you to come here and share it," he answers mournfully.

"You mean you do not know?" I ask. He shakes his head.

"Kelja went missing. By the time word reached us that Lekja had disappeared on the same day, in the same hour, we had given her up for dead," he answers. The door opens once more to Kurat's hand.

"You never found her? Either of them?"

Õnnev purses his lips.

"Kelja washed up on shore weeks later. Her pockets were full of rocks," he murmurs, eyes cast down to his empty hands. "Lekja," he shakes his head.

And then he breathes in deeply, squares his shoulders.

Õnnev makes to rise. I press a hand to his shoulder, holding him in place.

"My grandmother once told me that the Twin Queens did not give us their names because their reign had not yet ended in this world," I say. I need not go on. The old man's keen gaze widens, and I see myself in his eyes, a mouthpiece of Looklema, come to tell him that his daughter may yet play a part in all that is to come.

We are used to the awe, Wasters. We guard our words carefully. We do not give false hope.

But my grandmother and my mother are gone, as are their mothers and their grandmothers before them. It is I who decide now what we do with this legacy, from this day forward.

"Do not yet breathe your spirit into the sky," I murmur. "She might yet reveal herself in this world, if you have care to look for her."

After a moment, Õnnev nods. When he rises, I strengthen his aching knees.

War Council is perhaps not the correct term for what follows. It is rather a delegation of duties by my hand, aided in part by Õnnev's input and direction to his men. Kurat speaks only to insist upon leading the small array of men who will see Aemilie and I to the designated meeting place six miles across the Bay of Hapsaluu on its northern point. Should Õnnev's fear prove insight, and help not be enough, I do not want a fortress full of the sick and wounded, not to mention Saaremaa's seat of power, within the Norsemen's grasp. Better a barren strip of sand whose nearby villages have already been plundered.

I deny Kurat the position, and I confess that there is some satisfaction in doing so. In truth, my rejection is strategic rather than personal. It is enough to put the Chieftainess of the House at risk. I will not make the Heir vulnerable as well. Tuskjas may want him replaced. He'd likely as not see Kurat's death as a boon. For that reason alone, I will not risk giving him the satisfaction.

Kurat does not mount a defense of his position, but neither does he accept my denial or meet my eye during the exchange. We have returned from whence we came, pillars standing tall and separate with a kingdom between us.

We will meet the Norsemen an hour after twilight. Our departure from Hapsaluu is set for two hours hence. The War Council breaks up, and I go to seek out Aemilie.

Õnnev had been on the verge of calling her to the study to participate in the council, and Jaasa as well. I had insisted he not. The more ignorant Aemilie is to the inner workings of our designs, the more convincing she will be.

It is not my only reason for excluding her. I require that she hear her directives only from me. She must believe me to be sole authority and be prepared to follow my commands without question. I cannot have her bickering in the moment, drawing off something some idiot steward recommended simply to have his voice heard in a room of important men.

The door of their shared chambers opens to Jaasa's wretched face. She peels back her misery when she sees me, slamming all her anger and resentment over her features.

"She's resting," Jaasa says, opening the door no further.

"She is not," I refute. "She is just there behind the door."

Jaasa scowls but steps back reluctantly. I pass into their rooms, intentionally ignoring the comfortable way the space seems to shift around them. The familiar way they shift around each other. Mother and daughter, living in comfort and safety, having never known anything other than themselves.

"We leave in two hours' time," I report. "I have come to brief you on what will be required and when."

"The Kallas could have easily done so," Jaasa grumbles.

"And yet, it is I, not the Kallas, who offer myself to the mercy of your daughter's power," I respond coolly. "And so it is I who have come to ensure she understands what she is to do."

Jaasa works her jaw, assessing her options. But Aemelie places a small hand on her mother's arm.

"Let her be, Mama," she demands softly. "I have already agreed to this campaign. I would know how best to play my part."

Jaasa glares at me for a moment longer, then steps away deeper into the room, giving me her back. Aemilie offers the formal greeting with a demure bow. I return it brusquely. This girl has not yet earned it, but I need her to believe she can. I need her to believe I think more highly of her than I do.

SNAKE WIFE

She gestures to the room's finest chair, offering me refreshment. I refuse both, choosing to remain standing. Aemilie takes another chair close by, clasping her hands together in her lap and looking up obediently for my directive. It is a good start, even if I suspect it is not entirely authentic.

"There are those who would have me impress upon you the stakes of our endeavor," I begin, low but firm. "But I have insisted that you are no fool. You know what we risk, do you not?"

The girl nods.

"Then think no further on it. It is as my mother once told me – fear is rot to power. A warrior would not go into battle with his spear unsharpened, nor its shaft broken. You must treat your power the same. Do not go into battle with it weakened."

"So heard," she says, nodding with a new conviction.

"If there are those who would seek to remind you all that we have to lose before we board that boat in two hours' time, do not allow them an audience. You and your mother know who they are. I charge you both with preserving your composure."

"So heard," Aemilie says again, looking to her mother. Jaasa's eyes are fierce and dark on her daughter. She nods to her, an oath.

"When next you see me, I will be in the form of your elderly nurse," I continue. "You must treat me as such, giving me no undue deference. Consider me to be an item for your comfort, nothing more. I will take no offense to whatever you do while in this role, so long as it is for our mutual advantage. The Norsemen must believe you are in authority over me. I expect you to make it convincing."

Aemilie pulls a long breath in through her nose, sitting a little straighter in her chair.

"The Kallas will accompany us with a company of 40 men –"

"What about Kurat?" Jaasa interrupts. "You denied him a place but I would advocate –"

I shake my head.

"I cannot risk myself and the Heir," I explain, brokering no room for argument. "Should he fall, the House will be left without its future, and should I fall as well, then there can be no means of ensuring a new one."

My words are not entirely true, and Jaasa knows it. There is nothing to stop Tuskjas from taking for himself a new Chieftainess and getting a babe on her. But neither do I need to explain that such a child would likely not reach adolescence before his father's old age requires him to take the throne. A child Chieftain does not bode well for stability.

"Among our company will be no fewer than three Shade Walkers. They are Aabu, Höamee, and Härm. You are familiar with them?"

Both women nod.

"And you are familiar with what is required of them in order to use their power effectively?"

Both women nod again.

"Then you will understand that they are to be utilized only at the very end of our designs, when all subterfuge has been revealed and the truth of our intentions is known by the Norsemen. It will be difficult enough for them to navigate the water in the dark. If you act against my orders, you risk requiring their intervention too soon, which may hinder their abilities. We cannot put them into a position where they are forced to lie."

Aemilie's fingers are twisted into knots in her lap, but she sets her jaw and nods.

"There must be no end to your courage," I warn her. "If you call for rescue before the moment is right, you damn us, myself included. And if you damn me, the consequences of your actions will shake the foundation of this House. Do you understand?"

"Are we to deny you audience then?" Jaasa bites. "Is this not the very thing you warned her not to listen to?"

I do not acknowledge the mother, keeping my eyes on the daughter. Aemilie cuts her eyes at her mother.

"I would know, Mama," she says in response. "I will not dwell on it but I would know. In truth I had not considered it – that what we do here today could – might –" she loses her confidence, stammering at the thought of holding the future of the House in her hands. She will have to become accustomed to it. After a moment she gathers herself, turning her soft gaze on me and nodding once more. Then she croaks an unsteady, "So heard" when I do not go on.

"The Norsemen have agreed to come ashore with a single longboat of 40 warriors. They will unload the tribute in the Kallas' sight and, when it has been assessed for its value, you and I will be handed over to them. We do not know what they know of your power, nor do we know what they have heard about Estian power in general. It is very likely you will be gagged and I will be bound. You must prepare yourself for this."

Jaasa sucks in a ragged breath but says nothing.

"We will wait until the ship has departed. The War Council believes that the Norse will rejoin their fleet shortly after departing. We do not strike until we are within shouting distance of the other boats. I do not know how long this will take, nor do I know what manner of treatment we will receive in the meantime. You must prepare yourself to acquiesce, whatever their actions. I will do my best to disabuse them of physically harming us, but I will not risk exposing my power."

"That's hardly a comfort," Jaasa sneers. "Are you not there to ensure her safety?"

I let my cool gaze move to her slowly.

"No," I answer, spearing her. She narrows her eyes, scowling in disgust. We are a long way now from the momentary alliance of yesterday.

"The only safety your daughter can rely on is what she creates for herself," I continue. "And even in this, she must consider the safety of her people, their children and their children's children yet unborn, before she considers her own. I am not her shieldmaiden. She is mine."

I cut my gaze back to Aemilie, letting my words fall on her upturned brow.

"*I* am the warrior. It is *I* who will force spirits into the sky, or the sea, or wherever it is that Norsemen go when I kill them. I will get us off that boat. You will ensure they never return for you, or anyone else. You are a tool. You are *my* tool. If you desire to feel your mother's embrace again, you will allow me to wield you in the manner I see fit."

The silence beyond my voice rings with all the power held between us. We three women, daughters of nameless queens, with force of will rooted in our chests like oaks. We three women, the futures of hundreds wrapped around our necks like bridles, clenched between our teeth like bits.

Finally, Aemilie breaks the unquiet silence.

"I am no tool," she breathes out her conviction. "But I will be your shieldmaiden. Tell me what it is you require of me, and I will do it."

And so I do, praying all the while that there will come a day when my own daughter's voice will sound the same.

We have un-become what we had begun to be again. I know this because when I press my palm to the weathered wood of the door to my chamber, he is not within it. Yet, when I step through the doorway, he is.

"I have no time for this," I start in immediately, annoyed.

"I will be on that boat," he says.

"You will not."

"I will not sit here and wait, Liama," he insists.

"Whyever not?" I ask, brows high. "Because your niece goes into danger? It cannot be on my account."

"You have never been in battle. You know nothing of its nature."

"And have you?" I ask innocently. "Perhaps you have. Perhaps this is some other memory of mine that you have stolen from me on account of your pride. Did I stand on the ramparts and watch, tearful and simpering, as you strode with your men into the fray?"

"Don't be a bitch," he bites.

"I am a bitch," I bite back, unashamed. He lifts clawed fingers between us, growling through his teeth in frustration.

"I am beginning to think I preferred you better as Tuskjas' puppet," he spits meanly.

"Then put me back there!" I dare him. "It was you that put me there in the first place. Surely if I am so heinous to you now, you can put me back."

"That is the whole trouble!" he yells. "That is the whole trouble with you! You are not heinous. It would be better if you were."

In his words I sense a returning to the discussion of the night before, as if he hopes to finish what he left undone. But I left nothing undone.

"I have no time for this," I say again, reaching down to tear at the knot holding my skirts. I free it, unwrapping them from my waist in a furious flap of wool.

"What are you doing?" he asks dumbly.

"If I am to be an old crone in an hour's time, I had better begin now," I seethe, flinging down the skirts and stepping to the pile of worn servant's garb I brought in with me. I snatch up the long tunic, holding it up assessingly. I will need to reduce my height by a few inches. I reach back, throwing my braid aside and grabbing the fabric of my own tunic to lift it over my head.

"Stop!" he barks. I do not. I flip the clothing over my head, tossing it to the ground, then reach up to do the same with my shift. He takes a step towards me, hand extended to stay my arm, but then I am naked before him.

I turn, baring myself to his gaze. His eyes flicker, trying desperately to draw themselves up. His lips part on a whispered groan, as if I have squeezed the air from his lungs.

"For the last ten years I have only been what you have made me," I say, giving him no mercy. "Now I will become what I was always meant to be. What I suspect you intended for me to be when you first drew me out of that Wood. And you will not be there to see it."

"I cannot let you go alone," he wheezes brokenly, his mouth moving without his mind.

"If I am alone this day, it is only because you have chosen to hold yourself back from my side," I answer.

"But I would go with you," he murmurs. "I would shield your back until the last."

I shake my head.

"I do not want you there," I deny him. "I do not trust you there."

"Don't say that," he argues, his eyes finally climbing to my own. He searches my face, hoping, I am sure, for subterfuge. He will find none.

"You have given me nothing to refute it," I say. "You have not had the courage to be honest with me."

"If you knew – if you knew all that I have done –"

"You are a fool if you think I have not already discerned the truth of it all," I say. "And you are a fool if you think that I judge those sins committed in earnest long ago greater than those you insist on repeating against me now. I do not need your honesty, but I would have it, if only so that you can give it and this bitterness between us be done."

He stands there, his dark eyes desolate. I turn, taking my eyes from him, and begin to dress. When I have replaced the shift and tunic, their hems inches above my ankles, he comes to his decision.

"It is yours," he murmurs brokenly. I turn my eyes back to him.

"If it is within my power to give, or to return, you shall have it," he swears.

"Walk," I command. His head sags on his shoulders, ashamed, but he breathes in deeply and when he exhales, his breath is on my nape.

He reaches around me, showing me his cupped hand. Sand trickles between his fingers from the shore. I feel the delicate whisper of tiny grains falling on the tops of my bare feet.

I close my eyes against the shuddering relief.

My hand goes behind, searching. He slips his other hand into it, and I draw it around me, pulling him forward to my back. He turns the other palm over, letting the remaining sand trickle at our feet, then wraps his fingers around our joined hands at my navel.

"Will you take these from me again?" I murmur, opening his hand once more to trace his calluses.

"It is more difficult, when you suspect that I might," he whispers into my hair. "The mind has a way of locking itself around what it thinks might be taken from it."

"Like the heart," I say. He does not answer.

"Do not take them," I murmur, and as I speak I bring his open palm to my mouth, pressing my lips to the callous at the base of his middle finger.

"Liama," he breathes, half alarm, half warning.

"Swear that you will not," I whisper, flicking my tongue across his skin. He goes rigid with the sensation.

"Swear it, Kurat," I demand.

"I swear it," he breathes around the tightness in his throat. I nod, dragging the tip of my nose across his sensitive palm, feeling the grit of the sand trapped in its life lines.

"That will do," I whisper, pressing my lips into the soft center of his palm. "For now."

CHAPTER SIXTEEN
THE CRONE AND
THE NORSEMAN

A man stands apart from that which he worships.
He adores from afar, but fears to approach it.
Worship, my daughter, can rot from within.
Distance, my daughter, might save your skin.

I STEP FROM the safety of the fortress of Hapsaluu as a woman aged to near uselessness. It is deception, but it is not illusion. I ache. This time it is more than just my hands and face. Every step is a tax upon brittle bone and dry joints. My fingers curl in on themselves, decrepit. My skin sags from my face. I can feel its weight under my jaw, dragging.

Even Kurat does not at first recognize me when I approach him on the edge of the company gathering in the yard. He tells me he did expect me to look so like myself. I scowl at him, practicing the gesture on this aged face. There is the slightest upturn of the corner of his mouth, as familiar as it is faint.

We do not dare breathe even a glimmer of what has passed between us. Still, when he hands me up to the wagon that will carry us to the coast, he squeezes my gnarled hand, making me wince. I look back at him for only a breath, memorizing all the unspoken meaning pooling in his eyes.

He stands in the yard as we depart, his body tight and tense, looking for all the world like a man left behind.

Jaasa and Aemilie ride side-by-side atop two twin mares. It is not Jaasa's usual mount, nor is her long, fine dress her usual garb, but she has donned it nonetheless. The Norse have women warriors among them, to be sure. It would not surprise them to see Jaasa in her leathers with her spear. But we must withhold every weapon we have from them. I do not want them to see a warrior mother and begin to consider if they should tie Aemilie's hands and feet as well.

The journey is miserable in this body in this wagon on this forlorn coastal road, with the salt wind whipping our hoods back and loose hairs lashing across our cheeks. But I grit my teeth and endure it. It is nothing compared to what comes next.

At the end of a long peninsula we leave the mounts, the company folding itself into two small sailing vessels that rollick their way across the choppy bay to the northern tip of its mouth. There we retreat half a mile or so into the moor to await the twilight. Aemilie and Jaasa keep themselves far off from the men, whose bodies jitter and jerk with anxiety, even though they'll be doing none of the fighting themselves. After a while, I stumble away from them, putting a low rise in between my power and their inner workings. I do not draw the Shroud yet. I do not know how long or to what extent I will have need of it. I let flow the measured power required to maintain my appearance, a constant trickle, all the while keeping the well of what remains at bay.

Twilight nears. The moors begin to grow quiet. My body begins to deceive itself. My palms sweat. My heartbeat thunders. My chest tightens around it. I do not quell my instincts, though I do breathe deeply through them. The more I appear anxious and unnerved to the Norsemen, the more they will believe in the illusion of their power over me.

In truth, though my mother was a formidable sparring partner, Kurat is right. I have never been in battle. For all my talk of shieldmaidens, I hope desperately that this does not become a fight in earnest. My power will stay true, I have no doubt of this. But I do not know if my bravery will. When I had spoken to Aemilie about having no end to her courage, I had meant the words just as much for myself.

I tell myself that old tale. I bring myself the image of my grandmother's grandmother, though I know nothing of her appearance. I think of her standing straight and grim on this moor, watching the longboats beach their bellies on the sand. I grit my teeth around her rage. I shove her conviction into my belly. I draw the vision of the Norsemen fleeing from her wrath, their long braids like tails between their legs, throwing themselves into their boats and screaming for mercy, kicking up the sand and spray as they push themselves from her land.

A soft evening breeze, salty from the sea, bends the grasses gently away from the shore, pulling at the hood of my cloak. Her breath is on me.

A call goes up.

They have come.

"Mama," my daughter cries softly. "I cannot do it, don't make me try again."

"Of course you can, my love," I answer her calmly, putting my palm on her back. "Take a big breath and try again."

She does, shuddering a little through her tears as she inhales. Then she closes her eyes, struggling to wrangle the wild beat of her heart.

"Keep breathing," I whisper, running my hand in small circles on her back. "Loosen your body, listen to its sounds. Then when you're ready, draw the Shroud."

I sense a flicker of that peace in her chest, a tiny presence. And then it is gone. She keeps her eyes closed, scrunching her face to force peace into existence. Tears leak in fat tracks down her pale cheeks, her eyelashes thick with them, snot beginning to leak from her perfect nose.

"All is well, Maarja," I whisper, refusing to be like my own mother, even if I had mastered the Shroud under her stern guidance with barely any effort. "It will come, my love," I whisper over her head, ignoring the frustrated ache in my own.

"It will come."

I stumble coming back over the rise. Õnnev is there. He has come to fetch me himself.

He puts a hand out to steady me, and when I place my own over it, I notice that our skin, spotted and loose, and the knobbed shape of our knuckles is not so very different.

"They've come, Chieftainess," he murmurs, his voice still scratchy from overuse.

"Then let this be the last time you address me as such," I say to him quietly, wary that the breeze will snatch my words away to our enemies. Õnnev nods, guiding me back to the company.

"Remember, the leader, Vidar, speaks some Estian," he says. "This may be useful to you."

"Aemilie knows to try and draw his purpose out," I answer.

"I care little for what he wants with her," Õnnev growls. "He will not get it. But I would know how he heard of her, and what else he knows about the power of this land. I would not have him return for another."

"He may not desire an audience with her at all," I warn him.

"He was verbose enough when we negotiated," Õnnev answers. "I suspect if she is able to prick his pride he will be forthcoming. The Norse are not a civil kingdom as we are. Vidar will need to show his strength before his men to keep their loyalty. He will be boastful."

"Est is hardly civil," I huff a dark laugh. "And this Vidar is not so different a man than any other. I will bend him to my will."

"As you have bent my grandson?" Õnnev asks, his tone plunging. I do not look at him. I do not acknowledge his words. After a moment he speaks on.

"Know this, Chieftainess. Should you succeed today, whatever designs you and he have for the House, Saaremaa will stand for them," he swears.

"Do not speak treason before me, Kallas," I warn him, cutting my ancient eyes over to him. He stops, pulling me to a halt as well, and holding my gaze.

"He took my daughters from me," Õnnev breathes. "These are not the first words of treason I have uttered, and they will not be the last. My oath stands. Do with it what you will."

I turn away, trudging on alone, wondering when people will ever cease confiding their disloyalty to Tuskjas in me.

We form up before taking the last low rise to the shore. Õnnev and ten men lead, two of them Shade Walkers. Jaasa and Aemilie come next, shielded on both sides by another 20 men. I hobble along behind, trailed by the other Shade Walker, Härm, and the remaining warriors. Õnnev lights a bonfire on the beach, signaling the Norse to approach. Within minutes, the slender nose of a longboat breaks the sand. Thick, hairy men jump out to drag it to the beach.

We hear them now more than we see them in the waning light, splashing and grunting and signaling to each other in their sharp tongue. My power casts about, slipping from body to body. Here there is a man who is weak of seed. Here there is a man with a mass growing in his belly. Here there is a man whose blood is thin from long abuse of ale. He will be dead within a month.

A body breaks itself from the mass, and Vidar steps into the flickering orange light of the fire.

The man stands a head taller than Õnnev, his chest broad and unyielding, thick arms hanging stiffly from rounded shoulders. He has a weakness in the left one, where an old break to his collarbone has not healed correctly. The muscle has grown warped around it, layered over with a mass of fat that should not be there. I suspect he cannot lift his elbow above his head, but a war hammer hangs from his belt on that side nonetheless.

His too-bright eyes reflect the light of the fire as he scans our company, his gaze landing on Aemilie, the hood of her cloak thrown back to show her beauty. Jaasa's has been removed as well, and she shows all her rage and sorrow and despair on her face, and she is not beautiful.

Vidar grunts a directive over his shoulder, and his men stir to action once more. Goods begin to appear from the gloom. Chests that rattle when heaved between two men to the sand. Mismatched sacks of grain and seeds, undoubtedly stolen from Vidar's most recent conquests. Saaremaa's goods returned in exchange for her daughter. A sloshing barrel of krupnikas is deposited last before the men step back from the hoard.

Õnnev eyes it, sharing a look with another man, one of the stewards who has accompanied us. Then he shakes his head.

Vidar raises a thick black brow, narrowing his gaze. Then he grunts again. More items appear, a woven basket of summer cherries, a fat parcel that clinks and tinkles when it lands, and finally Vidar himself unwraps a silver necklace, fat with amber gems, and places it delicately on top of one of the chests, bowing dramatically with arms outstretched as he steps away.

Õnnev considers once more, looking again to his steward, who nods tersely. Then Õnnev raises his chin to Vidar, proud and straight, and nods his consent.

Vidar claps his hands together, a crooked smile splitting his face. Aemilie's heart hammers wildly before I feel her suck in a long, steadying breath through her nose.

"Now, my treasure," Vidar says in thickly accented Estian, gesturing her forward. "My Spider Silk."

What follows is exactly as orchestrated. Aemilie begins to quiver, losing her composure. Jaasa steps in front of her when Õnnev approaches, having decided at the last to deny her daughter's exchange. She is hauled away kicking and biting by two of Õnnev's men, one of them the Shade Walker Aabu. I feel them drag her, screaming, over the rise behind us, and then Aabu and Jaasa disappear from my awareness, the Heir of Saaremaa safely returned to Hapsaluu's thick walls.

I observe the bodies of the Norse carefully, watching for any awareness of what has just occurred not 40 feet from them, but there is nothing among them to indicate that they've recognized power at work.

Now Aemilie is being escorted forward, her great grandfather nearly dragging her as well. She is crying, reaching back for me. I hobble along behind dutifully, letting every misstep and limp convince my would-be captors that I am as docile as a doe.

Õnnev kisses Aemilie perfunctorily on the brow as she quivers, then turns her harshly and pushes her into Vidar's arms. Surprisingly, the big man receives her gently, pushing her back to take her hand and lay it over his forearm. He looks back at Õnnev with a lowered brow and narrowed eyes, but Õnnev is already ordering his men to gather the hoard in haste, turning his back on the Norse company. The deal is done. In only a few more moments, the Saaremaans have taken their goods and disappeared over the rise, leaving the fire on the beach to burn itself out.

Even Vidar seems surprised by their remorselessness. He looks down at Aemilie, who barely rises to his elbow, shaking and shivering below him. Then he looks once more to where the last of her kin are fading into the night, grunting something in his harsh language to his men. One or two of them offer a response, shrugging broad shoulders.

"You hear," he says, turning his Spider Silk to face him. Her head tips back, wide eyes going nearly to the sky, all her fear pooling at their edges.

"You not speak," he orders, putting his fingers over her mouth softly. "You speak, I –" and he makes a motion like stuffing something down his throat. Aemilie's face nearly crumples, but she manages to nod.

Then he flicks his chin at me.

"Her power?" he asks. Aemilie shakes her head furiously, turning her quivering hand on his arm into a claw. He narrows his eyes at her, watching her desperation, then nods, cocking his head towards the boat.

And so he does not gag her, nor bind me. Interesting, this man.

We are lifted at the place where the water meets the sand, Aemilie by Vidar himself and I by another man who smells of horse. They slosh through the shallow surf, delivering us over the low wall of the longboat between two brightly decorated shields. A lamp burns brightly from a central mast, casting the boat in striped shadows.

We are led under a sharply pitched covering at the vessel's center, recently vacated by treasure, to a little pallet of sorts and there offered some kind of spirits. Aemilie looks at me with her wide, surprised gaze, having expected, as I instructed, to be gagged at any moment. She takes the spirit, but I refuse it. They will not have gone through all this trouble only to poison her at the start, but they might welcome dumping my excess weight into the surf.

A heave, and suddenly bodies are sloshing back into the boat, settling themselves at the low benches and taking up oars. Another heave, followed by a sharp call, and the men begin to move as one, pushing us away from the beach.

From inside the little shelter, I cannot see the shore disappearing into the moonless night, but I can feel the hum and pulse of the bodies upon it growing distant. I tell Ameilie to sleep, and she places her head gently in my lap as if we have done the same a thousand nights before this one. I slip my bony fingers through her hair from scalp to end, humming the Song of the Daemon Prince.

Naught but shadow
In your realm
But shadow still, I love.
And would you come
And traipse the land
Of Shadow in the blood?
Walk with me and through the door
What wishes will be yours.
But hear me, lover, and give me not
A name to seal in lore.

It is not the lullaby but my power that slows her heartbeat and swallows her in sleep. I push her down, deep into herself, so that when Vidar crouches into the space she does not stir. I had told her that she would need to draw him out, but there is a reason Õnnev came to me as he did. A man like Vidar would never trust himself with a beautiful maiden of untold power. But with a crone, likely as not to die on the journey home, he might be willing to speak honestly.

He settles in opposite us, his long legs and booted feet only inches from my own. He spreads himself wide to take up space. He is a man who knows how to use his body.

I do not raise my gaze to his. I murmur the Daemon Prince's song, drawing Aemilie's dark, thin hair out from her cloak and spreading it over my lap.

"I know this song," he rumbles in crisp, clear Estian. His accent is still heavy, but not unwieldy as it was before.

"I suspected you might," I answer, keeping my chin low. His neck muscles tense with his surprise.

"Why did you suspect this?" he murmurs warily, his voice much lower now. I raise my face to his, looking out at him through crinkled eyes that he can barely see in the warm firelight that emits from outside the shelter. Even in the shadowed darkness his light grey eyes are disconcertingly sharp.

"I am an old woman," I say, tightening my voice to prove my claim. "I know many things, and many things have I known in lifetimes before. Are you not Vidar Grosson, who once made his home on the northern shores of Revala, until you were driven from there by the Kallas of that place?"

My husband had given the Kallas of Revala promises of greater influence at court in exchange for disrupting her long-held peace with her Norse residents. She had done so, opening her coasts up to violence. And Tuskjas had repaid her loyalty with abandonment. Though her invitation to court remains always open, he knew the Kallas would never be able to keep her position in Tarbatu, always being called away to defend her land. He had weakened her expertly, losing nothing himself.

And Vidar had been exacting his revenge against Revala for the loss of his homeland ever since.

Vidar shifts uncomfortably, but I know he will not be deterred by an old woman, no matter her strangeness. He cannot be, before his men.

"I am he," he grumbles. "And you are not what you seem."

"You think I have gained my age by ignorance?" I cackle, a senile old bat. "Perhaps I am cunning, or some have called me thus. But in truth I am simply hardy. And loyal."

"And so you come with your lady to my home," he concludes. I nod, returning my gaze to Aemilie's mane.

"Is she what they say she is?" he asks after a time.

"She is a girl," I answer. "That is all I can attest to. A frightened one."

"But is she powerful? Can she change the minds of men with her tongue?"

"Any maiden with coy eyes and clever words can change the minds of men," I defer.

"Then shall I dump you both into the spray?" he challenges, growing frustrated. "If she is not what they say she is, I have no use of her."

"Ah," I chide. "But you would do no such thing, power or not."

"You risk your life on my generosity?" he scoffs. "I thought you had heard tell of me, crone. Clearly you have not."

"I need not," I counter. "I need only to have seen your eyes when my master gobbled up your treasure in exchange for his own daughter's blood. You are barbaric, as is your nature. But you are not cruel, nor unjust."

He assesses me in the darkness. His fingers clench over the bulk of his upper arms. He adjusts his weak shoulder against the grain of the boards behind his back.

"What is your name, wise woman?" he says at last. I chuckle.

"You said you knew the Daemon Prince's song. But hear me, and give me not a name to seal in lore."

"What does your mistress call you?" he presses, impatient with my obscurity.

"Dittering bat," I cackle. "But only when she truly wishes to charm."

"This slip of a thing cannot be so cruel," he scoffs.

"Nor so powerful, some might say," I answer.

A harsh sound of impatience leaves his throat. He turns his head away in annoyance.

"Men make of women what they need," I go on lazily. "What is it that you need, Vidar of Revala?"

"A home for my people," he answers gruffly.

"And do you think this girl can spin such a thing into being?"

"Ack," he dismisses. "I do not need her to *make* such a place. Only to empty it so that we may fill it again."

"Your warriors cannot do this themselves? Is it not glory for your people to die in battle?"

Vidar's jaw stiffens. He glowers under a low thick brow, cutting his eyes to the shelter's opening, and the faithful rowers beyond.

"Ah," I answer for him. "They have no taste for bloodshed. They have lived among tame folk too long."

"I would hardly call your people tame," he grumbles, but does not rebut my insight. "You draw darkness with your tongue. You weave illusions as if on a loom. You twist your hands and a man's heart withers in his chest."

A flicker of alarm, or perhaps recognition, sparks in my belly at his words.

"So you have heard of our Wasters then," I croak, attempting to sound amused.

"Aye, I have heard of your Wasters," he sneers, saying nothing more.

"And yet, you still ravage our shores, knowing what waits upon them."

"My warriors may have lost their taste for bloodshed, but they are not so cowardly as that," he bites. "We pillage to survive, and to take back what was taken from us."

"And so you burn Saaremaa to acquire the weapon. And will you now take her back to Revala? You will turn her tongue on her own people?"

His jaw stiffens again as he turns it away.

"Not to Revala then," I conclude. "Nor back to your ancestral lands, I suspect. Your softened people would not thrive there. And so you aim to seek out a new home."

"Answer in truth," he growls, pivoting our line of discourse. "What is your name?"

And so I answer in truth, as he has demanded, if for no other reason than to be that much lighter when Kurat whisks me away.

"I am Liama, Chieftainess of House Est. And I am an Estian Waster, Heir to Looklema's throne," I answer seriously, holding his eyes.

"Sigrid's tits," he curses, rolling his eyes. He wipes a big hand down his face as I cackle.

"I'll call you Old Bitch," he growls.

"Half of that is true enough!" I answer, laughing all the more.

He pulls his big booted feet beneath him to rise.

"And what will become of this Old Bitch?" I ask. "I am not so agile as I used to be. I like to know what awaits me on the morrow."

He sighs, crouching low under the shelter.

"We'll be in sight of the rest of my boats in an hour or so. Then three days' journey by sea. Keep your mistress silent and you'll live to see it."

"One final question for you, master," I pester him. "Little it amounts to me, to be sure, and such I've told her. But she wants to know it, nonetheless."

"Know what?" he sighs impatiently.

"How you heard tell of her, of course," I ask innocently. "You've been gone from Revala's shores for years, and my lady has only just come into her full power. How did you hear of her?"

Vidar snorts through his nose, the sound sharp and humorless.

"You can tell your mistress she has her own to blame," he answers. "The Tale of Spider Silk came to me by raven from the Kallas of Revala herself."

With Vidar's departure, the ship settles in a mellowed rhythm. Oars strain through the water, swishing in unison. In the little shelter, I close my eyes and lift the Shroud. The pulse and thrum of the 40 bodies is amplified, hammering at my awareness. Heartbeats and gurgles, aches and creaks, and acid burning all tear at my focus. I let myself sink deeper in, pushing them out one by one, until nothing remains but my own body and a distant sense of another, far off to the ship's portside. If I were not so familiar with his essence, I would not feel him there at all. He is a glimmer, a spark, then gone.

Õnnev had assured me the Norse would stick as closely to land as possible without putting themselves at risk of attacks from the shore. That I can sense Kurat is confirmation of this information. Without the moon to measure by, I am not sure how long it has been since we cast off. Kurat and I had agreed on three hours, nothing more than a guess based upon where Õnnev's watchmen had last seen Vidar's fleet. But if the Norseman has spoken true, and we are an hour out from joining them, then the body following on the shore will arrive too late.

I lower myself deeper into the mists, feeling my power pool cool and become still around me. I breathe it in, swallowing a measure of it down into my belly. Then I set my focus on the place where that presence once was, not on the shore but in my awareness. And I wait.

The body reappears, its heartbeat hammering from exertion. I lash out at it, quick as a snake. The rhythm falters. I feel the bright flash of pain, and then the body disappears from my awareness once again.

The heart to summon him. The head to warn him away, as we had agreed.

Mere seconds later, he slips from the darkness, crouching before me, drawn by his familiarity with my essence.

"One hour," I whisper. He nods and is gone.

There had been so little time and the task before us great. When I had told him my designs, his doubt had become a palpable thing between us.

"I cannot Walk where I have never been," he'd argued. I'd pulled his hand to my chest.

"You have been here."

"A moving vessel, though," he'd said. "In the night, across open water. Liama, this is senseless."

"Could your mother have done it?" I asked.

"I haven't the slightest idea if she could," he'd argued. "She'd had no reason to do such a thing."

"So you think it cannot be done," I'd said.

"Not as I am," he'd admitted, jaw stiff.

"Then you had better begin the work of becoming something more," I'd challenged. "And quickly."

He'd narrowed his dark gaze at me.

"Is this another ploy to draw me out?" he'd sneered. "Have I not told you I will be truthful with you? Am I now to unravel ten years of deception in a single breath?"

"We've no time for that," I'd dismissed. "Perhaps a few of the weightier truths for now."

He'd scowled.

"I would not simply blurt these things out as if they mean nothing," he'd argued.

"Shall I ask you then?" I'd offered seriously. "Shall I ask you what I most desire to know, and when you have given an honest answer we will agree to speak no more on it until time allows?"

All the time we'd spoken his hand had remained in mine, pressed to my chest. He'd drawn it away then, crossing his arms like a shield.

"Do not make me despise you for this," he'd warned.

"If you were as changeable as that, you would despise me already," I'd answered. He'd turned his shoulder to me, a low sound of annoyance in his throat.

"Ask your questions then," he'd grumbled. "If you are intent on carrying their answers over your head."

"I would rather them over my head than dragging behind you," I'd said tersely, letting my own annoyance show. He'd stayed silent, staring intently at the wall, a fortress within himself.

"Did I go with you willingly from the Wood?" I'd asked. He'd sucked in a long breath through his nose before giving his answer.

"Yes."

Something fell away from him. I sensed it.

"Did you intend to overthrow Tuskjas ten years ago?" I'd asked next. He'd closed his eyes, his head hanging slightly lower.

"Yes."

"Is Tuskjas Maarja's father?" I'd asked, my voice faltering halfway through.

"No," he'd said, shaking his head.

And then I'd voiced what I had desired the most to know, and barely dared to consider.

"Are *you* Maarja's father?"

He'd turned to me, and I'd seen the remorse in his eyes and known his answer before it was spoken into the space between us.

"No."

And then something had fallen away from us both.

"She was a babe, barely a few months old when I met you," he'd murmured softly. "Whatever your memories of her father – I've never touched them."

The new vulnerability had been enough to let him Walk from the fortress where I'd left him to my side on the moor as we'd waited for Vidar's company to arrive. I'd known he would attempt it, but still, I had nearly jumped from my skin when he slipped from the air beside me, such was my anxiety in the moment.

He'd caught my shriveled shoulders, steadying the old crone's bones that I wore. When he'd looked down at my face, several inches lower now than his own, his dark gaze had softened.

"Is this what you will look like?" he'd murmured, tracing the lines on my face with his eyes.

"Aging is like premonition," I'd said, suddenly uncomfortable beneath his study. "It can unfold in a thousand different ways."

He'd looked on, lifting a hand to push the hood of my cloak back over my thin white hair.

"Let us try for more lines here," he'd whispered, tracing his fingertips over the corner of my mouth. "And here," out from the edge of my eye. Lines of mirth. Lines of laughter. Lines of happiness.

"That is much to hope," I'd whispered back through a raw throat.

He hadn't answered. After a moment more with me, he'd drawn in his breath and slipped once more from my awareness.

And vain creature that I am, I'd drawn the lines on my face that he'd hoped to see.

Wasting against the body's ability to heal, its vigor and strength and steadfast commitment to make whole what has been broken, is ultimately futile. My grandmother had insisted this be among the first things I was taught when my mother began to train me. All things of the earth may rot and ruin for a time, but life comes from death. What returns from the Waste is often stronger than what preceded it, just as the scar thickens the skin over the wound. It is the truth that drives the Little Hurt. It is why so much of Wasting ultimately becomes healing.

When I cut the line of power that I have turned upon myself, my face will heal, returning to what it should be. My body will straighten and strengthen. Its aches will dissipate and disappear. I will be younger and able and burdened once again.

So here, in the dark moonless night, within the huddled shelter of a Norse longboat, with this fresh slip of a girl sleeping on my lap, I allow myself to reside in old age and ancient bones as I know I never will again.

I allow myself to mourn the lines on my face that will never be.

It is as Vidar said it would be. After a time a shout goes up from the front of the boat. The rowers slow their measured pace. I reach out, twisting Kurat's heartbeat around my wrist and tugging once more. He appears faster this time. We exchange no words. He crawls to the shelter's opening behind the nearest row of men, rising high enough to slip his hooded head out from its roof and lay eyes on another longboat, its bright lamp like a warm bridge across the water. I feel the breath he inhales for only an instant, and then he is gone.

I reign in my power over Aemilie, letting her rise from the depth of her slumber. When her bleary eyes are on my own, I remind her of her directive. She nods, twisting her long hair around her wrist and then tucking it back into her cloak.

The rowers slow further, the men on one side suddenly switching their movement to push their oars forward. The vessel begins to turn. After a moment a voice rings out from beyond Vidar's boat. Vidar hails in return. The deep-chested voices converse for a moment in Norse. I open my awareness, still within the Shroud, to the voice's body on the other boat. I cannot understand their discourse, but his body's reaction will tell me if Kurat has been successful.

I need not have bothered. I have barely slipped my power around the man before Vidar is bellowing, his alarm obvious from the tenor of his voice. The other man responds with a defensive tone, challenging the leader with a barked question.

I clasp Ameilie's hand in my own, warning her, just as our boat begins to shake with the heavy footsteps of the Norse leader charging down its center towards us.

"What has she done?" He barks as soon as he reaches the shelter. He does not enter, but grabs the edge of my cloak, dragging me out of the space and into the open sea air. The Shroud collapses around me, and the oppressive force of my fear pummels through before I can snap it up again.

Aemilie scrambles after me, her eyes wide and terrified when she rises to see the blade held to my throat. She opens her mouth and the knife slips inside the skin of my neck, stinging.

"Do not say a word!" Vidar bellows. He jostles me back against his body, one massive arm wrapped around my chest, the other holding the blade.

"What has she done, Old Bitch?" he spits the nickname, squeezing me hard.

"She has not spoken a word," I wheeze. "I swear it on Looklema's name."

"She has done something!" he seethes.

"What?" I croak. "What do you say she has done?"

"My warriors are gone," he bites. His fear is tangy, his anger pushing the blood into his cheeks, the acid into his jaw. He holds it so stiff I can sense that it has begun to ache with the force of his rage. "My men are not where they were meant to be."

I know, of course, that it is Vidar, as well as this other ship, who are not where they are meant to be. That Kurat has Walked between them, catching their gazes only long enough to alter their memories, to rewrite their perceptions.

"Wherever your men may be, she cannot have done it!" I cry, letting my own sour fear into my voice. Suddenly, Vidar pushes me from him. I spin on creaking ankles, colliding with Aemilie. We both fall to the deck, tangled in each other's limbs and cloaks. I press her behind me, ignoring the raw ache in my hip, spinning to look up into Vidar's terrible gaze.

"I have been a fool," he seethes, pointing his blade down at us from his great height. "You say I am not cruel, now you will see what cruelty I possess."

"She cannot have done it!" I squeal again. "Her power works only in speech and only then to those who can hear. She is no goddess. Whatever has befallen your men, she cannot have done it."

"And you, Old Bitch," he spits, lunging forward to put the blade's tip once more against my throat. "I should have demanded to know what you are capable of before bringing you with her."

"Nothing!" I shriek. "I swear it. In my day I was a Shade Walker, common enough among my people. But the power has long since shriveled up. It is nothing now."

A sudden bellow goes up from the other boat. Vidar spins, striding towards the prow, his men scrambling up on their benches and forward behind him to cast their eyes out, following the cry. The longboat tips dangerously, men reaching out to steady themselves. I do not need to see what has drawn their attention. I could feel the shriveling sparks of pain long before the dull glow of fire on the horizon was spotted. In that place, just outside of our hearing, where Kurat has led the other Walkers to set fire to the Norse company.

Vidar curses, bellowing his men back to their positions like a beast. Warriors throw themselves to the oars, heaving in discord for a moment until unison is established once more. We slip through the water faster than before, leaving a putrid trail of terror and panic and confusion in our wake.

Aemilie and I are forgotten. We shuffle back into the shelter, both our hearts hammering, the spiky anxiety making my skin tingle.

"Let me do it," she whispers, shoving her mouth close to my ear. "Now, while they are distracted."

I shake my head firmly.

"You keep your mouth shut," I hiss.

"Is this not why I have come?" she presses. "I will do it. I will do it now."

She makes to rise, and I catch her cloak, hauling her back down.

"You are here as bait," I hiss, putting my face inches away from her own. "Nothing more. Keep your mouth shut. Show them nothing."

Her eyes narrow, shoulders hunching around her ears.

"You never intended for me to use it," she breathes, realization blooming on her delicate features.

"If they see it, if they have proof, they will never stop coming for it," I seethe. "If not these men then others."

"But I can make them forget they –"

"Hush!" I bite. And as I do, I cut the flow of power turned upon myself. Had I not tested her for this very purpose? To obey without question, regardless of the directive.

"And when they have forgotten their purpose in coming for you, what then? Will the illusion last forever? Will they not wonder why they burned Saaremaa? Will they not wake with a distant memory of great power in their dreams?"

She does not answer. She jerks her chin away, hiding her eyes.

"*What cannot be done with power can be done with fear,*" I quote the Waster's rhyme. "They must be made to fear what resides in this land, or they will never stop coming for us."

I do not have to raise the Shroud to pick Kurat's heart out among the fiery wreckage before us. I twist my sense of him around my wrist and tug. He is there immediately, reeking of smoke and blood and piss and a thousand other things the body releases as it dies in terror.

"Get her out," I growl at him, shoving Aemilie forward. He grasps her to him with an iron grip. She does not fight him, only glares at me with slitted eyes.

"I will take you both," he demands.

"Not yet," I say, pulling the Shroud around me once more. My body stills, sinking, all the while the thrush and hum and seep of the bodies around me presses in.

"Liama, no," Kurat argues, his breath thick with the smell of panic. I had not told him I intended to be left behind.

"They will return for her," I say, my voice drifting empty between us. In the Shroud I notice that it has lost the husky tightness of the crone. I can sense the youth returning now in force, aided by the Shroud's power.

"Then let them, and we will mount another defense," he presses, reaching for me. I know that if his fingers close around even an inch of my cloak, I will be gone.

And so I thrust his shoulder out from its joint, rendering his hand useless. He shrieks reflexively. Then realizing what I've done and why I've done it, he roars at me, a wordless raging howl.

A cry goes up from the rowers, one of them spinning on his bench, dropping his oar to unsheath his axe.

"Go," I command coldly. "Do not return until you hear their screams."

He sets his jaw, eyes ablaze, but sips in a steadying breath through clenched teeth and disappears from my awareness.

The warrior yells in shock, others turning now to see what has caused his outcry. I untie the knot that holds my cloak around me, standing on agile legs and stepping from the shelter, raising my head to meet the warrior's wild gaze.

It is the same horse-stenched man who lifted me onto the boat. He falters for only a breath at the sight of my unlined face, the empty shelter behind me. Then his chest expands massively, thrusting out a deafening roar as he steps forward, his arm cocking back to land his axe in my chest.

I catch his heartbeat around my wrist, but I do not tug. I whip my arm behind me, yanking the entire organ from its protective cage and onto the wooden deck at my feet with a wet squelch.

The warrior drops, his arm still extended behind him, his forehead coming to rest at the tip of my boot.

The fire on the horizon, the screams, just audible, of dying men, the bellows from the other boat, wondering why we've stopped, all of it fades.

Vidar stills midstep, having made his way forward at his warrior's cry. The dead man's body lies between us, all his men behind him.

His too-bright eyes rise to mine, the unspoken question sparking in the air between us.

And so I tell him once again.

"I am Liama, Chieftainess of House Est. Waster, Heir to Looklema's throne. You have sought to take what is mine. I will not allow it."

Vidar stares, nostrils flaring, one hand clenching and unclenching at his side, the other gripping the handle of his war hammer.

"What power is this?" he finally says. "What power is this that you would let another man rule this land while you possess it?"

I answer him with another of his warrior's bloody heart at my feet.

He stares at it, not bothering to turn his head to where the man drops loudly to the planks.

When he looks back at me, he knows he looks back at his death. But he raises his hammer, unbuckling a blade from his belt with his other hand.

"I would have made you a goddess," he breathes, lowering his big body into a fighting stance. Around him, the warriors do the same, unsheathing their weapons even as they bump elbows in the cramped confines of the longboat.

"I am no goddess," I breathe out into the last of stillness, letting myself drop further into the Shroud. "But I will lay you prostrate all the same."

CHAPTER SEVENTEEN
THE SHRIVELED TONGUE

Forged in blood. Breath of fire.
Death is the Waster's strongest desire.

VIDAR CHARGES, his war cry echoing across the open water. I turn, spinning low into the shelter and putting the structure between myself and the coming hoard. I drop the three bodies that greet me on the other side, making sure to break their outside hips as I smash their spirits into the sky. The bodies tumble outward into the water below, clearing the small space. Then I jump up onto the low bench, putting the dragon's tail at my back, and turn to greet the swarm.

They force themselves through the shelter a few at a time, Vidar first among them. I do not kill him, but I crack both his legs at the shin, sending him sprawling across the shelter's opening where his men must

259

clamber over his body to get to me. His mouth erupts with his scream, but I do not hear it over the war cries of his men.

The next body rises to its height, jumping over its leader in a long leap that brings it nearly to the bench beneath me. By the time he has reached it, he is blind. I swing under his wild axe slash, shoving his head aside and sending him sprawling into the dark water. Let him drown reaching for a shelter he cannot see.

Another follows. Another. I let them come to me one by one. I keep their line to me clear of their fellows' bodies, sending as many as I can into the water and the rest laying over the boat's low sides. I invite each body into its own hell, giving each its own terror. I do not know which of these men, besides Vidar, will survive this night. Whatever tale they have to tell about the night they faced Liama of Est, I would have them shivering in their scarred skin at the telling. I would have their remembered horror seeping out from their tight faces, their downturned eyes. I would have any and all who hear, who might be tempted by the power of this land to consider taking it for themselves, nothing but assured doom.

Still they come, Vidar's 40 men. Faster now that someone has dragged their leader away from the mouth of the shelter. Time is lost to me in the Shroud. I simply Waste the body in front of me for what could be hours or mere moments.

And so I register the twang too late.

A hot spark erupts across my cheek, just below my eye. The pain rips me out from the Shroud and I gasp for a moment, barely coherent enough to snap the neck of the man charging me, axe raised. I taste my own blood, bitter and metallic, as it seeps down my cheek, dripping from my jaw.

I sense Kurat, and then he is gone. The archer falling from the height of the dragon's head at the prow, a slash of red across his throat.

Twenty men or less remain on their feet. Bodies are strewn over the boat's sides like wet laundry, seeping their gore into the water below. I rally my power once more, preparing to lift the Shroud, when a pained bellow splits the air.

"Stop!" Vidar cries, trying in vain to lift himself on shattered legs by the low railing. His warriors do not hear him. Two more die.

"Chieftainess!" he screams, heaving. "Liama! Mercy! Mercy!"

The warriors hear him now. Some of them still looking to their leader. Others resist, shaking off their fellows' grips and trying once more to charge. I take another down gruesomely, pushing his entire spine out through the Wasted skin of his back. The men behind him are splattered in gristle and gore.

"STOP!" Vidar screams, and now tears roll from his small eyes.

"These are my brothers," he pleads, rage and hopelessness and despair. "Spare them. I beg you, spare them. They came on my word. They came for my greed. Do not kill them for it. Kill me. Kill me and take your justice."

"There are no terms under which greed can be satisfied," I repeat my grandmother's words. "They will come back, with or without you."

"They will not return! I swear it. They will not return," Vidar cries.

"And their sons? Their daughters?" I ask, my own breath heaving. Without the Shroud, my body aches for reprieve. I am coming to the end of my well of power. For the first time in my life, I feel the bottom.

Vidar shakes his head, hopeless.

"Didn't they tell you?" I press. "Didn't your grandfathers tell you what occurred when last your people met a Waster in battle? Didn't they tell you how she ripped their bodies apart? How they ran to their boats broken men?"

"They told us," Vidar pleads. "They told us and we did not believe them."

I lift my hands, fingers curled, between us.

"No more will your grandchildren believe you," I challenge.

"NO!" he screams, lunging forward on broken legs.

"And so, I will wipe it from your lips," I say, drawing the Shroud once more. It does not come with ease. It weighs as much as the bodies I have thrown into the sea and sits upon me like a tomb. Still, I descend into the power there, rallying for one final working.

Vidar is screaming, a broken, shattered cry.

And then he is not. The men begin to clutch at their throats, scraping their skin with their own ragged fingernails as their tongues shrivel to husks in their mouths. Dumb moans and gurgles, gagging and groaning and whimpering.

"Let there be no talk among you of power," I say, my final judgement. "If you do not wish your children to suffer the same, and their children after them, let the terror in your eyes be their only inheritance."

I sense him slip in beside me, and it is the only thing that keeps me standing while the last of the Norsemen gurgle into silence.

"Breathe, Liama," he whispers, his breath hot and heavy on my nape. I do, his good arm circling my waist, his face against my neck.

In the flicker of darkness that follows, I feel his lips press against the uppermost ridge of my spine. My head falls back against his, his fingers splayed out over my chest, holding me to him in the in-between.

I expect that we will be back on the beach. We are not. Nor are we within the fortress at Hapsaluu. Instead, he has Walked us high on a ridge overlooking the surf. Far out in the sea I can see the longboats ablaze, their eerie glow like dull lanterns in the night, dying slowly.

The wind buffets our faces, a cool, briny breeze that stings the slash on my cheek. For a moment more we stand still, breathing as one, looking as one out into the black sea. Then his hand moves to my shoulder, turning me to face him. His eyes are wild and sharp in the blue darkness as he searches my face, his one good hand running down my arm, my waist.

"Are you unharmed?" he asks, breathless. "How are you unharmed?"

"Why have you brought us here?" I ask, catching his hand in my own. The moment my skin meets his, I feel the wrongness in his body, its tense endurance of pain. One arm still hangs limp at his side.

"I didn't know –" he answers unsteadily. "If you had been wounded, I didn't want them to see."

"Where is Aemilie?" I ask.

"Hapsaluu," he answers, low and pained. "I threw her into her mother's arms and raced back."

As he speaks, I reach out, raising his elbow between us and setting my other palm against his shoulder. His eyes meet mine, tight with anticipation, and he nods.

I shove his shoulder back into place with an audible snap.

He grunts through his clenched teeth, bending in half with a hiss.

"I'm sorry," I breathe, a wild sob catching in my chest at the sound of his pain, words gurgling up to explain myself. "I couldn't let you take me. I knew you would, but I couldn't let you and I couldn't tell you before. I knew you'd never agree."

He stays bent double, breathing through his teeth.

"I'm sorry, I'm sorry," I whimper, the bubbling panic working its way up my throat. *Shock*, I remind myself. *This is shock.* I try and breathe through it, reaching for the Shroud, but it is immoveable, like a hood made of stone, hanging down my nape.

The squelching sound of the warrior's spine erupting through the back of his body is lodged in my ears like thick mud, my mind trudging back over it again and again, and I am rocking. Unsteadily rocking. Kurat straightens on a heaving inhale. Then he wraps his hand around the back of my head and shoves my face into his chest.

And I weep.

The waves rack my body like the surf below. I shake and shiver with them, clenching his tunic in my fists. On a heave, I shove away from him, vomiting spittle and acid and adrenaline. He steps up, bracing my side against his hips and holding me through the convulsions. He makes no sound. He does not shush me or tell me to compose myself. He simply breathes, steady on, until my own breath can fall into rhythm with his.

"I did not know," he starts, and I can feel the shake of his head above my own. "When I asked you to come, I didn't know –"

"You fear me now," I murmur, and though my own words repulse me, they fall right and sound in my chest. He should. He should have all along. They all should.

How weary I have grown of not being feared. More than I knew, pricking the babes of Tarbatu and setting bones and treating gout for men who'd cure themselves if only they'd give up ale.

Death is a Waster's strongest desire.

Kurat does not answer and I do not expect him to. But he lowers himself to the moist moss and brings me down sideways into his lap, pressing my head beneath his chin.

After a time, I begin to register a deep rumble in his chest, and when I still my body to observe it, I hear my name passing over his lips like a whispered chant.

I cannot bear it. It cannot be born, this wretchedness. It is like a wound grown swollen with rot. It must be punctured. The pressure released.

And so I pull back from the haven of his body, wrapping my arm around his head and smashing my mouth into his, an inhuman growl rumbling up from my throat.

In an instant his fingers are twisted through my hair, clutching me to him, his own wild groan trailing after mine. I push. He reaches back with one hand to steady us against the soft, mossy earth, locking my waist in the crook of his elbow. I claw at his neck, his cheeks, his ears, pressing my mouth into the darkness at his center.

Do not take this from me. Do not take this from me.

The mind has a way of locking itself around what it suspects might be taken from it.

He pulls his mouth from mine, heaving in a shuddering breath, then plunges in once more. I receive him, opening my jaw wide for his tongue, wrapping it in my own. He moans, pushing forward. I brace us, my body bending beneath his, taking his weight. He wraps his hand around my jaw and pulls my bottom lip between his teeth, flicking the tip of his tongue upwards over it.

There is an aching echo that clamors around in my chest. A knowing that he has done this before.

I shove him back away from me. He catches himself on an elbow, then pushes up again to take my face in his hands, fathomless eyes glazed and unseeing. I scramble up from the ground, fleeing backward.

"There is still a battle," I mourn.

"The battle is won," he groans, incredulous, sweeping his arm out to the orange light on the water. "Your enemies are tongueless and on fire. What more could you want?"

"Between us," I correct. "There is still a battle between us. There is still too much –"

"I am done with that fight," he barks, rising to his feet in haste. "I have surrendered it, and any other that comes between us."

He steps towards me, reaching, and I push my hands out, keeping him away.

"You cannot!" I order, holding him at distance. He sets his jaw, leaning against my locked arms.

"I do," he presses, his gaze wild and dark. "I do, Liama. Is this not what you want of me? Have you not insisted on my surrender?"

"You *would* see it as surrender," I accuse. "I wanted your honesty." My voice crackles over the words. He senses my weakness, pushing forward.

"It is yours," he pledges, wrapping a hand around one of my wrists and tugging my locked arm out from between us.

"I wanted your bravery," I plead. "I wanted it for myself. I wanted you to choose it over your fear, for me."

"I have," he murmurs, turning my wrist in his hand and kissing the tender place on its underside. "I will."

"I cannot be yours," I mourn.

"You need not be," he murmurs across the soft skin in the crook of my elbow. "Only do not be anyone else's."

"I am Maarja's" I whisper, belly quaking. He nods, sliding his nose up the sensitive underside of my upper arm. Slipping his face into the bend of my neck.

"You will always be hers," he breathes across my skin. Then he parts his lips over the bottom of my ear, grazing his teeth across it.

"I will betray you for her," I warn, closing my eyes. "If it becomes necessary, know that I will do it."

"You will," he affirms, just before his teeth clench gently over my earlobe, followed by his lips.

"Kurat," I breathe his name, sagging against his chest. "Nothing good can come of this."

"I tried to warn you," he says, dragging his mouth across my jaw.

"Nothing good ever has."

CHAPTER EIGHTEEN
THE WEEPING KISS

And what shall we say to the man who won't heal?
Who begs for health but whose will does not yield?
Say to this man, "Your healing begins
only when you cause a change from within."

"*TELL ME* about Saaremaa," I whisper into his tousled hair. He shifts lazily, rubbing his cheek against my breast, pressing his mouth against the tender skin.

"What would you have me tell you?" he murmurs, our voices low to keep from waking the babe tucked snugly in her basket beside our little pallet of pine needles and travelling cloaks.

"Did you not go there? With your mother? Did you not ever visit your kin?"

He sighs deeply, warm breath fanning across my belly.

"We went often. My grandfather was honored among the Kallas at that time. Saaremaa was honored. I spent many summers there with my cousin."

"Jaasa," I recall her name, sliding the tips of my fingernails along his scalp. His scent rises and I breathe it deeply. "Warrior woman."

He huffs a laugh.

"She would like to be thought so."

"She does not embody her name?" I ask.

"She is fierce, to be sure," he answers, sliding his calloused fingertips up the sensitive skin of my thigh. I shiver, and then I feel his smile against my breast.

"My great grandmother led warriors for Kotkas against the Slavs. When we were young, Jaasa imagined herself doing the same."

"And now?"

"I hear she has a child now," he muses.

"Fiercer still, I should think," I say quietly. "You have not seen her?"

He does not answer for a long time, though his fingertips continue their path up and down my thigh.

"I cannot show him that I love it." He murmurs after a time. I pull in a deep breath under his cheek, his hair tickling my jaw.

"I go when he sends me, which is little. Saaremaa lost his favor when my mother died."

"And if you did show him?" I ask, growing ever more curious about the man that I will soon slaughter. Kurat shakes his head, the bristle of his jaw scraping against my skin.

"Suffering, to be sure," he answers darkly. "Saaremaa would only suffer, and I the cause."

"Why does he hate you so?" I ask.

"He hates all, Liama," Kurat answers firmly. "You will know it to be truth the moment you behold him. He is all malice and greed. If I suspected he even hated himself, perhaps I could find mercy."

"Like Odypoeg," I say, smoothing the lines forming on his brow with my fingertips.

"Who?" He asks, rising from his leisure to look at me.

"Odypoeg," I say, surprised at his ignorance. "The clever-tongued leader of the Beings of Light?"

But his face holds no recognition.

"Have you not heard the story of the Door in the Glen, where the Mother Snake tricks the Beings of Light?"

"Perhaps your Waster's lore is different from my own," he shrugs.

"Then your education has long been neglected, for your Shadow Queen is a marvel in this tale," I say, drawing him back down into repose as I summon the story into my chest.

"By all means tell it," he smirks as he relaxes against me once more.

I breathe deeply, swallowing the taste of his skin, and begin.

"In the days after Looklema departed the Sacred Wood to live with her Daemon Prince in his undying realm, her daughters ruled in unity and in justice, at one with each other and with all their grandmother's kin, the Beings of Darkness, and all their grandfather's people, the Beings of Light. Yet, in time, dissent rose among the Beings of Light, for humans are changeable, capricious as the water's surface, and susceptible to greed..."

I hear his voice in my memory even as he presses his lips to my jaw. I stumble on weak legs, falling back, and he catches me by the hips, sliding his hand down over the curve of my back and below, jerking my leg up and around his waist. Then he turns us, cradling my body against his as he lowers me down to the moss and the heather and the mud.

"Don't take this," I moan, the weight of his body settling over my heavy bones.

"No," he breathes, sliding his thumb over my bottom lip. "Never again" he whispers, his mouth following his thumb.

My hands find the edge of his tunic, pulling it up and plunging beneath, searching out the heat of his skin.

"Why did you do it?" I murmur to the salt of his neck. He melts, sagging against my chest.

"You asked me to," he confesses, drawing himself back to look at me with his dark, despairing gaze. "I would never have done it. I would never have done it, I swear."

"Why?" I plead in a sob. He brushes his fingertips over my brows, down my cheeks, sliding his thumb gently over the scabbed slice left behind by the arrow, letting me see all his regret, his helplessness.

"We were never meant to be this, my love," he whispers, brushing his mouth over the tip of my nose. "When you left that Wood, you went willingly but not for any love of me. You went to restore Looklema's throne."

I pull his tunic out from below his belt, sliding my hands up to the peaks of his shoulder blades. He closes his black eyes over the sensation, hauling in a shuddering breath.

"What happened?" I whisper. The corner of his mouth tucks in, ever so slightly, on the hint of happiness.

"You irritated me. I offended you. You thought me arrogant. I thought you naive. And then your mouth was on mine, and I would have shredded my own mind to keep it there."

His black gaze drops to my lips. I raise my chin, inviting, and he lowers his mouth, brushing his lips over my own. I slip the tip of my tongue past, dragging it across his upper lip to the corner that held his half smile. He moans, low and wild, pushing his hips against me. The heat slips from my core, racing down my legs and then back up to my fingertips, my nails digging into the skin of his back.

There will come a night when you wake from the dream of this memory, and when you turn, it will be me beside you, and we will make it all over again.

I turn my head, breaking his kiss. He follows, rocking sideways, his mouth on the corner of mine, trying to draw me back in.

I pull my hands from his skin, bracing them on either side of his face and pushing him gently back. I would have his body. I would have it in memory and in truth. I would have it here on this moor under the moonless sky, the bodies of our enemies either sinking or burning in the distance.

But I would have his honesty more.

"What happened?" I ask, looking between his eyes.

He shakes his head in my hands, his eyes closing, then he lets it drop to my chest.

"He knew," he mourns. "Somehow he knew. Nothing good ever comes of this, Liama."

He pulls back, pushing off of me and rolling to his back in the moss. I turn my face to him, tracing his fine profile against the black sky, sensing the blue blood in his lungs turn red with every rise of his precious chest.

"I made love to you," he whispers. "In the shepherd's hut. We were to enter Tarbatu the next morning and demand he hand over the throne before all the court. I had Saaremaa and Revala and Vaiga, all sworn to stand with me. We thought that if we showed the others our powers, our links to Looklema, they would defy him too. But he knew, and he came, and neither of us –" he cuts off, staring into the sky.

"We were so lost in each other," he whispers, shaking his head. "And then there he stood in the doorway, with Maarja in his hands."

"Why didn't I Waste him?" I breathe, rolling to my side. "I could have killed him there. I would have, if he had threatened her."

For a long moment he says nothing, his eyes the same color as the starry void above.

"Kurat?" I whisper. He exhales slowly, bracing.

"You couldn't," he whispers. "You can't."

"That can't be true," I argue, sitting up above him. "I've Wasted him a thousand times, in ways he's never noticed."

Kurat's eyes come to mine slowly, and I understand.

"You've made me believe I can," I breathe.

"I nearly lost you to despair," he says, sitting up quickly. "In the months that followed, you were – you couldn't bear it. And I couldn't bear it, knowing I'd brought you to it. I'd brought you to his door. I saw – you were so like her, like my mother in those final months before – *before*. We were so young, Liama. *I* was so young. I thought if you believed you had power over him – if you believed there was a chance to overcome –"

"I asked you to change the memories," I say, the wretched misery of it stinging my eyes. "But I remember – I remember asking you not to take them."

He shakes his head, setting his jaw and turning away.

"I did not do it in one fell swoop," he explains defensively. "It happened slowly, over months, every time I met your eye, trying to remember what you remembered. Trying to rewrite it. Only knowing I'd succeeded when your bitterness towards me grew. But I could not – " He clenches his fists in the air, rubbing them viciously against his forehead. "Damn it all, but I could not let you go. I could not keep myself from you. And every time I would touch you, it would all unravel."

"That is how to undo it," I breathe.

He nods against his fists.

"I did not lie to you. I did not know how to undo it. I thought for years it was some scheme of your own power undoing it, undoing me.

Not until the night you met me again, when I cut a lock of Maarja's hair and put it in your hand."

I stare, slumped and empty and aching, into the wasteland of the moor for a long time. His hand taking my own, dropping Maarja's dark lock into my palm. That is when it had begun. The false memories, the ones that came to me in dreams, his touch had begun to untangle them from the truth.

And then he had taken my hand to Walk. And then he had held my face in his hands, asking me to save the House. And then he had wrapped his arms around me, and I had buried my face in the crook of his neck, for the hours it had taken us to Walk to Saaremaa.

After a long time, I turn to him, needing the story to bring itself fully forward. My story.

"He took me for his own that night," I murmur.

Kurat raises his head, the hard, twisted set of his mouth familiar. I reach across the space between us, touching my fingertips to his jaw. He sighs, reaching up to wrap them in his own.

"He took you that night," he murmurs, his voice hard and tight, his gaze as black as the bloodied sea. "But you are not his. You have never been. You cannot be."

"Because I am yours," I whisper, speaking what I have begun to know since he touched me those weeks ago.

"I am your wife," I say, pressing my fingertips to his lips. His brow breaks, his eyes close over my words.

"My grandmother married us at Looklema's shrine, in the heart of Her Sacred Wood. She blessed us there, and charged us to restore the Snake Daughter's throne."

He hangs his head, my fingers clutched in his hand.

"I called you Snake Wife," he murmurs, his voice unsteady.

"And I called you Shadow Husband."

He nods, breathing it in. They had begun as names we hurled at each other in anger. Then they became names we breathed over each other's skin in love.

I pull his chin up, sinking my mouth into his as I push away his still-fisted hands and crawl into his lap, straddling his waist. He takes my kiss as he takes the weight of my body, bending around me even as he presses back. I feel a tug as he wraps my long braid around his hand. I wonder if this is what his heart feels like wrapped around my wrist.

"I have been lying," I murmur against his mouth. He makes a sound of inquiry in his throat, but does not pull back from our kiss.

"I am an imposter," I breathe between his lips. "I am not the Chieftainess of House Est."

He huffs a dismissive sound.

"The throne has always been yours," he mutters, nipping at my bottom lip. "Regardless – as my cousin so eloquently put it – of who you bed."

"I have not bedded you yet," I argue, teasing. He grunts, taking my jaw in his hand again as he did before, sucking my bottom lip between his own and flicking his tongue up over it. I moan into his mouth.

"You have bedded me," he growls, "*in* countless beds, and out of them. Against tree trunks, beside streams – shall we add a moor to the list?"

"Tell me about the night you said we would make the memories again," I demand, pulling his hand at my jaw down by the wrist. I spread my fingers over his, sliding his palm to my breast. His fingertips curl over the collar of my tunic, tugging.

"I won't be able to tell you anything if we go on like this," he murmurs brusquely against the bare skin of my chest. When I look down, his eyes are wide and dark, staring at his own hand around the swell of my breast. I still and he drags his gaze to mine, waiting.

"What awaits us when we return?" I ask.

"Our enemies' ships burn on the horizon," he answers. "Word will have reached Hapsaluu by now, as well as whatever testimony Aemilie has to give. I suspect they think us dead. If we show them otherwise, then what awaits us is a fortress full of worshippers, and at least one Kallas at our back."

"And in Tarbatu?" I ask. "What awaits us there?"

He sighs, slipping his hand from my body and leaning back.

"It's been more than two days since we left," he says. "If we have been lucky, Maarja and Hariva are halfway to Vaiga under Rahuleid's guard. I do not think he will harm her, regardless. I believe his designs to marry her to the Slavs are meant for more than your torment. Still, he will know by now that we have gone, and likely that we have gone together, on the very night that I beseeched him for aid in Saaremaa. He will not be fooled by any subterfuge we might attempt."

"And so we will be punished," I conclude. He presses his lips together, scowling.

"Yes, but perhaps there is a way to lessen your due. If you claim I lured you under false pretenses, influenced your mind, perhaps I made you believe that Maarja was in danger –"

"That will not work," I shake my head, leaning forward to rub the tip of my nose against his own. He breathes me in, nudging my face up to capture my mouth.

"You could claim to have no memory of it," he reasons on after a brief kiss. "I could take it, even."

"You have sworn you will not," I argue, reaching down to slip my hands once more beneath his tunic.

"And have you no suggestions?" he asks irritably, trying to capture my hands beneath his clothing. "Shall we simply Walk in and declare our intent to murder him and take his throne?"

"Certainly not," I say, abandoning his skin to untie the thick leather of his belt.

"What say you then, Snake Wife?"

I smile down at him, sliding the belt from his waist and tossing it over my shoulder into the heather. Then I stand, his body between my feet, and slip the old woman's tunic and shift over my head in a single motion. His black eyes slip to the darkness between my legs, his lips parting on a stuttered exhale.

I drop back down to my knees, drawing his hand back to my breast. He palms its weight gently, reverence in the curve of his hand.

"Tell me, Shadow Husband," I murmur, my hands once more seeking his skin, "about the night you said we would make the memories again."

And so he does.

The moors grow lighter, dawn still far away but fast approaching. He breathes my name over my skin, his hands crafting the complex working of my desire with a familiarity that is both wonder and misery. His eyes follow his hands, fixated on every swirling touch, every hungry movement of my body against him. At long last I shatter, writhing and shrieking in his arms. And before I have drawn my mind back down to my body, he has slipped inside me with a heaving moan of disbelief. I know its meaning.

How can it be? How can it be? For so long it has never been. How can it be?

He rocks against me and I moan into his skin.

"Don't take this from me. Don't take this from me."

His mouth crashes against mine, sucking the words from my lips. His echoing groan is helpless, hopeless. The wet agony streaks from my eyes, rolling down my face and into my hair.

"A thousand times more," he pants, his eyes aching and desperate. "For every one I took from you, I will give you a thousand to replace it."

He wraps me tightly, flipping us so that I rise above him in the moss.

"Only make love to me, wife," he says. "Forget the other terrors and make love to me."

I move on him, gripping his shoulders as he drives his thumbs into my hips, moving with me. The memories surge, unraveling as he said they would, and I throw back my head, crying out into the dying night, and let them wash over us both.

"Where are they?" I whisper into his chest.

"We left your mother and your grandmother hale at Looklema's shrine ten years ago," he murmurs back.

"Why did you let me believe you had killed them?"

"You were only wisps of rumors," he explains, running his fingertips down the soft skin on the back of my arm. "I could hardly believe it myself when I found you. Three of you. I damned you, bringing you out of that Wood. I damned you all."

I sense him close his eyes over the crippling shame. It is a long moment before he speaks again.

"In truth, I knew you so little – there was so little time – yet, I knew you would rather die than betray them. But I could not be sure – you were unspeakably desolate. Your desperation –" he breathes in a long, sorrowful breath through his nose. "I thought it safer to take them. And if I could not keep myself from you, then I thought it safer that you believe something so heinous that you would never again allow me close."

"How long?" I ask him. "How long did we carry on?"

His silence lasts so long that I do not think he will answer, despite his oaths of honesty. But when he does, his voice is a strangled whisper.

"The night –" he swallows, rallying himself. "The night of the assassin, when he tried to mark Maarja."

Neither of us speaks, awash in the horror of the memory. Her screams. Tuskjas flipping the blade in his hands, preparing to carve.

The smell of my blood on the feathery down.

"I could hear you," he chokes. "You never screamed but you wept and I could hear the sound of him –" but he cannot say it.

"I Walked to your rooms and I held her. Hiida was there, and I thought I'd have to tie her down to keep her from running through to you. But I just held Maarja because I knew – I knew I would never hold you again. And I knew if I stopped him, he'd kill you both. I had to hold her. I had to make it enough that I had saved her, even though I couldn't save you."

I do not absolve him. I do not hold him tighter or brush the tears that I can smell on his face. I do not kiss him or soothe his sorrow in the warmth of my body.

This love has damned us. We can never be absolved.

"That is why she comes to you," I whisper. "She remembers."

He breathes a long sigh through his nose.

"I thought to take it from her, but she was so young. I thought perhaps she simply wouldn't remember."

"Perhaps not as you or I do," I answer. "But she remembers that you are safe, all the same."

"Then she remembers a lie," he huffs darkly.

"Where are they?" I ask again, picturing my mother and grandmother at Looklema's shrine, watching us as we disappeared together through the trees.

He shakes his head against the moss.

"I do not know."

Dawn breaks uninvited. We rise, aching, not bothering to brush ourselves free of the moss and heather and mud that clings to us. I bury my face into his chest, closing my eyes over the sound of his heart.

"Breathe," he whispers, wrapping my braid around his wrist and his arm around my waist. We inhale together and slip into darkness.

It is a distance he could not have managed yesterday, but when I open my eyes, we stand in the dim of my little chamber in Hapsaluu.

"Why have you brought us here?" I murmur, looking around. "Why not take us to the gates?"

"The longer jumps are easier when I have a strong draw to the destination," he explains, tucking his chin and capturing my mouth in an open kiss.

"What draw do you have to this room?" I ask, pulling my mouth reluctantly away. His black gaze sharpens, hunger lingering around his lips.

"The sight of you standing naked before me for the first time in a decade was heady indeed," he whispers, dipping his face into the crook of my neck.

The low flame in my belly rears up, sparking and smoking against my ribs.

But we are not youths anymore. There is more between us than desire.

I reach up to him, drawing his head back and placing his forehead against my own. We linger, cheek to cheek, breathing each other in, willing the heat to subside. Then I draw back from him, out of his arms, and slide my hand into his own.

And we Walk once more.

The guards on the wall shoot to attention, shouting down at us from above the gate.

"I am Kurat, Heir of House Est!" Kurat bellows back. There is no need for me to identify myself. I have no cloak, left in the shelter of

Vidar's longboat, and the crone's visage is gone. I wear the mask of the Chieftainess once again.

The gates creak open.

The yard is packed with refugees. Either word has not reached Hapsaluu of our success or Õnnev has decided not to trust it. Heads turn to us as we enter, a hurried murmur racing through the crowd. In less than a breath, my name is on a hundred lips. I begin to understand why the Twin Queens kept theirs to themselves.

A handful of Saaremaa's stewards, members of the War Council, come rushing out from the Hall, followed by Õnnev, moving slower on his stiff knees. His keen eyes fall first on his grandson, assessing him for injuries, and then they fall to me.

"Where have you been?" he barks. "We sent Walkers up and down the coast looking for you. We thought you dead."

Kurat steps forward. "The Chieftainess expended considerable power destroying Vidar's company. We took shelter in the moor and watched to ensure no ships made it to shore."

"We heard of fire?" Õnnev asks, his eyes bouncing between us. "And Aemilie said you refused to let her speak."

"Is this not a discussion better suited to your study?" Kurat asks, cutting his eyes to the open faces all around. Õnnev looks about, as if noticing the crowd for the first time. He shrugs.

"What use is that? They'll know within hours anyway. Better they hear it from your lips."

He levels Kurat with a heavy gaze, something passing between them. I remember his oath from yesterday. Õnnev is giving us a stage.

"Where is Aemilie?" I ask.

"I am here, Chieftainess," the girl's voice sings from above. I look up to where she stands on the balcony overlooking the yard, the strained face of Jaasa at her side.

"Come," I say to Kurat, striding forward past Õnnev and his councilors. "The time has finally come for Aemilie to use her power."

CHAPTER NINETEEN
THE HUDDLED MASS

Some have called us warriors.
Some have called us wan.
Some have sought for healing.
Some have sought for gain.

Some come on their knees.
Some come hands upraised.
Some come empty-handed.
Some come waving pay.

Some depart in glee.
Some depart in fear.
Some are granted wholeness.
Some lessen as they near.

Some on some on some.
And within them and without.
Always they come calling
for what a Waster will hand out.

AEMILIE SPINS the tale as we tell it, first from her own experience – the Norsemen on the beach, the threat from Vidar not to speak, the longboat with its oppressive shelter, and then the moonless journey to rejoin his fleet. I offer a brief summary of the words passed between the Norse leader and I, murmuring over her shoulder as she repeats them to the crowd. A huffing chuckle runs through the hearers when Vidar settles on calling me "Old Bitch," and I tell him that it is half true.

I have seen Illusionaries in Tarbatu, their bright-colored garb and expressive voices often more intriguing than the dim, hazy scenes they spin. Aemilie's power is far more adept. Certainly she uses her singsong voice well, pushing and pulling it, now low to mimic Vidar's gruff rumble, now tighter to mimic the voice of the crone. But it is not her primary tool. She casts her voice out from the balcony over the heads of its occupants, and in the grey morning light it spins itself into images, painted on the air in clear, crisp lines and colors. For all I have doubted her, and told her of my doubt, I must confess that she possesses considerable power. I have never seen anything the like.

She paints Kurat, Walking to me on the boat, and the people gasp at his boldness. When he departs, the story pivots, following him back to the shore to gather the other Walkers, who clasp onto his cloak and follow him through the darkness. They startle a warrior on the other boat as they appear, but Kurat changes the woman's memory as soon as she has made it. Then Aabu, Höamee, and Härm Walk to the boats drifting just out of earshot from Vidar, smashing the lanterns on their masts and setting them ablaze, before jumping back to the safety of the shore.

The audience cries out in wonder as the longboats are licked by fiery tongues above their heads. I gather my thoughts, assessing how much of what comes next I will tell – what transpired on Vidar's boat while the others burned – but Kurat does not lean away from Aemilie.

And then he tells the tale as one who has seen it.

They warp the story slightly, removing my dismissal of Aemilie's power and replacing it with a kind of matronly protectiveness that leads me to insist on her rescue, taking the risk all upon myself. Kurat of the illusion disappears with Aemilie in his arms, and the people clap, whistling and cheering for her rescue. Then he returns to the boat just as I am rising from the shadow of the shelter, my cloak discarded, my face young and frigid and terrible. Hands clasp each other among the listeners, breaths drawn in and held. Children are clutched suddenly to breasts, and all eyes are captured by my straight-backed form, standing alone before 40 vicious Norsemen, unafraid.

The warrior's heart falls at my feet. Several women scream. And then I declare myself, Liama, Chieftainess of House Est, and scattered yells echo my words. Vidar tells me he would have made me a goddess.

"*I am no goddess,*" I watch myself say, flat and indifferent and cold. The voice of the Shroud. "*But I will lay you prostrate all the same.*"

The crowd erupts just as Vidar steps forward to charge.

They shriek with every body that falls, tears streaming down enraged faces. Vindicated. I draw my eyes away from what I have already seen, watching the people of Saaremaa scream out all the terror and anguish and rage held inside of them. I gaze at them, enthralled, as they watch me deliver vengeance, deliver it into their hands. Hands which Vidar made to feel so helpless.

The arrow slices my cheek and Aemilie's illusion glows red at the edges, Kurat's wrath and fear coloring his telling. Her voice follows him as he Walks behind the archer, slicing his throat and throwing him into the sea to rasping cheers and bellows.

Vidar begs for mercy. Several voices scream out, telling me not to give it.

"Where was your mercy for my little Jaak?" a woman's voice breaks above the din, hoarse and broken and crackling with grief. My mother's eyes sting in response, shared tears rising.

"*There are no terms under which greed can be satisfied,*" I hear myself say. Wails rise, thrown upwards by sweet relief. And as I shrivel the tongues of the Norsemen, their groans are drowned out by the shaking, shuddering cries of my people, feet stamping the sandy earth, their faces upturned in surrender, giving me their essence, their very souls.

Kurat cuts his eyes to me once more, his gaze fiery. I told him he would not be there to see my glory. But he was. He is.

Aemilie draws out my final words, slamming them across the open yard.

"*Let the terror in your eyes be their only inheritance.*"

I step forward as my words echo back and forth between the stone walls. I raise two fingers to my brow, bowing lower than I ever have before. When I look back up, the people of Saaremaa have fallen to their knees.

Õnnev kneels at the forefront, looking up at me with his grandson's black, fathomless stare. Then he draws his fingers down from his forehead, placing them over his lips. The councilors behind him do the same, until a wave of salutes ripples out through the yard, hundreds of eyes locked on mine, the sign of Looklema, Snake Daughter, Goddess and Queen, on their lips.

Õnnev entreats us to stay, but I have been too long from my daughter. I have lived long enough with the man to know that Tuskjas always knows what he should not. I expect that the people's salutes – their claiming of me – will reach him, and may even now be rushing towards him. There is a new anxiety in my chest to hold Maarja in my arms. I am brittle with it.

Kurat folds me in his embrace, but I feel already the armor of the Heir going up around him, his beloved features sharpening and hardening into the facade of the man I once despised. Still, he kisses me softly before he inhales, and when he breaks away, we Walk.

It is not like before. On our stunted journey to Saaremaa we had seemed to fight against the wind, pressing on by sheer force of will. Now, it is as if the very air parts before us. We slip through it like sliding into a warm stream, tugging us gently towards our destination.

Kurat's arms fall away from me in the shepherd's hut, and I consider, perhaps too late, that I do not know when next I will have him with me as he has become.

"I know you do not like the place," he is saying, moving away towards the door. "But you will have to endure it. I'll Walk into town and bring horses from the stables. We need to appear as though we are arriving from a long journey."

He turns back, eyeing my still-soiled and bloody clothing. I had not wanted to spare the time in Saaremaa to change back into the clothes I came in. After a moment of consideration, he nods tersely.

"That will do. The more we can look as though we have been in battle, the more attention we will draw in the town."

"Wait," I breathe as he turns for the door. He stops, but does not turn.

"No, Liama," he says quietly, shaking his head. "Nothing good ever comes from this."

And then he inhales and is gone.

My eyes are drawn immediately to the little, sparse cot pushed into the corner of the shed.

I made love to you in the shepherd's hut.

We were so lost in each other. And then there he stood in the doorway, with Maarja in his hands.

But now I have made love to this same man. And now I have the memories of prior lovemaking. And I know myself, more than I ever have before.

No depth of passion would have veiled Tuskjas' approach to my power, nor the friction of his hands against the child of my womb.

Even in sleep, my power is searching, prowling, pulling in the sensations of other bodies. Always, always, never ceasing. Except for…

The sounds of startled horses come suddenly from outside. I push through the door, somewhat startled myself. I had expected him to lead the horses out under some disguise. But he has Walked them here.

Kurat runs gentle hands over the velvet noses, shushing and soothing as he slips blinders from around the beasts' heads. They calm under his care, stamping and jittery but no longer frantic.

"You Walked them here?" I say, shocked.

"It seems these are honest enough horses," he murmurs, his humor lame and flat.

"Did you – were you aware that you could?" I ask, looking back and forth between the mounts.

"Were you aware that you could kill half a company of Norse warriors before you attempted it?" he returns. And though I believe he aims for levity, there is none.

"Weight, size, these have no meaning in Shade Walking," he explains, turning back to rub his hand down one horse's long snout. "Only purity. And animals are far more pure than humans."

"The Beings of Darkness," I murmur, stepping up to give the other my affection. Kurat nods.

I step around the animal, putting my foot in the stirrup and mounting smoothly. He looks up at me from below, a half-guarded expression of remorse lining his features.

"You had never ridden when you left," he says after a moment. "I was required to haul you up into the saddle every time, like a bag of grain."

I look down on him, straightening my spine.

"We may have returned to each other," I say slowly, meaningfully, "but we are not the same."

"We are not the same," he repeats. And then he mounts, turning his horse's head towards Tarbatu in the distance.

"We enter as victors," he instructs now, the Heir returned to his voice. "We hide nothing. We act as though we were sent on his very orders, to do his bidding against his enemies."

I raise my chin even though the gates of Tarbatu are a mile away. He kicks his horse into a fast trot, and I follow, pulling the Chieftainess back around me.

Heads turn, whispers following, and some outright shouts. Alarmed marketgoers fall hastily to a knee, two fingers to their brows. Kurat had told the guards at the gate that we were in haste to the fortress to inform the Chieftain of our successful campaign against the Norse invaders in Saaremaa. Their eyes had widened but they'd spared no time in making a path for us, parting the crowded travelers moving through the entry and the wide courtyard beyond.

By the time we reach the market, the news has outpaced us. I sense the whispers turn to blurts, then shouts, and finally outcries of victory. Fingers leave brows to raise into fists as we pass. Our names are called out, racing ahead of us into the crowds. Children run alongside us up the hill to the fortress, leaving their parents puffing halfway up.

We careen through the fortress gate, sped along by the people's praise. Kurat leaps from his mount while it still moves, handing the reigns over to a startled guard and coming alongside to help me dismount. I let him, sliding as regally as possible to the ground in the bloodied crone's clothes, and then we stride wordlessly towards the open doors of the Hall.

We pass through, coming into the antechamber, and with the noise and shuffling of the bodies outside snuffed out, I am finally able to name what I have sensed since we came through the gates. I reach, trying to grab Kurat's arm to stop him, but my fingers brush against the rough wool of his sleeve and then he is through the door.

"My Chieftain!" he bellows, not waiting to be received. I grit my teeth and follow him, trying to keep my eyes from the huddled mass on the stone floor in the center of the room.

"I come bearing good tidings of our success against the invading Norsemen in Saaremaa. The Chieftainess and I have driven the barbarians from Estian shores. We decimated their fleet, killing most of them and leaving the survivors to the fate of the sea."

His voice does not falter, though his eyes now see what I have sensed.

Hariva, huddled over her swollen belly on her knees before the Chieftain's throne. Rahuleid is being held back by guards on the right, where he has just risen from his customary place among the court. Most damningly, the entire court is present, buzzing with anxiety at one of their own on trial before them.

I wipe all feeling from my face. I put my gaze on Tuskjas, my would-be husband, and let Vidar's cries ring in my ears. They will be his own, soon enough.

There is a flickering, shuffling silence filled with the sudden cuts of gazes and sharp inhaled breaths and shocked flutters of surprise.

And then Tuskjas leans forward in Looklema's chair, his meaty hands wrapped around the ends of its raised sides. His beady, dull eyes leave Kurat and crawl to me. I do not trust myself. I raise the Shroud.

"You have done well, Chieftainess," Tuskjas says, turning his large jaw ever so slightly away in a subtle nod. "I am relieved to hear of your success and of the rescue of the Kallas' great granddaughter from Norse hands. I understand you ensured they would not return in a particularly clever fashion. Shall you tell the court about what you did to them?"

I have prepared myself for this. I had expected word to reach him.

And so I raise my chin and lower my voice. If he thinks I will be ashamed or disgusted by my own power, or the perceptions of others, he has miscalculated.

"I shriveled their tongues in their mouths," I say clearly, letting my own tongue push my voice to the corners of the room. There is a collective recoil. I smile.

"I poured horror down their throats and silenced them forever to keep them from speaking a word about the power that lives in Looklema's land."

He does not like that I have referenced her. He narrows his eyes, calculating.

"And yet, you return so quickly," Tuskjas counters. "Is it not two days' journey to Hapsaluu?"

"Shade Walker, my Chieftain," Kurat answers, stepping forward. "Kallas Õnnev was kind enough to lend us the usage of one of his most powerful Walkers so that we could return promptly to deliver to you news of our success."

"Ah yes," Tuskjas says, nodding slowly. "My first wife's power. I remember it well. It must have been a powerful Walker indeed to have brought you *both* through the darkness."

"Indeed," Kurat says, knowing better than to offer additional information.

"I owe the man my gratitude," Tuskjas says, his eyes beginning to glitter maliciously. Now we come to it. His gaze returns to me. I brace.

"For you have arrived just in time to bear witness on a matter that greatly concerns you, my Chieftainess," he goes on, motioning to where Hariva has knelt, silent and aching, on the floor all this time.

"You are aware, of course, that this is Lady Hariva, wife of Kallas Rahuleid of Vaiga." He waits for me to acknowledge him. I refuse, keeping my eyes level and indifferent on his own. I let Vidar's cries ring once more in my memory for strength. I will not play this game.

Hariva has not been harmed, though her body aches with discomfort and reeks of fear. Yet, there is something else sluicing through her veins.

Rage.

"A very heinous charge has been brought against her this day, a crime that, if she has committed it, would surely call for her death," Tuskjas goes on, relishing every word.

I steady myself within the Shroud. I sip the acid from Hariva's aching hip, easing the tension in her body. I do not know if she looks to me, acknowledging my intervention, but the signals of discomfort abate.

"I am surprised at you, Liama," Tuskjas says quietly, as though he and I alone share the room. I raise my brows but give no other response.

"You have not yet asked after your daughter," he explains, forced concern bending his brows low.

"Is she not safe among your court, husband?" I ask flatly.

"Are any of us safe from betrayal?" he answers immediately, as if he has expected my question. "The Lady Hariva, is she not your dearest friend? And yet, she is accused of kidnapping your very daughter with intent to kill her and destabilize my marriage negotiations on her behalf with the Slavic king."

I tighten the Shroud, pulling my very skin close to my bones to contain my response. I give him nothing of my horror.

"And so, much as I abhor it, I must ask you to give witness in her trial. For there is no one who knows her as well as you do, save Rahuleid, of course," Tuskjas says sadly, nodding to the barely restrained man on the right of the Hall. "And he is hardly a reliable witness. We have already heard from Kallas Meevat's daughter, the young Lady Suita, who has bravely given testimony on how this woman has gained control of her husband through sexual means."

Suita, damn the girl. Sneaking into their bedchamber to watch their lovemaking and then using it against them. Meevat should never have allowed her to testify. But then he never should have denied Saaremaa aid.

"And what does Maarja herself say?" I ask, begging the best from my impressionable, terribly young daughter.

"That is curious, indeed, that you should ask that," Tuskjas answers, tilting his chin as though confused. "For when I questioned her, she seemed to believe that you yourself ordered Hariva to take her from Tarbatu under cover of night. Yet, such an account surely cannot be accurate, as you were sent by my very hand to Saaremaa and had no reason to suspect that Maarja would be in any danger here at court in your absence. Unless, of course, you did suspect as much?"

"I sent Lady Hariva a message via my lady's maid to keep Maarja out of trouble in my absence," I hedge. "Perhaps the message was misinterpreted."

"To the point of forcible seizure?" Tuskjas scoffs. "I should think it would take considerable misinterpretation of your intentions to force the lady to such a conclusion. Did she have any reason to believe you felt Maarja was in danger?"

"No," I answer honestly. I have never shared my fears about Maarja with Hariva. I have loved her from a distance, speaking to her always with my back turned.

"Think carefully, my love," Tuskjas says, allowing affection into his voice, yet spearing me with his malicious gaze. "It is your daughter's very safety we discuss."

Do not betray me. Do not speak a word against me.

"Prior to the message, I gave her no reason to believe I feared for Maarja's safety," I answer. Somewhere beneath the Shroud, I sense a wound opening. Beginning to seep.

"And so it is as I suspected. The lady acted on her own," Tuskjas nods slowly, his eyes narrowing. "Perhaps she saw your absence as an opportunity, thinking Maarja would be idle in the days, unexpected at her lessons and, therefore, could be slipped from the fortress unnoticed."

"I think it unlikely, my Chieftain," I counter. "Maarja has spent countless hours alone in Lady Hariva's presence, as well as with the child, Suita. Both children adore her. They think of her as an older sister or beloved aunt. If Hariva desired to take Maarja, she could have done so at any time. Why wait until she was heavy with child and barely able to travel to make the attempt?"

"Ah, a sound observation, indeed, my Chieftainess. Yet, one we have already discussed in your absence. Is the steward of Mustvee still among us? Ah, no, alas he has gone," Tuskjas directs his show with precision, pretending to crane his neck to search the gathered crowd and feigning his resultant disappointment.

"The steward, Kallas Rahuleid's very one, who has, for some time now, as you know, managed the Kallas' household in his absence, has already given testimony which I believe may clarify things for you. The man reported that for at least the last two years, the Lady Hariva has intercepted missives between myself and the Slavic king which unduly informed her of our marriage negotiations on Maarja's behalf. According to the steward, her disdain for the proposed union is well-known among her servants in her household. Tell me, Liama, has she given you any indication of her thoughts on the matter?"

"She has not," I answer firmly, steeling myself around the lie.

Tuskjas tilts his heavy chin to the side, making a show of studying me for several breaths.

"Approach, Liama," he commands, waving me forward to the dais. I stride forward, unabashed, rising the two steps until I stand against his presence, eye-to-eye. He reaches out, wrapping a paw around my upper arm. I refuse to recoil.

"My love," he whispers for all to hear. "It is a terrible thing, I know. Betrayal is a terrible thing."

His grip tightens.

"Do we not know each other, after all this time?" He murmurs lovingly. "Do you think I do not know when you lie?"

With the eyes of the court on my back, I let my hatred slip into the hot skin of my face, dropping my eyelids and setting my jaw.

"There," he murmurs. "There you are, my love. Let us proceed in honesty, as we always have. Let us do so, for Maarja's sake."

And then he squeezes my arm to the bone.

Do not betray me. Do not speak a word against me.

I will betray you for her.

I'd had the chance to warn Kurat. I never thought to warn Hariva.

He releases his grip on my arm, only to slide his hand down to my wrist. He turns me beside him, holding me to him as a man might hold a whip.

"What has she told you?" he asks quietly. "Surely you must have told your closest friend of your excitement to see your daughter so well wed. What did she say? Did she share your joy?"

I put my eyes on the far wall. The wound within me begins to bleed.

"She did not."

"What did she say?"

"She feared it would be the end of the Wasters," I say, giving her everything I can.

"Ack," Tuskjas scoffs beside me, squeezing the delicate bones of my wrist together in warning. "Surely Looklema's blood runs truer than that. Did she say you should not allow it?"

"She spoke from her love of Maarja," I defer.

"And yet, she advised you not to allow the girl to become a princess?" he asks, disbelieving. "Hardly the position of a loving older sister, as you called her."

"Whatever her opinions, they were spoken out of love for Maarja," I repeat. "And love for this House."

"Ay, yes," Tuskjas nods dramatically. "Yes, I believe you are correct in this. The Lady Hariva's love of the House is unquestionable. And yet, she herself has questioned my leadership of it. She and her husband, no doubt by her bidding, have spoken out against our daughter's union, when its very design is to benefit her own people, the people of Vaiga, who even now suffer under Slavic raids. And yet, she longs for something else, does she not?"

He stands slowly, dragging me forward down the dais. The Shroud slips, and my gaze goes helplessly to Hariva's prone form, her bowed head. I can sense the feverish shudders racking her body. She is shaking with rage.

"Stand, Lady Hariva," Tuskjas commands, sending his voice echoing about the Hall. The muscles of her jaw tighten, but she does not obey. I thrust my will on her, begging silently for her to obey.

"Stand, woman!" He thunders. Slowly, she unravels from her prone posture. She hauls her feet achingly underneath her swollen weight. Rahuleid leaps forward, trying to throw off his captors, but they haul him back, slamming him down into his abandoned seat.

She rises, letting her back curve, thrusting her belly out for all to see. And then she raises her eyes and damns herself.

There is nothing veiled on her sharp featured face. There is only withering hatred and wrath.

"Did you not intend to bear a child for the very purpose of arranging a marriage between it and my daughter?" Tuskjas accuses, all gentleness gone. "Is that not the reason you have insisted, against Looklema's obvious will, on bearing babe after babe though they do naught but die in your womb?"

And will I be doing any child rearing this time, do you think? She had asked me.

The babe is hale. He grows as he should. All is wholly well, I had answered her.

"You sought to gain influence, you sought to position yourself, and yet, you could not bear a son," Tuskjas goes on, laying his trap.

I know why you seek a son.

I had thought – if it had been the first time, or even the third...

She had wept over her dead babe, the baby boy born without breath. She had wailed, head thrown back, her mouth agape, face contorted in fathomless misery, the little, silent bundle clutched in clawed hands against her swollen breasts, heavy with useless milk.

She mourned the child that she hoped would wed my daughter, yes.

But, a thousand times more, she raged against the loss of the child that was to be her son.

"And so, when you saw that door closed to you, you sought to contrive another." Tuskjas speaks on. "You befriended the Chieftainess. You drew Maarja close to you. You gained their trust to further your influence."

"Stop this, Tuskjas," I say, helpless, holding in my mind the image of Hariva's open, sorrowful face when I'd told her it was too late. That the hale, healthy boy even now in her womb had come too late.

He squeezes my wrist with the hard, unassailable mass of his strength. The cry eeks past my lips, surprised and weak.

"My Chieftain," Kurat speaks, making to step between Tuskjas and Hariva. "With respect, this is considerable conjecture. I would advise caution before –"

"Silence!" Tuskjas roars, throwing his other arm into the air. Kurat leaps back from being struck by his flinging backhand, a new wariness in his eyes when they rise back to the man before him.

Tuskjas drops my wrist, throwing himself into motion, stalking the sides of the Hall like a panther, growling and snapping at the members of court.

"This woman has sought to murder my daughter!" Tuskjas bellows like a beast. "Your sister! Our beloved! And you advise caution? I will show no caution! I will show no mercy! Let anyone who seeks to come against what is mine remember this day!"

It is a clever show. They will remember, if not for themselves, then through the eyes of their parents, their grandparents. They will remember how Kotkas was said to fold his body into the shape of a giant wolf. How he stalked his enemies, devouring them. How he hunted the Wasters, driving us deep into the heart of the Sacred Forest. They do not know this man is no more able to take the shape of a wolf than a wolf to take the shape of a man.

And yet, though I know it to be an empty farce, Tuskjas' aggression is true. His violent hunger. My wrist aches with it.

Beware the powerless man, my daughter. Do not treat with him.

With the horrified eyes of the court on the Chieftain, Hariva steps forward quickly, snatching the front of my still-bloodied tunic in her small hand. She grips me to her with an unnatural strength, and in the half breath before Kurat comes between us, she shakes me, boring her livid gaze into my own.

"My son," she seethes through gritted teeth. A command.

And I know that she knows what is to come.

Kurat breaks her grip on me, putting himself between us and forcing her back. Rahuleid is bellowing from his chair, kicking and thrashing, but he has never been a warrior. He will not overcome the guards. Tuskjas has turned, prowling back towards us at speed.

"Guards!" he yells. "Hold her!"

Men stream from the entryway, far more than what will be required to contain Hariva. They grab her arms, wrenching her back and shoving her down to her knees. I sense the thudding jolt in her pelvis when she crashes to the stone floor, her breath catching over the pain.

"Lady Hariva of Vaiga, I will not abide your treason," Tuskjas spits. "You will die this day. You will die by the very hand you have sought to destroy."

And then he whips his red-rimmed gaze to mine, and I am not so sure there is not a wolf beneath it.

"Bring me Maarja."

CHAPTER TWENTY
THE MUCK OF THE WOMB

Muck of the womb, seeping down the leg.
Gore of the birth, coming to a head.
The blood of a woman is the only blood spent.
Not from want of violence, but for love's torment.

"MA–MA," I say slowly, letting my lips linger over the simple sounds. My daughter wiggles, her head lolling back and then tilting sideways, looking back at me with an enigmatic smile.

"Say, 'ma-ma'," I encourage, needing the words to come from her mouth more than I need my next breath. How odd this fascination with being acknowledged by our children by the names we give them to call us. How all-consuming.

"Maarja, say 'ma-ma'," I press. But she simply continues to giggle at my desperate face.

"No," I breathe.

"Now," Tuskjas seethes, stepping towards me.

"My Chieftain," Kurat tries to intercede.

"You shut your lying mouth!" Tuskjas bellows, striding into Kurat's face. "You hope to be Chieftain one day? You hope to be worthy of my throne? Then this is what you must do to earn it. This is what your mother did. You seek out my enemies and you destroy them."

I am unsure now how much of his performance is farce and how much of it is long-suppressed violence, that hunger he inherited from his warlike father but has never been able to fully indulge. And yet, I know that Kurat means nothing to Tuskjas, perhaps has never meant anything to him, and I will not add his blood to my clothes. They will be soiled ten times over before this is done, but not with his blood.

"I will do it," I say, raising my chin. I paint my features over with rage. I put Vidar before my mind. I become the thing that stripped a man of his spine with barely a thought.

Tuskjas whirls to me, his face mottled in true anger.

"I will do it," I repeat loudly before he can deny me. "It is my child she has sought to steal from me. I am the one she has sought to destroy. I will do it."

He glares at me hard, searching for the deception. The subterfuge. There is nothing for him to find. Hariva has given me her orders. She knows there is no other way. I will not fail her. Not in this.

"But," I add, sending my voice out to the corners of the room. "The Heir of Vaiga lives in her body. The babe is hale and healthy and innocent of his mother's crimes. I will do it, but I will not punish the babe. Nor should you seek to destabilize the very region that stands between us and the Slavs."

"No!" Rahuleid moans wretchedly somewhere beyond me. "Looklema save us."

"You would not punish a child for the sins of its parents were he standing before you. The babe is ready to be born. He will come any day. Stay your hand, and when he is delivered I will carry out your judgement."

Tuskjas stares and stares and stares, sucking in thick, chest-rattling breaths.

"No," he finally murmurs. A wave goes out from his denial in widening ripples.

"No?" I ask, shocked at this new depth of barbarity, especially before his court.

"No, I will not stay my hand," he says, his thick shoulders coming up around his ears. "She has desired a son. I will give her one. Take the babe from her womb."

A collective inhaled breath. The silence of terror.

He will push them too far, this court.

I will make sure of it.

"It is true. I can bring on the labor," I say slowly, giving myself time to design a way of doing so that will not kill Hariva. "But it will still take some time to ensure it is done well, my Chieftain. It may be prudent to allow the court to recess –"

"Have you forgotten, my Chieftainess?" he interrupts, letting my title linger dangerously between his teeth. "I care little how well it is done. I have sentenced her to death for her treason."

I stare at him, holding the collective disbelief of the room on my shoulders.

"Crack the babe from her womb, Liama," he orders, eyes glittering. "Do it now. Do it here."

In the terrible, ringing silence that follows his order, Hariva begins to laugh.

How many times have I heard her laugh? How many times has she cackled with glee at her husband's sharp-witted humor, her own quick tongue? It was her laughter that first made me love her.

But now it is warped beyond sanity.

She is deranged with it, wild and snorting and terrible. Its sharp barbs echo around the silent chamber, silent save for her husband's moaning sobs.

"I needn't have worried, Liama," she wheezes, tears streaming down her face.

And then she breaks once more into a fit of laughter before gaining control of herself enough to speak on.

"It seems I shall go to the sky with my breasts still full and perky," she titters, barely getting the words out. "My sisters will hate me for it!"

I had hoped to stay the bleeding, if only for a time. I had hoped to keep it to a warm trickle down my legs. But the wound inside of me wrenches open, and I pulse and thrum and gush and splatter. Every nasty thing inside of me stains the floor, even if I am the only one to see it.

I close my eyes, wrenching down the sob lodged in my throat.

And then I raise the Shroud.

"This is barbaric!" Kurat tries once more. Tuskjas rallies to bellow him down, but I slide my cool gaze to Kurat, finding his eyes drawn to mine.

"Do not take this from me, Heir," I say, watching him startle at my choice of words.

Do not take this from me. Do not take this from me.

Look at me, Liama.

I already have.

He will not abide it. I know that he will not abide it. There will come a point in the cracking of bone when he will break and all will be lost.

"Remove the Heir from the Hall," I give the order.

302

"No!" He argues, stepping towards me, his brow furiously low. I turn my gaze from him as the guards rush forward. "No!" he demands once more, but my word holds the authority here. He lets them force him back towards the door, but never turns, his dark eyes on the side of my face, which I do not turn to him.

And then he is gone.

Perhaps he allows himself to be led from the Hall because he understands what has passed between Hariva and I. But I doubt it. It is more likely he allows himself to be led from the Hall so that I may remain in his heart as the woman who made love to him on the moor. The woman who splattered the ocean's surface with the gore of our shared enemies.

You keep babies from being sick and give his enemies bad knees. My mother was slipping daggers into backs. She was pulling children from their beds.

And now I will pull a child from his mother's womb.

Hariva made her choice. She knew what I asked of her when Hiida delivered my request. Perhaps, I can hope, she remembered the sense of her power when we last spoke, poking at my untruths, trying to unveil what I held hidden from her. She is a keen woman, as Kurat claimed.

And I have chosen this. I knew what might come of our intimacy. And yet, I allowed it. The reasons do not matter.

Perhaps, as Kurat said, Hariva and I might overthrow Tuskjas still, though neither of us will be left to lay claim to what remains.

Our choices made, I do not hesitate. I begin.

Hariva howls with the first contraction, gritting her teeth. I Waste the thick lining of the sack inside her womb and her waters gush and splatter across the stones. The guards holding her jump back in disgust. I level unimpressed glances at them both, waving them away. There is no resistance Hariva can muster now. Both men look to Tuskjas behind me, who nods, and then they nearly sprint back to their safe distances at the Hall's entry.

Cowards.

The second contraction grinds Hariva down to her knees in the waters of her womb. She rocks and moans until it passes. Rahuleid is fighting again. His resistance seems to break something in the other members of the court. Several of them come to their feet, letting their horror out of their mouths.

He should have known. They will not abide it. No more than Kurat would have. He has miscalculated.

I breathe deeply, readying the working. The complexity of it pulls me deeper into the Shroud. Hariva's personhood fades, as does Tuskjas'. There are only bodies. Pulsing, thrumming, squelching bodies. I let my focus fall on the one before me, this little laboring mass of blood and muscle and bone and acid and water.

I let my awareness tiptoe along its spine, searching out the meeting place of mind and body at the base of the neck. And when I have found it, I sever it.

The body goes limp, collapsing face-down onto the wet stone. There will be no more pain. I step forward into the muck. I lean down and heave the laboring body over onto its back, then stand once more over it.

I wrap the heartbeat of the babe within around the tip of my smallest finger. And then I begin to tug.

Tha-thump tha-thump tha-thump tha-thump.

The tiny heart, no larger than the finger that pulls it, quickens. The soft, downy head meets resistance, and so I open the way before it. Bone cracks. Muscles snap like ropes pulled taut. But this deep inside the Shroud, there is only the little beating heart.

Tha-thump tha-thump tha-thump tha-thump.

The babe comes, sliding through its mother's destroyed canal. I whisper the Waster's Rhyme into the opening just as it becomes filled with the thick black hair of the emerging babe.

"The womb, the darling, the giver of life. Holy of power, riddled with strife. The body bears the womb as the womb bears the babe. Heavy the burden of birth and decay."

The child comes free with a squelch, blood gushing behind it. I flip it over onto my palm and forearm, my fingers sliding against the gore, and then I thump the boy firmly on the back.

A shuddering silence.

And then he begins to scream.

Bodies rush forward. A woman pulls the screaming babe from my arms. A man drags the mother's body back, out of its own gore. The body is slowing, its life blood flowing freely from the decimated womb. It will soon breathe its spirit into the sky.

I sense a nagging reluctance within myself. An unwillingness to let this body go. But the sensation lingers for only a moment and then drifts away.

I turn my awareness within myself. I seek out the wound I felt before. I can smell the metallic tang of my own blood. The rot beginning to fester.

Perhaps I am the man who will not heal. Poisoning myself from within.

In a marketplace, in a fortress on a distant shore, the people raise their fingers to their brows, then press them to their lips.

Looklema, they murmur. *Sacred Queen.*

You are a tool. You are my tool, I had told the girl there. *You will allow me to wield you in the manner I see fit.*

You ask too much of her, Liama, he had argued. *She tells stories.*

I am no tool, she had said. *But I will be your shieldmaiden. Tell me what it is you require of me, and I will do it.*

And I knew then that it was she, not I, who was chosen of Looklema. A childless woman. It would have to be a childless woman.

You are willing to leave your own daughter's fate in the hands of a being no one has heard from in a thousand years? Hariva had asked.

No.

No, Hariva. I am not.

Hariva?

Hariva.

"Do not take this from me," I plead. He rises from beside me, tossing the bed covers aside.

"Do not beg me like a woman starving," he spits, spinning back and spearing me with his black glare. His words of adoration from moments before dissipate in the air between us like smoke. "You asked this of me. You demanded it. I have taken nothing that you did not instruct me to take."

"I asked you to take the wretchedness!" I bite back at him. "I asked you to take the misery; yet, you take it all! You take the joy and passion and the very essence of what I am!"

"And what are you?" he demands. "What are you? I have begun to forget myself. Are you my wife? Or are you his? I see the way you take your place behind him. I see how you relish being Chieftainess. His Chieftainess!"

"Then you are blinded by your unfounded jealousy!" I seeth. "That is your own fear, your own anger. I will not take it on my shoulders. I have my own to bear."

"And I placed it there?" he asks, livid, his face now mottled in rage. *"That is what you are thinking, is it not? I dragged you here. I promised you power and gave you none, and so now you will take it for yourself. You will take what he offers you because I have offered you nothing!"*

For a breath my rage is so massive, so disjointed, that it cannot be put into words. And when the words finally form, they sound far too simple to contain the writhing mass of all I feel.

"You are a fool, Shadow Husband," I bite, my voice low and damning. *"A fool and a coward."*

"And you are a bitch, Snake Wife," he hurtles his words at me like a spear. I sneer at him, swallowing them whole.

"I am a bitch," I say, thrusting my finger down towards the floor below. Towards his chambers. *"Now get out."*

A painful grasp tightens around my upper arm, and I am dragged to my feet, the Shroud slipping from around me.

Chaos.

Tuskjas bellows, jostling me in his grip as he swings wildly around, taunting the members of court, daring another to step forward from their seats. The crowd whirls by in my foggy vision, my eyes furiously trying to blink the Shroud away. Tuskjas yanks me in front of him, his hands on my shoulders, shaking.

"Who will stand against me?" he yells. "Did you think her power myth? Do you think she only healed your babes? Now you have seen! Now you know what she longs for – the death this power craves! Who will dare stand against me?"

I feel their horror, their disgust, before my vision grows clear enough to see their faces.

Slowly, I become aware of my skirts clinging to my knees. Hariva's womb waters drip down my shins, pooling under the arches of my feet. Tuskjas swings me around again, like a shield before him, and when I step I feel the warm waters squelch between my toes inside my boots.

"I am the Chieftain of this House!" Tuskjas is bellowing. My hands are covered in the slimy, curdled coating of a babe who has come too soon. My eyes fall on Rahuleid, Hariva's lifeless body cradled in his lap, her slim legs splayed out over the stone floor, the blood between them beginning to congeal. The man weeps, touching his shaking fingertips to his wife's slack cheek, begging, begging, begging.

And a few steps away, the old manservant rubs the thick coating from the screaming babe's face, shushing and bouncing even as he swaddles the squirming child, wrapping it tightly and bringing the boy to his shoulder, as only a mother can.

Vappers cuts his gaze to mine, the little body squawking into his wrinkled neck, and I feel an old, familiar pull around my heart. Then he looks away, hobbling towards his master. He leans down, but I cannot hear the words he murmurs into Rahuleid's ear over Tuskjas' ongoing jeers. Vappers places a gnarled hand on his master's head. The younger man melts beneath it, his head dropping low, resting for only a breath on his wife's brow, all her rage smoothed over by death. And then he hauls her into his arms, bringing his feet beneath him.

He does not seek the Chieftain's permission to leave. Tuskjas screams on, and in only a moment the Kallas of Vaiga is gone, the black-red globs of thickening blood dripping from his wife's skirts marking his passage from the Hall.

Still, Kotkas' son rails his victory, his inevitability, into the ringing corners of his Hall.

I turn my eyes to Looklema's throne.

Empty.

Open.

CHAPTER TWENTY-ONE
THE TENDER EAR

Naught be your power if naught be your rest.
Enemies will wait.
Lay down your head.

"*WHY DO WE* linger?" *I ask.* "*Why do we not make at once for Tarbatu and deliver the Usurper his reckoning?*"

My new husband looks at me, a sneer tainting his fine features.

"*You are terribly naive,*" *he says, turning his face from me.*

"*Perhaps,*" *I say, unaffected. This is not the first time he has called me thus.* "*But you will answer me all the same.*"

He cuts his eyes back at me, then sighs, his lips pressed together. I am beginning to notice the patterns of his expressions. The stiffening of his jaw when he wants to conceal a truth. His lips pressing in on each other when he is deciding how much to reveal. He is a guarded creature. I suppose he has a right to be.

I am not a guarded creature.

"Do not make the mistake of assuming that Tuskjas is powerless simply because he does not possess power as you or I do," Kurat answers.

"I do not consider him powerless," I argue, narrowing my eyes. "But his power is surely derived from his father's conquest, not his own. Will the people not doubt him once Kotkas has been in the grave long enough?"

"Kotkas has been in the grave nearly 30 years," Kurat answers tightly.

"And so the time is coming when his legacy will be meaningless," I reason. "A dead man's old victory cannot hold the throne against Looklema's chosen Heirs."

"That is not his only asset," Kurat grumbles, growing impatient, but he does not continue.

"This is no time to be vague," I answer, pursing my lips at him. "You would do well to inform me of what we face. And you would do well to do so without tainting it with your bitter angst. I am not your enemy."

He rises to his feet in a burst of frustration, tossing aside the long stalk of wheat he has been absently shredding in his hands. He stalks away, putting distance between us, but not far enough to remove himself from my offending presence. I feel him inhale sharply through his nose, then he speaks in a measured, forced tone.

"Tuskjas is not just a body between you and the throne. He may be without power as we call it, but he is not powerless. No matter your opinion on his father, it is enough for most of the Kallas that he is Kotkas' son. There are those at court who believe he took my mother to wife in order to keep from having to reveal his own power, so that no one may hope to plan a challenge, as only a fool would do so without accounting for his ability."

"And you are sure that is not so? You are sure he is powerless in truth?" I ask.

310

He turns, casting his dark eyes into the flickering firelight. He is terribly handsome, and yet, I have a sense that he would be handsomer still if he were not so terribly bitter.

"There is a family in House Rezke to the south," he explains. "They call themselves Dampeners. They claim to be of Looklema's line, not her brother's, though they have made their home in his land. They claim to be descended from the Shadow Queen, like Shade Walkers. They can sense a person's power, all of it – its nature, its strength, its use, even at birth."

"How is that possible?" I ask. He shrugs.

"That is what they claim. And the claim is apparently well-founded enough that they have served the ruling family of Rezke for generations, assessing whether or not the Living Memory power has passed from Chieftain to Heir, and protecting the Chieftain from the mind sickness that plagues the Memory Keeper."

"How do you know of this?" I ask, knowing nothing myself of Living Memory or Memory Keepers or Dampeners in Est's southern neighbor. Kotkas had cut all ties between Est and Rezke when Rezke's Chieftain refused to give aid to Kotkas' campaign against the Slavs.

"That matters little," Kurat deflects. "What matters is this – I am acquainted with one such Dampener, a man named Aleksejs. He lives in a remote fortress on the coast of Rezke, very near the Sakalaan border. And in my younger, hopeful years, I paid him dearly to come to Tarbatu under disguise for the purpose of assessing whether or not Tuskjas truly had power."

"And he sensed nothing?"

"More even," Kurat sighs, running a hand through his dark hair. "He sensed a void. As though there may have been some kernel of power, perhaps in Tuskjas' youth, but it had been snuffed out, leaving emptiness in its wake."

"Like a phantom limb," I say.

"Except more," Kurat says quietly.

"More?" I ask. He stares a moment into the flame before answering.

"I brought Aleksejs to court barely a year after my mother died," he continues. "I had tried to remain faithful to her command never to use my power on Tuskjas. But her death --" he cuts himself off, turning quickly away. It is several moments more before he continues speaking.

"Suffice it to say I had grown somewhat wild in her absence," he bites at last. "I attempted what I had never attempted before."

"You tried to influence his mind?"

His jaw stiffens.

"It did not work," I prompt. He closes his eyes, shaking his head.

"He looked me straight in the eye," he murmurs. "He looked me straight in the eye and laughed."

"And so you brought the Dampener," I supply. He nods, crossing his arms over his chest.

"I had some inclination then that Tuskjas could sense power used against him," he continues. "But Dampeners are highly trained in subterfuge. I believe Aleksejs was able to assess Tuskjas without him knowing."

"How do you know he did not simply allow it?" I ask.

"I do not," Kurat shrugs. "I only know that Aleksejs and I both left court that day with our lives." I wait for him to go on.

"What Aleksejs sensed was a void, as I said. But he described it as something alive, something arcane. Something he'd never before encountered. As if the power that should have been there was not only absent, but Tuskjas' body was searching for it, pulling in power used against him, swallowing it whole."

"Stealing it?" I ask in horror. Kurat shakes his head. Beside me, my babe gives a sudden cry, jabbing her tiny fists against the swaddling clothes I have wrapped her in. I shush her, pressing my palm gently to her back and rocking her side to side until she settles once more into sleep.

"Aleksejs did not think he could use the power for himself," Kurat goes on in a hushed whisper.

"There is a Waster Rhyme," I murmur, casting my eyes up into the darkness of the canopy above. "Beware the powerless man, my daughter. Do not treat with him. For if you lay him open, you will disappear within."

"And yet," I continue, realization dawning, "Aleksejs himself was able to use his power presumably. Tuskjas did not absorb it, nor block his attempts."

Kurat nods, a strange light sparking in his dark gaze.

"And so you think it may not be all powers," I continue, speaking the words for us both. "It may not be my power."

"Why do you suppose I have sought you out?" Kurat answers. "My power to influence minds is an aberration. I do not know where it comes from. My father did not possess it, nor any before him. It is not pure. Not like Wasting and, if what they claim about their ancestry is true, not like Dampening."

"You have not tried Shade Walking?" I ask. He shakes his head.

"I have no way of knowing if a failure is the result of his unique ability or his extreme inauthenticity. And I have no desire to risk revealing my mother's gift with little to gain," he explains.

"And so you have sought me out," I say. He draws closer, sitting now beside me on the fallen pine. His eyes are tight and black and fathomless.

"There are countless reasons I have sought you out," he breathes into the air between us. It sparks, suddenly, with a nameless tension. "But yes, this is one of them. If my theory is correct, and Aleksejs' power worked against him because of its direct tie to the Shadow Queen, then it is within reason that yours would work against him as well."

My fingertips are on his jaw, pressing lightly against the acid I can feel building in the muscle just below his ear. I Waste it subtly, relaxing his face against his own will. His brows lower, but he lets me do it without comment.

313

"I will Waste him," I whisper the promise between us as I whispered my marriage oaths. *"Looklema has not abandoned us. She will give us a weapon against her enemies. I will be that weapon."*

I see now why Kurat so resisted the return of these memories.

How young we were.

And so very foolish.

"Go, my Chieftainess," Tuskjas breathes over me, electrified by his victory. "Rest. Bathe. We have won two great victories today. Tonight we will honor them."

The servants come to my rooms on his orders. I send them away, even Hiida, who goes reluctantly, but I cannot abide her just now. Killing a pregnant woman will surely damage the people's opinion of me. There will be no one lowering their fingers to their lips in the sign of the goddess. Whatever adoration I had cultivated in Saaremaa, it has been destroyed in less than a few hours' time. I cannot carry Hiida's disappointment. Her questions.

And I cannot give them answers, or I will crumble.

I strip myself at last of the soiled, bloody clothing I have been wearing. Within it I have been crone, Waster, lover, and murderer. It is discarded at last, and yet, I feel as vulnerable and aching as I did when I stepped from Hapsaluu's fortress yesterday afternoon aged half a life beyond my own time.

Maarja. Seek out your daughter, I command myself.

"You are a very good Waster, but you are not the only one," I answer my daughter, hoping that she is still too young to see the gaping hole below my words.

But she is not.

"Are you?" she asks, an accusation veiled in innocence.

I have killed for her this very day. There is nothing more that I can give her.

And so I wash the gore from my skin, sliding damp and naked into my bed.

I force my fingers from their clawed fists, feeling the sting of red half-moons left behind on the meat of my palms. I force down my heartbeat, force my lungs to expand, force the acid from my shoulders, my neck.

Naught be your power if naught be your rest. Enemies will wait. Lay down your head.

And so I do as Tuskjas ordered, yet surely does not expect.

I defy him.

I rest.

"You would have me do this?" I ask my mother. I have stalked her, leaving the Heir and my grandmother behind.

"My will is not the one you should consider, Liama," my mother chides, keeping her back to me.

"It should be you," I say, planting my feet for the fight. "I cannot go and leave the babe. Risk the babe and you risk the line. It should be you."

"I am not the Chosen of Looklema," she says dismissively.

"She has spoken to you?" I ask. An accusation veiled in innocence.

"She has spoken to your grandmother," she answers flatly, letting my dagger fly by.

"Because she does not speak to you," I sneer. "She does not speak to you, and that is why it must be me."

My mother turns, her face sharpened, but her rage carefully controlled.

"Do not pride yourself, daughter," she mocks quietly. "When you leave this Wood, her voice will be lost to you. You will have to go on without it. You will have to go on with little more than what you have been taught and that ambitious fool of a boy."

"So you would not have me do this," I accuse. "You think I am not able."

She scoffs, throwing her head to the side.

"You want me to confirm what you already suspect. You want to hear it from my lips so you do not have to hear it from your own. So that your doubts will come to you in my voice and you can dismiss them. I will not play the role, Liama. You show your youth in that you expect me to."

"I do not doubt myself," I say, raising my chin.

"Then you show your youth even more," she answers, shaking her head.

"I will go," I say. "I will wrap the Usurper's heart around my wrist and pull it from his chest and I will be Chieftainess."

My mother looks at me, but she does not need to. I can feel her intrusion. I can feel the delicate way her power observes my body, looking for my fear.

I yank up the Shroud, smacking her awareness away.

"I will pray for you, daughter," she says quietly. Sadly. "I will pray to Looklema that it will be as you say."

"But you do not expect it," I snap, my face burning from shame despite the Shroud around me. She pulls a long breath into her lungs. I can sense it held there, blooming red.

"No," she answers, turning away from me once more. Her Waster's honesty drops between us like the fall of an axe, severing.

"I do not expect it."

I consider the renewed memory for a moment in the stillness of my rooms. The dawn is breaking over Tarbatu, but I can see nothing but the pale blue cast of the light from my south-facing rooms.

I did not mean it then, but I *had* spoken truth.

It should have been her.

If it had been her, she and Kurat could have allied without the chaos of desire clouding their minds. Tuskjas would not have had her daughter to use against her. Even if she could not Waste him, she would never have consented to marry him. She would have allowed herself to be killed, knowing the line lived on, before she handed him her power.

I consider the memory along with shards of others that have come back to me. Out on the moor, Kurat had lamented that he could not stay away. That even after Tuskjas had taken me as his false wife, Kurat came time and again to my bed. And we must have moaned and shrieked and groaned in our lovemaking. And then we screamed and hissed and cursed each other in the aftermath.

All in my chambers, only a breath away from Tuskjas.

I call Hiida to me.

She comes bustling, looking ragged but purposeful as she knocks my door in with her hip and sweeps across the entry room with a tray of morsels from the kitchen, the teapot leaving steaming tendrils in the air behind her. A breath more and the room is sealed.

I do not let her speak first.

"What do you remember of the Heir and I, Hiida?" I ask her. She startles at my odd question in light of all that has occurred since last we spoke.

"Ah, oh, ugh, the 'eir?" she stammers. I nod.

"Is there somethin' I ought ta remember?" she asks, eyes narrowing over sudden suspicion.

"I am not sure myself," I answer her.

"I fel' quite certain ya 'ated 'im until only three days ago," she says, pursing her lips and moving to pour my tea.

"I have always told you thus?" I ask her. "You believe I have always felt this way, ever since my arrival?"

"I s'ppose there were times when I fel' ya'd grown, no' soft, but no' so angry with the man, I'd say. I just though' ya'd run dry o' hatred, after the time tha's passed. Tha's fine by me, I'd said to m'self. I'll 'ate 'im enough fer tha two o' us, no' ta mention all the folk 'e's wronged, like that per woodcutter's wife."

"Erga?" I ask.

"Aye, an' the poor child," Hiida goes on, now bustling about the tea tray. "Kurat's a fiend, Liama. Surely you 'aven't let 'im convince ya otherwise wit those dark eyes of 'is."

"He is a fiend," I answer honestly. A fiend fit for a bitch.

"I wouldna be surprised if it's been 'im all along, controllin' the Chieftain, forcing 'im about like a poppet on a string. And tha people tha victims. It's tha people what's sufferin'. Though why 'e doesna just take tha throne –"

"He will take the throne," I murmur, awakening.

Hiida stills, staring at me with lowered brows.

"'e's told ya this?" she asks. I do not answer.

"'e's told ya of 'is plans?" Hiida asks again, rounding the table and coming before my chair.

"Yes," I breathe, turning wide, innocent eyes on her. "He's told me."

"Wha' are they?" she demands, leaning forward. "Tell me wha' they are. We must –" and then she catches herself, softening her tone. "We must act agains' them. We canna let 'im take tha throne, Liama. He'll be even worse – even worse for the people."

I let myself grow small in her eyes. I let myself grow young. I was once so foolish. Perhaps I can convince her that I still am.

"You must help me, Hiida," I whimper. "I do not know – I cannot remember –"

"Shush, Liama," she says, smoothing her features and taking my hand. "Shush, now. Tell yer Hiida all ya can remember. We'll find a way, Looklema guide us. We'll find a way."

"Liama," Tuskjas murmurs, leaning to my side. "Eat."

I look down at the full trencher before me.

Muscle and bone and sinew.

I turn my chin from him.

There is mead. There is music. There is no blood and no womb water on the stone floor of the Hall. I am in good company, and yet, few members of the court seem to be able to bring the roasted flesh to their teeth.

Tuskjas had opened the feast toasting to the elimination of a traitor from our midst. There had been nothing about victory in Saaremaa. All the court had brought their cups to their lips, anxious eyes flickering back and forth as they'd pretended to drink, but there had been only a few true swallows.

He has pushed them too far. Perhaps they are tame for now. But the Hall is like a bone-dry forest after a long drought. The smallest spark will set it ablaze.

And I will be the one forced to extinguish it. More bodies. More blood.

And so I pass my low, menacing glare over them, catching scurrying eyes and forcing them to flicker away. I press my will against their throats, threatening them with little lashes of power. A knee that suddenly gives way, a mouth suddenly dry, a subtle headache, a cramping muscle.

And when eyes sneak to my place beside the Chieftain, they see what I want them to see. Whatever Tuskjas' original intention, there is nothing ceremonial about his Waster now. There is only a dog who has acquired a taste for blood.

Not yet. Not you. I press on them.

It is mine. It is mine to take.

When what will be eaten has been eaten, Tuskjas stands, towering above from his great height. And then, with a wicked grin splitting his thick lips, he speaks.

"I confess that I have not been entirely truthful with you as to our purpose for feasting this night," he begins, raising his hands before him. "For while we celebrate the death of the traitor Hariva, there is something more, something greater, that I would reveal to you now, good members of my court."

There is a bracing of breath, a stiffening of shoulders.

Tuskjas smiles, drinking in their attention.

"I had not meant to reveal these good tidings until I had done so to the girl herself, but the Chieftainess has rightly advised me that our daughter requires time to recover from the terrible ordeal she has experienced. And yet, I am an impatient man, as well my wife knows." He looks down on me with affection, and I grin up at him with the same. "And so I can no longer withhold the happy tidings of the day."

And then he reaches for his cup, though little mead remains, and raises it once more in celebration.

"It is with the greatest pleasure that I announce the betrothal of our daughter, the Lady Maarja, to the Prince of the Slavs, Matej Ninoslav, son of Premsyl, King of the Slavs."

He announces it on a roar, raising his glass. And yet, even the most loyal members of the court are unable to respond with their Chieftain's enthusiasm.

They had thought the charges against Hariva – that she sought to ruin a marriage alliance with the Slavs – trumped up, convenient, but impossible. Even if they had believed she'd intended to harm Maarja, they had thought her motivation born of paranoia.

And now they see that what she feared has come to pass.

He has miscalculated indeed.

To Tuskjas' right, the old Kallas of Ugandi slides his hand across his belt to the hilt of his knife.

I break his thumb.

He is warrior enough not to cry out, but his pain-lined eyes shoot to me. I catch them, squeezing.

Not yet. Not you. It is mine to take.

I stand, raising my own full cup before me. If Tuskjas is surprised by my support, he does not show it.

"We will put an Estian Waster on their throne," I call out, sending my voice out to the Hall's flickering corners. "And Looklema's blood will run in the veins of their kings for generations."

Eyes narrow. Shoulders clench.

What of Kotkas? they think. *What would he think of such an alliance? The girl is weak,* they think.

It will end with her, the very shrewdest among them consider. *The Wasters will end with her.*

Not yet. Not you, I press at them. *Forget these things for now. It is mine to take.*

And so, slowly, cautiously, they raise their glasses to their lips once more, feigning a toast.

This time, no one drinks.

"My Chieftainess," Hiida whispers beside me.

I turn my chin to her slightly, keeping my eyes on the court.

"Ya told me to come fetch ya a' the end of the sec'nd watch," she murmurs low, lying through her teeth.

I nod.

"So I did, but I will stay a while longer," I murmur back to her, playing along. She fidgets slightly, then I hear the soft pop of her power descending over us, sealing us inside it.

I flicker my eyes to Tuskjas beside me, but his focus remains on maintaining his farce of a celebration.

"There's a man a' the gates with a child," she whispers hurriedly. "Claimin' ya gave 'im leave to bring 'er to ya."

"Erga's husband? The woodcutter?" I ask.

"I 'spect so, though I ne'er laid eyes on the man when last 'e came," she explains.

"I told him to bring the girl to the Little Hurt. He is a month too soon," I say.

"'e said as much, but somethin's 'appened ta the girl," she answers. "'e said ya must come now. You an the 'eir."

I pull a long breath in through my nose, considering.

"Send him back to Acker's Inn and tell him to wait there. I will come as soon as I am able," I command, dismissing her. She hesitates, lingering.

"An' the 'eir?" Hiida asks nervously after a breath.

When I do not respond, she adds, "The man was insistin'. 'e'll no' go without yer word tha' the 'eir will come as well."

"He said this?" I ask.

"Aye," Hiida answers.

A breath passes between us.

"Did you see the child?" I ask, slipping my awareness back over to Tuskjas as I await her answer.

"Aye, m'lady, a wretched lil' thing, ta be sure," Hiida murmurs darkly.

"Did he say what ails her?" I ask. All the while I wind my power around the delicate workings of Tuskjas' inner ear. I did not tell Kurat that his retelling of the events of that night – the night Tuskjas took me for his own – were not wholly accurate. It is true enough, I cannot Waste Tuskjas. I have made a few small, delicate attempts since returning from Saaremaa. Nothing to draw his awareness to my probing and only in those moments when he is most distracted. Screaming curses over the court earlier this afternoon had provided excellent cover for a small exploration.

And yet, though I cannot Waste him, I have found, as I have always found, that my power, like the Dampener Aleksejs', is able enough to observe.

"Is she – does the girl no' suffer from, eh," Hiida stammers, surprised at my question. "Well, is she no' ailed but wha' the 'eir did to 'er mother?"

"Hiida!" I bark, careful to keep my body still, save for my raised voice. She jumps, startled at the sudden volume. But, of course, no one else hears me within her seal, save the man beside me.

Though he gives no indication that he has heard, I sense the little vibrations of sound striking the delicate surface of Tuskjas' inner ear.

"Do not dare speak against the Heir, not here," I hiss at her. "You know what he holds over me, and yet, I must have him if our plans for the Glen are to come to fruition. We cannot risk his anger."

"His – the Glen?" she stammers, rocking back a step.

"Hush," I whisper. Despite Hiida's power locked around us, eyes are beginning to take notice of the length of her stay. "Get word to the Heir but do not go yourself. We must give Tuskjas nothing to suspect I have aligned with Kurat, even to use him. I will slip away as soon as I am able."

"Aye, m'lady," she says, confusion still coloring her voice, but she slips away obediently, my ears popping as her power goes with her.

A few moments later, Tuskjas turns to me.

"You look tired, my love," he murmurs softly. "Perhaps you should retire?"

I flicker my gaze up to him beneath my lashes.

"Yes, husband," I answer. "I believe you are right."

And now there is nothing to do but play his game.

I ascend the stairs of the tower, my power bouncing from body to body in the rooms behind the doors I pass. Kurat was present at the feast only long enough to witness Tuskjas' announcement. I sense him now in his chambers. I do not know if Hiida has yet arranged the delivery of my message to him, but I suspect he will be reticent to obey it. He knows I would not risk even an indirect summons when I could more readily summon him myself with a subtle tug around his heart.

And so I pass his door for now, rising to the level of my own chambers, but I do not enter them. Instead, I turn left at the landing, following an even more familiar heartbeat.

Maarja is asleep when I press softly through her door. I kneel softly beside her, laying my head on the bed to watch her breathe.

I'd attended mothers who had complained of a constant, nagging fear that their children would suddenly and inexplicably cease to breathe. It had pulled them from sleep at night, frantic to place a hand on a back or below a nose, searching for life.

But even in sleep, my power had hooked itself around my daughter's beating heart, a constant awareness, the steady response to my own heart's call.

Are you there?

I am here.

Are you there?

I am here.

And as she grew, I could feel her power do the same.

Mother, are you there?

I am here.

And so she rises slowly from slumber, awakening by her power's awareness of my body's presence.

"Mama," she breathes, still lingering in that other place.

"I am here," I answer, smoothing the tousled dark hair from her cheek.

"Where did you go, Mama?" she asks, blinking. And then I watch her memory come into her eyes. She shoots up as only a child can from slumber.

"Mama! Hariva! They've taken her! The guards came and took her even though I told them she hadn't really taken me. I went with her – I wanted to go with her! Oh! Mama, Suita said the most horrible things –"

I pull Maarja's small hand into my own, weaving my fingers between hers and bringing our joined hands to my lips. I push my adoration into her skin, closing my eyes over her innocence.

"– I told her I would scratch her eyes out for what she said, and I would have, but the guards made me come here, and Hiida came and said you had come back and you would tell them it was all wrong and to let Hariva go. And I waited all day but you never came!"

I wait, my lips still pressed into her knuckles, for her little anger to burn itself out, as I know it will. I think of myself at her age. I think of how my wrath had burned through the Wood, dead creatures falling in my footsteps. And yet, Maarja's instinct had been to scratch her enemy's eyes out like any common girl.

And then I release the thought. My daughter is not like me. She never will be. What's done is done.

"Where have you been?" she asks again, her little furrowed brow low over her soft brown eyes. I pull a long breath in through my nose.

"You asked me once if I was a good Waster," I say, stroking my thumb along the furrow in her brow. Then I drop my hand and look in her perfect soft brown eyes.

I am a Waster. We speak the truth.

"Hariva is dead, my love," I breathe, steeling myself against her ever widening gaze. "I killed her. And I would have you know why, but first, there are things I must tell you. Things I have kept from you. Things that I have kept from myself. You must listen now, and you must not ask questions. There is little time, and I have need of you."

And so I peel back the skin of my daughter's sheltered existence and show her all the gore below.

I slip Maarja back to sleep, knowing she will be unable to find her rest again on her own. She'd shaken and denied and asked a thousand questions, but in the end she'd folded herself into my arms and promised to obey.

I cross the landing to my chambers, don my traveling cloak, and tug.

He holds himself back from me, standing fixed in shadows. There is death between us now. Perhaps with enough time, we could bicker our way back into each other's arms, but that time does not belong to us. He knows it as well as I.

"Did you send word for me?" he asks warily.

"We are exposed," I say in way of an answer. He steps forward into the flickering candlelight, eyes narrowed.

"Who?"

326

"Hiida."

"*She* gave Hariva over to him," he reasons, realization dawning. I nod.

"A trap."

"We knew that already," he says, jaw stiffening.

"Listen to me," I command, pressing my meaning into my gaze. "Consider. How long has Hiida been with me? It has *always* been a trap. He has *always* known."

He stares back, jaw stiffening and black eyes narrowing as the enormity of that truth flickers in recalled memories behind his eyes.

"All of it," he breathes at last. I nod.

"We have no way of knowing what he has ordained, every moment, every touch. Every memory," I warn.

"For all those years," he says. I nod.

"Hariva's trial was meant to expose us before the whole court," I say. "He has the marriage contract now. There is nothing stopping him from replacing you as Heir except the expectations of the court."

"I will go to Rahuleid," he says, turning to cast his gaze out the darkened window. "He will give us his allegiance now –"

"No he will not," I say, closing my eyes over the words. "I have killed her. There is nothing you can say on my behalf that will convince him that I am not exactly as I appear to be. And he will not risk his son."

"He must know there will be nothing for his son to inherit," Kurat argues. "Tuskjas will see him stripped of the title soon enough."

"I know him, Kurat," I answer. "Inheritance means nothing now. The babe is all he has of her. He will live a poor man in a foreign land if it means he keeps his son. He will not fight."

"We have Saaremaa," he goes on, designing his great rebellion in vain. "Barbüra has long been at odds –"

"Because I Wasted her child."

"Revala –"

327

"Whose Kallas gave Aemilie over to the Norse," I say, growing angry with his obstinance. "We have no way of knowing if the entire invasion wasn't another ploy by Tuskjas to draw us out!"

"The Kallas of Ugandi has no love for the Slavs," he argues back, trying desperately to hold his vision together. "He was willing to stand with us before. He will hate this marriage –"

"And yet, I have just broken his thumb in the Hall to keep him from acting on such thoughts!"

"Is there no one you have not maimed?" he seethes through his teeth, turning from the window, fists clenched in the air between us. "Is there no one you have *not* made an enemy?"

I do not answer him, leveling him instead with a flat gaze. After a moment he turns away.

"You see now that there is only one way," I say softly into the darkness between us.

"No," he answers, shaking his head.

"You see now, and it must be me," I go on. "I cannot be redeemed."

"No!" he denies, but he does not turn. He does not give me his eyes.

"He seeks to replace you with Maarja," I continue despite his refusals. "You must make him. They must see you as an alternative, not a continuation."

"Stop this, Liama," he says, but there is no strength in it.

"Do it publicly, for all to see," I say, stepping towards his turned back.

"I have made enemies as well," he argues.

"That will be forgotten," I say, coming to stand at his back. "When we are gone, Aemilie will make them forget."

He shakes his head.

"And so you have planned it," he murmurs. "How long have you planned it?"

I slide my arms around him, pressing my face into the dip of his spine. I inhale him, as though I pull his very being from his lungs and into my own. As though I could shuck his greedy soul from his body, like a nut from its shell, and take it with me to that place.

"*In the days after Looklema departed the Sacred Wood to live with her lover in his realm,*" I whisper, feeling my own breath against my face. "*Her daughters ruled in unity and in justice. Yet, in time dissent rose among the Beings of Light, for humans are changeable, capricious as the water's surface, and susceptible to greed.*"

CHAPTER TWENTY-TWO
THE OOZING LESION

Health does not settle lightly over every breast.
Oft times restoration cannot heal the brittle chest.
Do not be surprised, my daughter,
once the Working's done,
And coming right behind it, anger burning like the sun.

WE PASS through the small village where I attended the weaver, Erga. I have a mind to stop and see to her progress, but Kurat insists we must not be recognized as we make our way to Tarbatu. I ask him again why we did not simply Walk to its gates. Why take the risk of traveling on foot?

He gives the same response – Tuskjas is not without power. Other ploys are in motion. The timing must be perfect. We must proceed with extreme caution.

But I am coming to know him now. My new husband does not trust me. Despite how his eyes flicker to mine in the darkness. Despite how the *air between us grows tight as we lay sleepless in our pallets beneath the canopy, just beyond arm's reach.*

Despite the desire growing between us. Or perhaps because of it.

There is a huddled figure at the end of the path. Kurat puts his hand up, slowing. I try to reign the beast below me in, but it continues slowly clopping forward until Kurat reaches out and snatches the reins himself. I press Maarja in her sling to my chest, covering her exposed head with my free hand.

Seeing us halt, the figure comes forward, pulling back the hood of her traveling cloak as she does so.

"Hiida?" I ask in surprise. The round woman dips a small bow, her fingers on her brow. When she raises her pink-cheeked face again, she does so with an open smile.

"Varju Tütar," she says fondly. "Oh, Looklema bless me, I've found ya!"

"Is Erga well?" I ask.

"Oh yes, m'lady," she smiles deeper, huffing a laugh. "If ya can call 'eavy with child 'well' then my sister is well 'nough."

"What wonderful tidings," I answer her with my own smile, imagining the weaver's joy. "Yet, why have you sought me out?"

Hiida breathes in deeply, straightening her wide, round shoulders and clasping her hands before her.

"I mean ta offer m'self ta yer service, m'lady," she says quickly. "I am well able – as ya know, I was lady's maid ta the wife of the steward a' Gratu 'til she breathed 'er spirit inta the sky las' autumn, poor woman. I am – oh," and then her thundering heartbeat catches up with her, and she loses her courage.

"Linda's pit," she curses crudely, then slams her hand over her mouth, her eyes going wide. "Oh, m'lady, fergive me. I swear, I'm really very demure when –"

But I have already begun to laugh, much to Kurat's annoyance.

"You can hardly expect me to think you demure," I say, smiling openly at her embarrassment. "But I have no doubt of your capability."

"An' da not doubt my loyalty, m'lady," she rushes on, needing to get the words in. "You'll no' find a servant more loyal than Hiida, 'specially after all ya've done fer Erga."

"I've no doubt of that either," I answer. "But, Hiida, why should you think I have need of a lady's maid?"

"Oh!" she says, surprised. She looks back and forth between Kurat and me for a moment, trying to decide how best to proceed.

"Well, are ya not – that's ta say, is this man no' – eh," she stammers. I feel Kurat cut his gaze at me impatiently. "Well, it's jus' tha' I've seen ya b'fore, m'lord," she says, dipping her chin and giving a little curtsy. "It's been nigh on five er six years, but I was there, servin' tha steward's wife when ya came ta Gratu ta meet with tha woodcutters' guild. An' then, well, I saw ya again, jus' a few weeks back when I went ta the well fer water. I set Erga's boy to follow ya, begging yer forgiveness, thinkin' it strange for Kotkas' grandson ta be wanderin' about so near the Waster's Wood. An' tha boy said ya went in and ne'er came out, an' I thought ta m'self, well, they've 'ad their way with 'im then, fer all 'is grandfather did ta 'em. But then this mornin' tha boy came runnin' – I'd no idea 'e was still watchin' fer ya – clamorin' on about how tha Waster 'ad come out with tha man who'd gone in."

"You ought to make a spy out of her," Kurat murmurs low between us. I ignore him.

"An' then I saw ya an', well, I though' yer purpose could only be – well, are ya no' goin', goin' ta Tarbatu, m'lady?"

"Tell her nothing," Kurat whispers. I cut my eyes to him, remembering how he'd only this morning called me terribly naive. I would give him no reason to do so again.

"This man and I are simply enjoying the day," I answer her cryptically.

"Oh," Hiida says, her mouth holding the shape of the word. She does not believe me, but she pulls her eyes from mine, casting about awkwardly for something more to say.

"And yet," I say, giving her a small smile. Kurat's eyes cut to me yet again, his jaw stiffening. "Should you ever hear that I am in such a position to have need of a lady's maid, I would have you present yourself for the post, wherever that may be."

"Oh!" she says again, her brows rising. "Yes, yes, o' course, m'lady. I will. I swear it. Thank ya, m'lady."

"Good," I nod. "Until such a time, you honor your sister with your devotion to her. And to her children."

Something flickers over her soft, open face. And then it is gone.

"Yes, m'lady. I'll honor my sister," she says with a dip of her chin.

"Good day, sister of Erga the Weaver," I say benevolently as Kurat pulls our horses into motion again.

"Goodday, Varju Tütar," she answers, keeping her eyes low.

The door opens quickly, Erga's husband seeing our cloaked forms and waving us inside. It shuts behind us, and my ears pop. I lower my hood, Hiida doing the same behind me. The man's eyes widen in shock at the sight of her.

She had not wanted to leave the fortress alongside me. She had insisted on wearing her hood down as we passed through the gates.

"Where – where's tha Heir?" the man before me stammers. "Ya promised tha Heir –"

"We have no need of him," I say loftily, moving past him, feeling the sharp spark of Hiida's surprise. I had told her Kurat would meet us here. "I know what ails the girl and how to reverse it."

"Ya do?" Erga's husband says nervously, his eyes shifting to a huddled form on the bed behind him.

"Yes, the Heir has taught me how to reverse the effects of his influence," I go on, striding for the little body.

"Oh – tha' – tha's wonderful," the man follows closely behind.

"M'lady," Hiida says, moving to the other side of the bed. "Per'aps we should 'ave tha child moved ta –"

"That won't be necessary," I say. "If it is as you have said, then I can see to her well enough here."

I sit gently on the edge of the bed, careful not to jostle the little thing. Where they have found her and what they have done to get her here, I do not know. She is no more than Maarja's age, slightly younger, I would think. They would have chosen her carefully to align with the story, knowing I could easily detect her age.

And yet, I suspect, that is where their care ended.

"It's –" the man stutters, panicked. "It's taken a strange turn, m'lady. Use ta be she'd jus' be sallow an' wan. Now she's, well it's on 'er skin, ya see."

I make a show of pulling the child's limp hand out from the heavy cloak that covers her from head to toe. I turn it so that the wrist faces upwards, noting the worn rope burns. And beneath them, the visible signs of what I had sensed the moment the door was opened to me.

Leprosy. No wonder the man has her so heavily cloaked in mid-summer. He would have been terrified of contracting the illness himself. How he got her through Tarbatu's gates is testament to the depth of Hiida's manipulations. The blistering sores on her bare feet tell of her long walk here, likely sweating and feverish beneath the cloak. I can imagine the man leading her by the rope from a safe distance, perhaps dragging her behind a cart while he rode in comfort. And yet, the putrid smell of her rotting skin overcomes even the tangy scent of her sweat.

They had not expected me to get close enough to observe her. They had not expected me to make it through the gates of the fortress. If Kurat and I emerged together from its doors, they would have descended upon us. And if we had managed to travel apart and arrive at the inn, as soon as we stepped into one another's presence, it would have been over.

But the Heir is otherwise engaged. And the jostling, nervous guards posing as weary travelers in the rooms around us have suddenly fallen asleep.

That man at the inn is not what he claims.

I drop the man who calls himself Erga's husband, slamming him into unconsciousness before his head even bounces against the wooden floor. His body falls with an ungraceful slump. Hiida yelps in surprise, jumping back.

I pull the hood back from the girl's blotched face. The dark brown hair, once thick and long, has sloughed off of most of her scalp. I graze my fingertip over the worst of the wounds along what is left of her hairline. I do not have to touch her to begin Wasting the disease, but I want her to remember, however distantly, that someone touched her without fear. Someone touched her with compassion, blinking tears from their eyes.

"How is your sister, Hiida?" I ask gently, keeping my focus on the Working.

"My – m'lady?" Hiida stalls. She is still hoping, against all odds, that her master's men will come barreling through the door to save her.

"Your sister," I repeat. "Last we spoke of her, you said she was with child. How is she now?"

"I've no sister, m'lady," she denies, but she fails to veil the hardness in her voice.

"I suspect that that is true enough," I say, touching another of the pus-filled wounds on the little girl's neck. A thin lock of hair is plastered to her skin with dried gore. I pry it gently away, and blistered skin comes with it.

"I did not lie," I continue on in my mild tone. "The Heir *did* show me how to undo his influence, little use it will be to this child."

Hiida does not answer.

"How strange the memory, when it first returned to me," I say, pressing my fingertips to another of the lesions. "To remember how you offered yourself to my service all those years ago. To honor your sister, and all I had done for her. And so Erga is dead, in childbirth, I would assume," I continue in my mild tone. "And I am to blame, having made the way for her to become pregnant again."

Hiida is silent. I pull my gaze up from the girl, the sores on her cheek and neck beginning to harden into a yellow crust, and draw my gaze to Hiida slowly.

She is half terror, half rage. Her eyes glistening in fear. Her pink cheeks mottled.

"No, not childbirth," I say, studying her. "I suppose she never made it that far."

Hiida sneers, her silence finally breaking after ten long years.

"She wouldna let us call fer tha midwife three doors down," she hisses. "She insisted we call on you."

"Ah," I nod. "And I did not come."

"Yer bitch of a mother came at last," she spits.

"And told you a truth you did not want to hear," I finished for her.

"We did like they did in Husandi," she jeers, the smallest satisfaction in her crinkled eyes. "We buried 'er an' tha babe in tha road from tha Wood."

"But you couldn't kill the Wasters, could you?" I ask, titling my head. "You tried and failed, no doubt thinking you could catch them by surprise with that power of yours. But you never found them, did you? They had gone. And so you came instead to kill me."

But Hiida is no fool. She admits nothing.

"Kurat told me that day I should make a spy of you," I say. "Were you already in Tuskjas' hand, or did that come after, when you came to me again?"

Still she holds her tongue.

"No," I say, shaking my head. "No, neither is true. I denied you the most direct path and so you sought another way. You came here. You came to him. And you told him we were coming. You sealed the shepherd's hut so we would not hear his approach, so I could not sense him until he held Maarja in his arms. You made us believe you were sealing the room every time Kurat came to me. You told Tuskjas of my meetings with Vappers. You contrived the story of Erga's husband because you knew the guilt I carried on your sister's behalf, thinking Kurat had warped her mind. Yet, it was not enough to satisfy your vengeance. You knew I would seek to make it right, and damn myself in the doing. And then you gave Hariva over to Tuskjas."

I *tsk* at her, shaking my head sadly.

"So many traps, Hiida. And every one of them failed."

I gesture to the body on the floor.

"Who is this man? Is he your brother-in-law in truth?" I ask.

She has grown not only silent but still as I speak, a rat caught in my tightening coils.

"And how did you convince Kurat to remove you from my memory?" I ask at last, rising from the bed to face her across it. "Or did he do that on his own? Sweeping everything from the Wood, from our journey here, away?"

I stare at her, wrapping my power around her throat, squeezing gently.

"But you will not tell me any of these things," I answer for her. "You did not tell me all the long years that I lamented the loss of my memories. You were there for every moment. You possessed them all. Yet, you gave nothing away when I needed them most."

I come around the end of the bed slowly, letting the heels of my boots fall heavy on the wooden floor.

"But I do not need them now. Because Kurat has shown me how to undo it all. And would you like to know – or have you already guessed?"

Her face is beginning to bloom a dull purple at its edges, her eyes criss-crossed in red rivers. She brings her fingers up to her throat, tearing at something she cannot touch. I stand before her, gazing into her once-beloved face, drinking in her terror. She tries to kick, but I step aside. She tries to claw, but I slap her hand away before it can reach my face.

"There will be no final vengeance, sister of Erga the Weaver," I breathe into her face. A croaking gurgle comes from her constricted throat. Her pursed lips moving over empty air.

I shake my head at her slowly.

"How disappointed your sister would be in you. She, buried in the road to be trodden on forevermore. And ten years of attempted vengeance spent in vain," I whisper softly, tightening my hold on her neck until only the smallest gap remains. She rakes thick fingers over her throat, leaving angry furroughs in the pale skin from her own fingernails.

"And yet, vengeance is not so fleeting," I whisper. "Not for me."

And then I raise my fingers, the crusting paste of leprosy spread over their ends, and I tug her chin down, opening her mouth, and force her to wrap her swollen lips around my fingertips.

"Touch," I whisper, smiling. "It's as simple as a touch."

What little recognition is left in her red eyes swells.

"Don't worry, Hiida," I croon with a soft grin. "I have use of you yet."

And then she slumps to the floor.

CHAPTER TWENTY-THREE
THE WITHERED FACE

Draw the Shroud [inhale]
Lift the veil [hold]
She is with you in the pale [exhale].

Liama's child [inhale]
From her womb [hold]
Weaving power on her loom [exhale].

"*BLESSED CHILD*," Vappers breathes, his soft, gnarled hands holding my own in his gentle but firm grip. "Looklema is not gone from you. You know that She is not."

"But what if She is?" I cry. "What if all I have done – all he has forced from my hand –"

"You think She does not know?" he interrupts gently. "You are Her daughter. You are Her legacy. If the others are gone as you say they are, *then you are all that is left of Her line. You think She would abandon you for sins not your own? Would you turn your back on your own daughter?"*

"But they are my own," the condemnation spills from my soul. From all the shame at the center of me.

"Surely they are not, Varju Tütar," he squeezes my hands, warmth flowing through his touch.

"You do not know," I weep. "You do not know all I have done."

She is a slight thing, hardly more than bones. I tuck her into my arms, the cloak pulled tightly around her once more, and then I descend the stairs into the tavern at the front of Acker's Inn with a limp child in my embrace.

They stare. They stare from rough stools and chairs. And then when I pass through the front doors onto the street, they stare through the yellowed windows at my back. Only this morning I rode these streets, bloodied and battle-weary but victorious. And then they heard the rumors. The Kallas of Vaiga's wife wrenched apart by the Chieftainess on the Hall floor. And now I trudge up the hill with a body in my arms, sweating even under her slight weight. But I force my chin up, my eyes to the top of the hill, and I do not stop.

None of it will matter, soon enough.

It takes some time for the door to open at my knock. Vappers' aged eyes widen when he makes me out in the darkness before the door.

"My Chieftainess," he breathes. "What are you doing here?"

"I require your assistance," I say, trying to gain control of my breath.

Vappers looks around, then leans back into the House, searching behind the door.

"My lady, not now," he says. "I cannot – you mustn't – please –"

"You called me here. And I stand at your door with a half-dead child in my arms, which you well know. And still, you seek to uphold this farce?" I answer, stepping towards him and forcing him back.

"Farce, my Chieftainess?" he asks. So convincing. Incredible, really. For a moment I only look at him, marveling at the detail of his aged face.

"Whatever your designs here, they are done," I command. "I have greater need of you now."

"Forgive me, my lady, but I cannot abandon my master," he argues, bowing his head.

"This is ridiculous," I hiss, stepping forward again. But this time, he does not yield.

I am a child. I am nothing but a child as she takes my legs out from under me, dropping my weight to the stones even as she slips the girl from my arms and into her own.

"You have always been reckless," she says, her voice no different than it had been a moment ago, and yet, now I hear her in it as I did not before. "And a fine mess of Looklema's House you've made in all this."

I harden my jaw against her criticisms. I came to her. I will have to abide her scathing disappointment to gain her assistance. Or perhaps she is not disappointed. She made it clear she hadn't expected me to succeed.

So I summon all my resentment into my throat and look up into my mother's Wasted face.

"I have done what I can with what I was given," I say. She shakes her head, unimpressed with my defense.

"You have attempted to treat with greed," she scoffs. "And look what it has gained you." And then she turns her back to me, carrying the girl into the house.

I drag myself up and follow warily. Rahuleid is not here. I would not have sought entry if he were. Nor is Hariva's babe. Likely halfway to

Vaiga now. I wonder how my mother convinced him to let her stay behind, and why.

Rahuleid will not know, of course. She would never have revealed herself to him. But I understand now why she insisted on keeping separate quarters from her master.

"You summoned me," I say tightly, breathing out the tightness in my chest. "In the Hall. I felt your tug. It cannot have been only to provide your scathing opinion of my performance as Chieftainess."

"You are not Chieftainess," she answers, dismissing me with a shake of her head. We come into the wide receiving room, and she lays the girl gently on the couch there, peeling back the cloak.

"Leprosy," she breathes. "There was a terrible outbreak in northern Jaarva a year ago. The people begged Barbüra to send for you, but the bitch wouldn't do it. I'm surprised this child has lived as long as she has."

"I've already begun the Working, but it will need time," I explain. My mother nods.

"I'll take her with me when I join Rahuleid. It will be easy enough to claim I picked her up from some dead niece on the journey."

"How is the babe?" I ask.

"You did your work well," she answers, but even in praise there is judgement in her voice. "He's hale, considering."

"Where have they gone?" I ask. She turns from her crouch over the child, sitting down on the end of the couch.

"I'm not telling you that," she says, meeting my gaze and pursing her lips. She must have released her power as we've spoken. Already, I can sense her body opening and lengthening. The lines around her mouth and eyes have begun to smooth.

"What is your design, Liama?" my mother asks me. "Surely you have one, to have endured all of this, and forced the rest of us to endure it as well."

"I loved her too," I bite, unsurprised that my mother grew to care for her master's wife. Hariva and her laughter. Hariva and her cunning. Hariva and her coy, crude honesty.

When my mother looks at me, I can see her own eyes taking shape, the sloughing off of her disguise.

"Yes," she answers softly. "Unwise, but perhaps unavoidable."

"She told me to save the child," I murmur.

"Yes," she murmurs back. "What is your design, Liama?"

I pull a long breath in through my nose.

"The door in the Glen," I say. "He cannot be Wasted. He is truly powerless."

"*Beware the powerless man*," she intones. I nod.

"And what of Kurat – you have made known your intentions?"

"To the extent that he must know them to complete his task," I answer.

"To save the Waster Queen," my mother supplies.

"In a manner of speaking," I hedge. She lowers her brows over keen eyes, reading me as she has a thousand times in the lives we've lived before.

"Ah," she says at last, finding the truth. "The future queen."

She purses her lips. The only sign that she has understood my intent.

"And when will you do this?" she asks.

"We will leave for Ugandi in two days' time to finalize the marriage contract between Maarja and the Slavic Prince," I say. She looks up at me, narrowing her eyes.

"East?" she says. "That is not the direction of the Glen."

I shake my head.

"Then it is your grandmother's version of the tale you intend," she asks. I nod. Her jaw stiffens.

343

"Why not kill him outright? Why not drive a spear through his heart?"

"Why did the Twin Queens not simply kill Odypoeg when he came to treat with them?" I ask in return.

"I had thought you might outgrow your tendency to put too much in stories, Liama," she dismisses. "Even now you risk your very spirit on a tale hundreds of years old."

"I will not send his spirit into the sky," I answer simply.

"Revenge, then? You have always asked too much," she answers, shaking her head. "Kill the man and let it be done."

I give her no answer. I will not sway her. She will not sway me.

"It is not as we hoped," I murmur after some time. "I am not Looklema's Heir. I will not reign in her name. But another will. And I must clear the path for her."

My mother studies me before she speaks.

"I know what your grandmother believed, but I would not disregard the power of the blood, to be sure."

I nod. "I am accounting for it."

She nods in return.

"You will guide her," I command, letting some of the Chieftainess, which I am not and always have been, come into my voice. "You will train Maarja when I am gone. There is so much she has not yet learned. There is so much I do not remember."

I watch the recollection color my mother's eyes.

Fear not, Liama, she had said, my grandmother bobbing in affirmation behind her. *For when you teach your daughter, you will not be alone. What your mind will not hold mine will. And what my mind cannot recall yours will.*

She had promised once.

But now she denies me.

"Maarja is not the chosen of Looklema, Liama," she says softly. Sadly. "You have known this. She has been too long from the Wood."

"Then it is for nothing?" I whisper. My mother shakes her head, her Waster's honesty true to the last.

"But it does not change what you will do for her," she says.

"No," I breathe. "It does not."

After a time, I raise my head again.

"And what of my husband? What of Kurat? Has Looklema chosen him?"

My mother tilts her head, studying me.

"Your grandmother believed so. Otherwise She would never have consented to hand you over to him. But I have always been unsure. I suppose She has chosen him, in Her way. But that does not change what you will do to him."

We share our mirrored gazes. So alike. So known.

Too known.

"No," I breathe. "It does not."

"The Shadow Queen chose many descendents," my mother goes on. "She passed her blood to her children, and they to theirs, and they to theirs. You have seen it. There are as many Shade Walkers in Saaremaa as there are grains of sand on its shores. But the Wasting Queen chose differently from her sister. She chose to pass her power through only one. One daughter. One line. Pure. Powerful. And terribly fragile. Any number of things could have destroyed it at any time. Any number of things still can."

"Why do you tell me this?"

"To relieve you of the burden every Waster has placed on herself since the first," she says, lowering her brows, an uncharacteristic softness seeping into her gaze, something of the benevolent old man she had worn before.

"Perhaps her line ends with Maarja. Perhaps she always intended it to be so. Perhaps she meant it to end a hundred years ago. They did not give us their names, Liama. I do not think they wanted to be preserved forever, unchanging and unending."

"It did not end with *you*. It did not end with *me*. Maarja is not your daughter," I argue. "It is not *your* daughter's ruin that you speak of."

"Is it not?" she asks, eyes narrowing. I blink my eyes away.

"Do not forget," she continues after a moment. "*All* Wasting is ruin."

"Where is my grandmother?" I ask. Vappers' face has all but disappeared. The woman who raised me, who gave me all the stiffness in my spine, looks back at me, her eyes flickering over my features. Remembering.

"Waiting for you," she breathes at last. Her eyes hold my own fiercely. Longingly. I rest in their embrace, letting it fill me. So many nights she had held her hands out to mine, wrinkled and sun-stained, and I had taken them, thinking them someone else's, and she had Wasted my fear and anxiety and desperation and helplessness. And she had done it from the body of an old, benign man, knowing I never would have accepted it from her.

My mother is faithful. Whatever else she is, this is what I will carry with me into the cold.

In the distance, I sense a rising pulse of panic. A muffled shout carries in from the street.

My mother tilts her ear towards it, brows low. And then she looks back to me with narrowed eyes.

"And so it begins," she murmurs.

I pull myself away and rise.

"You will sense the severity of her treatment when you observe her fully," I say, nodding once more to the wretched child. "I have left one of her abusers for you in the high room at Acker's Inn. The other I intend to make use of. If it is within your power, find the rest."

My mother stands, now eye-to-eye with my height. A chill prickles my skin. I have a sense that I am looking at myself as Vidar's men saw me, their doom reflecting back to them in my eyes.

"I will do it," she says, low and damning. I trace her sharp, unmerciful features once more with my eyes. And then I turn away.

"Liama," she calls when I have nearly crossed the threshold. I halt, not turning back, the latch in my hand. "I know that you worried after your naming," she says from the other room. "You did not want to be like the Shadow Spirit, all womb and beauty and grace."

I had never known she knew. I had never known she was noticing.

"Do not forget that there are tales beneath tales, and within them and without," my mother goes on. "Whatever they say of her, she was made of a darkness deeper than the womb itself. No light could fade her."

"She was a void," I say caustically.

"No, *Tütar,Varju*" she answers in Vappers' gentle voice. And though I long to turn to it, I do not.

"She is the stillness. The well. The vast heart of power. She wraps herself around us all."

Now I turn, brows low. Vappers stands before me, hunched and aching with age, devotion on his wrinkled face.

"She is the Shroud, Liama," he says quietly. "We named you for the Shroud."

I nod, breathing deeply, and then I open the door to leave her forevermore.

CHAPTER TWENTY-FOUR
THE WHISTLING THROAT

Brittle the bone. Swollen the flesh.
Bright the blood that flows from the neck.
Wasting and Healing are oft times the same.
Starve the disease. Sever the vein.

FIERCE YELLS split the night.

The streets had been nearly empty when I'd passed from Acker's to Rahuleid's House, save for watching eyes from lighted windows. Now the call has gone out. People trickle into the street in their night clothes, flickering lamps held above them, casting about for the source of the rising din. I raise my hood, intending to slip silently into the mingling crowd.

I turn my face up the hill to the fortress. In the darkness, figures are spilling through the gates, the flash of steel and hard clap of boots growing closer.

And then the word, carried ahead of Tuskjas' descending guard, reaches us.

"The Chieftain is wounded!"

"The Heir! It was the Heir!"

"He tried to kill him! He came from Shadow!"

"Shade Walker! Like his bitch of a mother!"

And then the guards are upon us. They push the mingling bodies back against the houses, ripping off hoods and raising lanterns to blinking, startled faces. Several of them press into the houses, pushing the half-asleep owners to the side. A group of three break off from the mass, stepping towards the Kallas' house. I root myself firmly on the threshold, throwing back my hood.

"Stand aside!" one barks, not bothering to look into my face.

"You will not search this house," I answer firmly, wrapping his heart around my wrist.

He ignores me, making to shove past me.

I drop him.

His companions startle, looking up with wide eyes even as their hands go to the hilts of their blades.

"Chieftainess!" one of them barks in surprise, throwing an outstretched arm against the chest of his fellow, who is making to advance.

"What has happened?" I demand, giving him no time to question my presence here.

"The Heir, m'lady, 'e made to murder the Chieftain," he answers quickly.

"How?"

"In the Hall, at the feast."

"They're saying 'e's a Shade Walker, m'lady!" his fellow pipes up. "They're saying 'e stepped right out o' the shadows behind the Chieftain's chair and put a blade to 'is throat."

"What more?" I demand. "What stopped him?"

"I dunnow, m'lady," the first fellow says. "We weren't there. But the Chieftain 'as a ghastly wound, they're saying. They're lookin' for you everywhere."

Clever Tuskjas. Even with an open throat he has still taken care to expose my absence.

"You waste your time searching for the Heir," I say, redirecting. "If he is truly a Shade Walker, he'll be halfway to Saaremaa in a single breath."

"Ack, didna just say the same," the second fellow grumbles to his companion. The other man levels a furious glare at him.

"I'm sure you're right, m'lady," the other man says, not taking his eye from his fellow. "But we've our orders all the same." And then he turns an apologetic look forward. "If you'll, well – that is, can we have our man back? We're to search the whole town. We can't spare a single one."

"He's only asleep. Rouse him and carry on. But this house is secure. You will not search for it."

For the first time the guards look past me, noting whose house they stand before. The lead man nods. He is no fool.

"Aye, my lady," he says, kneeling to shake his slumbering companion. "We'll get 'im up and be on at the next."

"Looklema bless you this night," I say, touching my fingers to my forehead. The two men do the same, dipping their chins.

I step around them, lingering only long enough to ensure they follow my orders. And then I turn my face to the dark shape of the fortress above me. I must get to Maarja.

I am passing the last of the fine houses before the gate, my thighs burning with the speed of my climb, when his being flickers into the world beside me.

I spin, incredulity already barreling up my throat, when his fingers twist around my wrist and I am dragged into darkness.

I come out with a vice around my chest.

"Mama!" Maarja yelps, throwing herself back against the wall of her chambers. I shove Kurat's hold aside, rushing forward to shush her.

"Hush!" I croak, breathless, kneeling before her. "All is well. All is well."

She accepts my hands on her shoulders, but her eyes are as wide as river rocks, staring behind me. I turn, rising, keeping my open palm on Maarja's chest to steady her.

"You cannot linger!" I hissed at my husband. "You must go!"

"They've already come here, looking for you," he whispers, open palms held defensively before him. "Haven't they, Maarja?"

I look down at her. After a moment more of staring at Kurat, she turns her terrified eyes on me and nods.

"They know you are a Walker now," I whisper harshly. "They will come again. They will come all night."

"And I will be gone in a breath," he answers, stepping towards me. "But, Liama, when I opened him –"

For a moment, he struggles for words, his face open and vulnerable, disbelieving.

I understand what he has not said. What he cannot comprehend.

The final piece comes into place.

"I know," I say, giving him the truth in my eyes. He locks onto it, his black gaze begging me to make meaning of what he has seen.

"I know," I repeat. "Now go."

But he does not. He stares and stares and stares, drinking me in.

"Mama," Maarja murmurs, and I sense it too.

"They are coming," I warned him. He presses his lips together, turning slowly towards the door.

"What are you doing?" I hiss, stepping towards him. But then Maarja's door flies open, the first guard raising his head, meeting Kurat's eyes.

I brace myself, pushing back against Maarja, but the violence never comes.

The man and his companion behind him stand idle on the threshold, their eyes locked on Kurat's face. There is nothing but silence for several breaths.

"Tell me," Kurat orders after a moment.

"We saw tha Chieftainess pass in through tha gate," the man says flatly. "She ran through. She was screamin' that she 'ad ta get ta tha Chieftain."

Kurat nods. I watch his back expand as he pulls in a breath. Then he tilts his chin over his shoulder.

"I love you, Snake Wife."

And then he is gone.

The figure stands over me in the darkness. The fear rolls from her in spikes, glinting as brightly as her upraised blade in the moonlight. She had not expected me here. She has realized she was misinformed.

But she swallows the hesitation. Her mistress has ordained her. She will not turn away now.

I open my eyes.

Our gazes embrace.

And then I turn from her, giving her my back.

She breathes in. Three quick breaths booming red across her lungs. And then she tenses, the acid flooding into the muscles of her shoulders, her upper back.

With a final, bracing inhale, she slams the blade downwards, her own anguished cry vibrating in her ears.

I allow the tip of the blade to knick my husband's thick chest, and then I drop her, breaking her arms as she falls under paralyzed legs.

Tuskjas rises like a startled wolf, bellowing even before his eyes are fully opened. He leaps from the bed, grabbing the lame woman by the head and snapping her neck in one powerful twist of his arms.

He does not need to know who sent her.

Guards barrel into the space, candles lighting and voices filling my husband's chamber. But the big, heaving man turns his enraged eyes to me, livid with betrayal. A single trickle of thick foreign blood winds its way down his hairy, muscled belly. From somewhere I hear the sound of faint whistling, like a window cracked open in the wind.

I know that Tuskjas will not act against her now. She is his only Heir. And yet, I still cannot bring myself to leave her exposed and alone.

But all my allies are gone.

I put her in my chambers, tucking her quickly into my bed where I know she will be enfolded in all that my body has left behind. I put the two guards at the door with oaths of what I will do to them if they let a single soul pass through it, the Chieftain included.

They startle at that, looking between each other.

"He will not be sound of mind," I tell them. "He will look for enemies in every corner. If you have any loyalty to this House, to this line, you will not allow him to lift a finger against the only Heir remaining to us."

Another look passes between them, and I do not think that they will agree.

But then one of them turns back to me, dropping his gaze.

"I was there tha night tha 'ssassin came, m'lady," he murmurs. "I –, I–," he swallows, near to choking. "I was one of 'em what held yer daughter down."

Then he sucks in a wild breath, looking back up with a wet glisten in his miserable eyes.

"I'll never forgive m'self," he breathes over a sob. "Never. I praise the Goddess every time I see Lady Maarja, thank Her for sendin' the Heir to stop him, when I didna. I've babes of my own now, an'–" He cuts himself off, tears now streaming from his wretched eyes. He swallows again.

"I'll no' make the same mistake twice, Chieftainess," he breathes his oath to me, looking down at his boots. "He'll no' lay a hand on her, as long as I can still hold a spear."

I close my eyes over the shared sorrow of that night. And when I can speak again, I bless him.

"Looklema will not let you fall," I murmur. He nods, never looking back up at me. I turn to the other guard, who nods as well, putting two fingers to his brow, then bringing them down to his lips.

Oh, Tuskjas. How your grip is unfurling.

And then I descend.

I pass Kurat's chambers, the door thrown open, contents spilling across the shadowed floor.

When I reach the lowest landing, there are four guards at the Chieftain's door.

"Let me pass," I command. They do not step aside, but the man before the door reaches back, knocking firmly against the wood. After a breath, it cracks open.

"The Chieftainess," the guard murmurs. Another muffled voice passes the information on.

"The bitch is here?" Tuskjas thunders from within. "Get her in here!"

And now the guards stand aside, touching their fingers to their brows as I pass.

I pass through the threshold with a spine of carven rock, drawing the Shroud. The moment it passes over my head, I sense the clotted blood forming over the slice in the side of his thick neck. It is a minor wound, mostly muscle, as it was intended to be. Still, beneath it I sense the whisper, like a cool breath in the deepest part of a cave.

A healer has paused in her work of wrapping the wound. Tuskjas hunches below her, his blood drying on the fine embroidery of the chair that has always been too small for his size. His mother's chair, he'd told me once, his way of reminding me that I had nothing of my mother's.

"And so you come, wife, at last," he sneers when I stand before him. "Done roaming the streets then?"

I ignore him, nodding for the healer to continue her work. She does so in a hurry, eager to be gone from what her instincts tell her is coming.

We exchange no more words until the door is closed behind her.

"Where is he?" Tuskjas growls, his too-small eyes glittering.

"Saaremaa," I answer simply.

"I will burn it to the ground," he swears.

"You've already tried that," I answer, brows high. "Haven't you?"

He glowers at me, his disgust shriveling his thick-lipped mouth.

"Vidar told me he'd first heard the tale of Spider Silk from the Kallas of Revala," I begin. "And yet, the Norsemen have been gone from Revala for nearly a decade, far before the girl's power came to be known. They are bitter enemies now. I doubt the Kallas would be passing on gossip. Unless, of course, she was made to do so. You told the spy to damn her by whatever means necessary, truth or untruth. I suppose he did so, and you gave her a means to save herself. Betray Saaremaa. Draw us out."

"Do not pretend to be adept at these things, Liama," Tuskjas snarls.

"If you did not want that outcome, you should not have kept me trapped behind your throne, Tuskjas," I answered calmly. "Kurat came to you. You denied him aid. He came to me, as you knew he would. You could have let us go, you could have sent us yourself. But we would have gone wary. We would have suspected your trap."

His eyes glimmer with malice.

"Ah," I say, raising my brows. "I see I have surprised you, husband. Your father knew, of course. He tried to wield the Wasters himself. Perhaps you drank the vitriol he spilled when we denied him. Perhaps you did not believe in the warrior women of old. You saw me, cowled and obedient, and you did not believe me. You thought I would fail."

And then I smile at him with all my teeth.

"Bathed in blood. Wedded in violence. As lusty as a bitch in heat."

"You have done nothing but mark yourself out for death," he spits, rising to his height over me.

"An empty threat," I answer, shrugging, "considering how many times you have attempted to arrange it. How many traps you have laid, husband. You and your little spy. You meant to expose me through Hariva. You meant to expose me through the Weaver's child. Is that not also the purpose of this marriage with the Slavs? You think I will finally stand against you, openly for all to see. You think I will give you the blade to strike me down and rid yourself of Wasters forever?"

"I need no blade," he hisses, thrusting down into my face. "I can wring your neck with my bare hands, and there is nothing you can do to stop me."

"But you cannot," I whisper into his gritted teeth. "You have miscalculated, Tuskjas."

He roars, his massive hands wrapping around my throat.

What cannot be done with power can be done with fear.

It had never occurred to me that it could be done before I'd recognized my mother's power beneath Vappers' facade. She had not simply aged herself, as I had when I became the crone, she had wasted her features, warping them through a delicate working of decay. Thickening the brow, swelling the nose. Pushing water into the delicate nodes beneath the eyes, at the corners of the mouth.

I gaze at him as he gazes at me, seeing the exact moment, between one breath and another, that his growing alarm breaks through his rage. His fingers twitch around my throat, tightening. I cannot breathe, but I do not stop.

I Waste and Waste and Waste, lips swollen, chin weak, eyes too small, too close together, until Tuskjas, powerless son of Kotkas, Chieftain of House Est, holds his own face between his hands.

He knows it is an illusion, but he cannot escape his own body.

Finally, blackness swimming at the edges of my vision, I pour my power into the delicate chords of my throat, thickening them, dropping my voice to the depth of its own.

And with my final breath, I whisper my damnation.

"Powerless."

He flings me away from him. I fly backward onto the bed, heaving in gulping gasps of sweet air through a tattered throat. I flush it with blood so quickly my fingertips go numb, heaving myself up on shaking arms to face the wounded animal prowling in the corner of my vision.

He is dragging himself back together by sheer force of will, spitting and swearing but coming no closer to me.

"I will kill you!" he roars across the room, his rage flooding his eyes once again. "I will whore your pathetic whelp to that prince and make the boy my Heir, and then I will kill you in front of her! And then when she spawns her own brat, I'll kill her too and finish what my father started. The Wasters end with me! Do you hear me, Liama? You end with me!"

357

I stagger to standing, drawing myself up against the pummeling force of his fear, and look him in the eyes.

"Yes, Tuskjas," I croak through a burning throat, the Waster's honesty like honey on the tongue.

"I end with you."

CHAPTER TWENTY-FIVE
THE SEVERED RIGHT HAND

To touch what cannot be touched.
To say what cannot be said.
A Waster is free from the fear of rot.
A Waster is free from the fear of the dead.

WE ARE NOT permitted to ride. Instead, Maarja and I are confined to the carriage, a bow-laden man atop it, another beside the driver, and still another pair of soldiers on the back. Mounted men surround us on all sides. Our party is massive, clobbering through the dense forests and destroying even the driest of summer roads. Tuskjas had sent not a single man to pursue Kurat into Saaremaa, little good it would do. He had kept them all by his side.

The Chieftain is terrified, riding atop his great beast of a horse at the front of the column. His fear drifts through the company, infecting the men who ride with wary, alert bodies, hearts thumping, stress pooling in their bellies, searching every shadow.

I am no less a threat. He knows I intend to kill him. I suspect he has some inclination from Hiida as to how, but knowledge of the Glen gives him very little upon which to speculate. Little good it will do him. We are nowhere near the Sacred Forest, and yet, he cannot dismiss it from his mind.

And so I let him stew in all his anxious uncertainty, savoring the tang of his fear.

Maarja is not so young now as to be immune to the damp, dark weight of all the tension in our party. She dozes fitfully, eats little, and fidgets during my stories. She does not want to hear about the Twin Queens. She does not want to hear about the Beings of Darkness and the Beings of Light. Not now.

I have promised her, I have sworn to her, that I will never allow her to be sold in marriage to the Slavic Prince. That I will never allow our line to end with her. She believes my oaths. But she is not so young now as to be immune from doubts about her mother's ability to protect her. I have brought it on both of us, this mistrust, being as honest as I have been with her as of late.

I find that I can be honest, knowing she will not remember.

I find that I can ask of her what I have asked of her, knowing she will not remember.

She herself can hardly comprehend it, and that is why I know it will be done. Because she cannot yet understand the meaning of what her hands will do. She only knows that on the other side, we are free.

We left Tarbatu three days ago. We would have been across Ugandi in less than two on horseback, but Tuskjas' caution with the carriage and the size of the company has stalled our arrival, leaving us hour after hour in the thick, moist dimness of Ugandi's midsouthern pine forests. I should think it a perfect place for an ambush by a man who slips from

Shadow, but I know such a thing will never come, even if Tuskjas does not.

Not here. Not yet. It is mine to take.

But I know why Tuskjas lingers. He dares me. Even in his terror, he dares me to call my lover, to try and slip Tuskjas away to the Glen. He desires it done. He desires the trap sprung. Likely he has men in every glen and glade between Tarbatu and the Ugandi border, lying in wait.

He is like the Mother Snake, tempting me. Allowing himself to be captured, only to outmaneuver at the last moment.

I pay him no mind. I put myself and my daughter to sleep to wile away the long hours. I am at my leisure, unhurried and unaffected, and it is driving him mad.

We halt one final time at the border of the forest, the bald-topped mountains rising before us, the glittering Lake Peipus in the distance on our left. Through the gap before us is the Slavic Kingdom and Maarja's intended.

"Is there anything you require, my Chieftainess?" A guard asks from beyond the carriage's open window. I look down at him, yawning.

"Nothing," I answered. "Why do we tarry?"

"A short break for the men on foot, my lady," he answers.

"Tell my husband not to hold for long," I say lazily, leaning back into repose. "I am eager to see the mountains."

I know my words will be carried on to the Chieftain. That an eagerness on my part will be seen as a potential sign of my intentions. And so I extend Tuskjas' terror a little farther.

But though I appear to be at ease, my mother lingers on my mind.

I can see now that the delicacy of her subterfuge – what concealed the truth of her identity most effectively – had nothing to do with power.

It was her kindness.

There had been no time to ask her about her own designs – why she had left the Wood and taken the form of the old man in the den of our enemies. And I cannot recall when first I saw her, when first I noticed Rahuleid's aging manservant, to give me some inclination of *when* she came. And now I am left with no means of answering the question which harangues me the whole journey long.

Had she come for me – to aid me?

Or had she come to confirm what she already knew – that I would fail?

I reconsider everything I ever confessed to her in Vappers' form. I drudge up every remembered reassurance she gave me in his voice.

You are Her daughter. You are Her legacy. If the others are gone as you say they are, then you are all that is left of Her line. Would you turn your back on your own daughter? You think Looklema would abandon you for sins not your own?

We, all of us in the Wasting Queen's line, have had to answer the question of our purpose, the same one I finally answered for myself over Hariva's bloody womb.

Am I Looklema's Daughter, charged with her legacy?

Or am I the mother of my daughter, charged with her flourishing?

The subtle difference I can now see – it is the difference between my grandmother, who chose to be a mother, and my mother, who had always been Looklema's Daughter.

But perhaps my mother had found a way, through an old man's hands, to be for me what she could not be as a Waster in the Sacred Wood.

Or perhaps she had simply known, from withholding it herself, that compassion would tempt me the most.

The grandeur the Slavic King has gathered to complete a contract on the border makes me wonder what manner of opulence would be curated for a wedding. Amidst the sea of pale canvas tents in his encampment are four brilliantly-dyed crimson structures, the largest of which our company is directed to stop before. Despite her dread, I suspect notions of chivalric romance have not been entirely lost on my daughter, for she cranes her neck to peer out at the little group of bodies before it. It brings to mind Hariva's "more exploratory expressions of desire," and I am tempted to laugh, bitter though it might be.

Despite assuming the throne only three years ago, Premsyl, King of the Slavs, is a well-aged, well-fed man whose heart is laboring under his gluttony. I suspect being the son of a man who was the son of a warrior has left him far more comfortable in his wealth than his predecessors. His hook-nosed wife is more circumspect in both shape and appearance, looking on with half-lidden eyes and a faint look of disgust lingering about her mouth.

The boy, Matej, is not vile, nor is he handsome. He is, in fact, unremarkable and surprisingly young. I had not gleaned his exact age from Tuskjas, but he cannot be older than Maarja. A handful of years younger, based on the mass still left in his bones, waiting to expand. The Queen herself is not so young, and I wonder what manner of journey she has had in bringing him safely into this world at her advanced age.

He stands in his mother's shadow like a willow, drifting subtly in a non-existent wind towards a younger woman further back – his nurse, I suspect – who stands in a long formal line of servants to the left.

Tuskjas alights from his horse, the strain in his right knee bothering him from several days in the saddle. Still, Maarja and I watch him swagger forward from behind a drawn curtain in the window of the carriage, until he stands eye-to-eye with the king.

His cousin, I suppose.

A greeting is exchanged, both leaders dipping their heads respectfully.

And then Tuskjas turns, motioning to the man at the carriage door, and Maarja and I are put on display.

I descend first, mirroring the Slavic Queen's indifferent, unimpressed gaze.

And then Maarja steps down beside me, a practiced look of superiority on her young face. We step forward to be presented, not bothering with any genuflections of our own.

The Queen's eyes narrow at our lack of respect, but she says nothing. They would not have agreed to such a union without gathering considerable intelligence about us. She will have heard tell of our power. She is looking for it.

"We greet you," the king says, aspiring for something other than the flat boredom written across his pudgy face. "Your journey has been long. My steward will show you to your tents to rest and freshen yourselves. We have prepared a feast –"

"I require a demonstration," the Queen interrupts, looking down her long nose at Maarja, several feet below her height.

The bodies of our company stiffen at her tone, but the bodies of her own people do not. I need nothing more to know who rules here.

"If the girl is not as promised, then there is no need for us to proceed with any formalities of the agreement. She will prove herself, here and now," the Queen goes on. The King cuts his eyes at her but says nothing.

Tuskjas glowers, unused to commands, but turns to Maarja after a moment and nods.

She steps forward, and as she does so, I feel her raise the Shroud.

"What demonstration would you require?" she asks, her high child's voice flat and emotionless. The Queen recoils from it subtly, turning her long chin in surprise. Then she recovers, cutting her lidded gaze to a man at the head of the servant's line, who nods, stepping away between the tents.

I feel him returning before I see him.

He pulls behind him a man dressed in dirty rags. Maarja holds fast, aided by the Shroud, even though I know she can sense his Estian blood, as I can.

"This man was caught poaching at our border," the Queen declares. "The marriage contract requires that we will mete out punishment to our own when they are caught raiding Estian lands. Likewise, it requires justice be meted out by Estian hands to Estian criminals doing the same."

She pauses, spearing Maarja with her glare, looking for a weakness. I do not give her a chance to observe one.

"The contract stipulates several punishments, based on the severity of the crime," I say, showing my awareness. "The most severe of which is death. It is well known in Est, though perhaps you have not been informed, that an Estian Waster cannot kill a man," I lie. "It is beyond our power. Should you require it of her, we will know that you are either misinformed or in pursuit of a way to nullify the contract through deception."

I am aware that my lie puts Tuskjas in an untenable position, increasing his unease. He can expose the falsehood, making Maarja's power more attractive to her would-be owners and allowing him more leverage in the arrangement. But to do so would expose disunity in our rule, which could weaken his position, not only on the issue of marriage, but by exposing a larger instability in the House. An instability that might tempt an ambitious neighbor to invade.

And so he does as I expect him to do, and says nothing.

The Queen's upper lip nearly disappears into her large nostrils.

"You will find, Chieftainess," she spits my inferior title, "that I am neither a fool nor ignorant. I am aware of the *limitations* of your purported power. The criminal here was found absconding with food, not property. Thus, his punishment for a first time offense is the loss of his right hand."

I give her no response, looking instead to the man who holds the rope and gesturing him forward. He lingers, looking between myself and his Queen. She follows my gaze, sneering, and beckons the hesitant man and his captive forward herself.

The accused is thrown before us, smelling of long abasement and fear. There are several lash marks on his back, and the skin on his wrists is wildly inflamed from the ropes. He is long-starved, and I suspect barely conscious.

"It seems he has already met with punishment," I gesture to his bended back, though it is covered by a rugged tunic. If the Queen is surprised that I know about the lashes, she does not show it.

"The contract is not yet in place," she says through thin lips.

I open my mouth to argue that by her own logic she has no right to force Maarja to punish the man, but then Maarja steps forward.

"I am eager to show them, Mama," she says flatly. I pretend to study her a moment, considering, and then I nod, moving to stand behind her.

"If you would extend his wrist," she instructs the guard, who follows her orders immediately. Maarja turns her head just so, looking heavily on the boy she is to marry, who stiffens his shoulders but somehow looks all the younger for it. The Queen follows her gaze, cutting her eyes back with a new wariness. But Maarja has already changed her focus, setting her young gaze on the wrist stretched out before us.

"Stop," the Queen commands, raising a hand. Maarja's eyes flicker up to her, the Shroud slipping ever so slightly with her uncertainty.

"How will I know it is not the mother's doing?" The Queen asks haughtily, cutting her shrewd gaze back to me. "Do you not claim to possess the same power?"

I raise my brows at her.

"My Queen," I say innocently. "I confess I am surprised. For surely your informants must have told you how to identify the power of one Waster from another, and how to contain it, if necessary. And yet, you would have me reveal such here, before your court and servants who might, at any time, seek to use it against the future queen of your land? You must understand, certainly as a fellow ruler, I cannot reveal such a thing in present company, but more importantly, as a mother I would hardly do so. And yet, I am beginning to suspect my daughter's primary task upon her marriage will be to educate yourself and the King about the very power she possesses, which is known to even the lowliest child in Est."

I place a hand gently on Maarja's shoulder as I speak, sensing her controlled inhale, the Shroud tucked back in place once more with the time I have bought her.

The Queen's sneer turns into mottled anger, her cheeks reddening and eyes glittering with malice. And yet, there is nothing she can do. To call my bluff would be to chance revealing her own ignorance.

"Let my honor, as a mother and queen to my own people, be enough," I continue, nodding respectfully. "You and I know the methods to discern whether or not my daughter's power is her own. I beseech you to use that knowledge now and see the authenticity of her ability for yourself."

The Queen pulls in a long, tight breath through her hooked nose, glaring spitefully at me a moment longer. She knows she is being manipulated, but she stiffens her jaw, cutting her eyes to Maarja, and nods.

And Maarja puts on a show.

What a wretched shame it is to know, in this moment, that I have spent years doubting her – her power, her bravery, her boldness – thinking in the secret spaces of my heart that she is not as she should be. That in the absence of the Wood, she could not grow as she ought. And all she needed was an audience, and my trust.

She closes her eyes, raising her hands before her dramatically, palms downward, then flipping them quickly over, open to the sky, as if drawing the power to herself. A few onlookers twitch at the sudden movement.

Then she opens her eyes and crouches, drawing the man's hand into her own. He gives little resistance, muttering and wiggling his fingers reflexively, but letting her push back the stained sleeve over his forearm.

She opens his fingers, putting her pointer finger at the tip of his own and tracing, slowly, down into his palm, over the fat meat at the base of his thumb, then through the raw, blistered skin of his wrist and up the soft underside of his forearm, stopping several inches below the elbow and drawing a line from one side of the limb to the other, as if tracing out the boundaries of the Working.

Then she begins to hum. A low, toneless sound, meant solely as a distraction, that turns into a wordless chant in her high, child's voice. I feel Tuskjas' heavy gaze on me, trying to discern why Maarja is performing all sorts of unnecessary theatrics. But he can no more expose her than expose himself.

Maarja lingers at the line she has drawn for a moment, doing absolutely nothing, and the bodies around us begin to shuffle with impatience.

Then she raises her eyes to the sky, the warm brown color leached from their centers, leaving a void of grey nothingness, save the black center of her pupil. Gasps flicker through the onlookers. I cut my eyes to the Queen, seeing her confusion, but she does not dare ask.

"The power must be drawn from the sky," I explain, letting my voice carry out across the enclosed space. "It is where we believe all the souls of the dead go, and the source of all our power."

I hold the little tendril of my own power steady. Maarja has not inherited my capability with eyes. This part of our performance is mine.

My gaze catches on the poor slip of a prince. And yet, despite the horror and apprehension on his small face, he holds himself back from reaching for his mother, only inches away.

Then Maarja snaps her head down again, causing several people to jump. She is observing the Queen's body within her Shroud. She is waiting for the telltale signs, the flutters and thrums I have taught her to look for. She is waiting until the Queen's body believes what it sees, even though her mind might warn her against it.

And the time has come.

With a cry, Maarja snaps the man's bone directly beneath the invisible line she drew across his forearm. He screams, revived, but he is so weak that Maarja easily holds her grip on his hand. The flesh at the line begins to eat away rapidly, skin dissolving to reveal muscle and sinew beneath, blood beginning to drip from the open ravines. It is a scene not unlike the one in the marketplace those many weeks ago. And as she did then, she holds the man's heartbeat steady while I Waste. The captive screams and writhes and tries to shake her off, but Maarja holds him fast, aided by his captor.

The putrid scent of burning flesh and bright metallic blood seeps across the crowd. The sound of wretching comes from beyond us. The King, with a considerable amount to dispel from his stomach, is bent double, attendants rushing to support him. And yet, the Queen steels herself, refusing to acknowledge the tinge of green spreading across her face.

And then it is done. Maarja stands, drawing her gaze slowly and heavily up to that of the Queen, and I let the color flood back into her eyes as they stare at each other. And then she holds out the man's Wasted arm bone, cut cleanly at its midpoint and still dripping gore.

"His right hand, my Queen," Maarja says indifferently, her voice eerie coming from her soft petal mouth, her smooth childish face. "As you requested."

CHAPTER TWENTY-SIX
THE RUPTURED VOID

Waster woman, willing and free.
Go not from the Wood. Go not from me.
But if from the Mother your path must go
The whistle of wind will beckon you home.

THE PROCEEDINGS carry on without interruption from that point forward.

After a brief reprieve in another of the large red tents, we join the royal party in the largest tent for a small feast in honor of the contract now drying with my husband's seal. Tuskjas and I are placed across from each other at the heavy-laden table, Maarja on my left across from her betrothed, who barely looks up from his trencher. The Slavic King sits at the head of the table by Tuskjas, inhaling the decadent foods, as though he hasn't just turned out his stomach for all to see. His wife perches like a vulture at the other end, lording over the little party as if we are ten times our number.

The fare is far more fine than that which Cook serves in Tarbatu. I see Tuskjas eyeing the gilded trenchers and succulent offerings, thinking of the reward of his endeavors. Thinking of himself, no doubt, as the owner of a Slavic Princess. A Slavic Queen. And all the wealth that might flow to him through her.

The wine, I suspect, is among the goods he would like to acquire through his new riches. Not only for its taste, which lingers bitterly on my tongue, but for its status. The two big men have already emptied several carafes between them when the steward brings in another. The man fills the King and Queen's goblets first, then does the same for Tuskjas. When the steward silently offers to refill my glass, I shake my head.

"This is fine indeed," Tuskjas says, bringing his jeweled cup once more to his thick lips, which come away with a reddish tint.

"I confess I am relieved to hear you say thus," the Queen says, holding her own goblet below her and swirling its contents with a shrewd eye.

"We are not so barbaric as to be ignorant of fine drink," Tuskjas answers, swallowing another sip with a bitter smile.

"I should think not," the Queen replies, reading his tone and responding testily with her own. "It is only that I have never tasted this vintage myself, and I would never serve such illustrious guests something of which I myself had not verified the quality."

"It is only wine, woman," the King bickers, setting his half-empty goblet heavily on the table.

"And a very fine one," I say demurely, nodding to the Queen. "We are honored you would share it with us."

"That is just the problem," she says, unwilling to be dismissed. "I have not chosen to share it with you. I have not chosen it at all. I do not even know from where it has come."

And then she lifts her eyes from the dark liquid, shrewd and suspicious, and calls her steward forward.

"What is this?" she asks him, narrowing her gaze. "What have you served us?"

"Ah, yes, my Queen," the steward nods subserviently. "That is the Estian wine, my Queen."

"The Estian Wine?" she asks, her brow lowering in confusion. Beside me, Tuskjas' body goes still.

"Yes, my Queen," the steward answers, looking nervously around the table. His eyes flicker across my own and stick, begging me to clarify. I only look at him with the same confusion as everyone else.

"Uh, yes, from the Estian delegation, of course," he goes on, his words tumbling forth. "It was brought to the kitchens this afternoon. A gift from the Chieftain. The woman insisted we serve it with the feast."

"What woman?" Tuskjas growls, his too-small eyes cutting quickly to me, his hands clenching into fists.

"Ah, well, she said she was the Mistress of the Larder, my lord," the steward answers, pale with alarm. The Queen, seeing her husband raise the goblet once more to his lips, slaps his hand away, sending his cup across the table.

The wine spills, pooling just in front of Tuskjas' trencher, thick and congealing as it cools. He stares at it, his lip curling in disgust.

And then, slowly, his gaze raises to my own.

I smile.

And then I tug.

In a breath, the steward disappears entirely. The tent flap swings heavily down, and there is a subtle familiar popping in my ears. Tuskjas flies to his feet, his chair tumbling behind him, pulling his blade from his belt. The Queen, misunderstanding, screams a bloodcurdling cry, tumbling over her own chair to escape the table.

And then Kurat appears, his hands descending lightly onto Maarja's shoulders so as not to scare her. He leans down over the top of her chair, his eyes locked on Tuskjas, and whispers in her ear.

"Maarja, breathe."

Tuskjas bellows, charging forward, the tip of his blade extended towards my daughter's heart.

And then she is gone.

I slam my trencher down, trapping Tuskjas' blade flat against the table and leaning forward onto it with all my strength. It will never hold him, but I do not need it to.

Kurat drops Maarja right onto Tuskjas' back where he is splayed across the table. The breath stills in my chest as she slips the dagger from Kurat's hand, raising it high in both small fists above her stepfather's neck, her power searching out the narrow passage between bones.

Tuskjas bucks and kicks, jerking his blade free and pushing himself up off the table. Maarja slides from his back into Kurat's arms, disappearing from view. Tuskjas swings wildly, the blade cutting across the swollen face of the Slavic King, still gaping in his chair. Blood flings across the table, the Queen's screams ringing anew.

Tuskjas roars in frustration, spinning once more to face me across the table. With one giant step, he leaps onto its top, towering above me, and swings his blade.

I descend into darkness.

"We can stay here," he whispers.

"Do not take this from me," I answer.

"We can find another way."

I shake my head, letting its weight fall back onto his shoulder. He presses the hard line of his nose behind my ear, breathing me in. Somewhere, just beyond, there is a flutter of wind. like a cool breath in the deepest part of a cave.

"We can find another way, Liama," he whispers again. I raise my head, warmth spreading across my chest.

"Not now. It has already begun."

And then we step back into the light.

The Slavic King is facedown in a pool of his own blood. Tuskjas howls, spinning towards us where we have materialized across the tent. He launches forward, blade high, but slams to a stop when Kurat disappears from behind me. I relish the wild swing of his meaty neck, Maarja's dagger protruding from his back, frantically searching all the dark corners for a thing he will never see coming.

Kurat reappears, grasping the dagger's hilt and dragging it downwards with the full weight of his body.

What had been a flutter of cool breeze whips into a wind, lifting the tips of my hair. Tuskjas staggers, finally feeling the wound, reaching around himself for the dagger. Kurat flickers away, stepping out of Shadow beside me once more. He drops to his knees beside me, pressing both hands across my chest, and I only now realize that I am on the floor, my knees wet with my own blood.

Tuskjas spins, growling and grunting, the color draining from his big, square face. The whistling grows louder, howling. I close my eyes over it, listening for her voice – my grandmother's voice – within its squall.

Where is she?

She's waiting for you.

Beware the powerless man, my daughter.

There are tales under tales, and within them and without.

My blood seeps through Kurat's hands. I sense it, so recently a part of me, as it begins to slide across the dirt. Something crashes, a woman screams.

There are tales under tales.

"In another tale, there is no Snake Mother," my grandmother says, grinning her mischievous grin. I roll my eyes. I grow weary of the versions, and I have told her so.

"The Beings of Light are forced into the Realm of Daemons in the end to be eternally tormented for their greed," I complain. "It matters little how they got there. It is only a story."

"Ah," she says, smiling deeper. "But this particular story is the one that I believe."

I cut my eyes to her warily. She snickers.

"I have your attention now, I see," she says. I sigh, looking away from her to show her my impatience, but it does not fool her. She goes on.

"In another tale, there is no Snake Mother, or if there is, she is already dead – captured and killed by the Beings of Light when the Twin Queens would not bend to their will, even to save their mother's soul-sworn friend. This is the tale that I believe."

"Why?" I ask testily.

"Because," she answers with a shrug. "The Shadow Queen could not have lied. Daemons cannot do it. That is why Looklema took one as her lover. Despite his darkness, she fell in love with his honesty."

"But the Waster Queen was the child of the Daemon Prince as well," I argue, captured now.

"But not so much as her sister," my grandmother explains. "You know this. You have seen how one child takes after its mother and another its father. The Wasting Queen was Looklema's, but the Shadow Queen belonged to her father. Whose darkness do you think she traveled through when she stepped between shadows?"

"Then if the Wasting Queen could lie, why would she not have done so to the leader of the Beings of Light?" I ask.

"Perhaps she could have, but do not forget the cunning of Odypoeg. I do not think he would have believed one Queen while the other stayed silent. And so they knew they could not deceive him."

"Then what opened the door?" I ask. "What caused the Void?"

"Greed itself, my child. Desperation. Corruption. The lack of something vital, something meant to be, but absent. The powerless man is a void. He cannot be Wasted, for he is Waste. He cannot be Walked, for he already lives in Shadow."

"And so Odypoeg himself became the Void? It had nothing to do with the Glen, or the boulder, or the door?"

"In this version the Glen is not a place, but a way of being."

"Being powerless?" I say, disbelieving. "It's as simple as that?"

"Simple!" she cries sarcastically. "The Glen is simple? The door and the snake and the boulder are simple?"

"And so there is no power in the tale at all? The Waster Queen does not draw the leader's blood, and the Shadow Queen does not save her sister or push the men through. Odypoeg simply becomes the Void and everyone gets sucked inside?"

"Perhaps," my grandmother answers with a smug smile. I narrow my eyes at her.

"You do not believe it," I say. She shakes her head slowly, but offers no answer.

"What do you believe, then?" I press her. Her smile fades, a soft light in her wrinkled eyes.

Longing.

"The powerless man may have become the Void, but someone needed to navigate it. Someone needed to deliver the Beings of Light into Looklema's hands. Someone with the blood of Looklema herself."

Her soft gaze goes from my own, rising into the canopy above us, where spirits are breathed into the sky.

"I believe," she murmurs at last, "that the daughters missed their mother."

She turns to me, reaching out, pressing her soft palm against my cheek.

"I believe that it was time for them to return to her embrace."

I watch, enduring the searing pain, mesmerized by the slow slide of my blood across the floor.

"Mama!" Maarja cries, and now I feel her hands on my arms. Feel, with my skin, not sense, with my power. I drag my gaze up from the trail of blood, looking into her frantic face, tear-streaked and strained. And beloved to my bones.

I lay my eyes on her. Always my eye is upon her. Now flitting through the Hall on tiptoes. Now giggling into the cold air, her breath going before her. Now standing still, her back turned to me, watching the horses come into the stables. Now simmering in a near rage, refusing to eat the food growing cold before her.

My eye is always upon her in this world. And yet, it is not my only way of seeing. I see her in a second place, a place only a mother's eyes can go. I see her weeping in unknown arms, snot gathering below her nose. I see her walking silent stone halls, death in the corners, a loneliness like ice chilling her little bones. Hariva is gone. Suita has betrayed her. Her stepfather is gone. Hiida is gone.

I am gone.

A mother sees her own death in a thousand ways and at a thousand times. It is the echo after the cry of delight, happiness' shadow trailing just behind. For every wonderful moment, every breath of gladness, there is the threat of sorrow. The two cannot be separated. If there is joy, so too will there be despair.

"Hush," I whisper. "All is well. All is well. You've done well."

Her wet brown eyes are damning. She can surely sense the life pouring out of me. I had prepared her for what would be required of her. I had not told her what would be required of me.

"LIAMA!" Tuskjas screams, spinning frantically, and as his back turns, I can see the darkness, a spreading damnation. The Void devouring his broad back.

"Liama," Kurat whispers into my hair, holding me to his chest with his slippery, blood-stained hands. "Liama, Liama, Liama!"

I let him hold me a moment longer, my hand wrapped around Maarja's upper arm, letting their beings press into mine a final time. I let him hold me as the oozing bloom of emptiness devours Tuskjas' shoulders, spreading under his arms into his belly, his chest. He looks down at it, screaming now in earnest, my name shucked from his lips every time he bellows it out.

Like a nut from its shell.

And then I rise, sliding a little in my own blood. Kurat leaps up, supporting my weight until I can gather my numb feet beneath me, Maarja's fists are buried in my skirts, dragging and unyielding. She is screeching now, denying. She is throwing her weight to the floor, trying to drag me down with her.

I turn in Kurat's arms, stumbling on weak knees. His fine features are cracked open, his brow bent, eyes pleading in vain. It is done now. It was done the moment Tuskjas raised my blood to his lips and drank.

I raise shaking fingers to his cheek, ignoring their cold.

"Shadow Husband," I whisper. He closes his eyes over my words. I look down to my daughter, pale and shaking, her brown eyes as wide as the moon on the night I took her unnamed father to my pine-needle bed.

"I love you," I whisper, pulling her thick braid over her shoulder. *That is why I have done this,* I want to say to her, to make her understand the depth of that fathomless well, deeper than the well of my power. *I am willing to do it. I am happy to do it, for you.*

But I will not leave her as Kurat's mother left him, with all the weight of my horrible choices on her shoulders, shaming her to be worthy of them.

"I love you, my precious girl," I press my words into her eyes, knowing they will mean nothing until she holds her own babe in her arms. "But that does not change what I must do."

Her mouth bends, tears streaming down her face from red eyes, her lashes thick and dark with them.

"No, Mama. Please, Mama. No, no, no, no," she weeps, still clinging to my blood-drenched skirts, tugging viscously with all her slim weight.

Kurat's head drops to my own, his brow leaning into my cheek.

I reach out, laying my hand over Maarja's head. She buries her face in my side, screaming her rage into my hollowing frame.

And then I raise my head, and for the last time I put the Chieftainess into my voice.

"Put my blood on Her throne," I command of Kurat, dragging myself from both their embraces. I grab his eyes with my own as I untangle Maarja's fingers one by one from my skirts. I wrap his heartbeat around my wrist, clenching it tight.

"Put my blood on Her throne," I command again, giving a tug. "Or everything you fear will come to pass. I expect it to be done."

The sorrow hardens on his face, his black gaze narrowing, fierce.

"I will," he swears. And then his brows come together over shuttered eyes. "Haunt me, Snake Wife," he whispers, as close to begging as he will come.

The ends of Maarja's hair begin to lift. The corner of Kurat's tunic. My blood covering them both.

There is no answer I can allow myself to give him. There is no way, now, for me to stay, even as a shade.

"I will watch you from that other place," I say, stumbling backwards. "And when your oath to me is done, I will wrap your heart around my wrist and call you to me."

And then I push my daughter into his arms.

"Now Walk."

With an inhaled breath, they are gone.

I close my eyes over the image of Maarja's horrified face, knowing wherever I now go it will be burned into my memory, and there will be no Shadow Husband to erase it.

The edges of my skirts have begun to flutter. Tugging.

I turn, giving my body over to the current, and I face him.

There is very little of Tuskjas left now. The Void has devoured his big arms and violent hands, the blackness at his core flowing from the absence of something vital.

It is not hard to step towards him. I simply cease to resist the pull. His too-small eyes fall on my own, black and fathomless, even as his open mouth disappears, his screams sliding seamlessly into the Void's shrieking howl. Behind him, the thick, limp body of the Slavic King, his belly full of my blood, finally surrenders to the pull. It thumps fatly to the floor from its chair and slides beneath the table. Tuskjas whirls on waning legs, watching in horror as the King is dragged the final distance, disappearing into the abyss at his center. The Queen cowers in the corner behind the table, her body laid over her young son's, kicking and shrieking, tears streaking down her long face. But her clothes do not flutter. Her body does not slide toward the Void, nor does her son's.

Do not disregard the power of the blood, my mother had advised.

The Queen never drank of the strange vintage. As shrewd a woman as I thought. Kurat will have to see to her, once what's left to do is done.

"Tuskjas," I call to him, the wind whipping at my voice.

"Tuskjas!" I scream, blood gushing from my chest as it clenches. His eyes, frantic and raw, bore into my own. I extend a shaking hand, my bloody finger aimed between his eyes.

"You end with me!" I scream into what's left of his face. His brow slams down, malice and desperation and agony in his final glare.

Powerlessness.

"You end with me!" I shriek again.

And then his eyes are gone, though I can still feel his essence. His spirit, which I will drag with me to that cold dark place and deliver into Looklema's hands.

I let the Void draw me close. I send my awareness into its depths, searching.

She is waiting for you.

I do not know how my grandmother did it, how she gained that realm of the Daemons instead of breathing her spirit into the sky. But I have known the unique, familiar rhythm of her heart since before I filled my lungs with my first breath.

Are you there?

I am here.

Draw the Shroud, Liama.

I have always felt the same tug towards darkness.

Whose darkness do you think she traveled through when she stepped between shadows?

I know this place.

Breathe, Liama.

I pull in my last breath, relishing the feeling of it rattling through my throat, filling my lungs. I rejoice in the red bloom of it spreading in my blood, gushing, gurgling, thrumming, humming, spewing, spilling, thrushing, shushing, pulsing, pooling, wooshing.

Wasting.

And then I step into the darkness.

CHAPTER TWENTY-SEVEN
THE UNSPOKEN NAME

AT FIRST, as my tale began, there was nothing but outraged disbelief.

And then he began to remember.

By its end, I wish that he did not. I wish that the Snake Wife had stayed within the Void where she has lived for 13 years.

"She cursed me?" he asks, his voice broken. Cracked.

"In her way," I tell him, pressing my fingertips to his high cheekbone, grown sharper with age. "But you knew you would never Walk again. Not with the deception of what she did to gain you the throne hidden in your memory."

"And you?" he whispers, turning his dark eyes to me, half awe, half betrayal. "How did you know?"

"She told me," I answer simply. Smiling sadly. "On a moonless night, on a Norseman's boat. She wove her fingertips through my hair, and she told me what would be required – that I would need to spin one of two tales. The truth, if she failed. And if she should succeed, a lie."

I reach, forcing my weak bones into motion, pointing to the small, jeweled box I have kept with me all this time. He follows my direction, moving across the room to bring it forward. I gesture for him to open it.

There, on the top, worn by the oils of my anxious, unsure fingertips for 13 years, is the missive. I nod for him to open it, and he does so gently, reverently, reading the simple message in her hand.

Remember your oath, shieldmaiden.

Lie through your teeth.

How desperately I have regretted my words to her that afternoon as we prepared ourselves for battle. I had not known to what I was sworn. Kurat had tried to save me from her. He had said she asked too much. He had said I was only a storyteller.

And yet, I swore myself to her, thinking to show myself as more.

I shudder, aching under the weight of my corrupted power, long since gone to rot, and no one to Waste it away.

Aemilie will make them forget, she had told him. And I have.

But *I* have not forgotten. I have been the sole bearer of the truth for 13 years. And now I know I will die, my face still young, from the weight of the task with which she crippled me.

"It arrived with the same messenger who brought us word of the death of the Chieftain and Chieftainess by the hands of the Slavic King," I explain, indicating her missive. "A very strange messenger, to be sure."

As if I have summoned her, the worn wooden door of my inner chamber bumps open gently on her hip. My lady's maid slips quietly into the room, unobtrusive as ever, and sets a tray of steaming tea on the table beside my bed.

"Is there anything else you require, my Chieftainess?" she asks with a bowed head, though the deep pockmarks on her face cannot be hidden by her sheepish posture.

"No," I answer, smiling gently at her. My gift from Liama. "That is all, Hiida. Thank you."

She bobs a curtsy and goes.

Kurat's eyes stay on her, hawklike.

"What depth of deception have you employed, wife?" he breathes after a moment. "Do you lie to me even now? Do you still spin Liama's tale?"

I sigh. The tea will have to wait.

"Hiida knows nothing of who she was, or to whom she was once loyal," I explain. "You yourself did that, then sent her to me on Liama's orders. But she knew that you could rewrite only a mind at a time. The Slav Queen, the prince, Hiida, Maarja. And yet, you were the one she needed to be deceived the most."

"Why?" he demands, stiffening defensively.

"Because you were the one who must go on," I answer. He scowls.

"Did she think me so weak that I could not have done so with the full knowledge of all that had transpired?" he says, rising from the side of the bed to turn his back to me. "Maybe I loved her, as you claim, but did I not also love my mother and yet carry on after her death?"

I look at him a moment, unsure of what he asks of me. It has been my life's work, doing what he asks of me, even if he cannot remember asking it. I am always attuned to his needs. Always searching for his comfort.

The most dangerous of men is the one who will do for love what should only be done for the vilest hatred. Kurat is one such man. I am one such woman. You would do well to remember that.

She had warned me. I had not heeded her.

"I am not her," I say after a time. "I do not know any more than you what lay behind her eyes. I can only tell you what I have been told."

"And all of this? This tale you have finally revealed? How much of it is truth? How could you have known?"

"Because I heard it from your lips," I say. "And from Maarja's. And Liama's, of course. As for the rest, as for what can only be known by her, my mother always said I could speak with the Moon Tongue."

"The damned Moon Tongue," he spits, pacing away from me to the darkened window.

"You will either come to trust it or you will not," I say, the long-worn argument between us falling into its familiar rhythm. "You will either come to trust *him* or you will lose him."

"He cannot Walk," Kurat grumbles.

"Why should it matter?" I argue. "He is our blood, blood of Looklema's blood, twice over. Bring Maarja's girl and put them on the throne and be free of Liama's curse."

"And if it is not enough?" he says, turning his chin to me with slitted eyes. "Children on the throne, you dead, and I disgraced, mistrusted? And the power flowing out of the land faster than ever before?"

"Hear me, husband," I say, gathering my meager strength. "Perhaps the land had weakened before. Certainly Kotkas' usurpation, and Tuskjas' corruption after, might have weakened it. But it is Liama's curse and your unwillingness to fulfill your oath to her that cripples Looklema's House now. And it will be thus until you fulfill that oath and put her blood on Her throne."

"And yet, you sustained it!" he accuses, spinning towards me and striding forward. "An oath and a curse weakening this House, working against all I have attempted to strengthen it, and you knew! You knew, and yet, you have kept it from me!"

"You lie," I shake my head at him. "I have never taken your oath from you. It is the one thing I never touched, those words from your lips. So unless you have contrived a way to take it from yourself, you lie to me, Kurat."

He pulls a long, sharp breath in through his nose, turning his gaze from mine. He stands, hands fisted, black eyes on the darkened corner of my chamber, for a long time.

"We are, both of us, liars," he says finally. There is no heat in his voice, no accusation. Only honesty.

I nod, settling back under a wave of fatigue.

"Your lies have made you half of what you were," I say. "My lies will kill me. We are not Looklema's chosen. We never were."

He sits heavily on the bed, his greying head between his fine-fingered hands.

"It seems my wives have always been wiser than I," he sighs.

"That is because you have chosen them well," I put my hand on his nape, swallowing back the surge of miserable jealousy that rises up my throat. *His wives.* Before this day, there had only been one. "One Snake. One Spider."

"Do not call yourself that," he commands from habit. He has always hated the name the Norseman gave me. The name our people breathe behind the locked doors of their houses.

After a breath of long silence between us, he raises his head, staring blankly forward.

"Liama," he breathes, his mouth remembering the sound of her name after 13 years of its absence. The devotion on his lips drops my beleaguered heart into my belly.

"Why did she not want her name remembered?" he asks. "Why has it never occurred to me to wonder what it was?"

"She told Grandfather once that the Twin Queens kept their names from being remembered because their reign was not yet over, though they had gone from this world. It was not part of her instructions, but I suspected she would want the same, if given the choice. And so I called her only 'the Chieftainess' in my tales. The loyal, dutiful weapon of a beloved Chieftain in a time of great upheaval."

"One does not need to be living to be reigning," he murmurs to himself. "And so this is her legacy."

"For now," I say.

"And yours will be the same," he breathes, turning his black gaze on me. "The loyal, dutiful weapon of a Chieftain?"

"I am not like her," I say, tears springing to my weary eyes. "I do not have her strength."

"Do not speak thus, Aemilie," he says, pulling my fingers between his own.

I love him. Perhaps I always have, growing up with tales of the handsome Heir, my mother's cousin, conspiring against the wicked Chieftain in far away Tarbatu. And he has honored me. He has protected me. He has respected my power, its abilities and its limitations. He has placed me beside him, on a throne of my own.

And yet, he has never loved me. Not with the blistering light I saw in his eyes that morning in Hapsaluu, as he whispered his tale in my ear on the balcony for me to spin into legend. The Tale of the Crone and the Norseman.

He has never looked at me with the bone-shattering, oath-breaking devotion I beheld in his black gaze that day.

Liama.

The name that only I have remembered for 13 long years.

"Do not let them forget my name, Kurat," I whisper through a clenched throat.

"I will not," he says, squeezing my fingers. "You know that I have very little honor, but I will swear it on all I have left. I will not let them forget you, Aemilie."

"Good," I whisper, letting my heavy head fall back, my eyes searching for the sky.

"For I never wish to reign again."

EPILOGUE

THE CHIEFTAINESS OF EST breathes her spirit into the sky.

She does not come to this place. This place of Shadow. Still, her sisters gather at the realm's end to honor her passing.

Time does not pass here like it does in the Lighted realm. Yet, the Snake Wife can measure it by her daughter's growth. She has watched her Bitter One mature – once the forlorn and lonely child left behind, desolate with the memory of her mother and stepfather, loving, attentive, and good. Taken from her by the cruel hand of fate.

And now the girl is a woman, a mother herself.

And if the Wasting Queen, whose name the Snake Wife had finally felt on her lips, had slipped from the Darkened realm under the same moon as the new Waster's birth, then the Snake Wife had been little surprised. She had been warned, after all.

Why do you linger, Granddaughter? the beloved voice asks from behind her. *Spider Silk has kept her oath, and now her troth is done.*

And yet, the Snake Wife lingers still.

There is one more oath I am due, she answers.

Ah, her grandmother says knowingly, now beside her. They look down together into the lighted world below. *You still believe he will fulfill it, after all this time?*

The Snake Wife reaches out with her power, searching for the beat of his heart as she has a thousand times before.

Are you there?

Are you there?

Are you there?

A thousand times in vain.

And then the boy rushes in, his nurse on his heels. He throws himself over his mother's still form, brushing up against his father's knees.

In another realm, the Snake Wife stumbles back from the force of the sudden response.

I am here!

She straightens, turning her wide eyes on her grandmother.

Where is the Shadow Queen?

Her grandmother smiles, mischievous and achingly familiar.

I suspect, her grandmother giggles, *from this point forward we shall have to call that Being by another name.*

We shall have to call it the Shadow Prince.

AMANTHA BURGESS-SMITH

ACKNOWLEDGEMENTS

THIS WORK quite literally represents several years' worth of blood, sweat, and tears, not all my own, and not in the actual writing of the story, but in earning the right to tell it.

Virginia Woolf, in her infinite wisdom, said, "For heaven's sake, publish nothing before you are thirty." And though I've been writing stories since I was 11, I am thankful that Liama's is the first one that I am sharing with the world. I'm not sure it's possible to write a convincing main character that isn't a version of yourself, certainly not in a debut novel. Liama's losses, her laments, and certainly the feeling of being kept inches away from power by conniving men are all mine. I began this process in fury, much like Liama. And also like her, I end it now in a kind of patient and watchful peace that I've never before known.

But my reign is not yet complete.

I give thanks first to all my dead people.

How lucky I have been to have four grandparents and two parents who loved as fiercely and believed as fervently as they were able. I give thanks to "the first" Polly, my grandmother, who refused to let her story be written for her. Your legacy is in the very bones of three generations of Polly's who are doing the same.

To my grandfathers – J.B., whose love and pride was so enormous he never quite knew how to get it out of his chest and into words. And Bill, whose gentle fingertips on my back I know I will feel as I step into that welcoming darkness.

To my dad – Mike. You poked. You prodded. You subtly pestered. You knew I was meant to write stories and you never let me forget it. You are here in every keystroke, every line. Your heartbeat echoes in the breath after my own – *Are you there? I am here.* You are more present in death than you ever could have been in life, as if your spirit was liberated by the October wind that carried you away. You are in the faces of my daughters, their wild laughter, their effortless joy. You haunt my house merrily, my beloved ghost. And I know it is your voice I will hear calling when the time has come for me to breathe my spirit into the sky. I thank you, Daddy.

And now, for my alive people.

To my editor, Julie, who was also my Literary Theory professor and feminist idol. You made all of this real with your willingness to edit my monstrosity of an unfinished first project. Without you, I'd probably still be clacking away on page 1,892 of something no one wanted to read. I thank you heartily.

To my beta readers, Betsy, Sarah E., Sarah K., and Evan. Seeing your all-caps text messages and reading your enthusiastic feedback was magic in itself. Wild was the moment when I realized that my first reader had finished my first book for the first time. It will never happen again, and that surreal moment will be close to my heart for all the stories to come.

I give thanks to my brothers, the whole lot of them, who have helped me hone my unflappable arrogance by generally doing whatever I tell them to do. To Ryan, I'm sorry for that lame poem I put on Facebook because I was mad at you. To Will, I'm sorry for pushing you into the garage door on your pogo stick. To Jay, I'm sorry that I only ever serve you frozen pizza when you come to babysit.

I give thanks to the women that have made me their own. To my little sisterclan of sacrilegious Jesus women – Mellie, Betsy, Dawn, Gail, Amanda, Moriah, Merranda, and Laura. To my coven of low-key witchy moms just looking around and noticing – Sarah, Jaylin, and Alice. To the book club girls, who make me feel as legitimate as Ruth Ware. And to the Big Dirty Tee Mom's Running Club, who listened to me prattle on about this for literal miles – Val, Anna, Elise, Kerry, and Britney.

To my grandmother, Mary, the last of her kind. The matriarch. You are a precious gem, priceless and rock solid. I hope you heard yourself in Kallas Õnnev's words – *I carry a longing always to be with the ones that have made me who I am.* Forgive me for making you my muse. I can't help it. You're made out of poetry, Mississippi history, and dinner rolls. I love you.

To my mother and copy-editor, Tonya, who flat-out refused to "knock me down a notch" when it was suggested by a teacher that I was a little too confident for a 10-year-old girl. I always told you my first book would be an anthology of short stories about all the weirdos who somehow find their way to you in this wide world. Don't worry, I have more books in me. I'll get that one done. I love you.

And finally, I give the greatest thanks to my little bubbling cauldron of heaven on earth.

To Louisa Polly, *Famous Warrior*. To Charlotte Joy, *Free Woman*. Tales of enchantments and power and spells and spirits and Daemons and fairies and princesses and prophecies may tempt you to believe that this true world lacks magic, but hold fast. My prayer for you is that the day will quickly come when you embrace the radical, mythical, phenomenal power of choosing love, joy, peace, patience, kindness, goodness, faithfulness, self control, and (sometimes) sassiness.

With these spells you can fell corrupt kingdoms, break ancient curses, and rewrite the world. I have no doubt that you will, my warrior, my little liberator. That is why I have named you thus.

Sweet baby Jesus, Stephen, where do I even start? A careless reading of this book might lead one to believe that I hate men and long to slit all their throats. And if the arguments between Liama and Kurat about shame and guilt and pride and fear are convincing, you will know why. But it is my sincere hope that you see yourself in the places that I put you – in the listening ear of Vappers, the eager helpfulness and honor of the blacksmith, the soulful loyalty of Õnnev, the self-sacrificing courage of Vidar. If I have crafted a life where I can flourish and our girls can flourish, it is only because you, with your incredible mind and intuitive heart, have carved out a space in the chaos of the world for me to work (even if I have to move your dirty pants to get to my desk).

You are home, heart, hearth, and heaven. I sure do love you. Thank you. ***

And to the three-faced God – Vast Creator, Spirit Mother, and Rebel Son.

Not tame.

Not safe.

But good.

Want more from the world of Snake Wife?

The <u>She Who Reaches High Series</u> continues in
The Curse of Lore

Read on for an excerpt.

The small of his back is damp.

His nape as well, coarse hair sticking to it. Itchy. He wants to pull it away.

Something is wrapped in his fingers. His fist.

His fist. *His* fingers. *His* hair. *His* nape.

It is over, then. At last.

And he has lived.

"Miervaldis?"

The voice is so hesitant, so unsure. It will have been uncertain, then. It will have been chaotic, as they told him it would be. There will have been moments of doubt. Perhaps they will have huddled in the corner of his sick room, discussing alternatives. Assessing the infant. It does not often pass to two inheritants in a single generation, but it is not unheard of. They will have brought the Dampener Jaline to put her long-nailed finger on the babe's forehead – his step-brother – to read the tiny kernel of Kangars' power.

To see if it is the same as the one Miervaldis' father passed to his firstborn son.

"Miervaldis?" the voice again. And so he shows them that he is not yet dead, or insane. And that they are not yet in need of an alternative.

"My father?" he croaks. This he must know immediately. The voice comes closer now, leaning over him, though he has not yet opened his eyes.

"He lingers. There is not much time remaining."

Now he opens his eyes. The lightly-lined face of the woman above him is fuzzy at first, but even with an unclear gaze he does not miss her flinch.

It is all there then. It has been completed. He has known always that when the time came, he would not falter. It is not in his nature to do so. But others were not so sure.

"Take me to him," he breathes, pulling his chin up to rise. His stepmother does not argue. She rarely does.

He has never been sure if his father chose well for his second wife. Would one rather have a woman who has a shallow inner pool of thoughts yet speaks them openly, or a woman whose introspection is as vast as the western plains but speaks her mind only rarely?

A puzzle. One he will have to muse on at another time, though there is some comfort in knowing he still wants to do so. They had warned him that his own character might alter as a result of the task. He will inspect himself more thoroughly once he has seen his father draw his last breath. Once he is Chieftain.

Hands are beneath him, steadying and cool. Her hands are always cool. Cool and dry, like a scroll kept in the darkest corners of the library. It is something he has always liked about his stepmother.

He blinks to clear the fog from his gaze. The room is perfectly tidy. She will not have let it go to seed during his illness. In its corners, at the edge of his awareness, heavy drapes are being pulled back from windows. A dull grey sky is casting the room in dull grey light; impossible to tell the time of day.

"How long?" he murmurs, pulling in a long, rattling breath.

"Twenty-two days," she answers simply, providing no commentary.

He nods. He does not say that, to him, it felt at once like flipping through the pages of a book, each day flickering past too rapidly to be read, and like trudging in mud, progressing at the speed of a wagon caught in a torrential downpour.

"They have sustained him long," he says as he sits fully up, her arm behind his back. He turns his hips slowly, pulling his long legs over the side of the bed. His feet hit the floor with small thumps.

"He is in terrible pain, Miervaldis," she murmurs, close beside him. He nods.

What little she says reveals all that she does not say.

She does not say that, though Miervaldis is not yet Chieftain, the allegiance of the House has now transferred to him. She does not say that his father's comfort is a minor priority, compared to ensuring that Miervaldis' undertaking has been successful. She does not say that the Healers have kept his father alive, despite his pain, the long 22 days since his mortal injury in order to ensure that Miervaldis woke hale of mind, if not of body. She does not say that now Miervaldis has arisen from the mind-sickness, that it is time, at last, to release his father from his misery.

"Is he aware?" he grunts, pushing up to his feet.

"Not at current," she answers, holding him steady by his shoulders. "They will bring him up when you are ready."

He raises his eyes to her gaze. She does not flinch this time, but her keen brown eyes assess, as they always do. Not unkindly. She has always been too distant to be unkind. The thin silver circlet on her brow will not remain much longer. She will be relieved, he knows, to remove it forevermore, and return to her meticulously kept study in the scholar's tower, her duty to her House complete. He would not call her unambitious, but those ambitions have never been ones of political power.

He is terribly fond of her.

A nuisance really. He had hoped the transference would release him from affections. But at least from this self-possessed, intelligent woman who has been to him a strange but welcome companion over the last three years, he is not yet freed.

There are other affections, of course. And far more inconvenient for what he is becoming. But those, too, will have to wait for a quieter moment of introspection, when he can evaluate how to move forward.

"He will not be as you remember him," his stepmother warns quietly. He nods to her.

"I have been well prepared for this, despite the urgency with which it has been undertaken."

And as always between them, there is much that is not said, but is nevertheless understood.

She does not say, 'Most of what he was has been taken.'

She does not say, 'You are more your father now than he is himself.'

And he does not say 'All of this has been made known to me from my very first breath.'

They start forward. He leans heavily on her arm for the first few steps. But with movement he finds that his legs still shore up beneath him, and by the time they have approached the door adjoining his sick chamber to his father's, Miervaldis is moving on his own strength.

He straightens before the closed door to his full height, and his stepmother removes her arm from his. She knocks, and the door is opened.

This chamber is not like his own.

The windows remain covered, candlelight flickering across the gathered bodies therein. There is a slight tang in the stagnant air, that of stale blood. The big bed, with its carven owl wings stretching out to wrap around the head of the sleeper, is surrounded by five cloaked forms, all linked at the hands. Their feminine bodies, long and willowy, are hidden by their dark green capes, but their heads are uncovered in the presence of their Chieftain, bowed towards his prone form. The one at the foot of the bed raises her gaze as Miervaldis steps through the door.

"Hail to you, Heir of Rezke," she says formally in her familiar scratchy voice. Her hair is nearly all grey, the loose wisps of her curls catching warmth in the dim light.

"Hail to you, Healer on High," he responds.

"Quickly now, my liege," she says. "I fear we cannot hold him to us much longer."

Miervaldis approaches his father's bedside, and the Healer there moves to the side to let him pass, never breaking her handhold with her sister beside her. The Heir of Rezke kneels beside the Chieftain, gathering his father's bony hand between his own.

"Raise him," Miervaldis orders firmly. As one, the Healers nod.

The Chieftain rises slowly from the torpor under which he has been sustained for three-quarters of a moon. He moans, long and tortured, then hacks a crudy cough, his lean body spasming beneath the heavy wool coverlets. His grey hair is spread around his head like the glare of the moon. Grey, dull and varied. Not shining silver, as it had been.

"The Star's Blessing, father," Miervaldis says quickly, trying to pierce the veil of his father's awareness. But the man in the bed only moans again.

"Bring him higher," Miervaldis orders the Healers. They nod.

The moan becomes a cry. Like a babe, high and wailing. Miervaldis grits his teeth.

"The Star's Blessing, father," he says loudly, directly into his father's ear. The cry cuts off abruptly. The Chieftain's head swings to the side, towards his son, but his eyes do not open. He gasps something that Miervaldis cannot make out.

"Higher," the Heir orders the Healers again. There is no nod. Miervaldis cuts his glare towards the Healer on High at the foot of the bed. She is looking at him with her lips pressed together, undecided. He only glares at her with his new gaze.

"There is little left to bring him into," she warns. "Much further and there will only be madness."

"You would have me take the throne without the blessing of my father?" Miervaldis asks icily. He is surprised by his lack of composure. Something he will need to reflect on later. The Healer on High lifts her chin, looking down her long nose at him, but does not answer.

They will need to be tightened in, Miervaldis makes note to himself. If his father's primary legacy was to bring the famed scholars of Burtnieku's Tower under the rule of the throne, Miervaldis' legacy will be to bring beneath it the Healers. And perhaps the Dampeners as well.

But he can do none of that without the Star's Blessing. Not if he is harried with opposition from those very factions, as he will no doubt be without it.

But he need not worry. For his father is groaning once more.

"*Pucite.*"

Miervaldis turns abruptly back to the Chieftain, only to find the man's gaze upon him.

For a breathless, horrible moment, he is a child once more.

Pucite. Little Owl. And the reddened, pain-lined eyes that look upon him are a flat, muddy brown. As they had been when Miervaldis was a young child. As they had been when his father last called him by this name.

It is now, in this paralyzing instant, that Miervaldis begins to understand, not theoretically, but bodily, what he has become. Because the last time his father looked at him with this brown gaze, the man had been squeezing Miervaldis' small hand for the last time, readying himself to enter the transference chamber and take the mantle of the Living Memory from his own aged father's shoulders.

When Miervaldis' father had emerged from that chamber, weeks later, he never again called his son *Pucite.* And his gaze had been the pale, acrid yellow of an owl's.

"The Star's Blessing, father," Miervaldis croaks from a thick throat. The man's eyes flicker, like he is trying to blink away a fog. His empty stare rises above Miervaldis' head, to something beyond.

"Father!" Miervaldis barks, surprised again at his vehemence. Surprised at the flash of terror in his breast when his father looked away.

"Under auspicious stars," the Chieftain murmurs, barely intelligible, never looking back to his son. From the edge of his awareness, Miervaldis can feel the subtle lean of the Healer on High, straining to witness. "Blessed be the Chieftain, son of Erasts, in whom the Living Memory is made alive, and the –" he hacks a cough, blood dribbling out of the corner of his mouth. Miervaldis squeezes the knuckles in his grip to the very bone.

"– and the Gaze of the Remembered is in his eyes."

He could collapse against his father's bony shoulder. He ought to, from sheer relief. But he does not. Instead he rises, his father's damp hand sliding out from between his own.

"Release him," Miervaldis orders the Healer on High. She nods. As one, the Healers linked around the former Chieftain slowly unwind their fingers from one another, starting at the far side of the bed and moving around, until the Healer standing beside Miervaldis releases the hand of her sister beside her.

The moment the contact is broken, the Chieftain huffs a final, rattling breath, more blood leaking out of his open mouth. And then he releases his essence to those same auspicious stars that have taken the souls of all who have come before him.

The Healer on High bows her head, bending her long neck gracefully towards Miervaldis.

"Hail, Chieftain of Rezke."

The other women do the same.

Her study has been well-kept, despite how little she has been able to occupy it in the three years since she was made Chieftainess. There is a little layer of dust here and there. She will have it cleared away on the morrow.

As is her nature, she has been very little aware of her surroundings all the while she has walked slowly here from her former husband's chambers. Her thoughts have been taken with the events of the past several weeks. She would like to begin documenting them, if only to navigate her own perceptions through the comforting scratch of her quill on parchment.

She stops in her wanderings for a moment before the single window in her chamber. The dull grey afternoon has long ended, the clouds parting at last after days of winter dim. Stars have begun to spill out between the thin wisps of remaining clouds. Absently, she raises her hand to the small indentation on her forehead where a circlet only recently sat.

Far to the east, above a hovel on the banks of the mighty River Dauvaga, a star streaks across the sky. She sees it, of course, from her tower window facing east, though she does not see the place over which it arcs. She breathes deeply, to the full capacity of her lungs, perhaps for the first time in three years. She could make note of it, this auspicious star. She could consider, as was her craft before her Chieftain called her to his side, what it might mean for the House.

But her time as Chieftainess is done. She pulls the drape across the cold panes, breathing deeply once more into the comforting darkness of a space hers alone.

Miervaldis is the Memory Keeper now. He must be left to maneuver his own game.

Read more from *The Curse of Lore*

You could buy it on Amazon, which would be lame.

OR

Download for free at

Coming December 2026

SHE WHO REACHES HIGH
VOLUME 2

I have seen what men do to the things they worship.

Starburadze of the River Dauvaga has neither mother nor father. She has lived her life in the river's murky depths, where all is clear, emerging only for the caustic companionship of Vappa, an exile from the northern House of Est.

But the river woman's fluid life is dammed with the arrival of three men seeking the truth about a monarch's death seven years ago, and the murder weapon left behind.

When Starburadze is moved to save one of the men from drowning, she is submerged in a manipulative new current, worshipped as a goddess, and pressed into the service of the men and their mission.

Taken to the Slavic capital of Novgorod to negotiate with a boy king, Starburadze soon finds herself caught between formidable forces, including the charismatic Miervaldis, Chieftain of Rezke, and Aemilie, the enigmatic young Chieftainess of Est. With ulterior motives and ruthless intentions lurking in every bend, Star is quickly treading water, grasping at reeds.

But the River Woman is more than she seems. As plots thicken and games grow treacherous, Starburadze herself must maneuver the pieces on the board, rewriting the myth of her existence and the truth of three kingdoms before she becomes victim to a long-withheld tide.

Samantha Burgess-Smith is a writer of feminist fantasy fiction. Her works expand genre stereotypes to illuminate the world-shaping power of mothers, daughters, sisters, wives, and matriarchs.

Samantha lives the best of lives in Nashville with her husband and two daughters. She enjoys writing more than almost anything else. Also high on her list are hiking, cycling, travelling, sleeping, reading, thrift shopping, and watching professional cycling.

Visit www.samanthaburgess-smith.com for a list of Samantha's favorite books, her literary theory articles and critiques, and what she's working on now.

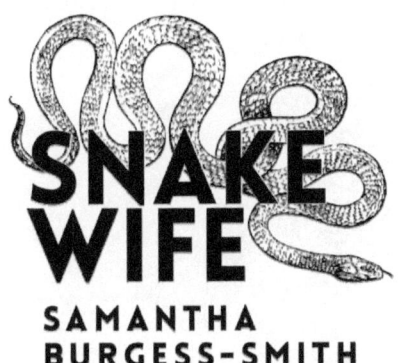

SNAKE WIFE

SAMANTHA
BURGESS-SMITH

Visit SBS at www.samanthaburgess-smith.com for
more from the author and to stay up-to-date with new
releases.

Scan this code to follow the author on Instagram.

@SAMANTHABURGESS_SMITH

www.samanthaburgess-smith.com